Mira's WAY

AMY MARONEY

ARTELAN
PRESS

Artelan Press

Portland, Oregon

This book is a work of fiction. Any references to historical events, real places, or real people are used fictitiously. Other characters, places, names, and events are products of the author's imagination, and any resemblance to actual events or places or persons, living or dead, are entirely coincidental. No part of this publication may be reproduced, or transmitted in any form or by any means, electronic or otherwise, without written permission from the author, except for the use of brief quotations in a book review.

ISBN: 978-0-9975213-3-7

ebook ISBN: 978-0-9975213-4-4

Cover design and formatting by Design for Writers.

Map by Tracey Porter.

Find more books in this series at www.amymaroney.com

For my parents

"My illustrious lordship, I'll show you what a woman can do."
—Artemisia Gentileschi,
Italian Baroque painter (1593-1652)

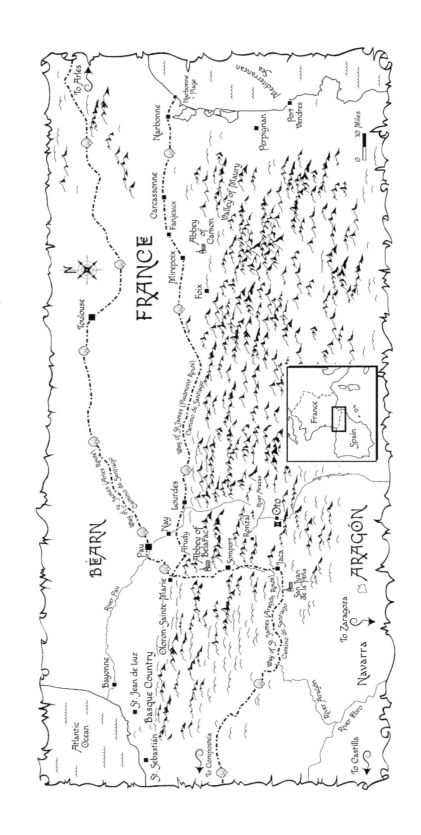

BOOK I

Respice post te, mortalem te esse memento.
Look around you, remember that you are mortal.
—*Tertullianus*

1

September, 2015
Amsterdam, Holland
Zari

ZARI FOUND AN EMPTY seat in a half-filled row near the front of the conference room. The latte she'd downed at the Amsterdam airport was still buzzing through her veins. It wasn't just caffeine making her jittery, she admitted to herself. It was nerves.

All around her, chairs were filling with people who mostly seemed to know one another. Art conservators, art historians, art dealers, journalists. Listening to the flare and ebb of voices swirling through the room, Zari imagined a day when she would walk into a conference and see dozens of familiar faces. A day when she would stop feeling like an outsider.

An elegantly-dressed man she recognized as a Swiss art dealer whose image appeared regularly in *Art News Weekly* sat down next to her. With him was a younger man, probably his assistant, carrying a laptop in one hand and the conference schedule in the other. Both of them nodded politely to Zari as they settled back in their chairs. The faint scent of a citrusy cologne wafted her way.

The lights dimmed. An expectant hush settled over the room.

John Drake strode onto the stage, clad in a slim-cut gray suit and a pair of truly spectacular black leather brogue shoes with tone-on-tone stitching. Zari smiled a little at the sight of him. In his laboratory at Oxford, John wore an all-black uniform of shapeless sweater, work boots, and jeans. But in public speaking situations, he showed a different side entirely.

Just before John launched into his talk, Zari caught a movement to her right. A reedy man with thinning sand-colored hair slid into a chair one row ahead. Her stomach lurched. It was Dotie Butterfield-Swinton. He crossed one leg over the other, eyes fixed on the stage, ignoring everyone around him. Zari exhaled. With a little luck, she could evade him for the entire day.

An image of two paintings appeared on the screen behind John. One was a portrait of a noblewoman standing against a plain black background; the other was a portrait of a merchant family, also against a dark background.

"These are early sixteenth-century portraits, oil on panel, unsigned," John said, gesturing at the images with his laser pointer. "Both were attributed to Cornelia van der Zee by experts in Netherlandish Renaissance art."

"I spent the better part of a few months analyzing the portrait of a noblewoman you see behind me," he went on. "It's the property of Fontbroke College at Oxford. The other portrait, the merchant family, is in France undergoing a similar analysis. The owner was kind enough to share the results thus far with me. And what we've discovered is extraordinary."

He clicked to the next slide. This time, the portraits' dark backgrounds had been replaced by elaborately detailed landscapes.

"The story these portraits tell is much more complicated than meets the eye. For instance, our work revealed these highly complex original backgrounds. This is remarkable because—as far as anyone knows—Cornelia van der Zee *only* used plain dark backgrounds."

Another click.

"We also found charcoal underdrawings—and words— beneath the layers of paint on the two portraits," John said.

Now the screen showed two charcoal drawings of the name 'Mira' with a whimsical image of a young nun forming the tail of the letter 'a'. Alongside one of the images were inscribed the words 'Pray for my mother'; a single word, 'Bermejo,' floated above the other image.

The next slide showed the back of each painting. A stamp bearing the initials 'ADL' was burned into the wood on both panels.

"Our analysis showed that these portraits are both painted on Pyreneen oak panels. In contrast, every verified Cornelia van der Zee painting is made of Baltic oak. And this stamp?" John's red laser pointer circled the initials 'ADL' on the screen. "It doesn't fit the pattern either. All of Van der Zee's known works bear a different mark entirely: the stamp of the city of Bruges."

A few people began murmuring to one another. Was it Zari's imagination, or did Dotie sit up a little straighter in his chair? Her pulse quickened.

John waited a beat, his eyes searching the audience. For an instant, his gaze settled on Zari.

"So," he continued. "Connoisseurship led these paintings to be attributed to Cornelia van der Zee. But then research and science intervened and called those attributions into question. Clearly the expert eye is not always reliable. But can it work in tandem with science? Absolutely. This should be a partnership, not a rivalry."

He paused to take a sip of water from the glass on the podium before him.

A woman in the front row raised her hand. "Who is Mira?"

"That's a question for Zari Durrell, not me." He pointed in Zari's direction. "Find her at the drinks reception tonight."

Zari felt the weight of Dotie's gaze upon her. Then his arm shot up.

"Perhaps we might be equally curious about Bermejo," he said crisply. "His name on one of the panels, plus similarities to his style in the paintings themselves, give us reason to hope that Bartolomé Bermejo himself may be responsible for these works."

Zari half-rose from her seat. "The prongs of the 'M' in one of the underdrawings we just saw contain the hidden script 'Mira, painter and servant of God,'" she asserted. "Mira was a painter, too—and her name is on *both* of the panels under discussion."

Dotie opened his mouth, about to launch a rebuttal.

"Please save comments about theories for the reception," John said coolly. "Let's get back to the subject at hand."

Zari clenched her jaw, heart thudding, and settled back into her chair. Beside her, the art dealer leaned over to whisper something in his assistant's ear.

Dotie folded his arms across his chest, turned his head, and stared in Zari's direction.

Studiously ignoring him, she concentrated on the man behind the podium. Using all the mindfulness tips burned into her brain after a lifetime listening to her mother spout New Age wisdom, she tuned back into the words John had spent weeks crafting—words he built around discoveries that had taken them both months to unearth.

The energy in the room shifted as John unspooled a tale of secrets long buried under layers of paint—of voices silenced by history that were only now being brought to light. Zari glanced sideways at the art dealer and saw a gleam of interest in his eyes. Even he was falling under the spell of John's storytelling.

She smiled. The adrenalin-fueled worry that had dogged her all morning was gone.

Somehow, she felt as if she had reached back through five hundred years of time and grasped Mira by the hand.

Zari stood in a little alcove in the reception room, fielding questions and showing photographs of her research findings to anyone who exhibited even the slightest interest. After an hour of nonstop conversation, she went to the bar for a glass of wine and stood alone for a moment, regrouping.

She scanned the faces in the room, searching for John. Could you technically buy someone a drink from a free bar? At the very least, she could thank him and offer to fetch him something.

Then Dotie stepped into her line of sight, clutching a tall glass filled with clear liquid, ice, and a slice of lime.

"Zari Durrell." He pronounced her last name the British way, with the emphasis on the first syllable.

"Hello, Dotie."

True to form, he made a quick head-to-toe examination of her body before returning his gaze to her own.

"You've changed your hair, haven't you? It looks longer since we last met. A cascade of pre-Raphaelite curls."

"Mmm. Yours looks different, too," Zari said thoughtfully, peering at the crown of his head. "I'm not sure why."

"That's quite a dress." Dotie's eyes roved south again. "One feels a bit dizzy looking at it."

Zari's indigo-and-black batik silk dress had been a find in a second-hand shop in San Francisco. Wearing it was like being embraced by an old friend.

"Then look away," she suggested, smiling brightly.

Dotie's jaw tensed. He took a pull from his drink. "I'd assumed you left Europe after your post-doc was over."

Zari shook her head. "Europe is still stuck with me. I'll be in France through the spring."

"Still hammering away at that theory of yours, it seems."

She nodded. "With as much enthusiasm as I imagine you devote to your own theory."

He gave a short, dismissive laugh. "Our theories have nothing in common. Bartolomé Bermejo was a living, breathing person. You, on the other hand, are conjuring up an artist out of thin air."

"Mira de Oto existed, too. I've seen the proof. She was an artist of great talent."

"Unfortunately, the historical record shows that women artists were rarer than golden eggs in those days."

Zari smiled. "The historical record is full of holes."

"It takes a connoisseur's eye and decades of experience to see an artist's hand in a painting." Dotie swirled the ice in his glass. "And you're no expert on Renaissance-era portraiture, if I'm not mistaken."

"I would never claim to have an expert eye." Zari felt the color rising on her neck. "I'm digging into history. That's where I'll find Mira. On the page, not on a panel."

"Ah, youth. There's so much more to this than you know." He leaned in conspiratorially, exuding an aroma of gin and sour lime. "Finding a paper trail from the Renaissance era takes expertise that one spends a career building."

"I may be inexperienced," Zari said, bristling. "But I managed to snag a Mendenhall Trust grant to do this work. I'm surprised you hadn't heard. With all your connections at Oxford."

The smile vanished from Dotie's face. "During my summer holiday I don't bother with institutional news unless it's of vital importance." His tone was clipped now. "And grants for junior academics don't fall into the category of vitally important, I'm afraid."

He muttered something about refreshing his drink and turned away.

Zari took a long breath and let it out slowly, watching him drift toward the bar.

Mira de Oto lived. The words pounded in her head, keeping rhythm with Dotie's footsteps.

Her story will be told.

And I will tell it.

2

Summer, 1504
Pyrenees Mountains, Aragón
Mira

MIRA EMERGED FROM THE cabin into the cool dawn air, filling her lungs with the scents of earth and oak. The night had slipped away with dizzying speed. If she slept at all, she had no memory of it. She smiled, her heart pounding a little faster at the thought.

Tilting her head back, she saw the pale glint of a star in the brightening sky. A hawk vaulted from the highest branches of a pine at the edge of the meadow and glided silently in her direction. The pulsating crown of the sun appeared over a ridge to the east, setting the grass ablaze with silvery light.

Mira stood spellbound for a few moments, watching the hawk chase its own shadow over the sun-dappled grass, waiting to hear the rush of its wings overhead. Then, slowly, she turned back to the cabin, already anticipating the warmth of Arnaud's arms around her.

A bank of lead-colored clouds advancing from the north made her hesitate.

"Do not bother to light a fire," she called out. "If we leave now, perhaps we can avoid the worst of whatever comes this way."

Arnaud appeared in the doorway, rubbing his eyes. "What comes this way is sunshine."

"From the east, yes. Come stand by me and look to the north."

He stayed where he was, leaning against the doorframe. "The people say this cabin's blessed by the gods. After last night, I've no quarrel with that claim."

"As much as I loved spending the winter with your family," she admitted, "I had been longing for a night alone with you since our wedding day."

"Let's linger here a while." He took a few steps forward, held out a hand.

She pointed at the approaching clouds. "It is never wise to tarry in the mountains—were those not your father's parting words when we left Ronzal?"

A gust of wind set the meadow grasses rippling, carrying with it the rumble of distant thunder.

Arnaud sighed, peering up at the sky. "I'll saddle the mules."

"By rights, we should have a long, mild summer after the winter we just endured." Mira swiveled in her saddle, checking the straps on the parcel secured behind her. "Instead it feels as if summer is already over before it has truly begun."

"That's the mountains for you." Arnaud swung up into place on his mule.

"Do you have all the pieces of your chair?" she asked.

"Every last one." He jerked his head toward the cabin. "Did you leave something for whoever comes next?"

Mira nodded.

The mountain people had an unspoken rule: shared spaces were always left tidy and stocked with necessities for the next visitors. It had been that way in the cave last fall. When she and Arnaud left, they had scrubbed it clean, erased all signs of violence, piled a neat stack of firewood by the blackened pit that served as a hearth. She shuddered, remembering the blood of her attacker pooling at her feet on the pitted limestone floor. Reflexively her hand went to the sheath at her waist. Arnaud had insisted she wear her dagger for the journey and she had pulled it from the bottom of her satchel with some reluctance. All winter in Ronzal, she'd had no need of the thing.

But only a fool would cross these mountains unarmed.

The mules ambled along the rocky trails through a fine mist, stopping at every opportunity for mouthfuls of tender grass. As they passed through a bowl-shaped meadow frothing with blue wildflowers, the sky darkened. In the space of a moment, the clouds unleashed a hailstorm.

"Let's stop under those beeches," Arnaud shouted, gesturing at a grove of tall trees crowned with pale green leaves. "We'll wait it out."

Mira urged her mule forward, her face stinging from the lash of the hail.

Just as they dismounted, the sound of men's voices and the discordant jangle of iron bells drifted across the meadow. A flock of sheep appeared through the hail, accompanied by several shepherds and large golden dogs. Arnaud cupped his hands around his mouth and whistled. At the sound, one of the men peeled away from the flock and approached them, carrying a long staff tipped with an iron spike. He was young, with heavy-lidded brown eyes and a thatch of curly black hair.

"The summer grazing season is upon us, even if the gods don't agree." He scraped hail from his beard and flung it on the ground. "The journey from Belarac to Ronzal is slow in the best weather. But this?" He eyed the skies, shaking his head.

"How do things at Belarac fare?" Arnaud asked. "The flock looks sound."

"Sound, yes, but smaller than it was. We had to slaughter some of our merinos for meat."

"Why?"

"One disaster after the next. The barn sprang a leak and the fodder got moldy, so there wasn't enough to last the flock all winter. Then two of the weaving looms broke—and no one knows how to fix 'em. To top it off, the dye came out strange this year. The cloth we brought to the Nay market wasn't black at all, more a grayish-brown. If it weren't for Carlo Sacazar, we wouldn't have sold a single length of the stuff."

Mira swallowed hard. "What do you mean?"

The shepherd looked at her for the first time. "He bought it all. For half the usual price."

She tried to put Carlo Sacazar out of her mind. "Surely the new abbess will address these problems."

"The new abbess?" His expression tightened. "She never sets foot in the washing station or the weaving room. Too busy praying, or whatever it is she does inside those gates."

"But none of the problems you speak of are beyond remedy." Mira glanced at Arnaud. "We can help right things there, Arnaud and me. He built some of those looms, and I know the proper way to dye wool."

Arnaud nodded. "We've got to pass by Belarac on our way to Bayonne. We'd be foolish not to step in and do what we can, for it benefits us all in the end."

"Bayonne?" the shepherd asked. "What's there?"

"Work, we hope," Arnaud replied. "And maybe a way to help Ronzal. Some of the villages in valleys to the west are hauling oak downriver from Pau to Bayonne, then shipping it north."

"I've a cousin who does it," the man said, nodding. "For great profit I'm told."

"It won't be easy," Arnaud allowed. "But the rewards will be worth the trouble."

"I'll pray to the gods that you succeed. I for one would much rather fell oaks than watch our flocks dwindle to nothing."

The shepherd embraced Arnaud, then hurried across the meadow. The hail had subsided, replaced by a driving rain.

"We should join them and help get the flock safely back." Mira watched the sheep plodding away, the men with their staffs, the dogs with their spiked iron collars.

Arnaud shook his head. "We stayed too long in Ronzal as it is. The safest thing for you is to be as far from Oto as possible when your father and brother return from war."

"Perhaps the order to kill me did not come from my father." She turned to face him. "Perhaps the steward was just possessed of an addled mind. He was a violent man prone to rages, by all accounts."

Arnaud put his arms around her. "Mira, as long as your father lives, I'll do whatever I can to keep you away from him. He wanted you dead. And for that matter, your brother may, too."

She stared at him bleakly. "The only thing I could not bear is you getting entangled in my family's troubles. If something were to happen—"

"I can handle myself in these forests. I've faced wolves, bears, lynx. But I'm no warrior," he said flatly. "I'm not schooled in swordplay, I've never held a pike. So the wise course for us is to leave these mountains before anyone from the house of Oto comes looking for you."

In her heart, she knew he was right.

Arnaud helped her back up into the saddle. She reached back and rested a hand on the canvas-wrapped oak panel behind her, imagining its layers of oil and pigment, its finely-etched underdrawings, its hidden words scrawled in charcoal—words no one would ever see.

All winter she had been fixated on the idea of a future in Bayonne. She and Arnaud would work side by side, artist and artisan, nestled in some respectable lodging near the harbor. She would collect wealthy patrons like so many shining pearls on a string. And he would craft furniture of such exquisite quality that foreign merchants would clamor for it, load it on their vessels, sail it north. But at this moment, shivering under a dripping beech tree high in the mountains, countless leagues from the sea, Mira felt a tendril of doubt unfurl in her belly.

The journey to Bayonne would be long and full of dangers. Once they arrived, they would have to cobble together a future piece by piece. They had no family there, no friends. If some crisis befell them, no one would come to their aid.

She squeezed her hands together until her knuckles ached. The flock and the shepherds had disappeared from sight, the jangle of iron bells had faded into silence.

For the first time, Mira wondered uneasily if the future she dreamed of would even come to pass.

3

Summer, 1504
Pyrenees Mountains, Aragón
Mira

THE SUN WAS BEGINNING its descent in the west when Mira and Arnaud arrived at the King's Road and the passage to Béarn.

A group of monks and a long mule train were assembled at the pass of Somport near a stone cabin occupied by a guard and a tariff collector. Behind them massed a group of muleteers, their animals weighed down by goods. Mira and Arnaud dismounted and led their mules to the back of the queue.

When it was their turn, the tariff collector searched the contents of the mules' panniers. His red leather armor was emblazoned with the herald of Queen Isabella and King Ferdinand. Meanwhile, the guard busied himself attempting to create order out of the shifting crowd of people and animals. He rattled his sword, shushing two muleteers who were arguing loudly in the mountain dialect.

"What's in there?" The tariff collector pointed at the can-vas-wrapped parcel strapped behind Mira's saddle.

"A painting," Mira said.

"Let's see it."

"It's not worth your trouble," Arnaud said, stepping between them. "It's damaged. Has no value."

"I'll decide for myself what its value is," the man snapped.

Arnaud carefully detached the parcel from its tethers and unwrapped it.

The tariff collector eyed the portrait, let out a low whistle. "A fine enough likeness of you, but what a mess."

"Of me?" Mira said. "No, I—"

Arnaud flicked her a warning look.

"Why haul something over the mountains when it's been destroyed?" The man examined the raw gouge in the center of the painting, shaking his head. "Someone dropped it on a pike, from the looks of it."

Mira draped the canvas over the painting again, annoyed to see a tremor in her hand. She wanted to tell him exactly how she planned to repair her mother's portrait: a plug of wool for the hole, layers of gesso and glue, then careful application of linseed oil mixed with pigment. In the end, the damage would be nearly invisible.

But she kept silent, her head bowed.

The man gestured at the bundle of parcels on the flanks of Arnaud's mule. "What about those? More ruined paintings?"

"Wood," Arnaud replied. "I like to whittle."

The tariff collector rapped on the parcels with his knuckles and seemed satisfied with the result.

"What business do you have in Béarn?" he asked, hand outstretched.

"Same as any other couple." Arnaud dropped several coins into the man's palm. "We go where the work is."

"Are you an artisan, then?"

"I work with wood, like I said. Cabinetmaker."

His response seemed to satisfy the tariff collector, who waved them on with a warning.

"Mind you be wary on your way down. The road north crawls with bandits and Cagots." He pointed to the necklace around Mira's throat. "If I was you, I'd hide that."

They proceeded down the wide, rutted road, keeping the monks' mule train in sight.

The pine trees here on the exposed ridge were spindly, their branches sparsely clothed with silver-green needles. The hillsides were covered in rocks and loose shale. A cold wind snaked down from the snow-covered peaks above them.

Mira glanced back over her shoulder at the gates, watched the tariff collector wave the next group of travelers forward. She put a hand to her throat.

"There are no rubies or pearls in my necklace. Just a bit of ivory on a thin chain."

"Anything shiny is attractive to a bandit," Arnaud said. "And the chain may be thin, but it's gold. Better to do as he says."

Mira sighed, fumbled with the clasp of her necklace and slipped it off. She held it in her hand a moment, pressed the carved ivory scallop shell into her palm. Then she pulled out her dagger and deposited the necklace in the bottom of the sheath. Anyone who wanted her mother's necklace would see the sharp end of her blade first. As an additional precaution she pulled up her skirts and strapped the sheath around her thigh. If they were ambushed, at least she would have a hidden weapon.

"What did he mean, 'Cagot'?" She folded her arms underneath her cloak, shivering. The air smelled of winter.

"They're a strange race of people. There are many in Béarn. You never encountered them, truly?" He sounded skeptical.

"When would I? My entire life was spent behind the gates of Belarac."

"You lived in Nay a time," he reminded her.

"In Nay, my world was the home of Carlo Sacazar, the convent of his sister Amadina, and the marketplace. I suppose I might have seen a Cagot there, though I did not know it."

"No. They wouldn't have mingled with the townsfolk. They keep to themselves, and others think of them as little more than beasts."

"Why?"

He shrugged. "Fate hasn't been kind to them, that's all I know."

The mules shambled along at their usual pace, searching in vain for tufts of grass to nibble. These hills were barren of life, Mira thought, save for those pines—and even they looked half-dead. Just ahead, the rocks on the slopes that bordered the road were stained the color of blood. As they got closer, she saw the rocks were covered with creeping red moss. Somehow it survived up here where no other plant would.

Wings churned the air overhead and a crow settled into a stunted pine, fixing its bright black eyes upon her. She thought of Elena and her hatred of the creatures. Mira closed her eyes a moment and whispered a prayer, overcome with a sudden wave of longing.

Please, God. Keep my Elena safe, wherever she is.

4

Summer, 1504
Basque Country
Elena

ELENA HAD NEVER BEEN this far west before. They had traveled on foot through the mountains for nearly a fortnight, following the shepherds' trails through meadows and forests that grew wetter and denser the closer they got to the sea. Each day beginning at dawn, she strode a short distance behind Xabi, breathing in the earthy, rich scents of the forest, half-listening to the trills and whistles of songbirds high in the canopy above them, charting the progress of the sun across the wide blue sky. If it were up to her, they would continue on this way until they reached the ends of the earth, where the rivers poured into the sea. But they were nearing their destination now. The quiet companionship of these days with Xabi was drawing to an end.

Afternoon was turning into evening when they came to the crest of a low hill that overlooked a grassy meadow. On the opposite end of the clearing, a broad-shouldered, bearded figure emerged from the woods and tramped across the grass. Two large white dogs wearing spiked iron collars padded alongside him.

He hurried toward them, waving both arms enthusiastically. Xabi and Elena descended into the meadow to meet him. The dogs settled back on their haunches, regarding their master with solemn eyes as he greeted Xabi and Elena in the mountain dialect. Elena realized this was for her benefit, since she could not understand a word of Basque.

As soon as the niceties were dispensed with the man placed his hands on Xabi's shoulders and said solemnly, "Your sister's dead, cousin. It happened last night, just after sunset."

Xabi lowered his gaze. "At least she's not suffering anymore."

Elena slid her hand into Xabi's, feeling a rush of sympathy for him. His mother had died when Xabi was a boy and his elder sister had been thrust into the role of motherhood long before she was ready. She never married, claiming the rewards of marriage were already hers: a brood of children and a whitewashed home with a peaked red-tiled roof that was every inch her domain.

But now it would all be Xabi's.

Xabi's cousin led them along the trail. A bear had been sighted near here not too long ago, he told them. That was why he had brought the dogs. It was odd, he said, a bear in summer. Usually bears stayed higher in the mountains until autumn, when they grew cranky and voracious, desperate to fill their bellies before winter silenced the land with its deep crust of snow.

"I suppose you'll be happy to live in one place," Xabi's cousin said over his shoulder. "The shepherd's life is no good when you have a woman."

Elena pressed her lips together and lengthened her stride, put out at the assumption that she belonged to Xabi. He turned, saw her expression, smiled. She felt her heart soften. The fact was, she did belong to Xabi—and he to her. They had wintered together too many times to count in their secret valley with its steaming pools, ensconced in a snug stone cabin.

Last autumn she started her journey to their secret valley too late. She'd had no choice but to stay at Castle Oto as long as Mira remained there, to watch over the girl. On the day when the steward Beltrán had unspooled Ramón de Oto's murderous plan and the arrow he launched at Elena hit wood instead of flesh, she fled to Ronzal. When Mira and Arnaud returned safely from the cave, she saw her opportunity to leave. But when they surprised everyone by announcing their intent to wed, she delayed her plans.

Mira and Arnaud were married on an autumn day that felt like midsummer. The Ronzal villagers slept under the stars around a bonfire that night, marveling at the sultry air. The next day began sunny and ended with snow flurries. Though Elena departed in haste, snow chased her west through the mountains all the way to the valley.

By the time she got there, Xabi had already resigned himself to a winter without Elena by his side. She smiled at the memory of their reunion, the quiet joy in his dark eyes at the sight of her.

Mira and Arnaud, for their part, must have been snowed in at Ronzal for the winter. If the gods were willing, they would soon make their way over the mountains. Before long they would be in Bayonne, settled into a new life by the sea.

Elena could never think of Mira now without thinking of her mother, Marguerite. From the beginning, Elena was convinced she could never love a noblewoman, especially not a member of the house of Oto. But she had grown to respect Marguerite. More than that, she had become fiercely protective of her. Despite the enormous gulf between them—a mountain woman and a high-born lady—they understood one another in the end. And the knowledge that Marguerite had sacrificed her own life so that Mira could live elevated the noblewoman even higher in Elena's estimation.

Walking along the quiet forest trail with Xabi's warm hand in hers, Elena wished for one more chance to talk to Marguerite, to tell her that Mira was safe, married to a good man, with a future full of promise. Just as she'd always hoped.

They rounded a curve and the whitewashed house came into view. Nestled in the crook of two sloping hills, the house was surrounded by fruit trees, a summer garden, and close-cropped grass. A flock of goats stood in a pen just outside the barn a short distance from the house. One of them began rasping excitedly at the sight of the dogs.

The broad, battered wooden door opened as they approached.

"Xabi," a woman cried. She ran to him and threw her arms around him, sobbing and talking a wild streak of Basque.

Soon Elena was longing for the quiet of their hidden valley. Xabi's family was loud and argumentative. They spent every evening picking apart discrepancies in stories, trundling out the same bits of family lore again and again, unravelling it all before the fire along with copious helpings of wine until everyone began to nod off under the weight of so many words.

Elena often found Xabi's eyes in the midst of these smoky, ear-splitting soirées, and he would shrug slightly, or raise and lower one eyebrow so fast that she wondered if that was really what she saw, or draw down half his mouth in a lopsided smile. She would take a deep breath and let it out, feeling herself grow calm under his gaze.

They were together, that was the important thing. These people roaring and screeching in their mysterious language— she would grow to accept their ways. Perhaps she would one day understand them, although there was a small comfort in her foreignness. It gave her the freedom to lose herself in her own thoughts while the rest of them were caught up in their stories.

"We'll have to marry," Xabi told Elena one night in bed.

She ran a finger up and down his forearm, tracing the slight furrow between two lines of muscle.

"What if I don't want to?"

He didn't answer.

"I'll be forced to wed with a dagger at my neck, is that it?" She rolled away from him.

He snorted, folding his arms under his head.

"I'd never force you to do anything."

She couldn't argue with that, but she felt like arguing anyway. The prickly side of her was outraged that his family would assume they could ram their traditions down her throat. The practical side of her knew that for all intents and purposes, she and Xabi were married. Formalizing things would not change their feelings for each other. But the idea that outsiders would press a union upon them—it didn't sit right with her.

"Do you truly want to live trapped in this house for the rest of your life? After all of your wanderings?"

"I won't be trapped here. There are plenty of others only too eager to take on the work. I could leave tomorrow, come back a year from now."

Now it was her turn to snort.

"Your days of following the flocks are over. You see how they look to you every time a decision must be made. Your sister led this family, but not one sibling other than you is capable of following in her footsteps. It's not hard to see."

"There are a few who can learn," he protested. "They just need the right training."

"But if you leave for a year, who will train them?"

He sighed. "Maybe a year is too much, but a season's reasonable. Next year I want to go to the coast again and help my cousin with the whale harvest. There's money to be had in that. We need it."

Her ears pricked up. "I've always wanted to visit the sea."

He slid his arm around her again, and she settled into the warmth of his neck.

"Marry me, and the sea with all its treasures'll be yours."

His hand slipped under her shift, his fingertips lazily following the curve of her hip.

"How can I say no to such a gift?" she whispered, relaxing under his touch.

A gentle rain began to patter on the roof.

5

September, 2015
Amsterdam, Holland
Zari

WIL AND ZARI WANDERED through the narrow streets of Amsterdam, the late afternoon sun warm on their faces. Zari cast covert glances at Wil from time to time, taking in the disheveled dark-blond curls that sprang from his head in all directions, his lanky limbs and tall frame, the confident grace of his movements. Being in his presence charged her entire body with delicious anticipation. She reached out, caught his hand in hers, and raised it to her lips.

On the arch of a bridge, they paused to watch a flotilla of swans glide through a canal's dark waters.

The swans floated to the open window of a small yellow houseboat, where a young girl leaned out with a piece of bread. The first swan snatched it from her hand with the speed of a striking snake. Screams ensued. A woman shooed the bird away with an umbrella and shut the window. Undeterred, it pecked at the glass with demented intensity.

"It's an attack swan," Zari whispered. "The most dangerous kind."

Wil looked at her, his eyes gleaming with amusement, and draped an arm around her shoulders. She leaned into him, breathing the scent of eucalyptus.

"You still smell the same. Thank God."

He grinned.

Zari's mobile buzzed with an incoming text. She pulled it from her pocket and scanned the words. "My presence is not required again at the conference until tomorrow," she announced. "I'm all yours. We can keep watching crazy swans, or..."

Wil pulled her in for a kiss. "I think 'or' sounds a lot more interesting."

At Wil's apartment building, they climbed the narrow, dimly lit staircase, the sounds of the streets and canal fading away with each step. Zari trailed her fingertips over the wooden bannister. It was so old and worn that it resembled polished stone.

Wil unlocked his apartment door and stepped aside so she could enter. Sunlight streamed in through the skylights, illuminating the centuries-old wooden floor. The white walls were crisp in contrast, and massive dark beams were exposed in the peaked ceiling. A simple kitchen outfitted with white appliances and matte gray wall tiles ran along the opposite wall. A table of rich honey-colored wood that Wil had made himself stood adjacent to the kitchen area.

Zari crossed to the table and ran her hands over the smooth, perfectly planed surface. She shook her head, smiling.

"What's funny?" Wil asked.

"Your apartment is exactly where I imagined my artist alter ego would live. The attic of a classic brick Amsterdam house, overlooking a canal. All it needs is some giant canvases and panels, maybe a standing desk filled with paints and brushes and charcoal."

"Your alter ego, whatever that is, is welcome to visit," he said, padding up next to her. "But even better would be the real you. Here. All the time."

He slipped his arms around her. Zari luxuriated in the caress of his fingers moving across her collarbone, sliding down each knob of her spine, exploring each indentation of her ribs. Then she took his hand and led him across the room to a door that stood ajar.

"I'm guessing this would be the bedroom."

He nodded.

"Why don't I start making myself at home right here in your bed?" She pulled him gently through the doorway.

With a wicked smile, he set about undressing her.

The next morning Zari found herself on a bicycle whizzing along a path behind Wil, feeling extraordinarily Dutch. The sunlight held a trace of summer's heat, but the wind on her face was cool. A gaggle of tourists clogged the sidewalk ahead, a few of them spilling into the bike lane. Wil rang his bike bell with vigor as they wheeled by the group. Zari kept his pace, coming within a hair's breadth of a woman wearing a bright red jacket, the familiar blue-and-gold cover of an American guidebook tucked under one arm.

"I could pass for one of you!" she called out to Wil. "No helmet, no light on my bike. Blatant disregard for pedestrians."

His rich laughter tumbled back at her.

"Why is your laugh so intoxicating?" she demanded.

"It's a Dutch thing," he said over his shoulder. "We have addictive laughs."

They dodged another group of tourists.

Part of her dreaded the meal tonight with Wil's best friend, Filip. Wil and Filip had once been "adventurists," working half the year to save money for huge expeditions all over the world. Their lifestyle came to an abrupt end during a disastrous skiing trip in the Arctic, when Filip had fallen into a crevasse and lost the use of his legs. Filip's sister Hana had been Wil's girlfriend for nearly a decade; their relationship was a casualty of the accident. Zari couldn't shake the worry that Wil's family and friends had written her off as a rebound girlfriend, a temporary distraction on the road back to normalcy and a nice Dutch woman. Maybe even back to Hana again.

Just be yourself, Zari. Her mother's voice floated into her head. *Because everyone else is already taken.*

She smiled.

It was as good a mantra as any for the evening to come.

Their meal was nearly finished. The small Indonesian restaurant was emptying. A few last spoonfuls of rice in peanut sauce sat on a plate in front of Wil, and he periodically shoveled a bite into his mouth.

Filip wasn't much of an eater. His plate was still half-full. He was on his third beer, though. He constantly made small adjustments to his position in the wheelchair, clearly uncomfortable. His dark hair was cut close to his skull and streaked with silver. His fine-boned face was pale and gaunt, with deep-set brown eyes that regarded her with wan detachment.

"How long do you plan to live in Europe, Zari?" he asked.

"I was only supposed to be here a year, but I got a new opportunity."

"She's looking for an artist from Renaissance times," Wil said. "A woman who painted in the Flemish style."

Filip looked doubtful. "A woman? From that era?"

"Women painted then," Zari replied, "but most of them were

never recognized. They weren't offered opportunities or were forced to work anonymously."

A defensive note had crept into her voice. She got emotional too quickly when she talked about this topic. It was a weakness, the kind of character flaw that a person like Dotie Butterfield-Swinton would pounce on and use to his advantage.

"If we can fill the holes in the historical record," she went on in a more measured tone, "if we can uncover those silenced stories, the question of whether women could and can produce truly great art will lose relevance."

Under the table Wil leaned his thigh into Zari's. A slow shiver of pleasure rippled through her.

The server approached and cleared the remaining plates, and talk turned to stories of Wil and Filip in childhood, of antics with siblings and cousins.

Hana came up often in the course of their reminiscing. Apparently she was even more of a thrill-seeker than her brother had once been. She was currently trekking on horseback through the plains of Mongolia, on break from her job as a disaster-relief coordinator for an international humanitarian group.

As the true measure of Wil's ex-girlfriend took shape, a feeling of uneasiness drifted over Zari. *Great*, she thought glumly. *I'm walking in the shadow of a badass do-gooder.*

Wil avoided the topic of the expeditions that had been the cornerstone of his relationship with Filip since their university days, that had defined both of them for a decade. Filip, for his part, was subdued. He occasionally sparred with Wil over a detail in a story, and twice he smiled with genuine delight, his eyes radiating joy. But each time the smile vanished so quickly Zari wondered if she had imagined it.

Watching the men dance around the subject of the adventures that had been their greatest passion, she felt a sudden jolt of despair for Filip. To be a person who reveled in taking his body to the limits of human endurance, trapped in a wheelchair for life—it was devastating.

"My brother Gus has a friend who was paralyzed in a skiing accident too," she heard herself blurt out.

Filip and Wil stared at her, astonished.

"He still skis. And he sails. He's going on a sailing trip in Croatia next spring, actually."

There was a long silence. Filip took a sip of his beer, his eyes unreadable across the table.

"He could be a good resource for you." Zari's mouth was suddenly dry.

Wil and Filip exchanged a glance. Filip shifted in his wheelchair again.

She faltered a moment, then found her voice. "I could send an e-mail introduction to you both."

Zari searched Filip's solemn face, fearing she had made an unforgivable blunder.

After a moment, he shrugged. "Okay," he said. "If you want."

Wil launched into a story about a decrepit houseboat the two men had purchased together and refurbished when they were in their early twenties.

Listening to him, watching Filip's face relax, Zari felt the tension slowly drain from her body.

6

September, 2015
Amsterdam, Holland
Zari

THE BEDROOM WAS NEARLY dark. Zari stared at the stars visible through the skylights, listening to the far-off thrum of engines and the occasional sound of voices in the street below. An emergency vehicle's siren whined in the distance. She turned over restlessly, her body coursing with energy. Jet lag had her in its clutches once again.

Wil slept on his side, facing away from her. His broad back rose and fell with each breath. She gently placed a hand between his shoulder blades, reveling in the warmth of his skin, the curve of muscle along his spine.

For a moment she was overcome with a desire to wake him, to lose herself in the circle of his arms. It was unsettling to admit, but she was attached to Wil in a way she had never been to any other man.

Instead she rolled out of bed, went into the kitchen, and

filled the electric kettle with water. Rummaging through the tea options, she found a foil-wrapped packet of chamomile.

Zari scrolled through the e-mails on her mobile, deleting all the junk. Then her eyes widened.

"Scuba diving?" she whispered.

She calculated the time difference between Amsterdam and California in her head and placed a video call to her mother.

When Portia answered, Zari could tell her mother was in the backyard at Gus's house, seated at the patio table. The setting sun had streaked the sky behind her with glorious brushstrokes of orange and pink.

"Zari, my girl! How are you? Isn't it the middle of the night there?"

"It's nearly morning, actually." Zari filled a cup with boiling water. "Mom, what's this about a scuba diving class?"

"So exciting, I know. Obsidian and I are doing it together."

Portia had a knack for attracting younger men. Obsidian, a mid-forties photographer she had met at a silent meditation retreat last year, had quickly become a fixture in her life.

"You don't like swimming," Zari pointed out.

"Scuba diving isn't swimming." Portia aimed her mobile's camera across the table at Gus and his children. "Look, guys," she said. "It's Zari!"

A collective roar of "Auntie Z!" rose up.

"Hello, my loves! Where's Jenny?"

"Mom's in Tokyo," Jasper informed her. "*Again.*"

"But she's bringing us back presents," Eva said cheerfully. "She always brings presents."

"Except for that one time—" Jasper began.

"Chop chop," Gus interrupted, winking at Zari. "Time to clear the table, kids."

Jasper and Eva scraped back their chairs and immediately began bickering about the number of objects they each had to carry inside.

"So, mom—the class?" Zari prodded.

Portia turned the mobile's camera on herself again.

"It meets in San Francisco, but our first dives will be in Monterey Bay."

"Are the teachers responsible people?" Zari envisioned a self-medicated pothead sending her mother into the Pacific with a nod and a peace sign.

"Of course! Honey, they do this for a living. They're total pros."

"Is Obsidian a strong swimmer?"

"He's a fish."

"I feel better." Zari dropped her tea bag into the cup. "How's the beading world treating you?"

"I don't want to brag, but—actually, yes, I do. The goddess has spoken. I'm on the road to riches."

"Seriously?"

"Who knows if this whole thing is a fluke. But my online jewelry sales doubled last month, thanks to your help with my website and social media. It's nuts. It took me nearly sixty years to become an overnight sensation."

The pride in Portia's voice made Zari's eyes sting with tears. After her parents divorced and her father all but disappeared from their lives, her mother had cobbled together rent payments through pet-sitting and house-sitting gigs combined with part-time jobs in yoga studios and health food stores. She never had fewer than three jobs at a time, and sometimes six or more.

"I've been hashtagging your stuff all over the internet, Mom. Anything to help your global empire."

Portia laughed. "What's it like there? Idyllic?"

"I don't want to jinx anything, but...yes."

Her mother beamed. "Is it the Wil Bandstra effect?"

"He's pretty great. Amsterdam's not bad, either."

"Well, enjoy, sweetie. I'm going to supervise dishwasher loading." Portia blew Zari a kiss. "Talk to your brother. He has a case of the chats, I can just tell."

Gus's grinning face filled the tiny screen of Zari's mobile. "Sissy boo!"

"How's the world's best dad?"

"Can't complain."

He began walking around the yard. Zari saw a terra-cotta pot of orchids behind him, its white blooms glowing in the twilight.

"You really are the orchid whisperer," she said admiringly.

"I have nothing else to do. Being a stay-at-home dad and all. I just sit around, tend my orchids, make smoothies. Pick up stuff."

He demonstrated by retrieving various kid-related items and piling them on the patio table. She watched him add a hula hoop, a plastic dinosaur, a troll, a tattered pair of fairy wings, and a seemingly endless assortment of Legos to the heap.

"Look at you tidying up. What a catch you are."

"What the kids don't know is that this is a burn pile. Tomorrow, it'll all be gone. Poof!" He snickered maniacally.

Zari's shoulders shook with laughter. Even on her darkest days, Gus never failed to make her laugh. It was one of the things she loved best about him.

She collected herself again. "So, Gus? What's going on with Mom and this scuba diving thing?"

"Just another one of her interests. Hard to keep track of them all."

"Yeah, but this one is different. She could drown."

"That's right, Miss Worst-Case-Scenario. Go straight to the potential disaster. You're worried about sharks, too, aren't you? Lots of great whites in Monterey Bay."

"Mom doesn't like swimming! Can you imagine her putting on a wetsuit?"

He chuckled. "I know. Those diving wetsuits are so thick you have to add weights to keep from shooting out of the water like a cannon."

"Thanks for the reminder. Jesus." Zari imagined her mother floating silently to the bottom of the sea loaded with an assortment of lead weights, while Obsidian and the scuba teacher chatted about New Age topics such as mindfulness, intention, and holding space.

"Reel in your freakish fears, sister," Gus ordered.

He always had an uncanny talent for reading her thoughts.

"Come on, Gus, don't tell me you're happy she's doing this."

"Why can't she have adventures and try new things? She loves to get pushed out of her comfort zone."

"I know. But it's just...dangerous," Zari said lamely.

"Here's what'll happen." Gus lowered his voice to a stage whisper. "She'll finish the class, do the ocean dives in Monterey, and then never scuba dive again. I bet you a million dollars."

Zari fought off another attack of laughter. "No way am I betting you," she said. "I lost a lot of quarters to you back in the day."

"Whatever. That's revisionist history."

"I just wish you'd take this a little more seriously. Why do I always have to be the voice of reason?"

He sighed. "Will I ever be a grown-up in your eyes? Doesn't being a dad give me any cred at all? Or will I never outlive my reputation as a deadbeat addict?" His voice had grown serious.

"Come on, Gus, no one thinks about that anymore."

"I wonder sometimes. I've been drug-free for ten years now. How much longer will it take for you to trust me?"

"I do trust you."

"Then see me—really see me—as the adult I've become, not the mess I used to be."

Zari was startled into silence. The tone of light amusement in her brother's voice had vanished. His eyes held a look of reproach she had never seen before.

Her nephew's high, sweet voice became audible. "Auntie Z! Auntie Z!"

Without another word, Gus handed the mobile to his son.

7

September, 2015
Amsterdam, Holland
Zari

Z ARI MET JOHN DRAKE the next morning for coffee at a
small café overlooking a canal. Through the plate glass
window, she saw cyclists wheeling across a bridge. Sunlight glinted off houseboats docked along the canal. Some were
freshly painted architectural gems, while others looked as if they
only stayed afloat due to a combination of glue, tar, and luck.

Across the table from her, John stirred his latte. He was
dressed in black jeans and a button-down black shirt, a nod to
his standard work uniform. His footwear was scaled down as
well—the fancy brogues he'd sported during his presentation
had been swapped out for high-topped Doc Martens.

Not for the first time, she wondered what his personal life was
like. He never mentioned a partner, and she had absolutely no
sense of his sexual orientation. The first time she'd seen him in
a suit she had assumed he was gay, but that was because most of

the straight American men she knew were incapable of putting together a sophisticated outfit. Things were different in Europe, she had soon learned.

His short-cropped black hair did nothing to soften the rough features of his face, and his skin was darker than it had been when she had met him a year ago, hunched over potions and gadgets in his workshop. That was because he'd spent most of his weekends over the summer surfing, it turned out. John surfed regularly in the frigid Atlantic off the west coast of England, and most of his travel revolved around the search for the perfect wave.

"Why aren't you staying at the conference hotel?" John asked.

"I'm staying with—a friend." Zari realized she didn't know what to call Wil. Long-distance lover? Boyfriend? Partner? She would have to pick a moniker and stick with it. "So how was your summer of surfing?"

"I got to know the Cornish coast quite well," he said. "I'm looking forward to branching out a bit. I'll be heading to France in the spring."

"Where?" Zari gave her own latte a stir.

"St. Jean de Luz. It's only an hour or so from where you'll be."

"Have you surfed there before?"

"A few times. There's a great community of surfers in the area. It has a strong Basque culture and a more relaxed outlook than you find in other parts of France." He put down his spoon and glanced at her. "So what did Dotie have to say to you at the reception? I saw you two chatting."

"I don't think chatting is the right description for that encounter. He talked about my hair and spent a little too much time examining my...outfit. Things devolved from there."

John shook his head. "Dotie does have a bit of a reputation, I'm afraid."

"So I've heard. I got prickly because he laughed at my inexperience. The thing is, he's right—I *am* inexperienced. I don't have dozens of well-connected colleagues on my side. I don't have an arsenal of experts backing my theory that Mira painted those portraits. What's the value of experts anyway, when technology and science keep proving them wrong?"

John took a sip of his latte. "Technology and science have taken the experts down a peg or two, but they still carry a lot of weight. Get a few of them on your side and Mira will rise from obscurity. Right now, she's a lovely idea based on a few scraps of evidence. You need to prove she's a maker of history. Try birth and death notices, church records. You'd be surprised how far back some of these things go. A lot of them are digitized these days."

"I know, and Laurence has offered to smooth the way with all of that."

Laurence Ceravet, who owned the portrait of the merchant family, was a curator at the art museum of the university in Pau, where Zari would be spending the next several months.

"Bureaucracy can be mind-numbing in France," John said.

"She's cutting through all that red tape for me. We've already got appointments lined up in Bayonne at the municipal archives to see the records on Arnaud de Luz, thanks to her. Whatever we dig up, I've committed to presenting it all at a conference on Renaissance-era portraiture in Bordeaux next spring. Can I count on you to share your findings from the Fontbroke portrait analysis for my paper?"

"Of course," he said. "I'll e-mail you all the documents as soon as I get back to Oxford."

Zari stared into her latte. Suddenly the thought of drinking it made her nauseous. Or maybe it was just the anxiety gnawing at her belly. "I wish I had your knowledge," she said wistfully, looking up again. "I worry that I'll find evidence that I can't even see because I don't know what to look for. Have you ever considered writing a blueprint for solving art mysteries?"

John smiled. "Tell you what. I'll make time for dinner in my busy surfing schedule when I come to St. Jean de Luz if you can tear yourself away from your research. You can share your findings and pick my brain. Wait—you surf, don't you? Why not join me in the water as well?"

She cradled her cup in her hands. "I'm warning you, my surfing skills are pretty rusty."

"Do you mind wearing a wetsuit?"

"Not as much as I mind hypothermia."

He laughed. There was a warmth in his eyes that Zari hadn't seen before, and his smile was broad and unguarded. John's cool reserve rarely slipped away, but this smile? It was evidence. He liked her.

And she desperately needed an ally like him in the art world.

8

Summer, 1504
Abbey of Belarac, Béarn
Mira

"WE DON'T HAVE TO go." Arnaud stood holding his mule's reins in the shade of a hawthorn tree, looking east to the green valley where the Abbey of Belarac lay.

"How can you say that?" Mira shifted in her saddle, swatting at a gnat that buzzed around her eyes. "We vowed to do it."

He reached up and took her hand, studying her a moment. They both knew she dreaded entering the gates and being swallowed up again by the measured rhythms, the silent discipline of the cloistered life. It was a world she had learned to navigate, but always resisted.

"In truth, the only person I want to see within those walls is Sister Agathe," she confessed. "Though I fear the reproach on her face. After all, I did abandon my duties at Belarac."

"With my encouragement," he said, kissing her palm. "You're married. You'll stay with me in the guesthouse." He squeezed her hand reassuringly. "You've a different life now, Mira."

In the morning, Sister Agathe took them on a tour of the workshop spaces where Mother Béatrice had created all of her industries. Sister Agathe had always been kind to Mira, and her warm smile had not changed. But now there were shadows under her eyes and lines around her mouth, evidence of her burdens. Mira felt a stab of remorse at the sight.

They entered the weaving room, which looked abandoned. Only one of the three looms Arnaud had built for the abbey still functioned properly. Arnaud admitted he was not surprised that his handiwork had proved faulty. He had copied the original loom gifted to the abbey by Carlo Sacazar as best he could, but with no instruction from anyone schooled in the engineering behind the contraption, he had relied on guesswork. He could reason his way through the repairs, but the real problem was that no one at the abbey knew how to fix a loom once it had broken.

Sister Agathe led them from the weaving room across the courtyard to the great iron gates, then to the orchards beyond. A basket under one of the trees was half-full of red apples. She plucked two from the pile and handed them to Mira and Arnaud.

"The new abbess—how is she faring?" Mira asked, polishing her apple on her skirts.

"She is from Gascony. She has filled the abbey with boarders, widows, and daughters of Gascon noblemen." Sister Agathe looked around, lowering her voice, though there was no one else in the apple orchard. "But she cares not for the complexities of the wool trade, or the business of paper-making, or the harvesting of hops for ale. Since Mother Béatrice died, it has been difficult to keep it all going." Sister Agathe sighed, her eyes on Mira. "Your presence is missed. You were raised under her wing, you absorbed the lessons of these industries, and you carried out tasks that were never taught to others."

Mira fell silent, overcome by guilt.

"What about the villagers? The shepherds of Ronzal?" Arnaud asked. "Do they still uphold their obligations to the abbey?"

Sister Agathe nodded. "Yes. The agreements made by Mother Béatrice and your father hold firm."

"We shall stay on for a time. We will do all we can to help you," Mira promised. "And we shall see that others are trained to carry out the work properly after we leave."

Sister Agathe looked from Mira to Arnaud, relief evident on her face. "My prayers have been answered, then."

"Will we need the permission of the abbess?" Arnaud asked.

"She is in Gascony for the funeral of a bishop—and to drum up more noble daughters to fill our bedchambers. I accept your offer of aid on her behalf. Truth be told, the abbess leaves the workings of our industries up to me."

Arnaud spent a fortnight repairing looms and helping the villagers with tasks in the orchards and the fields. He found a village boy skilled in woodworking and made him his assistant. Every day the boy was Arnaud's shadow. In time, he would be responsible for repairing the looms and whittling replacement parts.

For her part, Mira reinstated the systems she had learned from Mother Béatrice for wool washing and dyeing, for spinning and weaving. She kept two bright novice nuns by her side and had them write down the steps taken to accomplish each project.

"Sister Agathe," said Mira one afternoon while they supervised a group of young nuns boiling linen rags into pulp for paper. "Do the monks of San Juan de la Peña still stop here on their route north?"

Sister Agathe shook her head. "Not often. It was Brother Arros who used to convince the monks to detour into our little valley, and he no longer travels. His duties as prior forbid it now. And he is not as young as he once was. Riding a mule over the mountains is a burden to him these days, not an adventure."

"Mother Béatrice relied on his counsel for every aspect of the wool business. I hoped he could do the same for you." Mira peered into a steaming vat, then gestured to one of the nuns. "You can fit more rags in here," she told the young woman. "Add a dozen more, but slowly—so you do not get splashed and burned."

The nun nodded and hurried to the rag pile.

Mira watched her carry out the task, then turned back to Sister Agathe. "I would like you to write a letter."

"To whom?"

"To the merchant of Toulouse whom Mother Béatrice made a contract with before she died."

"Whatever for? He will not respond. We broke the contract, never gave him what she promised."

"But the product he desired is still made here. With the right price, he may yet take up the contract again."

"Seems a waste of time," Sister Agathe said in a tone that was both exasperated and doubtful.

"I shall help you compose the thing," Mira said briskly. "We will tell him our price is the lowest he will find for Aragónese wool. And if he points to a competitor with fabric of an equivalent quality, we will price ours cheaper."

Sister Agathe's face took on a brooding look. "How will that benefit us?"

"It will not—in the beginning. But that is not the point. The point is to get our fabric into the hands of a wealthy merchant of Toulouse. Once he has it, others will want it. Then we can raise the price."

Sister Agathe regarded Mira with admiration. "You sounded like Mother Béatrice just then."

Mira smiled. "So I did."

9

Summer, 1504
Abbey of Belarac, Béarn
Mira

ARNAUD SPOKE UP IN the dark one evening, perched on the narrow bed beside Mira in their chamber. They could see stars shimmering against the flat black sky through the open window. A trace of cool air drifted into the room. Mira wished they were still in Ronzal, closer to the stars, where the air was sweeter, scented with pine and wildflowers.

"Those looms were broken on purpose," he said into the quiet.

"What?"

"Someone pried the batten adjusters off the pegs on top of each loom."

"Perhaps they fell off."

"No," he said firmly. "It was deliberately done."

"Why would anyone do that?" Mira asked.

"I've been wondering too."

In the morning, Mira went straight to the servants. Often they were aware of transgressions that were never noticed by the nuns. One of the cooks who had been with the abbey since Mira's childhood still worked in the kitchens. She used to save charcoal sticks so Mira could draw on the cold marble steps of the old well in the kitchen courtyard.

"There are two nuns who came here from the convent in Nay," the cook told her. "Widows. Always keep to themselves. After you left, they asked for the job of keeping the weaving room tidy and stocked."

"Is that unusual?"

"For them, yes. We talked on it in the kitchens, for those two aren't known around here as worker bees. All they ever ask for is leave to go back to Nay."

"How often do they go back?"

"Not so much anymore. Used to be when Mother Béatrice was alive, they'd go back at least thrice a year."

"I do not recall other nuns having the same privilege."

"No. It's something Mother Béatrice worked out with the abbess in Nay, that foreign lady. Seems she had trained 'em to weave, and when we got the looms we needed weavers. So she sent them on, said she had a surplus of such women. But sometimes she'd call them back to Nay."

"Did she indeed?"

The image of Amadina Sacazar's perspiring red face floated into Mira's mind.

The cook nodded. "That's what they told us, anyway."

Next Mira ventured to the stables and found Gaston. He was as large as ever, his shock of thick yellow hair standing on end as usual, and he was occupied rubbing harnesses and bridles with oil. Nearby, a slight man with clay-colored hair filled a wheelbarrow with soiled hay, stabbing great piles of it with his pitchfork, the dull clatter of the metal against the cobblestones ringing out in a slow rhythm.

"Gaston!"

He turned and squinted at her.

"Miss Mira?" Gaston said uncertainly.

"Not miss. Madame Mira now."

"Ah. You've come back." His eyes brightened. "Where did you go?"

She smiled. "Too many places to count. I got married."

He widened his eyes, rubbed his chin with a meaty hand.

"To Arnaud de Luz."

He grunted in astonishment. "You and him...?"

"Yes."

She tamped down the feeling of impatience she always got when dealing with Gaston. The other man stared, leaning the handle of the pitchfork against the wheelbarrow.

"Come out to the courtyard with me, Gaston," Mira said.

"You, get back to work," Gaston ordered the man, following her out the door.

The tines of the pitchfork shrieked against the cobblestones.

Outside, Mira turned to Gaston. "What do you know of those two widows from Nay?"

He thought a moment. "I drive them back there sometimes. Not so much since the new abbess came."

"Where do you take them?"

"To the convent. Drop 'em off there of an afternoon and pick 'em up the next morning."

"That is not much of a visit," she observed.

"That's what they harp on. They talk all the way there and all the way back about how much they hate Abbess Amadina, how cruel she is, how she won't let 'em see their families."

"Do they?" Mira drew closer.

"It's a dull pair they make, complaining the way they do. Like a couple of flies buzzing about my ears." Gaston jangled a bridle for emphasis. "All she does is ask them questions about wool, they say. Questions about the washing and dyeing, the weaving and such."

"Is that so?"

He nodded. A donkey in the stable let out a bray that ended with a long, rasping hiss.

"I'd best get back inside, Madame Mira," he apologized. "They don't like standing in their own mess, the animals. And he's not much help." Gaston jerked his head in the direction of the other man, who stood in the doorway resting his chin on the handle of the pitchfork, staring at them vacantly.

"Thank you, Gaston."

Mira walked quickly away.

The day Mira and Arnaud began making preparations to leave, a reply came from Lord Esteven de Vernier. Sitting side by side at the long table in the main room of the guesthouse, Mira and Sister Agathe pored over the merchant's finely-inked words, crisp and black on linen paper. His elegant signature took up nearly a third of a page.

"See here," Mira remarked. "Lord de Vernier is also a merchant of woad, though he calls it pastel. One of the villagers grows woad on the farthest field down the valley, does she not?"

Sister Agathe nodded. "She makes pigment from it for dyeing homespun. A lovely deep blue."

They continued their study of the letter. The merchant was not prepared to reinstate the contract he had made with Mother Béatrice, he declared, but he would entertain a visit from a delegate and see samples of the wool—if someone could be dispatched to Toulouse.

"This is not an outright refusal," Mira said, chewing her lip. "It affords us an opportunity."

Sister Agathe looked up from the letter, disappointment on her face. "But who will go?"

Mira hesitated, her heart twisting. She had implored Sister Agathe to write the man in the first place. Yet there was no one at Belarac who could do this task with any chance of success—no one but her.

"I will go, of course," she said finally. "And Arnaud. We will see what we can do to convince the man."

"It is such a journey to Toulouse, Mira! What about Bayonne?"

Mira knew she should consult Arnaud first. But when she explained, he would understand. "Bayonne can wait."

"If you are certain, then I will have our most skilled weavers make up the samples."

"First we must dye a batch of wool blue."

"Why?" Sister Agathe leaned back, perplexed.

"I imagine if this man is a merchant of woad, he finds great value in anything blue. If we offered him a gift of fine blue fabric, he might look more favorably upon the abbey."

"He might. What can it hurt? I'll see it done."

"One more thing." Mira lowered her voice. "Those two widows who came from the convent in Nay—they're nothing more than spies for Amadina Sacazar. They report to her about the goings-on of Belarac's wool business."

"But why would Amadina Sacazar care about our wool? Her own fabric is renowned for its quality. She has contracts all over Béarn. There's nothing she can learn from studying us."

"The woman has an addled mind, and she is not inclined toward kindness the way her brother is. I suppose she sees Belarac as a rival to her own wool business."

Sister Agathe's expression tightened. "Are her spies to blame for the broken looms?"

"I cannot be sure, but it seems likely. Do not let them go in there without you. Have someone else tidy the room and stock it—and keep the door locked."

"But how will I—" Sister Agathe broke off. "Never mind. I shall find a way. There is always a method of persuasion."

Mira had seen since childhood how Sister Agathe, in her gentle way, planted seeds of influence and quietly watched them grow. This instance would prove no different.

"You were quick to volunteer us for this task."

Arnaud worked silently by the light of two candles. With slow precision, he shaved off a whisker-thin piece of wood from the batten adjuster he was making, then blew away a bit of sawdust.

"The merchant's letter tells of an inn near his home that will lodge the visitors from Belarac. See?" Mira waved the rectangle of linen paper at Arnaud. "A room awaits us in Toulouse."

He set the metal edge of his tool against the wood again, giving no sign he had heard her.

"Who else could do it but us?" She knelt at his side, one hand on his knee. "I set it in motion, this proposition, and I must see it through to the end. It will delay us only a season more. We shall still be in Bayonne by winter."

"I doubt that," he said after a moment, regarding her steadily. "It is a long journey to Toulouse, and every step will take us farther from Bayonne. Besides, who knows what lies in store for us there?"

"We shall deliver the fabric samples, strike a bargain with the merchant, and turn around again for the west. It will be speedily done."

He put aside his work, shaking his head. "You cannot foresee the future. There will be complications, Mira. Things we can't even imagine."

"I must do it, Arnaud. Mother Béatrice made the wool trade her life's work. Sister Agathe spoke the truth when she said Mother Béatrice had me at her elbow all along. I understand the business of wool like no one else here. Besides, who else in this place has the courage to travel abroad and strike a bargain with a foreign merchant?"

"We both know the answer to that," he said gruffly.

"You should be worried, too, for the abbey's fortunes—"

"Are tied up with Ronzal's," he finished, sighing.

"Please," she pleaded. "Let us go."

Arnaud let the block of wood slide out of his grasp and turned to embrace her. They sank down on the brown wool rug, Mira's skirts pooling around them. He unlaced the ties of her bodice, pulling the cords through each hole with gentle precision. A tingling ignited within her, gathering into a knot just below her belly.

"Husband," she whispered into his ear.

He buried his face in the warmth of her throat, finding the throbbing place that pounded under her skin.

"Wife."

10

Summer, 1504
Nay, Béarn
Amadina

T HE MAN STANDING BEFORE Amadina looked miserable.
Rain had pummeled him throughout the entire journey
from Belarac, and his hair was plastered to his cheeks
like wet string. A sodden flax shirt clung to his skin and a pair
of brown homespun leggings drooped around his thighs. His
bare feet were streaked with mud.

Amadina frowned. Two of the servants had spent the better
part of yesterday morning beating dust out of the red Moorish
rug that her unexpected visitor stood dripping upon. She leaned
back in her chair and tilted her chin up, staring at him with
narrowed eyes.

"What is it you've come all this way to tell me?" she asked.

He hesitated, his gaze sliding greedily around the room. A
person of his lowly stature would be astounded by the opulence
on display, she realized. The rugs, the gilt-framed portraits of

saints hanging on the walls, the silver plate displayed on the oak chests that flanked her desk, the tall beeswax columns in their polished silver candlesticks—all evidence of her power. She was sure no other abbess in Béarn had a parlor quite as grand.

If only she could have this parlor in Zaragoza, where the Sacazars had been a family of repute for generations. Zaragoza was her birthplace, the heart of the kingdom of Aragón, a city of elegance and dignity that bustled with nobles and merchants whose fortunes rivaled her own.

Here in Nay, the members of the so-called merchant class were laughably coarse, just a few notches up from landed peasants. She made it a point to shun them. As a result, she had no friends. Her brother Carlo, his wife Flora, and their two daughters were the only people she visited or entertained. But she had little time for socializing. Running a convent and overseeing the nuns who did the weaving and the lace-making took most of her time, and she was often away attending to the matters of trade. Her convent's merino wool fabric was coveted as far away as Toulouse, and she dreamed of finding a buyer for her lace in Paris one day.

Amadina glared at the sodden man before her. He worked the muscles in his jaw, twisting his hands together.

"Well, what news?" she asked.

"A man and woman with two mules bearing the brand of Ronzal came at the start of summer," he said finally, his voice barely louder than a whisper. "They'd all manner of things strapped to those mules. Made a big fuss about taking it all into the guesthouse, wouldn't be parted from it. Then they stayed on."

"What is that to me?" Amadina asked crossly. "And speak up. You've a terrible case of mumbletongue."

"It was them," he said, louder. "That pale-eyed girl who used to live at the abbey and the big shepherd, the son of the leader from Ronzal."

Amadina's pulse quickened. "What is their business at the abbey?"

"Fixing things, mostly." He swiped his nose with his sleeve. "Helping with the wool dyeing, the weaving…"

"What weaving? I thought their looms were broken."

"He repaired 'em. Handy, that one."

"What else?"

"Gossip is they're heading north soon." He flapped his hand toward the window. "All the way to Toulouse."

A trickle of rainwater rolled down his forehead. She watched the bead of water make its way to the end of his nose and dangle there, quivering.

"Why?" she asked. "Why Toulouse?"

He shrugged. "There was talk of 'samples' among the villagers. And we were ordered to prepare the woad for dye. Those Ronzal folk, they get out of the harvest work by tending to their flocks. All the worst jobs, the stinkiest and dirtiest, fall to the likes of me."

"Woad? What on earth?"

He held out his hands. They trembled a little. "I know not, other than my hands are still blue."

She stared. It was true. She had thought they were simply dirty, but his hands were a ghostly grey-blue, his nails edged with stains the color of the night sky.

"You have given me little information of value," she said.

He drew himself up. His cheeks flamed.

"That's not all!" he protested. "Your spies—they've been forbidden to leave the abbey."

"What?" Amadina felt a rush of anger. "How do you know that?"

"Heard it in the kitchens. They've been turned into kitchen servants and the cook's not pleased, for she hates 'em."

Amadina struggled to steady her breath. Her spies, relegated to Belarac's kitchens? It had to be Mira's doing.

She rummaged in a leather bag she kept in a pocket and drew out three silver coins. "Here."

"But that's silver."

"Gossip gets you silver. Give me something worth gold next time and I'll pay gold."

He pocketed the coins, a sour look on his face. "You only once gave me gold."

"You only once deserved it."

"Then give me another job like that one, when I went to the abbey in Arudy. I did exactly what you said. I took the vial you gave me and—"

"Enough!" Amadina rapped her knuckles on the desk. "Your blather is tiresome."

"I can do it again," he insisted. "Quick and quiet, just like the first time."

"No more of your impertinence. Away!"

The man slunk out the door.

Amadina heaved herself up and crossed to the window. Rain beaded against the leaded glass panes and splattered on the cobblestones in the lane below.

Mira had vanished from Nay last summer having finished only one of the portraits Amadina commissioned from her. Though Amadina dispatched spies south into the Pyrenees to search for the girl, they found nothing. Then winter clamped the mountains shut. One rumor did trickle back to her, though—a story that the girl had run off with that shepherd from Ronzal, crazy with lust, and the two of them lived like beasts in a tumbledown mountain hut.

Amadina stretched her lips back in a mirthless smile. If one paid close attention, one could see kernels of truth tumbling out of the mouths of gossips, glistening like rubies.

Her mind fluttered with memories of Mira, the novice nun who had grown up under the wing of Béatrice of Belarac, enjoying privileges shared by no other orphan in the abbey. When Mira had appeared in Nay after the death of Béatrice some years ago, casting herself as an artist of great skill, gossips whispered that she was the unwanted child of the Baron of Oto, spirited away to the abbey on the day she was born. Usually dismissive of rumors peddled by muleteers, Amadina had looked into the matter. And she had become convinced that in this case, the gossips had got it right.

Though her family had long mistrusted the barons of Oto, her brother Carlo had cultivated a relationship with Ramón de Oto in recent years. It was purely a matter of business: Carlo needed to exploit the man's influence with the royal family of Aragón in order to expand his own merino wool business to the north. Once established in Nay, Carlo had taken advantage of a Béarnaise tradition that allowed impoverished religious houses to sell their titles and holdings to the highest bidder. Now he was a titled man, abbot of two monasteries—and his sister was abbess of a convent.

The Sacazars owed a great deal to the house of Oto. And none of them had benefited more than Amadina. She was acutely aware that few women ever reached the pinnacle of wealth and power that she enjoyed. Therefore, she felt it was her God-given duty to share with Ramón de Oto the sordid rumor that had leaked over the mountains from Aragón into Béarn.

She had not dared sign her name to the letter she wrote, nor did she seal it with her own ring. She dispatched it over the sea to the Kingdom of Naples, where Ramón and his son Pelegrín fought under the command of the Great Captain. She had paid handsomely to get her message safely to the swampy, mosquito-ridden battlefields across the Mediterranean. No price was too high, really. After all, a man of Ramón de Oto's stature and reputation ought to be aware of the gossip that besmirched his name. Only God knew if anything had come of the letter—or if, indeed, Ramón de Oto was still alive.

Whatever the fate of Ramón de Oto, Mira's reappearance was a more pressing matter. Thanks to Amadina's subtle interventions, the Abbey of Belerac no longer posed a threat to her own convent's merino fabric business. In fact, she was currently negotiating a contract with the very merchant in Toulouse who had unceremoniously severed their long-standing partnership in favor of a contract with the abbey some years ago.

If Mira thought she could resurrect the wool business at Belarac, she was sorely mistaken. Amadina would discreetly put an end to her interference, just as she had done with the matter of Béatrice of Belarac. Her brother would be none the wiser, and the Sacazar fortune would continue to grow.

Amadina leaned closer to the window, her breath fogging the glass.

For the first time in ages, she was overcome by a sense of joyous anticipation.

11

September, 2015
Pau, France
Zari

Z ARI LET HERSELF INTO the apartment. It had been raining
in this part of France for four solid days, and the air in the
cramped space smelled musty. She dropped her bags and
looked around. There was nothing chic about the furnishings
or decor, but the apartment was well-lit and clean.

She went to the bedroom and opened the window. A group
of pilgrims wearing rain jackets and carrying hiking poles and
backpacks strode across the small square below, then disappeared up the winding road that led to the old palace overlooking
the city.

Zari smiled. Only a few months ago she had been one of them.

Showered and refreshed, Zari made her way down the curving stone staircase. She passed an elderly man wearing a beret,
slowly ascending the steps with one hand firmly clasping the

handrail. In his other hand was a string bag of groceries and a dripping umbrella.

"*Bonjour, Monsieur,*" she said.

Behind a pair of spectacles, his brown eyes flicked to hers. "*Bonsoir, Mademoiselle,*" he answered gravely.

After five o'clock in France, one said 'good evening,' not 'good day,' she remembered.

"May I help you?" she asked in her best French.

He gave her a startled look.

"With your bag?" she added, gesturing at his groceries.

He shook his head at her, frowning slightly, and continued on his way.

When she got to the ground floor, she glanced up. The man was still climbing.

Outside, Zari navigated the slick cobblestone streets, admiring the medieval stone buildings with their black slate roofs and narrow windows. Another group of pilgrims passed by, their hiking poles clacking against the cobblestones. Watching them, an urge gripped her to don hiking shoes and backpack again, set out into the green foothills, and follow the Camino trail all the way to the highest peaks.

Zari sifted through memories, remembering the long days of hiking, of watching Wil plant his trekking poles in the soft forest floor, listening to his tales of adventure in places she had only imagined. She yearned for him with sudden fierceness, then comforted herself with the thought that he was coming to Pau in a month.

Four weeks was not so long.

Even though it was raining steadily, Zari and Laurence sat outside at a café on a quiet side street. In fact, the outdoor seating area—protected by an orange awning—was completely packed.

Most of the patrons had cigarettes in hand. A haze of smoke hovered over their heads, trapped under the awning.

Zari admired the bubbles spiraling up through their rose-colored drinks. Laurence had insisted on ordering festive cocktails, and these *Kir Royales*, tall glasses of champagne doused with black currant liquor, fit the bill.

"I've been looking forward to seeing your painting in person for a long time," Zari confessed. "When did it come back from the lab?"

"The wait is not over, I'm afraid. My portrait is still in Paris at the conservation laboratory." Laurence rummaged in her handbag for a cigarette and lighter.

Zari put down her glass. "Why?"

"There are more tests to be done."

"What else is left to do? At this point, the paint's been analyzed, the wood panel's been dated, the infrared and x-ray images are done."

"True, but there is also elemental mapping, false color imaging, liquid chromatography..."

Zari leaned forward, eyes wide. "Liquid chromatography? Really?"

"Yes."

"But that's so expensive!"

"I am not paying for it."

"Who is?" Zari asked.

"Herodotus Butterfield-Swinton."

Zari felt her mouth compress into a thin line. "How generous."

"You did not know?" Laurence shook her head, one eyebrow raised in surprise. "He is now working with a Spanish expert on Bermejo. They plan to analyze a Bermejo work with the same tests and they want to compare my painting to it."

Zari regarded her uneasily. "I didn't realize he's been involved in the restoration of your painting."

"No matter who pays for it, the tests will only reveal more of the truth." Laurence lit her cigarette. "Isn't that what you want?"

"Of course." Zari tried to keep her voice light. "I'll be patient. In the meantime, I'm looking forward to Bayonne."

She watched smoke spiraling above Laurence's head.

"I forgot." Laurence smiled. "You're afraid of smoke."

"I'm afraid of lung cancer."

"I quit smoking once. Then my husband died and I started again."

Zari regarded her across the table a moment.

"You could try now, while I'm here," she said. "As an experiment. I'll get nicotine gum for you. You can run with me instead of smoking."

"Run?" Laurence balanced her cigarette in the ashtray on the table, grimacing. "In this rain?"

"I love running in the rain. You like to hike, right?"

Laurence nodded.

"There's not that much difference. You just start slow and combine it with walking. You kind of trick yourself into it to get through the hard part in the beginning when it feels awful. Then, one day, it feels good."

Laurence looked skeptical. She picked up the cigarette again, took a puff, and blew the smoke out in a long stream.

"I'm going running tomorrow morning," Zari said, shrugging. "Text me if you want to join."

As soon as Zari got back to her flat, she made a video call to Vanessa Conlon.

Vanessa, the mentor who helped her secure this research grant, had an adversarial relationship with Dotie Butterfield-Swinton, to put it politely. He was a fixture at Fontbroke College in Oxford. His father had been the dean. And Vanessa was an outsider, an Irishwoman who was one of the first female professors in the college. Dotie slid upward through the ranks of academia with ease, his path oiled by generations of wealth and social connections. Vanessa battled her way up, as she liked to put it, with imaginary mentors keeping her sane in her darkest hours.

When Zari had come to Oxford last year to kick off her research on Cornelia van der Zee, she found an ally in Vanessa, who encouraged her to pursue the idea that Mira de Oto—not Cornelia van der Zee—may have been responsible for Fontbroke College's portrait of a noblewoman. The fact that Dotie had a competing theory about the true creator of the portrait seemed to amuse Vanessa as much as it distressed Zari.

"Dotie's like a dog with a bone, Zari," Vanessa said now, twisting her long dark hair into a bun on the back of her head and stabbing a pencil through it. She was curled in a battered-looking leather armchair, a cobalt-blue wool throw draped around her shoulders.

"I don't get it. In Amsterdam he acted like he had no idea about my new grant. But he must—he's the biggest Oxford insider there is."

Vanessa shook her head. "Oxford is huge. Dotie doesn't step out of the cozy confines of Fontbroke College very often. Unfortunately, I think learning that you're being taken seriously has made him get serious about this Bermejo idea."

"Great."

Vanessa paused, chewing her lip. "He needs a big win right now."

"What do you mean?"

"This summer he let it be known that he wants to become head of his department. But he hasn't had any big scoops lately. His research is lackluster. He hardly publishes at all. If he can prove that Bartolomé Bermejo painted these portraits, he'll walk on water at Oxford."

Zari sat up straighter in her chair. "There's absolutely no proof that Bermejo painted them!"

"Yeah, but there are some similarities to his work in those portraits. The extraordinarily detailed backgrounds, particularly. Plus the fact that his name is written on one of them."

"Mira's name is written on *both* of them," Zari groused. "Doesn't she get any points for that?"

"Try to keep emotion out of this. Look at it logically. You're raising someone from the dead here. Even when they're cloaked with mystery, artists usually at least have a body of work to catalogue."

"Mira does too! I know it."

Vanessa rolled her eyes.

"I'm sorry, Vanessa. The important thing is I have the opportunity to do this work—it never would have happened without your help."

Vanessa smiled. "How's your French?"

"Getting better all the time. I didn't realize how lucky I was that Laurence speaks English so well—most people here don't. It turns out she spent a year in Ireland as an exchange student."

"She's lived among my people? That's a blessing. At the very least, we know she speaks English properly." Vanessa reached for the cup of tea that sat on a table next to her. "You made connections in your research last year that elude seasoned academics. You're curious, Zari, and you're persistent. Just keep doing what you've already shown you can do well."

Zari felt a rush of relief. The tightness in her shoulders eased. Even if she was feeling insecure at the moment, Vanessa seemed to have faith in her. That was something.

"But you should know that your proposal was an outlier for the Mendenhall Trust," Vanessa went on. "I did a fair amount of cajoling on your behalf. And I called in favors."

Zari's moment of contentment evaporated.

Whatever happened, she could not let Vanessa down.

12

September, 2015
Pau, France
Zari

I T WAS THREE DAYS after their first run and Zari had convinced
Laurence to meet her again, despite the weather. She waited
under a tree on the riverfront street that cut through central
Pau. When she spotted Laurence's slight figure approaching on
the rain-slicked sidewalk, she smiled. The Frenchwoman had
grimly plodded alongside Zari for the duration of their inaugural
outing, the total running time of which was approximately seven
minutes. But here she was again, back for more misery, dressed
in an all-black ensemble of athletic tights and fitted rain jacket.

"That is an interesting look," Laurence said as she approached,
her eyes glinting with amusement.

Zari glanced down. Her long-sleeved purple T-shirt decorated
with yellow handprints had been a gift from her niece Eva.
Periwinkle-blue shorts, running shoes sporting various neon
hues, and a lime-green rain jacket rounded out the ensemble.

"I'm all about safety," she said. "Visibility."

Laurence chuckled. "You don't care what people think, do you?"

"In some situations I care very much. But not this one."

They began running along the river, which was swollen with rainwater. Zari watched a branch floating downstream, bobbing madly in the swift current.

"The reality is that I'll never pass as a French person," she pointed out. "Even if I copied your style exactly, people would know I'm not French."

"You could pass," Laurence said, casting a sideways look at Zari. "Your mother is Basque, no?"

Zari nodded. "Half Basque, half Greek. And my dad's mostly French. So if I could just get a perfect French accent, learn how to tie a scarf, and walk on cobblestones in five-inch heels, you're right—I could definitely pass."

"I can teach you how to tie a scarf. Walking on cobblestones... that is just practice. And your accent is good."

They crossed over a bridge and entered a market street lined with cafés and shops.

Halfway down the street, Laurence's mobile rang. She slowed to a stop and took the call under the green awning of a bakery. Every time a patron pushed open the door, the scent of buttery croissants floated outside. Zari's mouth began to water.

A conversation in rapid French ensued between Laurence and her caller. Zari strained to understand the spirited exchange. When Laurence ended the conversation, she turned to Zari with a sober look.

"The archives in Bayonne have flooded," she said. "They are moving everything into a warehouse on higher ground."

"We'll still be able to access what we need, though, right?"

"I am sorry, Zari. Not until next summer at least. Some of the documents are damaged and will have to be repaired."

Zari stared at Laurence, taking in the enormity of her words. Bayonne had been her north star, the centerpiece of her plan, the starting point of everything. If only the archives of Bayonne were fully digitized. It was such a frustrating time to do research. Digitization was happening in fits and starts, and some museum and city collections were available online, while others were still years away from starting.

"That was my one solid lead," she said softly. "Arnaud de Luz and the cabinetmakers' guild in Bayonne."

"You are not looking for Arnaud de Luz, you are looking for Mira," Laurence reminded her.

"They're connected. I saw the proof."

Before she could go on, Laurence held up a hand. "I know you are disappointed. But I have something else to tell you. A friend who works in a museum in Perpignan saw some of your posts about Mira online. She called me last night. There is a prayer book in her museum with artwork that looks similar to Mira's. A prayer book like the one we saw here."

In the archives of the University of Pau that summer, they had examined a sixteenth-century prayer book from the Abbey of Belarac that contained a tiny self-portrait of a young nun, along with the Latin words '*Mira pinxit hunc librum.*' The same day they had found Mira's signature in a parchment mortuary roll that commemorated the death of the abbey's leader, Béatrice.

The disappointment crushing Zari's chest eased a bit. "Where is Perpignan?"

"On the Mediterranean coast. And we must go soon. My friend begins maternity leave in two weeks."

When they set out for Perpignan a few days later, the rain had finally stopped. Laurence's gray Renault wove through the curves of the narrow road, taking them deep into the green foothills of the Pyrenees. The air was cool, the sky capped with lacy clouds. Leaves swirled on the roadside in their wake.

Laurence kept one hand on the stick shift, smoothly down-shifting around each turn, then slipping the clutch and switching into a higher gear on the straightaways.

"You're a good driver," Zari said admiringly. "I don't know very many people back home who can drive a stick shift."

"Can you?"

"My mother had an ancient car when I learned to drive. I had no choice but to figure it out. Which I'm grateful for now, but at the time I thought it was very uncool."

She left unsaid the fact that she had been ashamed of her mother's car, a rattling old Toyota truck with an accumulation of flotsam and jetsam inside that would test the excavation skills of even the most ardent archaeologist. Most of her friends drove their parents' spotless minivans and SUVs. Some of them had been gifted shiny new convertibles for their sixteenth birthdays.

Zari had been hyper-aware of her own family's unconventional story all through her childhood. Her parents had been hippies in the seventies, but when the eighties hit, her father transformed himself into a polo-shirt-wearing commercial realtor, disdainful of the meditation retreats and drum circles that once obsessed him.

He divorced Zari's mother and remarried a much younger woman, also a realtor. They had two daughters in quick succession and rose to prominence in California's central valley as businesspeople of repute. As the years wore on, he made little effort to stay in touch with Zari and Gus. He hadn't remembered Zari's birthday in more than a decade, and her calls to him often went unanswered. She had made peace with that, but what she could not abide was the fact that he was equally neglectful of his grandchildren, Gus's kids. That broke her heart.

Outside her window, the sun burned through the clouds and sent long pale rays into the fields. Zari watched the light shimmer against the grasses, transfixed.

Her reverie was broken when Laurence turned off the road and followed a narrow graveled lane to a Romanesque church, rolling to a stop in a small parking area.

"This is one of my favorite places in these hills," Laurence said by way of explanation.

They entered the church and walked around the perimeter, admiring the jewel-toned stained glass in the high windows, their footsteps echoing on the rutted stone floor. When they emerged from the church, they traced a circle around the exterior, examining the time-worn details that stonemasons had chiseled carefully into the rock centuries ago. Zari stopped at a small door on the south wall that was bracketed by two whimsical carved stone faces.

"That door was for the Cagots," Laurence said. She peeled a piece of nicotine gum from a foil packet and popped it into her mouth.

"The Cagots? Who were they?"

"No one knows where they came from, but they lived in these mountains. They were not treated well. They had to enter churches through these doors and drink from their own holy water fonts."

"Were they a different race?"

Laurence placed her hand on the weathered cheek of one of the carved faces.

"Some think yes, but others say no. No one agrees on what they looked like. They had to wear red marks on their clothes."

"Why?"

Laurence shrugged. "I don't know."

Zari went back inside the church through the main doors, which were flanked by holy water fonts each containing a small amount of water.

She paced down the aisle along the south side of the church until she reached the other, smaller door that had been reserved for Cagots. Next to the doorway stood another holy water font.

Unlike the water fonts by the main doors, this stone basin was dry. Zari ran a finger over the surface of the vessel.

It came away covered in a film of dust.

13

September, 2015
Perpignan, France
Zari

AFTERNOON WAS STRETCHING INTO evening as they approached Perpignan. The landscape was markedly different here from the wooded foothills of Pau. It was drier, the vegetation sparser, the colors more muted. And the air was sultry, heavy with moisture. The blue waters of the Mediterranean shimmered in the distance.

Laurence parked the Renault in an underground lot just outside the historic heart of the city. They walked along a concrete canal lined with green-painted container boxes overflowing with geraniums.

"This used to be a river flowing from the mountains to the sea," Laurence said. Despite the long drive and the heat, she looked fresh and rested, her sleeveless white blouse spotless and unmarred by wrinkles.

Zari watched the gray-green waters flow languidly through the confines of the canal's walls. Glancing down, she noticed a grease stain on the front of her blue shirt. She and Laurence had both eaten croissants this morning at a café. Maybe this was another skill Laurence could teach her: the art of eating flaky, butter-drenched croissants while remaining totally crumb-free.

"But why turn it into a canal?" she asked.

"Floods," Laurence said simply.

They turned a corner. Just ahead loomed a massive crenellated tower built of faded red brick.

"The gates to the city," Laurence said. "All of Perpignan was once surrounded by brick walls. This is all that is left."

They passed through a cool, dark archway at the base of the tower and entered the stone labyrinth of Perpignan's medieval streets.

After a quick lunch in a café on a large, somewhat grungy and dilapidated square, they hurried to the museum. Stepping inside, Zari sighed with pleasure at the coolness of the air, a welcome relief from the harsh afternoon sun outside.

Deep in the bowels of the museum, Laurence's curator friend, her belly swollen under a chic black maternity dress, led them to a brightly lit room outfitted with a long metal table. She removed a leather-bound book from a cardboard box and placed it on what appeared to be a miniature bean bag chair upholstered in velvet. The contraption, she explained, allowed delicate books to sit open without straining their bindings.

Laurence donned white cotton gloves and began to carefully turn the linen paper pages. On one of the first pages was the mark of the bookmaker: a swooping, long-tailed 'R'.

"Albrecht Rumbach's mark. He had a bookmaking shop in Perpignan for many years," the curator said. "Later he had a workshop in Barcelona."

"Why did he leave?" Laurence asked.

"We don't know. Where he came from, why he came, why he left—it's a mystery."

Laurence turned the page.

"Ah—the frontispiece. When I saw your posts online about the prayer book you found in Pau, my mind went immediately to this," the curator said to Zari. "Look at this miniature of a woman."

The small likeness she pointed to did have some similarities to the prayer book from the Abbey of Belarac that Zari and Laurence had examined that summer in Pau. The dark-haired woman's face in this image was round, with almond-shaped brown eyes and wide, red lips.

"We assume this is the patron who commissioned the book, since most of the female images in the book show her face," the curator added. "That was typical of the time."

She directed Laurence to turn several more pages, then held up a hand. "But look at that miniature of Judith slaying Holofernes. I always stop here because something is unusual about it."

Zari slipped a camping headlamp on and picked up a magnifying glass.

"There is a tool made for this job," Laurence remarked, her eyes on Zari's headlamp.

"Yes, a magnifying visor. John Drake has one. It's slightly out of my budget."

"Ah."

"This looks like Mira," Zari said excitedly, peering at the image of Judith.

Pulling a folder out of her bag, she retrieved a color photocopy of Mira's self-portrait that appeared in the prayer book at the university in Pau. She held it up.

"See? The faces are exactly the same."

The curator looked at the two images, nodding. "It's true," she said after a moment. "Every other image of a woman in this book is the patron's. This is the only one that has a different face. And it is a scene of great violence, of a woman murdering a man."

"Is this book dated?" asked Laurence.

"Yes, 1505."

"That's about the right time," Laurence said.

"If Mira was in Perpignan, working for this man," Zari said, "how could she have gotten here from the Abbey of Belarac? It's so far away."

"Pilgrims, shepherds, merchants—they all traveled through the region easily," Laurence said. "The roads go back to Roman times, Zari. This has always been an area of movement, of pilgrimage, of trade between cultures."

Laurence's friend pointed at a rolling table stacked with several other cardboard boxes. "Everything with Albrecht Rumbach's mark is there. You can work until six. But I will tell you now, this is the only book with a high level of artistic skill. The others will not impress you as this one does."

Zari checked the time on her mobile. "Four hours, Laurence. How's your gum supply?"

Laurence patted her handbag. "You bought me enough to last a month."

Nearly three hours later, after examining each page in every book, their eyes were strained and their backs ached. The very first one they had been handed was the only book from 1505. The curator had been right—none of the other books boasted artwork even approaching the level of mastery in that one.

"Let's go back to the first book. The artwork is Mira's," Zari said. "It's identical in style to what we saw in Pau."

"I agree, it looks like hers." Laurence gently placed the book in the support again. "But where is her name?"

In silence they pored over the pages. Somewhere outside the museum, a church bell struck five times.

"One hour left!" Zari lamented. "Turn back to the pages that begin with 'M'."

The minutes ticked by as Zari examined the decorative artwork surrounding each capital 'M'. One page contained a curious cross-hatching of black-inked geometric designs surrounding the letter. Zari bent down, her camping light illuminating the markings through her magnifying glass.

"Aha!" she exulted.

An 'i', an 'r', and an 'a' sat neatly hidden in a thicket of black pen marks as slender as hairs. Through the magnifying glass, her eye followed more letters down and across and back up again, making a neat square.

"'*Mira pinxit hunc librum.*'" Zari whispered the words reverently. "Mira illustrated this book."

Laurence regarded Zari, her face breaking into a radiant smile. "You found her. Again."

14

Summer, 1504
Pyrenees Mountains, Béarn
Mira

O N THE ROAD NORTH from Belarac, Mira and Arnaud fell
in behind a party of Aragónese traders. At midday on
the outskirts of a village, the traders stopped under a
hawthorn tree to spread a picnic. They invited Mira and Arnaud
to join them, laying out copious amounts of dried ham, bread,
olive oil, and salt on a cloth and passing around a wine sack.
After lunch, the traders lay back and tipped their caps over their
eyes while Mira and Arnaud readied their mules again. The
traders said they would catch up after a brief nap and directed
them to a village ahead where the mules could drink from a
fountain in the square.

Passing into the village, Mira and Arnaud heard shouting. The
square was alive with movement and noise. A mob of people was
gathered around the steps of the stone fountain at the square's

center, shouting abuse at something or someone in their midst. Three dogs barked crazily at the outskirts of the crowd.

A woman barely taller than a child stood a bit to the side, one hand over her mouth, watching the scene. Her cap was askew, revealing hair the color of straw.

Mira approached her. "What is happening?" she asked.

The woman would not meet Mira's gaze. "They cut off his hand," she said dully.

"Why? What did he do?"

The man's moans were audible now, drifting over the heads of his attackers, deep and guttural and thick with pain.

"He drank from the wrong holy water font. His hand was nailed to the church door in punishment." She pointed across the square.

Mira could make out an object attached to the front of the church's tall wooden doors. A dark smear trailed down from it.

"He lost a hand for such a small offense?" she asked, incredulous.

The woman turned and held up her arm. "Look." A scrap of red cloth was sewn onto her sleeve. "We Cagots are marked with a brand. We live apart from the rest, and follow the rules they give us. If we fail..." she jerked her head at the mob. "That is our fate."

A light rain began to fall. The change in weather seemed to dampen the fury of the crowd. People sidled away, huddling in small groups or disappearing into their homes. A few passed Mira and Arnaud, glancing curiously at them. The man's body lay sprawled on the cobblestones. Two dogs approached him, sniffing and lapping at his feet.

"Be gone!" Arnaud shouted, handing the mule's lead to Mira. He strode over to the fountain and waved his arms at the dogs. They growled, but fell back.

At the sound of Arnaud's voice, the priest on the church steps turned his gaze on them.

"Who are you?" he demanded.

"A traveler who is used to seeing justice done." Arnaud's voice was like ice.

The priest walked back across the square to the fountain, his hands clasped at his waist. "This is justice, traveler," he said. "The Cagots know the rules. Yet this man broke them."

"You cut off his hand for drinking out of the wrong vessel? That is not justice."

The priest pressed his lips together. "I did not do the cutting. You're a foreigner. You know nothing of this place, nor of our customs."

Mira stepped forward, her lips quivering with rage. "You will simply leave him here to rot? That is Christian mercy?"

"His people will carry him off soon enough." The priest waved a hand dismissively. "Should you not also be on your way?"

"We will rest here, let our mules drink, and be off," Arnaud said.

Mira urged her mule ahead. It shambled over the cobblestones to the fountain, plunged its nose into the cold water, and began to slurp. The dogs paced a short distance away, whining, eager to resume their exploration of the bleeding body.

The priest folded his arms over his chest and scrutinized them in silence for a moment. Then he whirled and tramped across the square to the church. When he slammed the door behind him, there was a faint thud as the dismembered hand slapped the wood.

Mira stared after him. "We cannot leave this man here."

Arnaud made a show of inspecting the baskets strapped to his mule's back and redistributing the goods within them. "We'll tarry a while," he said under his breath. "Maybe his people will come fetch him."

"He bleeds on the outside and most likely on the inside as well. What madness lives in this town?"

"The Cagots are hated. I have heard it said many times. But only now do I truly believe it."

The half-timbered houses that overlooked the square were all shuttered, but they knew that eyes were peering through the slats, waiting to see what happened next.

"Why did he drink out of the wrong font if he knew this was the punishment?"

Arnaud shrugged. "Perhaps he is simply a fool."

Storm clouds moved in, unleashing waves of pelting rain. A group of ragged people darted out from the alleys that radiated from the square. They surrounded the injured man, rolled him into a cloak, and hefted him up. Silently they hauled him away—all but one of them.

It was the yellow-haired woman they had spoken with before.

"Not many would risk aiding a Cagot," she said to Mira and Arnaud. "We will not forget your kindness to my husband."

Mira nodded. "What is your name?"

"Deedit," said the woman. "And yours?"

"Mira, and this is Arnaud."

"My husband was pushed to that fountain with a knife at his back." The woman's voice trembled with anger. "He would never be so foolish as to break a rule. The blacksmith blamed him for the theft of some tools. He did not take them. But a Cagot's word means nothing. We knew he would pay for the crime one day, though he was innocent."

"You do not have to stay here," Mira said, stepping closer. "When he is strong again, go someplace you are welcome."

"There is no such place for us."

"Any convent or monastery on the pilgrim's route north must offer hospitality to travelers. You will find shelter."

Deedit frowned. "My husband's hand is nailed to the door of a church. A house of God offers us no comfort."

"The ancient pilgrim's routes are different. Say to them you are a pilgrim. Away from here, who will know you are a Cagot?"

Deedit let out a bleak laugh. "They always know."

"Rip that red patch off your sleeve. Pretend you are a pilgrim from a foreign land," Mira insisted. "Say your husband was hurt in a threshing accident."

"Cagots aren't allowed to thresh. Our men are carpenters, the women seamstresses. We've no other work."

"His hand was hurt some other way, then—some accident with a mule."

Arnaud stood silent, his eyes roaming over each shuttered window in the square. Loud voices floated out from the top floor of a half-timbered house. Mira saw the worry on his face and gave him a look that meant, "Wait."

"Truly," she went on. "Follow the shells and you will see. They are like stars in the sky, pointing the way north and south. We shall follow that path ourselves, all the way to Toulouse."

"Toulouse?" Deedit backed away a few steps, shaking her head.

A movement in a narrow passageway caught Mira's eye: a man standing with his legs spread wide, watching them.

"Shells and stars are no help to Cagots," Deedit said. "You are kind, but what you talk of is impossible for us. We don't slip through the world so easily as you."

She turned and disappeared into the rain.

"By morning the entire village will know our destination," Arnaud said, his voice tight with irritation. "Be stingier with your promises, Mira." He pulled on the mules' bridles, setting them on a course back to the road. "This is one you'll not likely keep."

"I wanted to give her a bit of hope," Mira protested. "To let her know there is more to the world than this place."

The man observing them had not moved. She stared back, willing him to see there was no fear in her eyes. He ran his tongue over his lips and made a crude mock-kissing noise.

"Look away, Mira." Arnaud pulled the mules forward, blocking the man's view. "You're a stranger who's not welcome here and has no allies in this place."

She yanked the hood of her cloak low over her forehead and stalked along beside Arnaud, fuming. The Cagots endured their harsh treatment because they had no experience of the world. All it would take was one brave soul to abandon this life for another, to strike out along the pilgrim's road, to prove that misery was not their only fate. Imagine if she herself had not summoned the courage to leave, first from the Abbey of Belarac for Nay, and then to track down the truth about her own origins high in the mountains of Aragón. She would still be illustrating manuscripts at Belarac, preparing for the life of a nun.

A dissenting voice in her head pointed out that nothing in Deedit's experience had given her reason to hope. Why would the woman trust a stranger after enduring a lifetime of treachery and abuse?

Mira quickened her pace to keep up with Arnaud.

"You wish her the same freedom that you enjoy," he said after they had put a considerable distance between them and the village. "But open your eyes, Mira! A Cagot woman and a daughter of barons are worlds apart."

There was a current of anger in his voice now, a dark, coiled emotion that he rarely revealed.

"Elena taught you to defend yourself, showed you there was life beyond the convent's gates," he went on. "Your mother, with her sacks of gold, made sure you had other...privileges. Deedit's not so lucky."

Arnaud was right.

Mira had been denied her birthright as a noblewoman. She never knew what it was to grow up in the ancestral castle under the wing of her baroness mother. But her childhood in the abbey—copying manuscripts, stirring the great copper wool-washing vats, bathing the feverish limbs of pilgrims in the infirmary—was a privileged one.

She felt a rush of shame, remembering something Amadina Sacazar had once told her: *Someone paid for your life in gold coins.*

Deedit, like most women and all Cagots, had no such benefactor.

15

Summer, 1504
Pyrenees Mountains, Béarn
Mira

IN MID-AFTERNOON, THEY CAME to a place in the road where
a narrow trail led to a monastery. At the intersection of the
road and the trail was a tall marker stone decorated with a
carved scallop shell.

Mira traced the outline of the shell with a finger. She recalled
Deedit's haunted face, the sodden hem of her cloak dragging
over the cobblestones as she melted into the shadows.

Arnaud led the mules up the trail toward the monastery.

"They do have to accept all travelers, do they not?" she called
after him.

"Ask the monks and see."

The monastery was on a high outcropping of rock overlooking
a narrow valley. Clustered ferns waved in the breeze at the base
of the staircase that led to the monastery's arched entry doors.

Climbing roses clung to the stone balustrade, their petals long dead, their leaves beginning to wither and yellow.

A monk gestured to Mira and Arnaud to follow him, while another led their mules to the stables. As they walked around the periphery of the courtyard, they watched a group of monks working in the kitchen gardens that took up the entire rectangular space. Several men were bent over preparing small beds for crops, while others were on their knees, weeding.

Their room was tiny, with a narrow bed made of rough alder planks covered with a straw-stuffed mattress. A square hole was cut into the door at eye level. The monk opened a small chest next to the door and pulled out two brown hooded robes made of rough homespun cloth. Another man appeared lugging two pails of water, one of which was steaming. From his pockets he plucked towels of flax cloth and a square of yellow soap flecked with lavender flowers.

Mira hung her cloak over the hole in the door and the two of them did their best to bathe without slopping too much water on the stone floor. The soap was rough against their skin, and the sharp scent reminded Mira of the lavender oil her mother loved. One day, Mira vowed, she would have a limitless supply of lavender oil herself and anoint her body with it every day.

Dry, she slipped the brown robe over her head. "This is not the most flattering dress I have worn," she observed.

"Then take it off again," Arnaud said, watching her from the bed.

"I do not think the monks would appreciate the sight of an unclothed woman when we go to fetch our supper."

"On the contrary." He beckoned to her. "My wife," he whispered, sliding his hand under the coarse cloth.

"Husband, it is not seemly to embrace within the walls of a monastery," she whispered back, her fingers tracing the ridges of his cheekbones. "Let us go in search of what is sure to be a savory meal."

She pulled the cloak away from the door and gasped. A monk was staring through the hole directly at her.

The man widened his brown eyes, whirled and disappeared down the corridor. Mira turned to Arnaud.

"What was that about?"

"They do not see many women, I'd imagine."

Mira quickly pulled the hood of her brown robe over her head. She hated the feeling of being scrutinized. It was something she had become sensitive to in Nay, when gossips had begun circulating the tale that she was no mere orphan raised by nuns, but the daughter of an Aragónese baron. How confidently she had rejected that rumor! But in that instance, when the gossips' tongues wagged, the truth came out.

As she and Arnaud padded barefoot down the stone corridor to the guesthouse kitchens, her mouth twisted into a wry smile. To think she, this shoeless creature in a shapeless homespun robe, was the child of barons. Stumbling on a crack in the floor, she suppressed a wild urge to laugh.

They sat on a bench at a long wooden table and were served barley porridge, mugs of ale, slabs of cheese, and a hunk of dry bread. The porridge was tasteless, the cheese stank of mold, and they had to soak the bread in ale to soften it.

Mira had grown up on a diet not much superior to this in the abbey. But Arnaud's village of Ronzal was rich in flocks, situated near trading routes, and home to a people who knew how to glean the treasures of the mountains. He was accustomed to plenty of meat, to salt and olive oil, to nuts and fruit and wild honey, to creamy cheeses made from the milk of sheep and goats. She watched him swallow a gray hunk of bread, resignation on his face.

"Hunger is the best sauce," she whispered.

He shot her a sardonic look.

The prior entered and sat down next to Arnaud. He had a high forehead and a long nose, and his brown eyes were wedged under thick black brows.

"I hope your meal suffices," he said. "We bake bread but once a week, and our cheese stock runs low."

"Our thanks to you, prior. We're grateful for your hospitality," Arnaud said. "We were in sore need of a bath and a meal."

"It is my God-given duty," the prior said. "Where are you traveling to, if I may ask?"

"Toulouse," said Arnaud.

"What do you know of the city?"

Arnaud glanced at Mira.

"It is a city of merchants," she asserted. She imagined the high walls of Toulouse, the great houses glittering like dark jewels against the dun-colored plains of the north.

"Have you been to Toulouse before?"

"No, but we have a contract to fulfill with a merchant, and a bed awaits us in a fine inn there."

"How do you know it is fine if you have never been there?"

Mira felt a prick of annoyance. "Lord de Vernier would not lie to us. He said it is where all the merchants lodge their suppliers, the Inn of the Blue Ox."

"Ah. I have heard of the place. He spoke the truth."

The prior turned his gaze to Arnaud. "You will be oddities there. An Aragónese mountain man and his high-born wife."

Arnaud put down his mug.

"I don't mean to offend," the prior continued, "but one of you is clearly of mountain stock, while the other is just as clearly not. This will raise questions."

"We'll keep to ourselves," Arnaud said. "As soon as our affairs are organized, we'll be on our way."

"Let me offer you some words of advice." The prior looked pointedly at Mira. "First, discretion is an excellent idea."

Mira stopped chewing her bread a moment and glanced at Arnaud. She felt chastened for the second time that day. The tips of her ears began to burn.

"I have heard it too many times to count from travelers of every stripe," the prior went on. "Toulouse is a place where greed is only equaled by jealousy, a city filled with untrustworthy people all intent on making a fortune off the color blue."

"You speak of the woad industry?" Arnaud asked.

The prior nodded. "Those who grow rich from it call the stuff pastel, not woad. If you plan to involve yourselves in that business, put your confidence in no one. And remember—the Aragónese are not beloved by the French. I trust you are aware that the King of France only lately lost the war for Naples to your Queen Isabella. All the more reason to keep your origins to yourself."

Mira gave a start of recognition. Her father and brother fought in that war. Who knew how many Frenchmen they killed on the battlefields. Perhaps they themselves had died, torn apart by some French knight's sword. Or perhaps they were even now sailing home to Aragón, intent on returning to Oto and finishing the job that the steward Beltrán had failed at when he killed her mother and then tracked Mira to the cave. She stared into her porridge, remembering the man's fingers on her neck, his foul breath in her face, the covetous gleam in his eyes.

"How do you come by this knowledge, prior?" Arnaud asked.

"Pilgrims stop here, as you know," he said. "They bring us news from the outside world. If what I have learned can help others, I share it."

"If Cagots were to stop here," Mira asked, "would you let them lodge?"

"Of course. We turn away no travelers."

"Is that true of every place on the pilgrim's way?"

"It is how things should be. But only a fool would say yes. Why?"

Mira told him of the gruesome sight they had witnessed in the mountain village.

"There are strange customs governing the lives of Cagots. I have heard of such unjust treatment before. Who cut off the man's hand?"

Mira and Arnaud looked at each other.

"We did not see," Mira admitted. "The priest denied doing it. But the man's hand was nailed to the church door."

"A priest is overseen by others more powerful than he," the prior said after a moment. "Perhaps he was carrying out their bidding."

"Perhaps." Mira tilted her head, hesitating. "Are you subject to the same...obligations?"

"There is little on this scrubby mountainside to invite the interest of bishops," the prior said. "We scratch a living from the earth, keep a few mules, a small herd of goats. We are not like the monasteries over the mountains in Aragón, with their fleeces of merino piled like snowdrifts. For us, poverty and isolation beget a bit of freedom."

He leaned forward, a new intensity in his tone, his eyes fixed on Mira's.

"Priests feel the scrutiny of their superiors, but they also endure the judgement of the townspeople who fill their coffers with coin. Perhaps that priest was simply complying with the demands of his congregation. I imagine judgement is a force you, too, shall reckon with in Toulouse. You would be wise to remember it."

16

Summer, 1504
Pyrenees Mountains, Béarn
Mira

MIRA SHIVERED. THE CHILL of evening was descending, though the western sky still glowed amber above the ridges. Dawn and dusk were always marked by a stillness that drifted down and clung to the land. Or perhaps the quiet was always there, but she only noticed it when night melted into day or day faded into night.

Their journey north was slow, hindered by the pace of the mule train that they were bound to follow for their own safety. Now the mules ahead were no longer in sight, for they had turned off to the guesthouse of the monastery at St. Anne's. Still, they heard the faint sound of the pack-animals' hooves striking stones on the road.

"Nearly there," Arnaud called out from behind her.

At the edge of her vision Mira saw a shadow move in the trees just off the road.

She turned, eyes wide. "Arnaud, look—"

Three cloaked figures rushed out from the forest. Mira and Arnaud scrambled for their weapons too late and were dragged from their mounts. Mira drew a breath to scream with all the volume she could muster. Perhaps the mule train was still in earshot. Perhaps someone would raise an alarm and send out a party to investigate. No sooner did she open her mouth than one of the men leaped forward and slapped her face. She staggered back, the metallic taste of blood filling her mouth. Arnaud shouted in outrage, scrambling to his feet—but he, too, was silenced with a mighty blow to the head. He sank to the ground.

Mira swallowed her own blood. She stood on wobbly legs, trying to calm herself, trying to ignore the terror that rose in her throat.

The third man busied himself with their mules, taking each by the bridle and leading them into the woods.

"What do you want with us?" Arnaud tried to stand.

He was rewarded for his words with a savage kick to the gut.

"We are under the protection of barons," Mira said with all the confidence she could muster. "If any harm comes to us, you shall meet your end in a dungeon."

"Shut your trap," the man closest to her growled. "It's your own end you should be worried about."

He spewed a gurgle of laughter and prodded Mira forward. The men pushed and dragged their captives through a grove of pines to a meadow that was divided by a wide stream, its banks swollen by snowmelt. A log lay across the stream, forming a rude bridge. In the half-light Mira saw a stone cabin on the other side of the water.

Ahead of her Arnaud stumbled and nearly fell, then righted himself. What would they do to him? To her? She choked back a sob.

The group paused before the stream. One of the men edged across the log and jumped heavily to the ground on the other side, turning to face them.

"Come on then," he shouted. "Get over here and be quick about it."

Arnaud stepped out on the log and began to move slowly across it. The dark water pulsed by, rippling and whispering. Mira stopped on the streambank and made a great show of gathering her skirts. She took a hesitant step forward. Then she sprang up on the log, snatched Arnaud's hand, and dragged him with her into the icy water.

There was a tremendous splash.

The swift current pulled them downstream faster than Mira had imagined. She tried to touch the bottom with her feet but it was too deep. In the next instant, she was sucked under.

Their attackers let out a barrage of outraged shouts, racing along the banks, trying to keep pace. But the stream curved around a bend thick with willows where the banks were steep and impassable.

Mira fought her way to the surface, the shock of the cold water paralyzing her lungs. She forced herself to draw a breath, then another. Water flooded her mouth. She coughed, kicking her legs the way Elena had taught her all those years ago.

The water pulled her under again. She flapped her arms, forcing herself back up as the current pulled her along. They were sluicing through the forest now. Tall pines closed in on either side of the stream. She imagined a great waterfall ahead, a bubbling pool beneath it spiked with jagged stones.

"Arnaud!" she cried, panicking.

"It's wider here," he shouted from somewhere ahead of her. "Swim to the rocks!"

She saw a group of boulders and willed her body to move toward them, spluttering and gagging, her heavy wool cloak dragging her under again. Somehow she clawed her way to the rocks and wedged herself between two of them. Arnaud was draped over a flat rock nearby, face down, heaving.

After a few moments he sat up and put a hand on her back. She felt the reassuring weight of it through her sopping clothes, and thanked God he had survived her reckless act.

"By the sun and stars, why did you do that?" His words came at intervals between gasping breaths.

"That cabin. They would have killed you, and as for me..." Mira shook her head against the rush of dark thoughts in her mind.

"We nearly drowned," he rasped. "Would that have been better?"

"Yes!" For a moment Mira busied herself trying to wring out her skirts. Her hands were too cold to be of much use, and she soon gave up. "Do you think they followed us from the village?"

"We made ourselves targets, no denying that. But bandits ply these roads, and to my mind these men were no villagers out to teach a pair of strangers some lessons."

"They have everything. My mother's portrait. The chair you carved. The fabric samples for the merchant!" Mira's voice rose in panic.

He enfolded her in his arms and for a moment she sat listening to the thump of his heart.

"We're alive." He looked up at the towering pines, at the stars that glimmered faintly in the narrow strip of slate-blue sky visible overhead. "As far as the rest—we've just misplaced those things. I've no intention of letting them go."

17

Summer, 1504
Pyrenees Mountains, Béarn
Mira

AT DAWN, MIRA AND Arnaud walked shivering in their sodden clothes back to the site of their capture. They retraced the the stream's route through the woods, struggling through the dense groves of willows along the banks. Fresh signs of mules and men led them up a winding smuggler's path into a narrow valley.

It was not long before they spotted the mules across a small meadow that was bracketed with birch groves. A short distance away, a smudge of smoke curled up from a rudimentary camp. Mira and Arnaud slunk around the birches toward the mules.

In the distance one of the men bent over the fire, poking it with a stick.

The mules' ears pricked up when they heard Mira and Arnaud approach. They began to shift restlessly. Mira and Arnaud took hold of the ropes that bound the animals to a birch tree and quietly worked at the knots.

One of the mules stepped on a dry branch, startling the other into a high-pitched whinny.

The man tending to the fire stood up.

"What's spooked you?" he shouted, moving across the meadow. His companions were slow to rouse themselves. One propped himself up on an elbow, rubbing his eyes.

Mira slipped her dagger from its sheath and slashed the ropes. Arnaud held out a hand to help her into the saddle.

But the man was moving quickly now, closing the distance between them. He yelled hoarsely for his companions, a blade in his hand.

Arnaud stepped in front of Mira, evaded a thrust of the man's dagger, and felled him with a swift kick. The man got hold of his ankle and yanked him off balance. The dagger tumbled to the ground, but the bandit snatched it up again.

One of the mules bolted across the meadow to escape the fray.

Another man was crashing through the underbrush toward them, fully awake now, a short sword in his hand. Mira's fingers closed around her dagger. She stepped behind a tree trunk, into the shadows. The man lunged past her toward Arnaud, who still grappled with the other bandit.

Mira stuck out a foot and tripped the man as he raced past. He rolled, seized one of her legs in his hand, and gave it a sharp tug. As she fell, she saw the flash of his blade in his free hand. With a desperate yank she wrested her leg from his grasp, sprang up, and turned on her heels. He caught hold of her skirts and dragged her back toward him. She twisted and arched, straining to get away. But it was no use. The dark shape of his arm rose up over her head, the blade glinting in his grasp. Just before he brought it down on her, she jammed her dagger into the side of his neck.

He grunted in surprise, fell heavily to his knees. Blood spurted from the wound, splattering the earth with dark, glistening stains.

She threw a glance at Arnaud. His dagger was buried in the other man's ribs.

They both stood panting, shoulders heaving, watching the life drain out of their attackers.

The third man had stopped halfway across the meadow. For a moment he stood unmoving, his eyes on the forms of his fallen companions. Then he sidled backward and fled to the mule that now stood nonchalantly grazing the lush green grass. He pulled it up by the reins and leapt on its back, digging his boots into its belly and urging it forward into the woods.

"After him!" Mira cried, rushing forward.

"No," Arnaud said, putting out an arm to stop her.

"But he has our things." She frantically searched through the goods strapped to the remaining mule. "The painting is not here. Nor the pieces of your chair. Just the fabric samples and our satchels."

She listened to the trampling of the mule as it ascended the smuggler's trail. The sounds faded with each passing moment.

"Arnaud!" she beseeched him.

He stood his ground.

"What good will it do us to chase him? We've only the one mule between us, and look at its burdens. We're lucky to be alive. Let's get back on the road north and finish the job we've been tasked with."

Mira knew he was right.

"But the painting." Her voice was small.

It was the only record she had of her mother's image, of their fleeting time together. She could not bear the thought of parting from it.

"Don't despair, Mira," Arnaud said, drawing her close. "There's always a chance that it will come back to you."

He winced, putting his palm to his side. Mira stared at him in alarm.

"You're bleeding!"

She pulled his vest and blouse up. His opponent's dagger had made a long, thin gash in the flesh over two of his ribs. Thankfully, the wound was not deep. But it bled profusely.

"Sit!" she ordered.

Yanking up her skirt, she ripped a length of flax cloth from her shift. She folded it in a square and pressed it against his wound.

He grimaced. "Don't make it worse, now."

Mira shushed him. "It bleeds too much. We shall have to turn back to the monastery."

Arnaud shook his head. "We're closer to Nay than we are to the monastery. Let's call upon Carlo Sacazar for aid."

Mira stared at him, biting her lip.

"Carlo Sacazar has always been a man of honor in his dealings with us and with the abbey," Arnaud reminded her.

"But his sister—"

"He can't help being bound to her. But he's nothing like her. You know it's true!"

She took a breath to argue.

Arnaud went on before she could speak. "Even if we return to the monastery, what can they do for us other than offer me a healing salve or two? We have only one mule now. We've lost everything of value save that wool fabric. There are many days of travel ahead to Toulouse. Who knows if we'll be ambushed again? The road crawls with bandits, bears, and wolves. Look at me, Mira." He gingerly lifted the blood-soaked padding and eyed his wound. "Nay is our best hope."

A bluejay landed in a branch overhead and shrilled a warning at them.

Mira swallowed her words, the fire dying within her at the sight of his blood.

Her own fears, whether they were warranted or not, would have to be put aside.

18

Summer, 1504
Nay, Béarn
Mira

"L ORD SACAZAR." MIRA'S SMILE was forced. She hoped it did not betray the anxiety roiling in her stomach. "It is an honor to be welcomed into your home once again. Please may I present my husband Arnaud de Luz—"

"Señor de Luz, of course, we are well acquainted!" Carlo made a little bow to Arnaud. "I have often conversed with you and your father in the course of a market day."

Arnaud bowed deeply in return. "I am honored." When he straightened, a bloom of fresh blood showed on the fabric of his blouse.

"The saints and stars above, you are injured!" cried Carlo. "Allow my servants to tend to you at once." He clapped his hands and several servants came running.

"Would you be in possession of butterwort salve to stop any infection?" Mira asked him.

"I am sure I possess everything under the sun that can cure a man," he assured her. "We have accumulated an arsenal of potions and herbs for every conceivable ill."

Mira murmured her thanks, watching Arnaud disappear from the room.

"They will have him in fine form again within the hour," pronounced Carlo. "Let me offer you refreshment. All I ask in return is the favor of a story."

"A story?"

"Yes, the tale of your predicament. Whatever course of events led you to my doorstep. I shall be quite mesmerized by it, I imagine."

"But first let me inquire after the health of your wife and daughters," Mira said.

He waved her into a leather-backed oak armchair and poured a thin stream of red liquid from a pitcher into a tiny silver glass, which he placed on a polished wooden table at her elbow.

"My Flora is a rose always in bloom. And our girls have their mother's constitution, praise God. They are all three ensconced in our summer residence near Zaragoza." He poured himself a cup as well.

"And your sister?"

"She, too, is in good health. Off on her annual wool-buying trip along the pilgrim's route. It is her summer custom. Keeps her apprised of the competition."

Mira felt the fear in her gut begin to unknot itself.

Carlo sank into the chair opposite hers and fixed her with an encouraging smile. "I must tell you," he confided. "I was quite worried when you disappeared from Nay. As were others in the town who had hoped for works as fine as this one on their walls..."

He gestured at the portrait that hung over an oak sideboard. Mira glanced at it, then dropped her eyes.

"It was a family matter that took me away from here. I had no choice but to leave." She broke off, her mouth suddenly dry.

"Oh, dear." He held up a hand. "You grow distressed. Let us speak of other things. Such as the adventure that led you to my doorstep once again. I only mean to say how delighted and relieved I am to see you well. Please, begin."

By the time Arnaud joined them again, Carlo had downed several cups of wine. Two spots of color adorned his plump cheeks, and his dark eyes glistened as he ushered Arnaud into a chair and offered him a drink.

"Your wife has told me the most astounding tale," he said. "I assure you, when I rose today I had no inkling what excitement was in store for me."

Arnaud raised his cup. "To your health, Lord Sacazar, with my gratitude."

They all drank.

"It seems you find yourselves in a quandary," Carlo said. He set his cup down and leaned his elbows on the arms of his chair. "All in the name of helping the Abbey of Belarac. I feel a tug of sympathy in my heart, for I greatly admired Mother Béatrice. I often said she had the soul of an angel and the mind of a merchant. There aren't many women like her. She took in so many widows, so many orphans. And her end came far too quickly. There was much more she could have done." He smiled sadly, gazing at the cherubs carved in stone that frolicked over the massive hearth. Then he fixed his eyes on Arnaud.

"I hear the bandits made off with the chair you spent all winter carving?"

"Yes." Arnaud put his cup down. "I planned to take it to the cabinetmakers' guild in Bayonne when we arrive in hopes of finding a place in their ranks."

"But now you are diverted to Toulouse instead."

"Yes, but only briefly. Once we conduct our business there, we leave for Bayonne."

"Ah. The loss of the chair is of course a disappointment. But the accepted practice these days when approaching a guild is to present a letter of recommendation vouching for one's talents. It's near impossible to gain admittance otherwise. How does this strike you: I'll write such a letter to the cabinetmaker's guild of Bayonne, send it off, and by the time you reach the city it will be in the hands of the guild master."

"I would be much obliged," Arnaud said gratefully.

"It will be an easy letter to write." Carlo shifted in his seat. "But I wish you would reconsider the offer I made you last year to work here in Nay. There is an endless supply of quality wood in these mountains, and I now have a furniture-making work-shop to complement my other businesses. Few possess skills like yours. I could use you here, and pay you handsomely."

Arnaud dipped his head in thanks. "I am flattered, Lord Saca-zar. My wife and I have made up our minds, though. Bayonne is where we'll seek our fortune. We're bound to help Ronzal with a new venture to pole-barge oak down the river Pau to the harbor there."

"Indeed? Yes, a hunger for good oak grows in the north. Word is they've cut down all the forests in those lands."

Arnaud nodded. "Others in the mountains already do this, at great profit."

"And great peril," Carlo said. "Felling oaks, carting them to the river—that is not easy work." He stared at Arnaud thought-fully. "Why not build up your wool business instead? There is no end to the demand for fine merino fabric."

Arnaud glanced at Mira. "Our Ronzal flocks are bound to overwinter at Belarac, it's written in the ancient agreements. But if there's not enough fodder for them under this new abbess, we'll be lucky to hang on to the animals we have. Building up our flocks would be impossible. No, it's better to try something new."

"Bayonne it is, then, if I cannot persuade you otherwise." Carlo looked at Mira again. "I know the terror that roadside bandits can inspire, and I wish I could allay your fears. The least I can do is send you on your way with another mule so that your journey progresses with haste." He held his hand up to ward off their protests. "No, no, I insist. And I also give you my assurance that what we've spoken of today shall remain a private matter."

With that he stood. "May I offer you a room for the night? I shall call for my notary and have him write up the letter of recommendation in the morning." He paused, searching for the right words. "I do not wish to offend you, Señor de Luz, but can you write your own signature?"

Arnaud nodded. "No offense taken, my lord. I read and write."

"In several languages," Mira added a trifle hotly.

A broad smile creased Carlo's face. "My apologies. I know your father is learned, so I might have assumed the son was as well. But I also know that assumptions are often wrong."

Mira was instantly contrite. "We are in your debt, Lord Sacazar."

He shook his head. "It is I who is indebted to you, Mira— pardon me, Señora de Luz. The portraits you painted are priceless to me. They bring me joy every day. I am glad you came to me for aid. If you ever need my assistance in the future, you have only to ask. And should you ever require a recommendation from a patron, please think of me first."

Mira searched his eyes and found only kindness. It was true, he had always been a man of his word. He had been a friend to Mother Béatrice and had helped the shepherds of Ronzal sell their wool in Nay. Why, then, did the sight of him set her pulse racing? It was his sister Amadina whom she did not trust, after all. Not him.

As she and Arnaud left the parlor and followed a servant up the curving staircase to their chamber, she worried over a thought that had long tormented her.

How could one Sacazar be so good-hearted and the other so cruel?

19

Summer, 1504
Nay, Béarn
Carlo

ARLO STARED AT THE door long after Mira and Arnaud had left the room, his arms folded across his chest. He gazed unseeing at the polished oak panels, the ironwork spiraling out from the door's massive hinges, his mind sorting through a lifetime's worth of memories and coming to rest, as it often did, on his sister Amadina. His brain churned so intensely that he failed to hear the crackle of wood in the hearth, the coo of a dove on the windowsill. The entire world dropped away as he riffled through the past.

Something had happened last summer between Amadina and Mira, he was sure of it. He and his family left Nay expecting Mira to be in her chamber at their home when they returned that autumn. She had a full schedule of portraits to paint, after all: two for Amadina and several for Nay's other leading families. And yet, when they returned from Zaragoza, Mira was gone, leaving her contracts unfulfilled. The town gossips said she ran off with a shepherd. There was no point dispatching servants to investigate, for winter soon sealed off the passage through the mountains to Aragón.

He had questioned Amadina, but she fluttered her eyelashes at him the way she always did when she was being evasive, claiming ignorance of the entire matter. Carlo had listened with his customary skepticism. He knew his sister too well, better than he even knew himself. He had spent a lifetime studying her, trying to discover what made her happy. It had taken far too long for him to realize that happiness was out of Amadina's reach. For her veins flowed with as much bitterness as blood.

He had tried since they were children to mollify her, to ease her anger. Yet as soon as she was soothed, another eruption bubbled forth. She thrived on rage.

In his campaign to appease Amadina, Carlo had developed a habit of placating her with money and gifts and contraptions for her growing industries. There was no end to the stream of widows and fallen women who made their way to her doorstep. No sooner had Carlo delivered another loom to Amadina than it was put to use in her workshop. Lately she was consumed with lace-making and sat for hours overseeing the nuns who worked their threads of silk into lace by candlelight.

She had taken an intense interest in Mira, had grasped onto the rumor bandied about by muleteers that the girl was a child of the barons of Oto. Carlo tried his best to dissuade her from spreading such gossip, though in his heart he believed it was true. After all, he had spent enough time with Marguerite de Oto to see how much Mira resembled her. It was mostly in their pale gray-green eyes, as watchful and wide as the eyes of a cat.

He had wondered last summer if Amadina frightened Mira away from Nay with some cruel trick of the tongue. And it was obvious just now, when Mira asked about Amadina, that something troubled her. There had been a shadow on her face—not fear, exactly, but apprehension.

Carlo sighed.

Whatever the truth regarding Mira's origins, Carlo had no desire to dig into the matter. He despised gossip. His wife Flora's interest in salacious stories was the one thing about her that he disliked, and he was quite stern with her when she indulged in such talk.

But since Béatrice of Belarac died he had been plagued by an irksome feeling of responsibility toward Mira. It had settled into his bones and become another burden to carry around. So he was heartily relieved when she appeared healthy and whole on his doorstep today—and yet he fretted anew, imagining the dangers she faced in the world outside the abbey's gates. Surely Béatrice would have wanted Carlo to intervene in some way, to help the girl and her husband find security in their new life together.

Slowly he turned and regarded the portrait that hung on the opposite wall. He in his fur-trimmed cloak and matching cap, his fingers adorned with gold. Flora and their two young daughters, dressed in identical red gowns. The whimsical background with its balcony, its twining vines, the snow-covered mountains in the distance. He had brought the portrait to Zaragoza years ago, but at Flora's insistence he had returned it to their Nay residence last autumn. She had argued, rightly, that since they spent so little time in Zaragoza, it made no sense to keep their most treasured possession there.

He approached the panel and reached out a finger, stroking the gilt-covered frame with satisfaction. Yes, Mira had created a masterful image of his family. He would cherish it until the day he died.

Carlo went to his desk and removed a sheet of linen paper, his pot of ink, and a quill from a drawer. The letter to the cabinetmakers' guild would wait until tomorrow when his notary could be present, but another note was already taking form in his mind. He would write to the man who taught Mira to wield a paintbrush with masterful skill—and see if there was something he could do to nurture her fledgling career as an artist.

He glanced at the portrait again, working the muscles in his jaw. *Had* Amadina done something to frighten Mira off last summer? Carlo frowned. One thing was certain—he would never get the truth out of his sister.

Overcome by a growing sense of urgency, he dipped his quill in the ink and began to write.

BOOK II

Tu ne cede malis sed contra audentior ito.
Yield not to misfortunes, but advance all the more boldly
against them.
—Virgil

1

October, 2015
Pau, France
Zari

IN HER SUBCONSCIOUS MIND, Wil's face appeared in the dim light, his unruly hair a soft halo around his head. He found the pulse point in her neck with his lips, then turned his attention to the hollow at the base of her throat. Her eyelids fluttered, and she breathed in deeply, letting out her breath in a long exhalation of contentment. His lips traced a path down her body, his ministrations to her most secret and sensitive spots made in silence. In a moment, startled by her own cry of pleasure, Zari felt herself surfacing from sleep.

Wil's deep, languid laugh sounded in response. She sat up in bed, her body tingling with luxurious aftershocks. He rolled back, one hand propped under his head, one hand on her naked thigh.

"Not a bad way to wake up," he said, grinning.

"I'll say." She pulled him up next to her and settled into the crook of his arm. "I had no idea you were so schooled in the art of surprises."

"I said I would be late getting in, you left me a key, the rest is history."

He drew a circle around her belly button with a finger.

"How long do we have?" she asked.

"More than forty-eight hours."

"That's something to celebrate. I think I'll start by giving you a taste of your own medicine."

She kissed him with a ferocity and tenderness she never knew she possessed until Wil entered her life. Zari had never been in love before, had resigned herself to the idea that she simply wasn't built for it. And then one winter night in Amsterdam, this tall, wild-haired, bespectacled Dutchman had knocked her off her feet. Literally.

It had been her fault. As he was quick to point out that night, she committed a typical tourist error: walking in a bike lane. She smiled, remembering the terrible first impression she'd had of Wil. He seemed superior and dismissive, blaming her for the accident. Her temper flared and she stalked away. Concerned that she was really hurt, he insisted on walking her back to her hotel. Then, out of nowhere, came his rollicking laughter. Its infectious warmth and richness seemed completely at odds with his stern demeanor. And she knew in that moment with utter certainty that she had to hear him laugh again.

The next morning dawned gloriously crisp and bright. They rented bicycles, rode to an outdoor market, and filled their baskets with cheese, bread, fruit, and wine. Pedaling along a narrow lane through fields that bordered a winding river, they watched amber-colored leaves spiral down to the ground, shorn from tree branches by a strong breeze. The white peaks of the Pyrenees loomed over the hills to the south.

When they found the perfect place for a picnic on the river-bank, they spread out their jackets and unwrapped their market goods. Wil's keychain sported a multitool with a tiny corkscrew. He made a dramatic show of popping the cork out, offering Zari the first swig.

"French people would never drink out of the bottle," she remarked.

"Everyone drinks out of the bottle if they have to," Wil said sagely. He cut a slice of goat cheese and handed it to her with a chunk of baguette.

"What was your favorite kind of adventure, back when your whole life revolved around travel?" she asked.

"The cold-weather trips are bad memories now, because of what happened to Filip," he said after a moment. "I always loved water adventures. Sailing, kayaking. I love the sea. Our sailboat became a tiny world. And I'm a bit obsessed with maps and charts. Tying rope knots, too. Filip and I used to spend hours figuring out these complicated knots." He smiled, caught in a memory. "We met an Irishman in a harbor once, I think in Greece, who had a ring that looked like a rope knot. It was actually three or four rings that were twisted together."

Zari nodded. "Puzzle rings. I've seen them at art fairs in California." She remembered his neatly packed backpack on their summer trek along the Camino. "You're so organized. That's probably why you love the miniature world of a boat."

He caught her hand in hers. "Speaking of boats, thank you, Zari."

"For what?"

"For making the connection with Filip and your brother's friend."

"Did they make contact?"

"Yes. Filip's been invited to join the sailing trip in Croatia next May."

"Do you think he'll go?"

A swallow glided past them and swooped to the water line, skimmed something from the surface of the river, and winged away.

Wil propped his head on his hand and followed the movement of the swallow with his eyes. "His family is worried about him. They don't think he's ready for a trip like that."

"What do you think?"

"He wants to go. He told me. But I don't know if he has the confidence."

"Why don't you go with him?"

Wil glanced at her, surprised. "But it's an adaptive trip."

"I'm sure not everyone on the boat will be disabled. There has to be a support crew, right? You have tons of sailing experience. Ask if you can help out, be a volunteer sailor."

"That might work." He pulled a blade of grass from the soil and twirled it between his fingers. "I'll look into it."

"My presentation in Bordeaux is in May, too. I hope the dates don't clash, because I'd love for you to be there. You can run interference with Dotie Butterfield-Swinton at the reception."

"Is that what I am to you? A bodyguard?" He grinned and stretched out on his back.

She watched his face relax under the warmth of the sun. Beyond him the river pulsed and shimmered, its murky waters carrying snowmelt from the highest mountain peaks west to the sea. The swallow returned after a while, followed by another. They dipped and glided, tracing complicated patterns in the air, then vanished into a clump of willows on the opposite bank.

Zari rested her head on Wil's chest. The sun filtered through her eyelashes. Within minutes she was asleep.

After a while she became aware of Wil's voice in her ear.

"What are you dreaming about?" he whispered.

"I'm not sure if I should tell you." She sat up, yawning, and pushed her hair out of her face. "Drinking wine during the day is never a smart move."

He rested his head on his hands and looked at her quizzically. "You can't help your dreams. It's your subconscious brain making things up."

"My subconscious brain doesn't usually come up with anything this good. I dreamed about beautiful Dutch-American babies, to be perfectly honest."

A slow smile spread over his face. The tenderness in his dark blue eyes made her pulse tick up a notch.

"How many?" he asked.

"At least two. Maybe three."

"Move to Amsterdam when this project is finished and we can work on making your dream come true."

Zari laughed. "You have more imagination than I gave you credit for."

"What do you mean?" He sat up.

"I think we'd have to try living together for a while before we add any babies to the mix." She brushed a clump of dried grass off his shirt.

"Live with me, then." His expression was sober.

Zari sighed, shaking her head. "What would I do there? I have to go where the academic jobs are. I'm on a career path, remember?"

He nodded. "If nothing works in Amsterdam, find something else in Europe and I'll come to you."

"Really?"

"Yeah. I can sublet my place for a while."

"What about your furniture design business?"

"I can do it anywhere. I can just bring my tools and rent a work space."

She regarded him thoughtfully. "Are you serious?"

"I'm always serious about what I want, Zari."

He reached out and gently laid his hand on her cheek.

2

October, 2015
Pau, France
Zari

AFTER DINNER IN A small restaurant near Pau's university, they wandered through the dark streets to a long, narrow park on the campus that was planted with meticulously trimmed shrubs. Zari pointed out to Wil the building at the opposite end of the park where, last summer, she and Laurence had discovered Mira's traces.

That was the moment, she realized now, when Mira had truly come to life for her. Combing through ancient documents in a climate-controlled laboratory, she heard Mira whispering to her across a yawning divide of five hundred years.

"I existed," Mira's words and images told her. *"I lived and loved, worked and grieved, in these mountains. This is the proof. What will you do with it?"*

Just weeks ago in Perpignan, Zari had felt Mira's presence beckoning her back in time again. But in the intervening days, searching fruitlessly through digital archives on the list Laurence had given her, she had begun losing hope.

She and Wil left the park and walked along a narrow lane that took them past lovingly preserved medieval buildings constructed of cream-colored stone. Zari glanced up at an arched doorway that was illuminated by a streetlamp and saw a scallop shell carved into the wall above it.

She paused. "This must have been a stop on the Camino at some point."

"Maybe it was a convent or a monastery," Wil agreed.

Zari looked at the shell in silence for a moment. "In her self-portraits, Mira's wearing a nun's habit," she said finally. "That makes sense. She grew up in a convent. But in the prayer book I saw in Perpignan, she's Judith slaying Holofernes. Was that literal? Was it symbolic? Was it meaningless?"

He shrugged. "Why did Judith slay Holofernes?"

"To protect her people."

Wil waited for her to sort it out.

"So maybe it's not literal but symbolic," Zari said slowly. "Mira saw herself not as a killer but as a Judith. A protector. I like that." She sighed. "Another theory with absolutely nothing to back it up. Why was she in Perpignan, anyway?"

"For now, Perpignan does not make sense. Think of it as..." He searched for the English word.

"An outlier?"

"Yes, an outlier. The Abbey of Belarac was on the Arles-Aragón route of the Camino, and so was San Juan de la Peña. The prior there signed the mortuary roll you found, right?"

During the summer, Zari and Laurence had also examined a parchment mortuary roll that commemorated the death of Béatrice of Belarac. Mira had signed it, and Zari was convinced she had been responsible for the artwork on the document as well.

Zari nodded. "Marguerite de Oto signed it, too. And others."

"Have you looked into those names?"

"Yes. The most intriguing possibilities are Carlo and Flora Saca-zar. They were wool merchants from Aragón who had a home in Nay. It's a museum now. It's closed for renovations until January."

"Too bad." Wil thought a moment. "What did Mira write in the mortuary roll? About Béatrice, the mother abbess?"

"'*The Abbess gave us refuge when we did not have homes, food when we went hungry, skills when we had none. She was a mother in deed as well as name. Death visited her too soon.*'"

"You memorized that?"

"It's all I have of her voice."

"Maybe use the Camino as your guide. Start with the things you are certain of and cast your net from there. The cave. The monastery. Belarac."

Wil had been at Zari's side when she discovered the ancient foundation stones of Belarac, when she found Mira's self-portrait and Arnaud de Luz's mark carved into the wall of a cave that had been used by mountain people for hundreds, maybe thousands of years. And he was with her at the monastery of San Juan de la Peña when she unearthed the lineage of the Oto family.

"What about Bayonne?"

"Arnaud is the one connected to Bayonne, right? As far as you know, Mira was never there. So throw that out for now."

Zari glanced back up at the weather-worn shell carved above the doorway. Had Mira journeyed along the pilgrim's way, seen that shell with her own eyes? The crumbs of evidence that she left behind were frustratingly few. But Wil was right. Zari needed to focus on the evidence she did have and find connections to it, radiating outward like the grooves in a shell.

The next morning, Wil left the apartment early and came back with a map. It contained an east-west subsection of the

Pyrenees, northern Spain, and southern France, and it showed all the known Camino routes. He tacked it to the wall and highlighted the routes in various neon shades. Finally he plotted the locations of the Abbey of Belarac and the Castle of Oto and marked them as well.

They stood shoulder to shoulder regarding the pink line that followed the Arles-Aragón route of the Camino, which passed through Toulouse and Pau, then climbed over the Pyrenees into Spain. Zari traced it with her finger first north, then south, then north again.

"I'm going to start at the northernmost point, the city of Arles," she announced.

"Wake me when you find something good," Wil replied, heading to the bedroom.

Flipping open her laptop, she began to search through the digital archives of Arles. She could hear the creak of footsteps overhead from time to time. Her elderly neighbor, the man who wore his midnight-blue beret at a jaunty angle and took the stairs one slow, determined step at a time, lived directly above her. He was a night owl, but his muffled footsteps were never loud enough to wake her. Zari took comfort in the knowledge that another human nearby was awake during the loneliest hours of the night, when she sometimes got lost down research rabbit holes so deep that she didn't come up for air until three in the morning.

After an hour and a half, she had found nothing useful and got up to stretch.

Wil was still asleep in her bed. She was tempted to join him, but instead did several yoga poses and chanted a series of her mother's positive affirmations. Then she examined the map again. Toulouse was a lot closer to Belarac than Arles was. She gingerly settled back in her seat. The hard plastic chair was not ergonomically correct by any conceivable stretch of the imagination.

Zari pecked out the address for the archives of Toulouse, then clicked through various pages until she found materials from the years 1500-1510. Zoomable photographs of centuries-old documents presented themselves.

One at a time, she scoured the faded script and accompanying notes for each document. She circled back to a book containing records signed by the same notary, a man named Jean Aubrey. The most intriguing was a note written in ink the color of dried blood. The words were unintelligible to her, the script so faded in places she could barely make out the individual letters. Scanning down to the bottom of the note to see the signatures, Zari drew in a breath and held it. One of the names, in bold, blocky letters, was Arnaud de Luz. Next to it was another name in much smaller, more delicate script. The first word was quite faded, but it began with an 'M'. And the last name contained an uppercase 'L'. Zari zoomed in on the image until it became too pixelated to see. Reverting it to the original size, she held her pocket magnifying glass up to the screen, but the faded rust-colored letters refused to give up their secrets.

She leapt from her seat and did a silent, exultant dance. Then she padded to the bedroom clutching her laptop. Wil slept on his side, his face smashed into a pillow. Zari felt a glimmer of guilt at the thought of waking him. She fidgeted in the doorway a moment, wrestling with her excitement.

"To hell with that," she said at last, bringing the laptop to bed. "Wil! Wake up."

He blinked at her with bleary eyes. "What is it?"

"I think I'm back on Mira's trail."

3

Autumn, 1504
Toulouse, France
Mira

I T WAS EVENING WHEN they arrived at the gates of Toulouse. Traders from the south waited in a ragtag queue, their mules burdened with ceramic vessels bearing wine, spices, olive oil, and salt. Interspersed with the traders were farmers leading oxcarts piled with bags of pastel, the blue dye made from woad.

Mira and Arnaud led their mules to the back of the queue.

"Compared to the others, we are a sad little group," Mira said.

She pulled the hood of her mud-spattered cloak down over her eyes and crossed her arms against the cold.

"A humble appearance can be an advantage," Arnaud replied, looking at her sideways.

His beard was covered in a film of fine brown dust that matched the color of his skin, she saw. And his cloak was not only smeared with mud but ripped in several places.

She raised an eyebrow. "We shall see."

When it was their turn, Arnaud dismounted and explained to the guards that they had business in Toulouse. He went to unlatch their panniers but the guards motioned him to stop, already focusing their attention on the Aragónese merchant behind them whose mules were loaded with wine. They would skim a little off the top of his load, Mira guessed. Within minutes she and Arnaud were riding into the walled city of Toulouse, the chatter of traders and farmers fading away with each step.

She was grateful now for their miserable appearance.

When the day of their appointment arrived, Mira and Arnaud stood waiting in front of Lord de Vernier's home. Above them soared three stories of stone and brick. Diamond-shaped glass panes glittered in tall, narrow windows. The house was crowned with a hexagonal brick tower that soared into the sky—an architectural marvel envied by all of Toulouse society, according to the innkeeper at the Blue Ox.

Mira straightened her shoulders, making a mental inventory of her appearance. Clean, simple homespun skirt and flax blouse. Dark green fitted wool bodice. Hair braided and pinned under a clean white flax cap. Arnaud, for his part, had been up late cleaning and oiling his boots. His hair was neatly drawn back and secured with a leather cord, and his black beard was trimmed close to his jawline.

A stray dog trotted up and sniffed at the hem of Mira's skirt. She clapped her hands, shooing it away. Nothing must interfere with her appearance on today of all days.

One of the heavy doors swung inward. A servant beckoned them inside. They walked through a dark entry hall paved with cobblestones, then through another tall door into the interior courtyard. It was immense, ringed with a series of stone balconies supported by tall, decoratively-carved columns.

The servant knocked at a broad oak door.

"Come!"

Inside, Lord de Vernier sat at a leather-topped desk that was strewn with paper. He put down his quill and waved them into the chairs opposite his.

"I am a very busy man," he said abruptly, bypassing the usual pleasantries. "I am beginning to regret I ever agreed to meet you. Especially in light of this." He brandished a piece of linen paper that was covered with tiny script and numerals. "It is an offer of sale from a merino fabric merchant with whom I've had dealings before—at a price no other wool seller can match."

At the bottom of the page Mira saw the florid signature of Amadina Sacazar. A sick feeling twisted her gut. It took all her effort to focus on the man's words.

"Amadina Sacazar," he said, jabbing the paper with a long, ring-laden finger. "Someone I disentangled myself from years ago, after I agreed to the Abbess of Belarac's proposal. The woman is about as pleasant to deal with as a donkey." His tone grew sour. "For all her faults, she has a better grasp on the concept of contractual obligations than your Béatrice did."

"With all respect, my lord," Mira said, "Mother Béatrice was the most honorable of women. Her death was unexpected and threw the abbey into confusion for a time. But now that has been remedied."

"Excuses are nothing to me." The merchant's tone and flat expression implied he was entirely unmoved. He dropped the contract on his desk and made a tent of his fingers, elbows on the arms of his chair. "Business requires fulfillment of contracts. When they are broken, no matter the reason, merchants lose money."

Mira hastily pulled a sample of black merino wool fabric from her satchel and placed it on his desk, unfurling the roll so it spread over his pile of paperwork. He leaned forward and stroked the fabric, examining the quality of the weave.

"What is the origin of this wool?"

"My village has raised merino sheep in a high valley of Aragón for generations," Arnaud responded. "We drive the flocks to the Abbey of Belarac each fall to overwinter on their fields. In summer we take them back to the mountains to graze along with the abbey's own flocks."

"So the abbey purchases wool from you and finishes it? Or does the abbey own the sheep outright?"

Arnaud hesitated.

In truth, Béatrice had purchased a flock of merino sheep from the shepherds of Ronzal long ago. It was a deal she had brokered with Jorge de Luz in her early years as abbess of Belarac. In return, she allowed Ronzal to populate the homes of the village in the valley of Belarac with its excess sons and daughters. Since the sale of merinos to foreigners was forbidden by Queen Isabella, the agreement had not been recorded on parchment. Officially, the merino sheep that overwintered at Belarac were all the property of Ronzal.

"The ancient peace accords guide such things," Mira said to break the silence. "The shepherds of Ronzal care for the sheep and the abbey processes the wool. They share the proceeds from the sale of the fabric."

"I see. Do the tariffs that normally inflate prices of Aragónese wool apply to this?" He tapped his fingers on the length of fabric.

"No," Arnaud said.

"It is quite unfortunate that the arrangement I made with your abbess did not come to pass," the merchant admitted, "for this is wool of the highest quality. But I cannot abide uncertainty in my business dealings." He picked up the contract from Amadina Sacazar again. "The safer bet is this one, I suppose."

Mira half-rose from her seat. "Whatever she sells her fabric for, we will sell ours for less. And I can assure you, my lord, that no uncertainty will befall any future dealings with the Abbey of Belarac."

"Ah? How so?"

"Both my husband and I have overseen the necessary improvements to the production and finishing of wool at Belarac. We have trained assistants to ensure the operation runs smoothly. And we developed something new. I hope it is to your liking."

Mira pulled a sample of the blue wool from her satchel and placed it on the merchant's desk. The fabric was the color of the lapis lazuli pigment she used for painting. It glowed with a luminous sheen, the weave tight and even. Sister Agathe herself had operated the loom, and she had done a masterful job.

"This was dyed with pastel," he said, examining the fabric closely. "I trade in pastel as well as wool. But this gift implies you knew that."

"I read your letter carefully," she acknowledged. "If this blue wool is to your liking, we can make more. There is a field of woad in the valley of Belarac. We could earmark it all for you, the villagers can process it into pastel, and each summer the abbey can send as many bolts of fine blue fabric as you wish to Toulouse."

He leaned back in his chair, a slight smile creasing the corners of his mouth. "Perhaps it is indelicate to say, but you neither look nor speak like a shepherd's wife. No offense to you, sir," he added, looking at Arnaud.

"None taken," Arnaud said.

"My husband is no mere shepherd," Mira objected. "He is a skilled woodworker. He built the looms that these fabrics were woven on."

"Ah?" The merchant's fingers were tented again. "A man of many talents, then."

"As for me," she went on, "I grew up in the abbey, learning the wool trade at the elbow of Mother Béatrice."

"If that is so, why did you not pick up the threads of the connection she had made with me when she died?" He sounded faintly annoyed again.

"I left the abbey soon after her death."

He glanced at Arnaud. "To tend to matters of the heart, I suppose."

Arnaud stared levelly back at him, silent.

The merchant's thin red lips twitched. He shifted in his chair, causing the leather backing to squeak.

"If you can provide fabric of this color and this quality in the amounts I desire, you need look no further for contracts. The desire for blue wool fabric of the highest quality is soaring in Paris."

"Why's that?" Arnaud asked.

"The French court demands it. Our king is quite interested in the trappings that befit his station." He tapped a finger on the contract that lay on the desk before him. "Oh, it will be a headache to extricate myself from this woman again. But merino wool of such quality is quite rare in Béarn, and I have seen no blue fabric to rival yours." His expression grew stern. "I do have one condition."

"Yes, my lord?" Mira said.

"You must stay in Toulouse until the wool is delivered next summer and await my satisfaction. If I am unhappy with the product, or if the terms of our agreement are not met by the Abbey of Belarac, I will hold you and your husband personally responsible."

Mira and Arnaud exchanged a look.

Just then the sound of children's laughter floated in from the courtyard. Three little girls ran by the open doorway, giggling. One caught sight of Mira and stopped. In an exaggerated whisper she called out something in Aragónese to her sisters. They gathered in the doorway, staring at the strangers.

"Hello girls," Mira said in Aragónese. "How are you, little ones?"

Their eyes grew even rounder. Then they all flinched at the sharp sound of hands clapping. The girls turned their heads, eyeing their pursuer, and fled. A plump woman with a black veil over her hair bustled after them, clucking her tongue. Her dour expression made it clear that she was not pleased with her charges.

Lord de Vernier drummed his fingers on the desk. "The girls are under of the care of our housekeeper Madame Heloise these days. We are in between governesses."

"I used to care for the children at the convent," Mira said. "I taught them their lessons."

"Is that so?" he said, clearly unimpressed.

"I could teach your daughters to read and write in Aragónese," she went on.

Lord de Vernier's eyes swiveled back to her. There was something in his gaze—amusement? Irritation? She could not decipher it. She fought the rising color in her cheeks, tried to steady her breathing.

"If we are to stay in Toulouse, we must work," she added. "We wish to accommodate you, my lord, but there are practicalities to think of."

"My wife is Aragónese. Instruction in that tongue is not worth paying for," he said, narrowing his eyes. "It is becoming a language of peasants, she tells me. Our children speak it enough with her, I've no desire to see them learn to read and write it."

Mira's throat was dry. "I could teach them Latin and arithmetic, if it pleases you and your wife. And drawing."

"Whatever skills you have, I am afraid there is one requirement of a governess that you do not possess: noble birth."

He stood up, indicating that the interview was over. Arnaud followed suit. But Mira stayed in her chair.

"My lord, I must respectfully disagree," she said. "I am of noble birth."

Mira felt Arnaud's eyes boring into her. She stood and faced the merchant, clenching her fists to keep them from shaking.

"I am a daughter of the house of Oto, one of the great families of Aragón. I was placed in the convent for protection, and I was raised with an education that befits one of my rank. If you need proof of this, write to Brother Johan Arros at the monastery of San Juan de la Peña. He will vouch for my honesty."

The merchant was silent for a moment. "I know the name. He is renowned for his knowledge of the wool trade. But the passage to Aragón over the mountains will soon close. Even if my letter gets through the pass, his reply would not arrive until the spring thaw."

"If we stay in Toulouse through the summer at your bidding, that is time enough to learn the truth from Brother Arros," she pointed out. "He can speak to my character, and that of my husband too."

The merchant looked back and forth between the two of them.

"Why would a noble-born girl marry an unpedigreed man?"

"Fortune is fickle," Mira said, keeping her voice light despite the sting of his words. "Not all daughters have dowries that attract the attention of titled men. That is the way all over the world, if I am not mistaken."

He nodded slightly, seeming to accept her explanation.

"I shall have you meet Madame Heloise, then. Perhaps you shall make a fitting governess for my daughters after all."

"Thank you, my lord."

"But heed this," the merchant warned. "I am not a trusting man. Your commitment to do as we have agreed will be taken down in writing and witnessed by my notary. I shall hold you both accountable if this wool does not appear as promised, or if it is of inferior quality to these samples you've shown me. And I shall write to Brother Arros immediately."

Mira bowed to him.

"As you see fit, my lord," she said. "I promise we shall not disappoint you."

4

Autumn, 1504
Toulouse, France
Mira

ASTOUT WOMAN DRESSED in blue sat at a broad wooden
table, a leather-bound book open in front of her. In one
hand she held a quill poised over the page. She looked
up.

"Ah! The girl is here." She put the quill back in its holder and
stood up. "Come, approach."

Mira walked to the desk.

"Take off your cloak."

Mira untied the strings of her cloak and slipped it off her
shoulders.

"Yes. Good." The woman walked around her in a circle, looking her up and down. "Plain, modest. Except for that bauble." Her
gaze lingered on the scallop-shell necklace around Mira's neck.

"It was my mother's."

"Pilgrim, was she?"

"My mother was a baroness."

"That's right. You told the lord you're noble-born."

"Yes, I am."

The woman's mouth slanted in a smirk. "Bastard, are you?"

Mira stared, her anger rising. "No."

"You may call me Madame Heloise," the woman said curtly. "I am the mistress of the household, though not mistress of the *house*. They are two entirely different things, of course. Lady de Vernier is the mistress of the house. It is possible that you may never meet her. And if you do, only speak to her if she addresses you first, do you understand?"

"Yes."

"Your trial begins today. We will see how the children like you. If they do not like you, no matter how well you teach, you will be let go." A fleck of spittle shot out from Heloise's mouth and Mira felt it come to rest on her chin. Resisting the urge to wipe it away, she took a deep breath.

"Thank you. I hope I do not disappoint Lord and Lady de Vernier."

"As do I." Heloise walked across the room to another door and pushed it open. "The nursery." She swept into the sunny, open space and held out her arms as if surveying it for the first time. "Books, paper, quills, ink." She pointed to a table and a chest near a window.

Mira went to the table and picked up one of the books, a collection of poems. She smiled.

"Why that is worth smiling about I cannot fathom." Heloise squinted at Mira.

"I smile because I love poetry."

Heloise pursed her lips and made an unintelligible noise that Mira decided to interpret as a grunt of approval. She nearly laughed at the thought, and felt a slight loosening in the tension between her shoulder blades.

Another door opened on the far side of the room, and three young girls burst through it. In a blur of glossy dark curls and swishing blue skirts, they rushed forward and stopped an arm's length from Mira. The morning sun passed through the glass panes of the tall window, bathing the girls with golden light. Three sets of dark eyes stared at her.

"Girls, I am Madame Mira, your new teacher."

They regarded her in silence for a moment, then all three spoke at once, raising their voices in an effort to be heard. Above the chatter Heloise's voice rang out.

"Girls!"

Silence fell over the room.

"You will speak when spoken to," she snapped. "You will ask no questions of your teacher. She is here to teach you, not listen to you babble."

The children kept their eyes trained on Mira, ignoring Heloise's scolding.

"They are, in order of size from smallest to biggest, Blanca, Sophie, and Sandrine. Now I will leave you to your work," Heloise said to Mira. "There is a switch to slap their hands if they grow insolent."

She jerked her head toward the table. Mira saw a slender birch rod next to the pile of books.

"Thank you, Madame Heloise."

When the door closed behind Heloise, the smallest girl stuck out her tongue at it, then glanced at Mira.

"That is not polite, Blanca." Mira composed her face in a severe frown.

Sandrine turned to her sister. "Why are you so rude? It is a stain on our family when you do such things."

"Madame Heloise is a sour rotten cabbage." Blanca folded her arms across her chest.

Mira stifled a laugh.

"She is trying to help you become a lady," Sandrine said.

"I do not want to be a lady."

"Too bad. You will be one. As will I and Sophie."

They both turned to Sophie, whose eyes had never left Mira's face.

"Why did you not use the switch on Blanca when she stuck out her tongue?" Sophie asked.

"I see no need to."

"Why?"

"I have taught many children to read and write, and I have never used a switch on any of them." Mira pretended to consider something for a moment. "Unless, of course, you believe that you require the switch."

"We do not! But if you do not use it, she will think you are a bad teacher," said Sophie. "She will tell our parents to turn you out."

"If you learn your lessons, she will have no choice but to believe I am a good teacher. Switch or no switch."

A slow smile spread across Sophie's face, and she nodded, pleased.

"Now, Blanca, Sandrine, and Sophie," Mira said solemnly. "Let us begin."

5

Autumn, 1504
Toulouse, France
Arnaud

IN THE QUIET BEFORE dawn, Arnaud and Mira lay in the dark on the narrow, lumpy straw mattress in their chamber above the inn's dining room. Cold air leaked in from the wooden shutters. The past few nights, they had spread their cloaks over the thin blanket, and still Mira shivered. Arnaud enveloped her in his arms, willing his body heat into her.

There was a scuttling sound and a faint squeak. Mice. They scurried around the floors at night. Occasionally one climbed up the legs of the bedframe. More than once Arnaud had woken to the sensation of tiny claws on his skin.

"Silence," he said softly. "I almost forgot what it sounds like."

Their nights were marked by the voices of men raised in argument or laughter rippling up from the dining room. When the tavern closed, groups spilled outside to the alley, continuing their drunken discussions and disputes under the window.

"With my pay, we'll soon be able to find lodgings of our own," Mira whispered. "And perhaps you'll soon have work from the guild."

"I've no letter of recommendation. And I'm a foreigner." Arnaud shifted in the bed and the webbing of flax rope that supported the mattress creaked. "I wish now I'd asked Carlo Sacazar to give me that letter he wrote vouching for me, instead of sending it to Bayonne. Who knows when we'll get there now?"

"When the guild master sees what you can do, he will not care where you come from."

Arnaud did not answer, just turned and found her lips in the dark.

The next afternoon Arnaud visited the cabinetmakers' guild in hopes of convincing the guild master that he was a journeyman worth taking a chance on. There was no shortage of skilled work to be had in Toulouse, the guild master explained, but without an endorsement the guild would be breaking its own bylaws if it hired him. It was an unfortunate predicament, but his hands were tied.

Arnaud returned to the inn and found a table in a quiet corner. Supper was not yet being served, and the crowd was composed entirely of men. An ale wench dressed in a tight blue bodice that was unlaced at the top, exposing a pair of breasts that were pushed unnaturally high, plopped a wooden tanker of foaming ale in front of him. She held out a hand while he fished for a coin.

"Handsome one, you. Where's your companion today?"

He dropped the coin in her palm.

"My wife, you mean? She'll be back soon."

The woman pocketed the silver. "Where've you come from, then?"

"The south."

"What brought you north?"

"Work."

"Not a very talkative one, are you?"

He raised his tanker and saluted her with it, and she flashed him a wide smile, exposing two gaping holes where teeth had gone missing. She whirled and was swallowed up by the crowd.

A group of city guards sat in the center of the room at a broad table, their blue uniforms unlaced at the throats and their black caps pushed away from their brows. It was clearly their customary gathering spot, for guards joined them and melted away at regular intervals. Arnaud made it a point not to stare at them overtly, but his eyes flicked their way as he regarded the rest of the crowd, watching the ale wenches evade the busy hands of the drunkest men and expertly sidling away from troublemakers.

From his perch in the shadows, he heard snippets of the guards' conversations.

"...My two brothers fought in that war and only one came back. It took him nigh on a year to make the journey home."

"Their queen's the one who started it all. Isabella. It was her who sent that general over the sea. The one they called the Great Captain."

"Sparks and steel, that's how he won. Lead balls and powder, shot out of a..."

"To hell with Aragón! To hell with Spain! To hell with Naples!"

There was the loud clacking of wood as they all slammed their tankers together, splashing ale over the table. An ale wench laughed, a coarse, brassy sound that ended on a note so high that Arnaud winced.

He glanced around at the other patrons. Two middle-aged men sitting nearby were engaged in a conversation that caught his interest.

"Those guards talk of war," said one, a slight man clad in a black felt cap and a wine-red vest studded with carved wooden buttons. "But what we should be concerned with is the Spanish trade in blue dye."

"What? No land south of the Pyrenees can match our woad production." His companion, a thick-set, curly-haired man with a luxuriant beard, set his tanker down with a thump.

"I said blue dye, not woad. Grown in some foreign land across the sea."

"Across the sea there is only plague and drought and war," came the drawling response.

"Not the Mediterranean—the other sea." The smaller man's voice rose in exasperation. "The one that licks at the shores of the trading port Bayonne."

"Trade ships can't navigate those waters. They're too fierce. And full of monsters."

Arnaud watched the big curly-haired fellow take a long pull of ale.

"And yet the Spaniards have found a way to do just that," the small man insisted. "Merchants from the south trickle through these city gates talking of crops across the sea, and slaves who do the farming and harvesting for them. The indigo plant, they call it..."

The ale wench's face appeared in Arnaud's line of vision.

"Ready for another?" She cocked her head and ran her tongue over her lips, peering into his tanker.

He shook his head, shooing her away. "No, I'm not yet half done with the first."

The word 'indigo' floated past again, this time as a question. The ale wench stood her ground, leaning slightly forward to ensure he got a good view. He covered his tanker with a hand, scowling, until she sauntered off.

But the two men had changed topics from the indigo plant to the trade in wool. Now this was something Arnaud knew intimately. He sighed. No more news would be gleaned from this conversation.

"I am owed six dozen bags of washed merino wool—I paid for it two summers ago, and it never arrived," the smaller man complained. "I had a good source, a reliable source, that came over the mountains through the Col du Somport."

Arnaud's ears pricked up again.

"One of the Jaca sheepbreeders? A monastery?" asked the other.

"No, no. A nobleman. God knows I thought him a man of his word. Ramón de Oto was his name. I paid in advance every summer for ten years. And now his shipments have ceased altogether. I can find no word of him, no explanation for this."

"Did you write to him?"

"Of course. But it is nearly winter—nothing crosses the mountains until the spring thaw. I must resign myself to the loss and find a new supplier."

Arnaud stood, tanker in hand, and crossed to the two men.

"Good sirs, I couldn't help but overhear. I know the man of whom you speak."

"Who are you, then?" The red-vested man kept one hand wrapped around his tanker of ale but the other fell to the hilt of his short sword.

"Arnaud de Luz of Ronzal."

"I know your mark," said the man, relaxing his grip. He pointed at the stool next to him. "You sell your wool at the market in Nay, do you not?"

Arnaud sat. "Yes—or I did. I am a cabinetmaker now." He saluted them with his tanker, and they returned the gesture.

"I heard that Ramón de Oto crossed the sea to fight at the battle of Naples," he said.

"Foreign wars!" said the heavy-set man in disgust. "A waste of lives and money."

"But what the king wants, the king gets," his companion said. He fixed his gaze on Arnaud. "I paid in advance. I suppose I'll never get my wool now."

Arnaud shrugged. "Could be he's back now, as the war's over. In the meantime, I know another source of washed merino wool. The Abbey of Belarac near the pilgrim's route, just south of Nay."

The man's expression brightened. "Merino wool from Béarn? That's a rarity."

Arnaud nodded. "No tariffs to pay. Plus, I can vouch for its quality. You won't find better wool."

"Why did you come to Toulouse?" the large man asked.

"To oversee a business affair for the wool trade. But my skills lie more in making furniture."

The smaller man regarded Arnaud thoughtfully. "Member of the guild, are you?"

Arnaud shook his head. "I lack the proper credentials. Though there seems to be work aplenty."

"I have some carpentry that needs doing," said the red-vested man. "It's not fancy, but if you work quickly and your crafts-manship is fine, I might keep you on for better work."

Arnaud knew the unspoken implication. If he worked for the merchant on the sly, the man would not have to pay fees to the guild. The repercussions if the arrangement was discovered would be severe, but he had no other choice.

The man's companion scoffed. "Why would he do the work of a Cagot?"

Arnaud shook his head. "I'm not too proud to do honest work." He gulped from his mug. "Are there many Cagots in this city?"

"Their settlements are outside the city walls. They keep to themselves," said the large man. "Stick to the side alleys and the shadows, they do. Sniffing out the work in their weaselly way."

A round of rough laughter went up from the guards' table.

Arnaud drained his ale and stood, his eyes on the man in the red vest. "Thanks for the offer. Where can I find you?"

"Come to the main square on market day at first light." The man set his tanker down. "I'll be at the wool stalls."

6

Autumn, 1504
San Juan de la Peña, Aragón
Brother Arros

THE FINAL DAYS OF autumn were upon them. There was so much to do. Yet try as he might, Brother Arros could not keep his thoughts straight today. His mind felt wrapped by moss. A headache plagued him, pounding fiercely in his temples, as if some creature had burrowed into his skull and was now attempting to force its way out with fury.

The end of autumn meant harvesting the last of the vegetables, pressing the olives, drying the beans, stacking the fodder. It meant preparing the winter enclosures for the flocks of sheep that would soon wend their way down from the summer grazing pastures in the high valleys. For Brother Arros, it meant corralling and organizing the monks and the servants to carry out all of their jobs.

Then there were the cycles of prayer, chapter meetings, care for the ill in the infirmary, ministering to the travelers in the guesthouse. Since he was the prior, he was ultimately responsible for all of it.

Brother Arros patted the pocket where a letter lay crinkled between the folds of his brown homespun robe. He tugged the paper out and held it aloft, his back to the sun, squinting at the darkly inked letters, tracing the embossed design of Lord de Vernier's wax seal with a stubby finger. The letter had languished in his pocket for days. There had not been a moment to spare, let alone the substantial allotment of time writing a letter required. Even if he neglected all his responsibilities and wrote a response today, he had no way to send it. He had got word yesterday that the pass of Somport had been sealed shut by a blizzard.

A strong breeze blew in from the north just then, tugging the letter loose from his grasp.

He bent to pick it up, but a curious thing happened. His fingers would not close around the paper. He tried again. No, his fingers did not heed the call of his mind. They just dangled weakly at the end of his arm. He reached for a stone that lay near the letter. But it was no use. Experimentally, he flexed the fingers of his other hand and was relieved to discover that it worked as it always had. He reached for the letter with that hand, then wished he hadn't.

His head pounded anew. A wave of bile rose in his throat. Slowly he sank to his knees.

The last thing Brother Arros remembered before losing consciousness was the soft kiss of the north wind on his cheeks, and the sight of the letter skittering away from him in the dust.

7

November, 2015
Pau, France
Zari

L AURENCE OPENED THE DOOR to her apartment and ushered
Zari through.

"Tea?" she asked. "You prefer Irish breakfast, yes?"

Zari nodded, slipping off her boots.

Laurence headed into the kitchen. "Meet me in my office,"
she called back over her shoulder. "I'll be there in a moment."

Zari padded down a long, narrow hallway covered with
Moroccan rugs.

In the living room, a recessed series of shelves held a
collection of carved stone sculptures. The ceilings were high
and the wooden parquet floors were at least a century old,
though they appeared to have been refinished recently with a
honey-colored stain. Three tall windows looked out over the
city. A dark, billowing cloud moved rapidly north, pushed by a
brisk wind coming off the mountains. While Zari watched, two

more clouds materialized behind it. Rain was sure to follow.

She entered the office, which was connected by two glass-paned doors to the living room. One wall was lined with shelves, each stuffed with books. The wall opposite, lit from above with bright directional lights, was hung with artwork. At its center was the portrait of the merchant family.

Zari gasped, put a hand to her mouth. Then she slowly approached the portrait.

The round-faced man and his equally plump wife stood in front of a balcony, their two daughters standing between them. The father, wearing a short black fur-trimmed cloak and matching cap, had a warm expression in his dark eyes, the barest hint of a smile on his full lips. The mother held herself regally. Her dress was a deep scarlet, her throat and fingers laden with jewels, her hair covered with a pearl-encrusted veil. The girls, also clad in red dresses, were miniature versions of their mother, their dark hair braided and pulled back from their heart-shaped faces.

Zari stared into the eyes of each family member, mesmerized. They seemed to watch her as much as she watched them.

Laurence came to her side. "How do you like my painting?"

"They seem so alive," Zari said. "They know they are seen—and they look back. That effect is missing from all the Cornelia van der Zee portraits I saw in person—all except the one at Fontbroke College."

The background of the portrait showed a low balcony of stone covered with lush, twining vines. Beyond it were pale green hills studded with rocks. Various species of trees—Zari picked out oak, pine, and beech among them—were depicted on the slopes, and flocks of sheep grazed on the lush grass. In the far distance towered snow-capped mountains.

The level of detail in the background was what bolstered Dotie Butterfield-Swinton's theory that Bartolomé Bermejo had painted it. Unlike his contemporaries, the painter had zeroed in on real-world details in his backgrounds to an astonishing degree. One of Bermejo's works had been found to contain nearly two dozen different species of clearly identifiable animals and plants.

"The conservators believe this background is the southern Pyrenees, in Spain," Laurence said. She gave Zari a searching look. "And—I'm sorry, Zari. But Dotie contacted me yesterday. He told me he is collaborating with a scholar from Spain, an expert on Bermejo."

Zari stared at her in apprehension.

"At the moment, a Bermejo painting is being analyzed at the Prado Museum in Madrid. Dotie said the underdrawings are quite similar to those in this painting and in the Fontbroke College portrait."

Zari took several steps backward and sank onto a low couch upholstered in soft mocha-colored fabric.

"Oh, no." The words were barely more than a whisper.

Laurence perched next to her, eyes full of sympathy.

Zari put her hands over her face for a moment. If the underdrawings had been markedly different, Dotie's theory would look even shakier than it already was. Instead, he'd scored a coup, and Mira's ascension to the pages of history was rendered more fragile.

"There's so little known about Bermejo that Dotie can just fill in the blanks about him," she said bitterly. "But the few facts that exist about Bermejo don't support Dotie's theory, and I keep coming back to those. Bermejo disappeared from the face of the earth in 1495, and much of his work was created far earlier than that. This painting and the Fontbroke College portrait date to 1500 at the earliest. The dates don't add up."

"Carbon dating is not precise enough to tell us that this panel is from the year 1500 exactly," Laurence reminded her. "It might be a bit older."

"I know. I wish there were more evidence about the origin of the wood he painted on. Bermejo's work was sometimes on pine, sometimes on oak. But we don't know where the wood he used came from, although I found one source that showed a patron ordered him to use 'Flanders oak.'"

"He painted like a Flemish master. He must have lived for a time in Flanders," Laurence said. "How else could he have learned those techniques? No one else in Spain at that time painted like he did."

Zari shrugged. "Maybe some of the Flemish masters traveled around dispensing wisdom and one made it all the way to Spain. All of the documents referring to Bermejo during his lifetime—plus all of his known works—originated in Spain. There's no evidence he ever spent time in Flanders or France or anywhere else."

She sprang up and scowled at the portrait, arms crossed over her chest.

"The provenance of this painting is clear: all the owners have been from this area, not from Spain. So if Bermejo painted it in Spain, wouldn't the first owner have been from there as well?"

"It could have been a commission from someone on this side of the Pyrenees."

"Am I the only one who's noticed that Bermejo's existing works are mainly large religious pieces painted for church altars?" Zari asked. "The few smaller pieces attributed to him are also religious subjects. Sometimes his patrons were depicted in those scenes, but never with this level of skill. He may have been a master at detail, but he wasn't exceptional at painting human figures. And then there's the huge red flag that not one portrait like this exists among his works."

Before Laurence could parry, she held up a hand.

"I know, I know. There could have been portraits. A lot goes missing over the course of five hundred years."

Zari returned to the couch and sat down again, aware that two spots of color burned on her cheeks.

"Have courage, Zari," Laurence said gently.

"I've contacted every owner of a painting by the man," Zari said, a tremor in her voice. "None of Bermejo's works have Arnaud's mark on the back. That's got to mean something, right?"

"I hope so." Laurence reached out and squeezed Zari's hand. "It's time for some tea."

She got up and went to the kitchen.

Zari stared hungrily at the painting. What had she missed? What was hiding in plain sight? She stepped closer and closer, until her face was just inches from the panel.

Outside, the shifting clouds partially obscured the sun. The room grew dim.

Laurence reappeared and handed Zari a ceramic mug of steaming tea. "Milk, no sugar, yes?"

Zari smiled her thanks. Someone in France knew what kind of tea she preferred, and how she liked it. Whatever happened, she was grateful for that. Tears stung her eyes and she blinked them away impatiently. How could gratitude make her cry?

She gestured at the painting. "Who is this family? If we can learn that, we're getting somewhere. Find them, and they could lead us to the artist. Paintings of this era always held clues or symbols that were meaningful to the subjects. Like the wife's ruby necklace. And this ring on the merchant's finger."

The gold ring on the man's finger had a square face that bore a swirling design made of some dark material. Enamel, perhaps. A buzz of excitement crept up Zari's spine. The ring had to be significant.

"Discovering their identity will be very difficult," Laurence said, shaking her head. "I'm sorry, Zari, but it is probably impossible."

The storm clouds swelled, sucking what was left of the sunlight into their dark embrace. Everything in the room fell into shadow except the artwork on the wall.

Brightly lit from above, the merchant family gazed steadily out into the gloom. Their luminous eyes flickered with stories untold, with long-buried secrets, with memories sealed in a forgotten past.

"That's perfect," Zari said softly. "Impossible is turning out to be my specialty."

8

November, 2015
Toulouse, France
Zari

THE PINK BRICK BUILDINGS and tall church spires of Toulouse gleamed on the horizon. A stiff wind careened across the plains, buffeting the Renault with eerie unpredictability. Miniature cyclones of dust rose up on the road ahead.

Laurence's posture was tense. When she picked up Zari that morning, her eyes showed evidence of a sleepless night, and her navy blue blouse had an uncharacteristic wrinkle down the front. Most of Zari's attempts at conversation had fallen flat. And the brooding, preoccupied expression on Laurence's face seemed to deepen as their journey progressed.

"The wind comes from all directions and does not know which way to go," she complained now, slowing the car as they came to a toll crossing.

Zari produced some change and Laurence tossed it in a metal

basket that emptied into a machine. The coins rattled as they slipped into the mechanism.

"Gum, please." Laurence jerked her head at her handbag.

Zari fished around for the foil packet of nicotine gum and handed over a piece.

They drove the rest of the way in silence.

The city archives were housed in a nineteenth-century former water reservoir that had been modified twenty years ago to store municipal documents.

Inside, an artificially blond, middle-aged archivist examined them with cold blue eyes, explaining tersely that she—and only she—would be turning the pages. Laurence and Zari agreed to her terms, flanking her at a narrow metal table.

The notary's record book was not nearly as ornate as the prayer book they had examined in Perpignan. The thin cover was bound with rust-red paper painted to resemble marble. The yellowing pages were fragile, their brittle edges flaking away. Each page was filled with the notary Jean Aubrey's slanted script, the ink a faded brown. Under each description of a transaction or agreement was his mark, a complicated and whimsical design that resembled a coat of arms with long feathering tails shooting off in four directions. The other parties' signatures appeared below or alongside his, if they appeared at all.

When they got to the entry that Zari had flagged, Laurence had a whispered consultation with the woman. Reluctantly, the archivist peeled off her magnifying visor and handed it to Zari.

"*Tenez*," she said gruffly.

"Oh! *Merci*," Zari said in gratitude, slipping the contraption over her head. She stood and awkwardly leaned past the archivist's shoulder to get a better look.

Her eyes were drawn immediately to the signatures. The notary, Jean Aubrey, had made his flamboyant mark below the lines of script. To the left of that, three names were listed. First, another swirling concoction of self-promotion that was the signature of Lord Esteven de Vernier, one of the governing leaders of Renaissance-era Toulouse. And under that, in simple, faded letters, Arnaud de Luz and Miramonde de Luz had inked their own signatures.

Zari pulled the magnifying visor off and thrust it at Laurence. Between them, the archivist, whose intensely floral perfume could not mask an underlying scent of stale cigarette smoke, sat silently. Her white-gloved hands gently held the edges of the book open on its squishy bean bag support.

"Are there other records from this notary?" Zari asked the archivist.

"We have one more of his register books. But it is in very bad condition. We don't allow it to be handled."

"I didn't see that one in the digital records," Zari said.

"Because it is not there. As I said, we don't allow it to be handled."

Zari looked at Laurence.

"I'll talk to the director," Laurence said.

They took photographs of both documents. Finally, after offering their thanks to the unsmiling archivist, they headed downtown to find a café.

Laurence forbade Zari to pore over the photos while they ate.

"It is not healthy to do anything else when you are eating," she explained. "Americans are so proud of this 'multitasking.' It is a sign of a cultural malady."

Zari looked at Laurence's stubbed out cigarette in the ashtray between their plates. "Smoking and eating is multitasking."

Laurence rolled her eyes. "It is not the same."

Zari nearly blurted a retort, but thought better of it and stabbed a forkful of *salade frisée aux lardons* instead. The plate was beautifully arranged: bitter greens, perfectly balanced vinaigrette, thick crumbles of bacon, and two toasted slices of baguette spread with goat cheese. She ate rapidly, eager to get back to the document.

"Zari!" Laurence held up a hand, her eyebrows furrowed in disapproval. "Calm yourself. Those words are five hundred years old. They can wait a few more minutes for you."

"I can't help being excited." Zari jiggled her leg under the table. "I'm freaking out over here, to be honest."

"Freaking out?" Laurence pushed away her half-eaten salad and lit another cigarette. "Why do Americans say such things?"

"What about you?" Zari retorted. "*J'ai le cafard*, for example. Explain why 'I have the cockroach' means 'I'm depressed.'"

Laurence fell silent. The thin gold chain around her neck was strung with a simple circle of gold. A wedding ring, Zari suddenly realized.

"It is not easy, Zari." Laurence's voice was low and halting. "Look around."

Everyone but Zari seemed to be smoking at the tables clustered around them.

Zari watched a man at the next table light up an unfiltered *Gauloises*, the stench of which never failed to nauseate her. "Yes," she admitted. "It must be torture."

Her eyes fell on Laurence's necklace again.

"My husband's wedding ring," Laurence said absently. "I wear it on our anniversary."

"Today...?" Zari put down her fork.

Laurence nodded. "Yes."

All at once Zari understood why Laurence had been so testy. Grief threatened to engulf her, an all-consuming sadness that she tried to mask with a cloud of smoke.

"I'm sorry, Laurence," Zari said. "Smoke to your heart's content—I won't say another word, I promise."

Laurence stretched her lips into a thin ghost of a smile. She closed her eyes and tilted her face to the sun, the cigarette dangling from her fingers.

Zari settled back in her chair, her mind on the swirling rust-red letters scrawled across the notary's book. Whatever message they contained, Laurence was right. Those words could wait a few more minutes to be discovered.

After their plates were cleared, after their tiny cups of espresso had been served and drained, Laurence nodded at Zari's messenger bag. It was time.

Zari fished her laptop from her bag and slid it over to Laurence.

"*Sale of wool cloth: Folio 70r, dated July 26, 1504,*" Laurence read aloud. She stopped and glanced up. "I will do my best to translate, but this is not modern French."

"*In the year and on the day aforesaid,*" she began, "*we, Arnaud de Luz, journeyman cabinetmaker of Ronzal, and my wife Miramonde de Luz, sell to you, Lord Esteven de Vernier, merchant of pastel and wool, each and all of the bolts of fine dyed merino wool fabric which were made from the fleeces of sheep from the Abbey of Belarac...*"

Laurence's voice faltered and she looked up at Zari for a moment, her eyes aglow. "*We promise to deliver and to transport this fabric to you in the summer of 1505,*" she went on. "*If the fabric is not of the same quality of the samples we provided, we obligate ourselves personally and all our present and future property.*"

"A sale of fabric to a merchant in Toulouse," Zari said blankly. "I thought we were onto something huge. But this?" She slumped in her chair. "Fabric?"

"This *is* huge, Zari. First, we know they were married. We were never sure before exactly what their relationship was. Now we have proof."

Zari stayed silent, but she sat up a little straighter.

"We knew from the mortuary roll that Mira had a close relationship with the abbess of Belarac," Laurence said. "You thought the abbey might have raised merino sheep. Now we know that is true. This helps your case, do you not see?"

"Thanks for trying to make me feel better, but—"

"This woman, Mira. She was forgotten, lost to history," Laurence interrupted. "And think what you did. You learned she was a nun. And then you learned she was a member of the family of Oto. And then you learned Arnaud de Luz made panels for her and went to a cave in Aragón with her. And now you find out she was married to him! All of this, about a person who lived five hundred years ago. It is fantastic, what you have done."

"Why are you suddenly the optimistic one?"

"Because I have a reason."

"You do?"

"When the archives open up again at Bayonne, you will know that every bit of evidence you find about Arnaud means something, because he was Mira's husband. That alone is something to celebrate."

"But that's not until next summer." Zari's voice flared with worry. "I need to have a solid paper to present in Bordeaux this spring."

"No one will accuse you of being lazy. You are studying the archives in every city and museum in the entire region. Just keep searching, Zari. Keep asking questions. That is all you can do. And you're very good at it."

Laurence lit another cigarette, took a long drag, and exhaled.

They both watched the thin plume of smoke twist upward into the blue sky and disappear.

9

Winter, 1505
Toulouse, France
Mira

THE COLD HAD BURROWED into Mira's bones. Even in the luxury of the merchant's home, with its fires burning in multiple hearths, she was never warm. Here at the inn, she shivered all night long.

The inn was crowded with woad farmers and peasants eager to contract with the city's growing ranks of merchants. During meals at the downstairs tavern, Mira and Arnaud became students of the woad industry through a series of long-winded monologues delivered by the innkeeper, whose chief pleasure appeared to be the sound of his own voice.

The merchants in Toulouse who invested in woad were obliged to pay out years in advance, he explained, for the process of turning the plant into blue pigment was long and laborious. It took a year from planting to harvest, then many months of washing, soaking, crushing, grinding, and fermenting.

He told them that the tall brick tower built by Lord de Vernier was being copied by the newly wealthy all over Toulouse. Rich merchants were sprouting like mushrooms, he said. And why wouldn't they? The demand for blue dye grew stronger with each passing year. The ambitious and the greedy flocked to Toulouse, hoping to reap their own reward from the woad industry. If Mira and Arnaud were lucky, he said, they would benefit too.

They had found a lodging house near a quiet square that had two rooms to let, and soon would have enough money saved to move there. Listening to the scrabbling of rodents and the noise in the tavern night after sleepless night, Mira longed for that day.

This morning, snow swirled around her as she shuffled through the alleyway to Lord de Vernier's home, slipping now and then on the icy cobblestones. She had taken to first visiting the cellar kitchens for a cup of steaming cider spiced with cloves. She stood with her hands wrapped around the hot ceramic cup, staring into the shifting flames of the kitchen fire. When her fingers began to redden and swell it was time to put down the cup and climb the three stories of the servants' staircase to the nursery.

She had quickly learned to stay a few paces ahead of the grumpy housekeeper, Heloise, whose lip curled in a sneer every time she caught sight of Mira. Apparently her installation as the new governess had been a personal affront to the woman, who never tired of reminding Mira that though she might claim to be high-born, she was no better than any other servant in the employ of the family.

It was late in the afternoon. The girls had been bundled up and sent to the courtyard to play. Their mother believed in daily time out of doors, and though Mira had never met her she agreed with the philosophy—it was the same one that Mother Béatrice had instituted at Belarac. All the children raised there had spent time each day playing in the cloisters' gardens, or if it rained, in the covered arcades that lined the inner courtyard.

Mira closed her books and tidied up the room. On her hands and knees, recovering a quill that had rolled under a bookcase, she did not hear the door open. When she stood up, a woman dressed in layers of shimmering blue silk stood in the center of the room. Her dark hair was covered with a fine lace headpiece encrusted with pearls, and a glinting red ruby dangled from a gold chain around her neck. Mira dropped into a low curtsy.

"Please, rise." The woman's voice was low, and she spoke in Aragónese.

"Yes, my lady."

"You are my kinswoman, I hear."

Mira was startled. Then she realized what the woman meant. "Yes, my lady. I was born in Aragón."

"Of what house were you born?" The woman walked to the table and opened a book. She turned the pages with elegant fingers. Mira counted four gold rings on her hands.

"I...the house of Oto, my lady." She was in France now, Mira reminded herself. Far from Aragón. A whole kingdom away from anyone who cared.

"The barons of Oto. I have heard of their exploits. They say a war cannot be won without the house of Oto."

"Do they?" Heat began to creep up Mira's neck and color her cheeks.

The lady tilted her head to one side, her dark eyes never leaving Mira's face.

A cough rose in Mira's throat and she swallowed it away. Why hadn't she made up a name? By telling the truth, she would tangle herself in more lies.

"I myself was born in Zaragoza," Lady de Vernier said. "My father and his father before him were advisers to the king."

Mira nodded, not daring to speak.

"Noble-born in Aragón. Then fate led you to France and a life of service." A hint of curiosity swelled in the woman's voice.

Mira tried to keep her voice light. "Fortune is capricious, my lady, even for the noble-born. Our names do not always help us find a way in this world."

At that moment, Heloise bustled into the room. Her eyes widened with shock at the sight of Mira conversing with her mistress.

"My lady!" she burst out. "I apologize for this rude interruption to your day. She has been instructed not to speak to you."

"I spoke first. She was only being polite in answering my questions." The woman's voice was mild, but there was a firmness in her tone that neither Mira nor Heloise missed.

"I see." Heloise glared at Mira. "The children have returned from their play." When Mira made no move to go, she jerked her head toward the door. "Hurry along, then."

"Madame Mira." Lady de Vernier's voice rang out with authority. "You shall no longer climb the servants' staircase to reach the nursery. You will walk through the great hall and up the family staircase. Your noble-born status demands it. Heloise, though she means well, is ignorant of such matters."

Heloise stiffened. Her eyes raked over Mira, glistening with anger.

The lady of the house ignored her housekeeper's obvious discontent. She nodded to Mira and swept out of the room, her silk skirts whispering over the wool carpet.

Mira began toting a pouch of charcoal sticks to the nursery each day, along with a stack of linen paper remnants that she had bought from a bookseller. Drawing soon became the girls' favorite activity. They clamored for their turn with the charcoal each morning, and Mira's greatest challenge was keeping them from ruining their dresses with charcoal dust. She took to wrapping them in linen dishcloths that she cajoled out of the kitchen staff in exchange for quickly sketched charcoal portraits.

A fortnight into the drawing lessons, Mira was putting the finishing touches on a sketch of Sandrine, who was seated in front of her while the other two girls watched at Mira's side.

"Ooh," said the smallest one, Blanca. "That is a good likeness."

"Mmm. But you've made her much prettier than she truly is!" added Sophie.

"That is not amusing," said Sandrine, frowning. "But then your little jests are never amusing to anyone but yourself."

"That is not true," Blanca protested. "I laugh at her jests."

"You laugh at anything."

"Do not."

"Do too."

"Girls!" Mira warned, putting her charcoal down. "Who wants to draw me?"

They all glowed with excitement at this. She handed out paper and charcoal to each girl, then took her place on the chair while they stood three abreast at the polished walnut table, sketching intently.

Their mother entered the room. All three girls turned and bobbed curtsies to her, while Mira stood and bowed.

Lady de Vernier went to the table and looked over the girls' shoulders. Then she picked up the sketch Mira had made.

"This is no idle drawing." She glanced up at Mira. "You have some schooling in the arts."

"I trained in the abbey as an artist, first illuminating prayer books, then painting portraits."

Lady de Vernier studied the sketch again.

"If the artist we commissioned for our portraits was this talented, he might be worth half what we paid him."

"Ah?"

"Indeed. Every merchant in this city desires their images captured in portraits these days. The best artists are booked out for years. My husband did not want to wait, so he commissioned an artist whose work, I fear to say, is inferior. The man trained neither in Flanders nor Florence."

"I can paint portraits in the Flemish style," Mira said boldly. "My teacher was from Flanders."

Lady de Vernier's eyes lit up. "As a gift for my husband, you shall paint my portrait, then. If the quality lives up to your promise, you shall have more work than you can imagine."

That night in bed, telling Arnaud what had happened, Mira's gleeful recounting of the conversation was felled by a sudden wave of doubt.

"I have no supplies, no tools, no panels. How can I do this?"

He did not hesitate. "I can make the panels and the brushes. There's a bookseller in the weekly market who hawks pigments and artist's tools. We'll have everything you need in a week's time."

"But we had just about saved enough to pay for our own lodging," Mira objected. "If we buy all those things, we shall have to stay on here another month, perhaps more."

"I've got more work from the wool seller I met in the tavern. He's having me build chairs for him now. Keeping it on the quiet, because I'm not a member of the guild."

"On the quiet?"

"He pays me, not the guild, and saves himself money. The guild collects extra for tariffs and such."

"But what if he is caught? You will be jailed—or worse."

"It's the risk I must take if I want to work. The guild won't have me, I've told you that. I've no recommendation."

She rolled over and propped her head on her hand. She could just make out the outline of his face in the dark. "Why did you not tell me of this plan?"

"Because I knew you'd do what you're doing now." Arnaud was rarely irritated with her, but the exasperation in his voice was plain.

Mira sat up and crossed her arms, fuming. She nearly asked three more questions and just as quickly knocked them back down her throat. Only the knowledge that she might step on a wriggling mouse's tail if she jumped out of bed kept her sitting at Arnaud's side.

When she had finally got hold of her patience again, she heard the faint whistling of a snore. Arnaud had fallen asleep. Soon dawn would bear down on the city and the streets would come alive again. A bit of sleep was too precious to spoil with an argument.

She lay down and pressed her cheek against his chest. The steady thud of his heartbeat soon lulled her into unconsciousness.

10

Winter, 1505
Toulouse, France
Mira

WITHIN A FORTNIGHT OF moving into their rented rooms, both Mira and Arnaud felt rested for the first time in months. Their rooms were small but clean, and overlooked a quiet square. The bedchamber contained a wood-framed bed and chest. They turned the sitting room into a workshop of sorts. It was furnished sparsely, with an oak table, two chairs, a stool, and a small chest. Piled on the floor were their wood panels, tools, and painting supplies.

They quickly fell into a routine, leaving early for work, meeting at a tavern for supper, and returning home for an hour or two of work by candlelight in the sitting room before retiring to their bed. The square was blissfully quiet at night. Only at dawn, when housewives and servants traipsed to the fountain at its center, did it come alive with voices and movement.

Late one evening there came a pounding at the door. Mira and Arnaud looked at each other. No one had ever knocked for them before. They both sprang out of bed.

"Yes?" Arnaud called.

"Someone asks for you." The landlord's voice was gravelly with sleep. "Come at once."

They scrambled in the dark to shove their feet into slippers and pull on their cloaks. Downstairs, in the guesthouse's entryway, a woman lay on the floor curled on her side, a screaming baby in her arms.

The landlord nudged the woman with a toe. "They sent her from the inn. She asked for you there and they told her you'd come here. Walked in babbling, fell on the floor, and now she's gone silent."

Mira sank to her knees at the woman's side. She drew back the hood of her cloak and took in a sharp breath. It was Deedit, the Cagot woman from the mountain village, the one whose husband lost a hand for drinking from the wrong holy water font. Mira glanced up at Arnaud, shocked.

"Poor thing," she said when she finally found her voice. "She needs a bed."

The landlord frowned. "She looks ill. The sweating sickness has taken hold in the eastern quarter of the city. I'll not allow it in my property."

Mira put a hand on Deedit's forehead. "She has no sweating sickness."

The landlord opened his mouth to protest.

"I nursed hundreds of pilgrims in a convent infirmary." Mira said more forcefully. "I know what sweating sickness is, and this woman does not have it. She is hungry and exhausted, that is all. Please, let us take her to our rooms. We shall pay for her lodging."

The landlord jerked his head at the sobbing baby.

"We'll pay for hers as well," Arnaud said, plucking the baby from her mother's side and handing her to Mira. He slid his arms under Deedit's slumped shape and scooped her up.

"Very well." The landlord yawned. "On a temporary basis only, mind you. And bring me payment tomorrow, before you exit these doors. I'll be waiting."

Arnaud made a nest for Deedit and her baby in a corner of the sitting room. When Deedit awoke in the morning, Mira kneeled at her side, feeding her spoonfuls of broth and boiled millet. The baby was able to sit up on her own, and she reached for the spoon so many times Mira finally let her feed herself, though the mess was eye-popping.

"What happened?" Mira asked, nestling the baby at her mother's side again.

"My husband got sicker and sicker. His stump never really healed. Nothing I did helped. One day he died."

Deedit's pale yellow hair was plastered to her head. She was so thin Mira could see her skull pressing through the scant flesh on her face. The day they first met, Mira had been struck by the woman's cornflower-blue eyes, fierce with anger. Now they were bloodshot and dull, circled with dark shadows.

"My belly swelled. When my baby was born I was frightened. I had no husband, no one to feed us. The other Cagots gave me what they could, but they had so little themselves." She shifted her position, stroked her baby's head with a small, calloused hand. "I kept thinking on what you said. I decided the only way I could help my baby was to leave that place. So I tore the red badges off my sleeves and crept away. I thought we'd die on that first night. But I managed to find a place with the shell over the door just as you said. The monks were kind, and the prior remembered you. He told me where you planned to lodge in Toulouse. And then I followed the shells all the way here, sleeping and eating by the grace of nuns and monks."

"And no one mistreated you?"

Deedit shook her head. "I told no one what I am." She glanced around the room. "Do you make things here?"

"Arnaud makes tools for his work and supplies for my work." Mira saw Deedit's eyes rest on a stack of paintbrushes. "I am an artist," she explained.

"What do you mean?"

"I paint portraits."

"And you get paid for that?"

Mira nodded.

Deedit took that in silently. The baby squalled and she gathered the infant in her arms, putting her to a breast.

"She cries because my milk's dried up some, from all the journeying."

"We'll soon put that to rights. And she is ready to wean. You saw her with that millet and broth."

"But how will I pay you for the lodging? I've got no money."

"Do not worry about that now. Rest, eat, and regain your strength."

The wary look on Deedit's face washed away. She settled back into her blankets.

"What is your baby's name?" Mira asked.

For the first time, Deedit smiled. "Rose."

They fell into a new routine. Deedit and Rose slept in the front room surrounded by painting supplies and tools. Once Deedit had regained her strength, she became a maid of sorts for them, attending to laundry, meal preparation, and marketing. She carried Rose in a wrap on her back.

Rose's screams gave way to smiles as she gained weight and flourished under the attention of all three adults. Deedit was an accomplished seamstress and she began taking in work from the landlord and neighbors.

They strolled out together on market day, traipsing from stall to stall in the great square, observing all the craftspeople hawking their wares. They would buy warm buns from a bakery on the way, then wander at their leisure watching the crowds and the bustle of activity.

From time to time they caught sight of Cagots on these outings, identifiable from the red fabric badges sewn onto their sleeves. They were rarely in full sight, nor did they mingle with the market day crowds. Rather they crept along the side alleys, melting into shadows when they needed to, trying not to attract attention to themselves. Mira found herself staring unabashedly after them, trying to catch a glimpse of their faces to see if they all looked like Deedit and Rose, with cornflower-blue eyes and hair like straw.

One day on her way home from work, Mira cut through a narrow alleyway to avoid a mule cart with a broken wheel that blocked the lane. A dark-haired man about her height approached from the opposite direction. His eyes were downcast and he walked with quick, scurrying steps. His clothes were patched and worn, and there was something red on his sleeve—the distinctive badge of a Cagot.

The next morning she mentioned the encounter to Deedit.
"He looked nothing like you," she remarked.
"Why should he?"
"You are both Cagots."
"We don't all look the same."
"The red badges are the only way to tell, then?"
"Yes."
"But why?"
"It's the way things have always been for us."
"I do not see a difference between you and any other woman." Mira leaned forward, plucked Rose from the floor, and settled the girl on her knee. "It makes no sense."

163

A shadow crossed Deedit's face. "I feel deceitful, knowing I'm one of them who's meant to walk in the shadows and keep my eyes down. I pretend to be like you, but in my heart I know what I truly am. It makes me ashamed."

Mira reached out and took her hand. "What you truly are is a fine mother and exceptional seamstress."

Arnaud emerged from the bedchamber, buttoning his vest. "Who's ready for market day?"

Rose screeched in excitement at the sight of him, raising her arms. He swung her up and twirled around, eliciting a stream of laughter.

"You'll be a good father one day, sir," Deedit said, her face creased in a rare smile.

"Call me Arnaud."

"As you wish, sir."

He winked at Rose, who let out a squeal of glee.

Mira felt a queer sort of yearning in her chest. She imagined Arnaud with another baby in his arms. Their baby. It wasn't for lack of trying that she was not yet with child. A tingle of desire took hold of her at the thought of Arnaud's body next to her in the dark, his hands exploring her most intimate places, his mouth claiming her, possessing her. It was the only time she felt truly at ease in Toulouse. All the worries of the day, of the future, dropped away in those moments.

"Mira?"

Arnaud drew close, looking at her with the smile that she treasured the way other women treasured pearls. It had been his gift to her since they were eleven years old.

"Tonight?" he whispered.

The sly look on his face told her he knew exactly where her mind had been.

11

Winter, 1505
Toulouse, France
Deedit

DEEDIT WALKED THROUGH THE streets, head up, her small feet in their new shoes of soft tanned leather silent on the cobblestones. She wore a thick brown wool cloak and matching mittens, gifts from Mira. In her basket was a pile of linens to be embroidered and returned to customers by the end of the week.

It had not been difficult to find work. People they encountered on the way to the market complimented the intricate embroidery along the hem of little Rose's skirt and on the sleeves of her blouse. Deedit quickly gained a reputation as a fine seamstress who could make a plain garment look like something of quality with the addition of decorative stitching. Her earnings helped with rent and food, but Mira always insisted she keep a few coins for herself.

Each evening after Rose was asleep, Deedit lit two tallow candles and sat in silence, pushing a needle and thread through linen and flax, thinking of nothing but the desire to make fine, careful stitches. The murmurings of Mira and Arnaud behind their chamber door were a reminder that she was safe here in Toulouse, under the care of kind people. Those were the only moments of the day when she was free of the worries that churned constantly in her mind. She treasured them.

Just ahead was the small square where their lodgings were located. It was a fairly quiet place, though the fountain sometimes attracted servants fetching water for laundry or workers washing off after a day's toiling in the trades. As Deedit passed into the square she noticed two boys in a narrow alleyway standing over a prone body on the ground. They were jeering and shouting. The only intelligible word she heard was 'Cagot.'

Instantly she stopped.

Keeping her eyes fixed on the fountain, she willed her feet to move, to continue home. Yet she could not get the image of her deceased husband out of her mind. His poor, dear body bleeding on the slick cobblestones while villagers stood by, taunting him. Now here she was walking through the streets of Toulouse as if she were a true citizen, wearing fine clothing, working at a trade, living in a safe and warm dwelling.

What has she done in her life to deserve such a fate? What made her any better than the Cagots who were doomed to creep in the shadows, shuffle past the citizens of the city, always in fear of being noticed? And when they were noticed, the outcome was always the same: ridicule, torment, abuse.

She wheeled and approached the alleyway.

"Leave the poor thing alone!" she shouted.

The boys turned and appraised her. They must not have been much older than twelve, poor themselves, if their stained clothing and dirty faces were any evidence. Yet because they were not Cagots, she knew they still felt superior to the man trembling behind them.

Slowly he rose, shivering in the cold. The red badge on his sleeve was florid, a vulgar flash of color on his timeworn shirt. Perhaps it had been white once, that shirt, but now it was the faded gray that poverty bestowed upon the clothing of the destitute. She noticed a ragged hole on the other sleeve, and wished she could mend it for him.

Instead of heeding her words, the boys laughed. One of them, the taller of the two, with hair the color of silt and eyes that were hooded like an old man's, reached out and yanked her basket so it fell on the ground, spilling out its contents.

"Seamstress, are you?" he said, eyeing her closely. "You're dressed fine." He bent down and picked up one of the blouses that had fallen out of the basket. "I'm in need of something new myself. This looks like a good fit."

His companion pawed through the other items. He had a broad face and wide, thin lips. Squatting there before her on his spindly haunches, he put her in mind of a toad.

"Cagot women are the best seamstresses, they say." He squinted up at her. "Ain't that so?"

"I don't know," she said. "Get off my things!"

The one clutching the blouse stepped closer. "You're small. Like a child, you are. Cagots are like that. Look at him!" He jerked his head back toward the slight man, who had pressed himself against the wall of the alley, his eyes round with fear. "Only a Cagot would defend one of their own. Show us your sleeve!"

"Thief!" she screamed as loudly as she could. "Thief!"

Her voice floated out over the square, high and insistent.

A merchant woman and her servants stopped by the fountain, observing the scene.

"Are those boys abusing you, madame?" the merchant woman called.

Deedit locked eyes with the boy who had the blouse crumpled in his fist.

"Are you?" she hissed. "Do you wish to feel the sting of the bailiff's whip?"

He flung the blouse at her. His companion sprang back and the two of them melted into the shadows. From the darkness came the tall boy's mocking voice again: "Cagot."

Hands trembling, she stuffed her linens back in the basket. When she looked up, the Cagot man was gone.

She quickly returned to their lodgings and said nothing of the encounter to Mira or Arnaud. But now she would have to be on her guard, watching for those taunting, ragged boys, each time she passed through the square. The familiar, sickening sensation of anxiety and fear returned, pressing down on her even when she took up needle and thread and stitched her patterns.

For Rose's sake, Deedit knew she would never come to the defense of a Cagot again.

12

Winter, 1505
Toulouse, France
Mira

MIRA GATHERED HER SKIRTS in her hands and took the steps two at a time. Lady de Vernier desired her presence at once. Heloise had delivered the news breathlessly, an eager light in her eyes, as soon as Mira entered the kitchens that morning.

"I wonder what you've done," she added as Mira hurried away, loud enough for all the kitchen servants to hear. "I'd brace for the worst if I were you."

Striding along the red wool carpets past polished oak chests, displays of silver plate, and gleaming beeswax candles, Mira prayed her error was something forgivable.

When she entered the chamber door her mistress was standing at the window, staring up at the soaring brick tower across the courtyard. As usual Lady de Vernier was dressed entirely in blue, her bodice encrusted with tiny white pearls.

"Mira," she said, turning. "Approach. I have something to discuss with you."

She spoke in Aragónese, in a soft, pleasant voice. This was a good sign, surely.

"I have studied the completed portrait to my satisfaction," she said, "and I have arrived at my conclusion. Your work is exquisite, my dear. It rivals anything executed by the artists other families import from Flanders and Florence. I could not be happier." She smiled broadly.

Mira was overcome with relief. Her knees felt weak.

"Oh, my lady," she said. "I am honored to hear this."

"Tell me how you learned your craft."

"I studied under a master painter called Sebastian de Scolna. He was from Flanders and happened upon our convent after a grave injury. I helped nurse him back to health. After his recovery he stayed on at the convent and painted the frescoes in an old chapel that had fallen into disrepair. He offered to teach me to paint proper portraits in the Flemish style."

"But surely it must have taken years for you to develop these skills."

"The truth is I began to draw as a small child," Mira admitted. "I had a basket of charcoal and when I could steal a few moments I would go to the old well in the kitchen garden where there was a marble step that served as my drawing surface. When the mother abbess saw what I could do, she put me to work illustrating manuscripts in the library. In that way I learned to use a brush and pigment, although my first and best skill was drawing. The master Sebastian taught me to use my drawing skills to aid my painting. Do you recall how I used that lead stylus to make underdrawings before I even put a drop of paint on the panel?"

"Yes."

"The underdrawings are the foundation for the portrait, then I add layers of paint on top of them. Master Sebastian taught me the tricks of light and shading that make a portrait come to life."

She gestured to the painting. Lady de Vernier was depicted from the waist up and wore a blue silk dress with a square neckline. A double strand of glowing pearls was wrapped around her neck. Upon her dark hair lay a gossamer-thin veil stitched with the finest gold thread. In the background, visible through an open window, was the pink brick tower that every other merchant in Toulouse envied.

"Does your master still live?" Lady de Vernier joined her in front of the panel.

"I know not," Mira said. "He returned to Flanders when the scars from his injuries had healed. I pray for him each day. He is a kind man, and patient. He taught me how to wield a brush with more skill than I knew I possessed."

"My husband has not seen this yet, but I know that when he does he will invite you to make more portraits of our family. Once that is accomplished I imagine he will share the news of your skill with other merchants in Toulouse. You could have a long career painting here, for this city bursts with wealthy merchants who want their portraits painted in the Flemish style. And yours is the best I have seen. Believe me, I have seen many."

Mira looked down at her hands. "Your compliments mean a great deal to me," she said. "I only wish I could stay on, but after the fabric arrives and is examined and approved by your husband, we are obliged to leave for the west."

"Why is that?"

"Our future lies in Bayonne."

"How unfortunate," said Lady de Vernier. Disappointment was evident on her face. "I shall miss you, for speaking my native tongue with you gives me comfort. And my girls adore you. I cannot imagine finding a suitable replacement when you leave."

The warmth in her brown eyes made Mira miss Elena desperately.

"In the meantime, what say you to painting miniatures of myself and my girls? As keepsakes for my husband."

Mira smiled. "Nothing would give me greater pleasure."

13

December, 2015
Pyrenees Mountains, France
Zari

T<small>INY WHITE FLAKES FELL</small> from the sky and landed, tingling, on Zari's cheeks. The sky was pale silver, the evergreens on the ridges that surrounded the valley iced with snow. She took a deep breath, luxuriating in the sharp, cold air, admiring the trail of teardrop-shaped impressions Wil's snowshoes had left in the powdery whiteness ahead of her. He moved fluidly, with athletic grace, never stumbling or wavering in his course. He carried a backpack topped with a mysterious box wrapped in brown kraft paper. It wouldn't be Christmas, he said, without presents.

Zari had a present for him, too, but it was nestled in a side pocket of her own pack, in a bag too small to attract attention. She shivered with anticipation at the thought of Wil opening that bag.

Two months had passed since they last saw one another. This holiday trip to the backcountry had been Wil's idea, but Zari had found the cabin, which belonged to a work colleague of Laurence's. It sat just a few miles past the site of the Abbey of Belarac.

They had snowshoed through the frozen silence of the narrow valley of Belarac, pausing by the stream where, last summer, they discovered the abbey's ancient foundation stones sinking into the earth.

Now there were no stones visible to spur Zari's imagination, but she didn't need them. She stood next to the rushing water, constructing in her mind the structures that had once dominated this landscape: chapel, dormitory, refectory, stables, kitchens, guesthouse. Delicate icicles hung from the bare branches of willows that grew along the stream. Zari broke one off. It looked like an animal's curved claw. Had Mira stood on the stream-bank in wintertime, watched icicles take shape on the willows? Where had she slept? Where had she learned to draw, to paint?

When Zari had daydreamed long enough, they forged on. Now, sweaty after a long tramp up a steady incline, they had finally reached the meadow where the cabin stood.

"Hey!" Wil pointed ahead. A crow flapped across the meadow, its black wings stark against the pale sky. "He's probably keeping an eye on us in case we turn into dinner."

Zari shuddered. "That's not a good visual."

The crow cawed at them from a branch in a pine tree.

"What?" Zari called out. "Are we invading your space?"

The bird fell silent, its shiny eyes charting their progress across the snow.

The cabin was constructed of stone, its roof made of slate tiles. It was just one room, with a self-composting toilet in an attached outhouse. Inside was a fireplace with a stone hearth, next to which was a stack of fresh cut pine logs and kindling. A pair of bunk beds were wedged along one wall and a table with four chairs sat opposite them. A worn wool rug occupied the center of the room, and on either side of the door were rectangular windows darkened with wood shutters. In one corner sat a wood-burning iron stove with two round burners on top for cooking.

Wil set to work building fires in the hearth and the stove and opening the shutters. Zari unpacked her things. She had brought a Provençal tablecloth and a few Christmas ornaments that she had picked up in an outdoor market. They stashed their food in a wooden cupboard and put their perishables in an outdoor cache fitted with a bear-proof lid, then took stock of the place.

"Cozier and warmer by the second," Zari said.

"It's still missing something." Wil handed Zari her jacket.

Outside, she strapped on her snowshoes and followed him into the woods. He stopped after about ten minutes and tugged at something in the snow. A branch from a black pine tree, freshly fallen by the sight of it, with a long crack on one end and luxuriant growth on the other.

"This is good." He shook the snow off the branch.

Zari smiled. "A Christmas tree. Now we've got everything we need."

On the way back to the cabin, the snow began to fall harder.

They leaned the tree branch against one wall, bolstered at the base by their empty packs. Then they pulled the mattresses off the lower bunks and made them into one large bed on the rug in the center of the cabin. Snuggled into their sleeping bags, they watched flames dance in the fireplace.

"Two months apart is rough." Zari propped her head on her hand and turned to face Wil. "It can get lonely in Pau."

"I know it's hard for you. I feel the same way." He twisted a strand of her hair in his fingers. "I wish we could be together all the time."

"We've got Bordeaux to look forward to in May. Although it probably won't be much fun," Zari admitted. "I'll be a nervous wreck. And you'll be exhausted from your trip."

Wil had secured a position as a volunteer crew member for the adaptive sailing trip to Croatia with Filip.

"I won't be exhausted. Sailing gives me energy—and so do you." He smiled. "Why will you be nervous? Are you afraid of speaking in public?"

"No, I love it. But I'm worried about the strength of my research. I don't have enough yet to present a convincing case about Mira."

"You will."

Zari threaded her fingers through his. "We'll need to come up with at least one more destination before May where we can meet. Five months between visits is way too long." She felt a stab of longing for home. "I feel so far away from my usual support crew," she said quietly, pressing her cheek against his shoulder.

"What does your family normally do at the holidays?"

"We're not a huge Christmas family. My mother doesn't like the holiday hoopla. I think once my parents divorced, she dreaded this time of year. So we traveled. We camped in Mexico one year, got a cabin in Yosemite another. Once we drove up the coast to Oregon and stayed in a yurt."

"What about your dad?" Wil's dark blue eyes regarded her steadily. "Did you spend some holidays with him?"

"He moved in with his girlfriend the day he left my mother. They got married and had two kids, and he kind of went dark on us. His second wife is not a fan of his first family."

"So your mom worked hard to make holidays special for you and your brother."

"I'm really proud of her. She's making money from her creativity at last. She made thousands of dollars in online sales last month. She's sixty and she's just launched a career."

Wil got up to add another log to the fire, then settled at Zari's side again. "Why didn't you choose a creative life?"

She hesitated. "I was always drawing as a kid. I loved art. Even though I knew I could go down a commercial path and do graphic design or illustration, I somehow got it into my head that art wasn't a responsible choice. Becoming an academic who studied art was my compromise."

He raised an eyebrow.

"I know," she said. "The academic life isn't a road to riches, or even a steady job. Building websites on the side nets me more income than I'll ever make as a professor, unless I get tenure at some fabulously elite school. Still, I love the idea of opening up these dusty doors into the past. Mira is a true obsession to me. There are more women like her, waiting to be discovered. I don't know, I just—I want to be the one doing the discovering." She traced his jaw with a finger. "Thank you."

"For what?"

"For coming here with me. You're sacrificing your own Christmas with family."

"They won't miss me. There's so many of them. We don't all stay home for Christmas, anyway."

"What about your grandmother? I'm still worried that I'll never fill Hana's shoes in her eyes."

"Worrying about what my grandmother thinks is not the best use of your time." He leaned over and kissed her. "This, on the other hand, is."

The next morning they awoke to a white-out. Snow pelted the windows with fury. When Wil stepped outside to fetch the milk and butter, he returned covered with a thin layer of icy flakes.

Zari put a pot of water on the stove to boil for coffee, then brushed the snow off Wil's sweater.

"Merry Christmas," she said.

"Merry Christmas."

They opened presents while eating clementines and chocolate and drinking coffee.

Zari carefully unwrapped her gift. Inside the box was a magnifying visor, the type that John Drake wore for his art conservation work. She gasped.

"I've always wanted one of these!"

"I know."

"But I don't remember telling you that."

He smiled. "I have my sources."

She picked up a small box containing several lens plates of different focal ranges.

"Interchangeable lens plates. I'm going high-tech. No more hand-held magnifying glass and camping headlamp for me. It's like having a superpower."

Wil reached into his pocket. "I have something else for you."

The jewelry box contained a pair of silver scallop shell earrings to match the necklace that Laurence had given her last summer, which Zari had worn during their trek to Oto.

She immediately put the earrings on. "I love them."

Wil's eyes gleamed with quiet joy.

Zari thrust a small box at him. "Now your turn."

He peeled off the tape and lifted the lid. Inside were four bands of silver, each forged in a slightly different way.

"Four rings?" He held one up, looking at her for an explanation.

"Try one on," she encouraged him.

The ring fit perfectly over the third finger of his right hand. "How did you know?"

"I measured your finger when you were asleep. My mother has a jeweler friend who makes these in a tiny studio on the California coast. I sent him your size a few months ago."

"But why four?"

"It's actually one ring. A puzzle ring. You need to figure out how to fit them together."

His face lit up. "You remembered!"

"Now's your chance to figure it out. There are no instructions in the box, I'm sure you noticed."

"It can't be too difficult."

She smiled. "Try it."

Thirty minutes later, Wil pushed back his chair and ran a hand through his rumpled hair. "I give up."

Zari reached for the bands. In a moment she had them locked together. She grasped Wil's hand and slipped the ring over his finger.

"It looks just like a sailor's knot." He twisted it back and forth, tested its stability. "You have to work hard to get these pieces apart."

She nodded. "They belong together."

He wrapped both his hands around hers. "Like us."

They sat quietly like that for a while, holding hands across the table, while the fire crackled and hard pellets of snow ricocheted off the windows.

Winter's grip was tightening outside, sending a deathly hush across the landscape. Listening to the rattle of the snow on the glass, Zari imagined the cabin as a bubble of light hovering in a dark world—a private, sacred space where love unfurled minute by minute.

A place aglow with promise, with possibilities.

14

January, 2016
Nay, France
Zari

ZARI STEPPED OFF THE bus by a stone bridge that arched over a swiftly-flowing, narrow river in the town of Nay. A light rain fell as she walked over the bridge and onto the glittering wet cobblestones of the ancient streets. The air was chillier here than in Pau, even though the bus ride had taken less than an hour. She thrust her hands in the pockets of her jacket, wishing she had remembered to bring gloves.

Steep foothills rose up just behind the town, which was nestled at the base of the Pyrenees. The medieval character of the central square was perfectly intact, dominated by a town hall that faced north and surrounded by buildings with half-timbered facades. A long arcade with graceful Romanesque arches wrapped around the entire square.

Zari approached the wide double oak doors of the Sacazars' home and paid her entry fee to a woman in a glassed-in kiosk.

Crossing the threshold into the courtyard, she was confronted with the sight of three stories of arcaded stone balconies. The balconies were supported by columns carved with decorative flourishes. Under her feet, rocks in various shades of gray, black, and white formed complex patterns on the courtyard floor.

A series of descriptive placards were affixed to one of the walls next to a pair of faces carved in stone that were identified as Carlo and Flora Sacazar. According to the text, the Sacazars had been a family of importance in the late 1400s and early 1500s both in Aragón and Béarn. Their ancestral home had been in Zaragoza. They had two daughters and had risen to prominence as traders of wool and makers of fine fabric.

Apparently the Sacazars had taken advantage of their status as sheep-breeders in Aragón by shipping fleeces over the mountains and having them processed in Nay, then selling the fabric in the town market to buyers from the north. They also traded in oil, wine, olives, and iron from Spain.

One of the placards listed the items in Flora Sacazar's will. Zari stared at the words for some time, her lips moving as she worked out the English equivalents. The list was mostly made up of clothing items: dresses of silk and wool, sleeves, hats. Then there was some jewelry, followed by other items she could not decipher.

Near the bottom of the placard she made out the words, 'Two portraits painted in oil.'

Her heartbeat ticked up a notch. She took photos of the placards and texted them to Laurence.

Zari's eyes were drawn to the carved faces on the wall again. The stone was stained and darkened, and the features of the couple were blurry, pocked with deep pits and grooves. The man's face, particularly, was nearly flattened in places, as if someone had taken a sledgehammer to it. His nose was missing entirely.

She scaled each set of stairs, slowly wandering the rooms. The only sound was the gentle slap of her shoes on the cold stone floor. The exhibits traced the growth of Nay's industries. The town had become a hotbed of fine wool fabric finishing in the Renaissance era, and dye houses had sprung up along the riverbanks. Satellite industries had taken root: notions, ribbons, lace, buttons. Meanwhile a burgeoning woodworking industry developed, with the seemingly endless forests of the Pyrenees providing the foundation for high-quality furniture making.

She saw massive wooden looms, spindles and distaffs, mannequins dressed in replicas of eighteenth-century peasant garb. All the tools and trappings of the region's wool fabric industry were laid out before her, housed in glass-fronted cabinets, or presented in tableau fashion behind cords of rough rope.

On the third floor, she went outside to the balcony. The sun had broken through the clouds and a flood of light illuminated the courtyard below. A group of schoolchildren was massed below her, chattering excitedly. Several of them formed a line and, balancing on their toes, they followed the patterns laid out in the stones. Zari watched the children hop from one stone to the next, drinking in their energy and unselfconscious exuberance. Her thoughts turned to her niece and nephew. She missed the high, clear timbre of their voices, the immensity of their hugs.

After a few moments, the teachers managed to corral their charges into a line and they trooped inside the building. The courtyard was suddenly silent. An orange cat appeared below her, stepping daintily across the stones. Zari watched it, transfixed. Then she took a photo of the cat and its shadow.

Sitting at a café on the edge of the square, Zari sipped a tiny cup of espresso, watching clouds move across the sky. She loved this kind of weather—dark and rainy one moment, sunny the next.

When her mobile buzzed, Zari jumped.

Laurence wasted no time with pleasantries.

"You understood most of the text?"

"Yes."

"The part about three silken dresses, two fine wool dresses? The sleeves?"

"Yes, I got that part. I didn't understand the specifics about Flora Sacazar's jewelry or the paintings."

"She had pearl necklaces. A gold and ruby necklace. Ruby and gold rings. Silver plate. Jeweled caps."

Laurence drew in a breath. Zari knew she had gotten to the important part.

"Two portraits made in oil on panel," Laurence read slowly. "With gilt frames."

"Portraits of whom?"

"It says nothing else about them."

Zari drained her espresso. "We need to see that will. The entire document."

"*Absolument.*"

"I'm going back to the museum."

The woman in the museum kiosk shook her head. "Those paintings? They are not here. Nothing belonging to the Sacazars is here. This is a museum of industry now. The building is just a space for museum exhibits."

"Still, I would like to see the will."

"It is impossible for a tourist to see such documents."

Zari fished through her bag for a business card. "I am not a tourist."

The woman peered at Zari's card, frowning.

"My colleague Laurence Ceravet is helping me with this research," Zari added. "She is with the university in Pau."

"Have her contact the museum director, then," the woman said carelessly, pushing Zari's card back through the slot in the glass window that separated them.

Zari turned away, frustrated once again by her reliance on Laurence as 'fixer' for every bureaucratic maze she entered. It rankled her to be so dependent on someone else.

She ambled out to the center of the square and fixed her eyes on the Sacazars' home. In her mind, the square was transformed into a bustling market, full of townspeople doing their weekly errands. She ran her eyes along the empty arcades that faced out toward the square, imagining them filled with the stalls of various artisans. Purveyors of wool, wood, grain, oil, wine. All hawking their wares to the people of Nay and the itinerant merchants who traveled up and down the pilgrim's route of the Camino de Santiago.

She saw the merchant Carlo Sacazar leaving his home, making his way through the crowded square to the wool stalls, examining the quality of the fleeces brought by his competitors, comparing it to the fibers of his own wool, from his flocks raised in Aragón.

A bank of gray storm clouds moved in, obscuring the high peaks of the mountains that rose up to the south. Rain softened the sounds of traffic and people in the maze of narrow streets that radiated away from the central square.

Zari stood motionless, raindrops rolling down her face, immersed in the world she had conjured up. Imaginary scenarios rippled through her mind. She closed her eyes, going over the stops on the Camino from north to south and back again. She saw Béatrice of Belarac's parchment mortuary roll, the signatures of Carlo and Flora Sacazar in the long list of mourners.

For a moment her shoulders sagged. She felt the pessimism that had gripped her in Toulouse flooding back. Why had she ever believed that she could resurrect Mira from history's sealed-off archives? What use was there in pinning her hopes on a five-hundred-year-old will from an Aragónese merchant?

Then her eyes flew open. The Sacazars' ancestral home had been in Zaragoza. If there was anything valuable preserved about them in the historical record, it was likely to be there.

She wheeled and strode quickly back to the bus stop.

15

Spring, 1505
Basque Country
Elena

XABI'S SISTERS ARGUED OVER the wedding plans without end. It was just as well, Elena thought. She had never planned a party in her life. These Basque people had celebrations for every conceivable event, and the sisters spent days jabbering about menus, guests, music, dancing, and other details that Elena found bone-crushingly dull. She withdrew more and more into her own memories just to keep herself entertained on long evenings.

The family settled on a summer wedding during the time of the full moon. Soon they would fan out across the hills and inform their neighbors of the festivities. Endless arguments transpired about the merits and disadvantages of including various far-flung relations. Apparently some were kind, upstanding, and generous, and some were stingy, sly, and rude. The problem as far as Elena could tell was that none of the siblings could agree on which relatives held which of these characteristics. If her Basque was better, she would stand and inform them that most people carried around a blend of all these qualities, and how they were seen depended entirely on the person who did the seeing. Therefore, they were doomed to argue forever.

Since her Basque was weak, she settled on a brief comment, given one evening after Xabi roared a long, decisive "Hush!" at his siblings and their offspring.

She smiled her thanks to him for the courtesy, and stood facing the assembled group.

"All are invited," she said.

Blank stares ensued.

"All the relatives are invited to the wedding," she managed to elaborate.

Eyes turned to Xabi. He nodded his agreement.

One of the sisters let loose with a high-pitched protest. Xabi held up his hand to silence her.

"You've argued long enough," he said. "Elena's right. Best to invite all of them. Yes, some of you hate some of them. You don't want them drinking our wine, eating our cheese and our hens and our pigs. Well, it's my household now, and my wedding, and I say we share what we've got with all the relatives. Even the ones you don't like."

There was a tense, simmering silence. One by one, the siblings edged away from the great hearth, refusing to meet Elena's eyes as they said good night. She knew they blamed her for the decision, and she did not care.

On an afternoon in early spring there was a knock at the door. A traveling monk on his mule had made the long trek from the valley to the east, where a monastery lay. He claimed he had a message for Elena.

They sat him at the long oak table and plied him with soup, with rabbit stew, with wine. Neither Elena nor Xabi could read (well, truth be told, Xabi could read a little, and he knew how to write numbers and figure a sum, for a shepherd who hires himself out to the rich had better know if he's being cheated). But it did not matter—the monk had no letter; there was no seal for Elena to break.

He ate his fill, then looked at her and said, "Brother Arros is very ill. A monk from San Juan de la Peña sent word to all of the monasteries in the west, seeking you. There is no one else in these mountains who can heal one so ill. And no one who knows him so well as you."

"This can't be." Elena's words were barely a whisper.

He nodded solemnly. "I swear by all the saints, it is the truth. He cannot walk, they say. He talks, but in an odd, babbling way."

"Does he have fever?"

"That I do not know." The monk slurped from his cup.

"It is a sickness that comes with old age, I reckon." Elena's mind shuffled through memories of people she had healed, people she had watched die. "When did he fall ill?"

"In the autumn."

"And he still lives. There's still time, then."

Xabi looked at her, startled. "Time?"

"To cure him of this ailment. Come morning, I'll travel with the monk back to his monastery and stay the night in the guest-house. The snows are gone, it will be quick riding to San Juan de la Peña. I'm sure I can find a monk or two—maybe a whole mule train—to ride along with. It's the spring rush, after all."

As soon as spring came, the monasteries sent wool, grain, and other goods over the mountains into Béarn. While snowmelt swirled down the mountainsides in rivers gray with silt, the King's Road swelled with pack animals on their way to market towns along the pilgrim's route. Elena always took hidden tracks through the woods, avoiding the mule trains, and she had every intention of doing it again. But the idea of her traveling alone always worried Xabi.

She stood.

"Where are you going?" Xabi rose from his chair.

"For my things. We'll leave at dawn."

"But the wedding..."

"It's waited this long. It can wait a while more if need be."

"My muscles are sore from the journey," the monk complained. "Surely a longer rest is due me."

Elena strode to the doorway and turned. Her gaze slid over the monk, his frowning face, the bulge of his round stomach pressing through his robes.

"You'll rest when you return home," she told him flatly. "Your belly is full, you're warmed through. A good night's sleep and you'll be right as rain."

16

Spring, 1505
San Juan de la Peña, Aragón
Elena

DESCENDING THE ROCKY MOUNTAIN path above San Juan de la Peña, Elena catalogued her finds with pride. Honey, herbs, roots, bark, leaves...she had filled two satchels with the mountain's bounty. Brother Arros would have a full supply of the medicines he needed.

At the thought of him her pace quickened. She worried about him as if he were her own father. In fact, the idea of Brother Arros suffering made her knees go weak.

A snow finch trilled a warning from the high branches of a pine tree. She looked up, squinting into the brightness of the noonday sun, and saw the outline of a great brown bird overhead. It was a griffon vulture. The wingspan was broader than an eagle's—Xabi had taught her that, back in the days when they argued about such things. He was right more often than not about wild creatures. For her part, Elena was an expert in the green growing things—the silvery plants that crept along the highest cliffs, the flowers that burst forth from meadows each spring in great shows of gaudy color, the roots and tubers that lay hidden under the dark rich soil of the forests.

The mountains had given up their secrets to her long ago.

When she laid her goods in a pile on the roughhewn table before Brother Arros, he beamed.

"Such treasures," he said. "You've outdone yourself."

"It was all done in the name of selfishness."

He looked surprised.

"I can't abide the thought of you in pain." She scrutinized his posture. "Have you been doing as I told you? Strengthening those limbs?"

"I would never disobey my healer." He swayed slightly and struck his walking stick against the stone floor to steady himself.

She crossed her arms over her chest.

"Think on it—when you arrived, I was nothing more than a lump of flesh in a bed. And look at me now! It is all thanks to you. I can walk again. But one side of me is broken, Elena, there is nothing you or anyone else can do about that."

His words ran together in a long, blurry string. Whatever remedies she gave him did nothing to improve the quality of his speech.

"That can't be helped," she said. "The other side of you is perfectly capable of everything it did before. Don't let it go weak, even in winter when you can't get out and walk the path to the clifftops."

"I am picking up all the threads of my life again," he assured her. "With help, of course. My writing hand still works, praise the saints. The pass of Somport shall open soon and I've a mountain of correspondence to attend to."

"Writing is not as important as walking."

"Oh, I disagree entirely. Writing is of the utmost importance when the letter concerns young Mira," he teased.

"What?" Elena's eyes widened.

Brother Arros nodded. "She is in Toulouse with Arnaud, in the employ of a merchant. He wrote in the autumn asking if I would vouch for Mira's character. I owe the man a reply."

"But they were meant to go to Bayonne. Why on earth..."

"It was an affair of the Abbey of Belarac that took them to Toulouse. Something regarding the wool trade. I do not recall the particulars, as I lost the man's letter the very day I fell ill."

Elena frowned, chewing her lip. "The important thing is that they've left Ronzal," she said after a moment. "And they're safe." She returned her gaze to Brother Arros. "Promise me you won't sit inside writing all day."

"With my stick at my side, I'll click and clack my way around this valley from dawn to dusk. Next time you visit, I shall be strong as an ox."

She snorted. "I'd take a mule over an ox. Strong enough, and smarter."

"As you wish, then. I shall endeavor to have the strength and wisdom of a mule."

His chest heaved, wracked by a fit of coughing. The coughing fit grew worse and worse, until finally Elena led him to his chambers and helped him settle into his narrow bed.

In the kitchens she placed a glob of honey and a smear of pulverized herbs in a ceramic cup, then poured boiling water over it. *There, that should do the trick*, she thought, carrying the cup through the silent corridors to Brother Arros's chambers.

One candle burned on a table next to his bed. Elena placed the cup on the table and rummaged in a small wooden trunk for a blanket, then tucked it around him. She perched on the edge of his bed and reached for the cup.

"Sit up and take a drink."

He scrabbled and clawed until he was in a sitting position. His hand collided with the cup and liquid sloshed over the rim, burning her arm. She sucked in her breath at the searing pain.

"Oh, my child," he cried. "What have I done?"

"Drink," she said curtly. "I'm fine. It was not so hot."

He gingerly slurped some of the brew. "Not so hot? I've peeled the skin off my tongue," he grumbled.

"You exaggerate."

He drank again, his eyes on Elena's arm.

"That is where you were burned as a child."

"Yes." She carefully returned the cup to the table and rolled back her sleeve. The silvery ridges of her old scar now had a pinkish cast from the new burn. "I've Ramón de Oto to thank for this."

"Why did he do it?"

"Because he was a cruel boy, just like his father before him."

Elena stared unseeing into the tiny flame shuddering atop the candle.

"If I had known the Otos would return to Belarac I never would have sent you there," Brother Arros said sadly. "I thought you would be safe across the mountains. I tried to protect you from your mother's fate."

"I know."

"The Otos had not honored their duty as patrons of Belarac for a generation," he went on. "I thought—we all thought—they would never set foot in the place again."

Elena blew on her arm, turning it over in the candlelight. The pain was diminishing a bit.

"Did he attack you?" Brother Arros had never pressed her for details about the incident. She wondered why he did now.

"Ramón?" She shook her head. The memories came racing back like a pack of yellow-eyed wolves snarling inside her skull, converging on her mind from all directions. "Not with his hands. With words. He came upon me in the kitchens, chopping vegetables for a dish that was meant to serve his parents. They were off with the abbess, getting a tour of the place. He wandered in, spied me. Called me a stupid waif, ordered me to make him a stew right then. I did my best to drag a kettle of water into the hearth to heat. But then he said the vegetables had to go in before the water, ordered me to start again. I grabbed the handle of the kettle not thinking of how hot it'd be. The water went everywhere. My arm got the worst of it."

"What did he do?"

"He watched me scream. Laughed at my pain. When the cook came in he told her I'd been stealing food. I don't think she believed him, but it was the end of me at the Abbey of Belarac." She shook her head. "I thought I'd never clap eyes on that family again. Instead I've become entangled with them too many times to count."

"You've been treated kindly by Ramón de Oto in recent years, though. You've told me so often enough. So why are you still angry at the man?"

"There's plenty to be angry about, beginning with the way he treated his wife. And his kindness to me was only because of you."

"I may have influenced things a bit," Brother Arros admitted, a gleam of pride in his eyes.

"Your letters to the queen—I would not have thought you capable of that."

"Why on earth not?"

"Because you lied."

Brother Arros looked affronted. "I did not lie."

"You told Queen Isabella I was a good Christian woman, a healer who was devoted to God and my queen. Those are lies."

"Well, you *are* a good woman and a great healer. That's the truth I set forth in my letters, perhaps with a few small embellishments. And Ramón was so eager for the Queen's favor in those days. It was the only way I could send you to Castle Oto in good conscience. I knew he would never allow harm to come to you if you were under the Queen's protection." He frowned. "Even with my intervention, if he was truly such a cruel man, he never would have heeded my words."

"He does love his sons, I'll admit that, and I saw him toss a scrap or two of generosity to his wife, but not enough to make up for the bruises he beat into her."

"Still, there is always time for forgiveness, as long as one walks the earth."

Elena fixed him with a stony look. "The barons of Oto have brought nothing but grief to the mountain folk. Ramón de Oto was born cruel and bred cruel, and I'll be glad when he's dead."

"Elena, you should know..."

"No!" she broke in harshly. "I'll never forgive the Oto family for what they allowed that devil priest to do to my mother."

"That was so long ago," he sighed.

"It might as well have been yesterday. Maria saved countless lives and the mountain folk loved her for it. The priest was jealous. He was an outsider, a city man, obsessed with his one great God. He wanted what she had—the respect of the people. So he concocted a lie about her, branded her a witch. The baron and his son could have put a stop to it all. But instead they sat astride their horses and watched her body go up in flames. I saw the smile on Ramón's face. He took pleasure in the sight."

Brother Arros looked anguished. "Maria was already dead. Don't you see? God had spared your mother the agony of being burned alive."

Elena shook her head, feeling weighted down by sorrow, as if her heart had been replaced by a lump of granite.

"God had nothing to do with her death," she said softly. "Even a small child can change the course of fate, Brother Arros. Maria went out of this world peacefully, I made sure of that. And I've never had a day's regret in my life."

Brother Arros studied her expression for a long time. Then he buried his face in his hands and wept.

17

Spring, 1505
San Juan de la Peña, Aragón
Elena

THEIR LAST NIGHT TOGETHER, Brother Arros invited Elena to join him in the parlor, a room normally reserved for high-born visitors. She had only entered it once before.

He was already seated at the oak table, a trencher of walnuts and a pitcher of ale before him, his face illuminated by the guttering light of two stubby candles. Behind him a small fire burned in the hearth. The room smelled of woodsmoke and tallow.

Elena settled across from him and poured herself a cup of ale. He watched her in silence with a look that unsettled her. Each time he seemed on the verge of blurting something out, he swallowed his words again. Finally she could stand it no more.

"What is it, Brother Arros? Say what you will. I'll not think worse of you." She tossed a handful of walnuts in her mouth and chewed vigorously, eyeing him across the table.

"The saints above. What am I to do?" A leather pouch was slung across his shoulder. With his good hand he set it on the table between them. "I don't know if I should say it, but God only knows what the future holds. And I would never forgive myself for not telling, should we never meet again."

"Then say it, by the sun and stars!"

"Very well." He leaned forward. "Mira is family to you, is she not?"

"Of course! As you are."

"Well, Pelegrín is too. And Alejandro."

"I don't see it that way."

"It doesn't matter how you see it." He passed a hand over his face, closed his eyes for a moment.

"What do you mean?"

He sighed, his eyelids fluttering open. "Mira and Pelegrín and Alejandro are your niece and nephews. You are the baby girl who was cast out to die by the Baron of Oto and taken to the village of Arazas. The girl Maria found in a houseful of corpses."

"Maria found me, yes. But I am no baron's child. What has got into you, Brother Arros?"

Elena watched him cautiously, her annoyance giving way to genuine worry. Perhaps this odd illness had truly rattled his mind after all.

"No, no, it's true." He used his left hand to pull his right arm up and prop it on the table in front of him. "I have known since you were a girl. Maria told me. When she found you in Arazas, she discovered a gold chain around your neck strung with a medallion that bore the mark of the Otos."

"I loved Maria," Elena declared. "There was no better mother in the world. But she spun yarns with the skill of a muleteer. You know that as well as I."

He unlatched the clasp of the pouch, drew out a glittering object, and placed it on the table between them.

"A circle within a circle, overlaid with a cross," Elena said slowly, picking up the medallion. Her heart thumped insistently against her ribs.

He fished a folded rectangle of blue wool from the pouch and handed it to her. "The blanket your mother the baroness wrapped you in when she gave you up to the guard."

Elena shook out the fabric and spread it on the table. Numbly she touched a finger to the fine stitches of red silk that adorned one corner. They formed the same design as the medallion. She picked it up again and weighed it in her palm.

"Maria gave me these things to keep them safe," Brother Arros went on, studying her across the table. "She made me promise to tell you one day, when you were ready." He shook his head sadly. "It seems to me you will never be ready. But I cannot put it off any longer. You are Ramón de Oto's sister, Elena. You were that baby girl cast out in the woods to die, the one saved by a kind-hearted guard. That is the truth, and may God help you accept it."

Elena stared at him, horrified, closing her fingers around the medallion. A tremor started somewhere deep inside her. She felt as if her spine had turned to liquid. Her mind raced, flitting back through memories of Castle Oto, of Ramón and Marguerite, of Mira and her brothers.

She took a long, ragged breath.

A memory pushed its way to the forefront of her mind—an image that had haunted her for twenty years. It was the moment she first caught sight of the Baroness of Oto tottering vacantly through the great hall of the castle, surrounded by servants and helpmates. Elena had developed an abiding scorn for the woman that day. Addicted to poppy milk, adorned with pearls and rubies, clad in silks and furs, the baroness glided around the castle like a ghost.

"Was I their only girl child?" she whispered into the silence.

"The only girl who lived."

She dropped her head in shame, thinking of the contempt she had harbored for the woman who had given birth to her, whose baby daughters were torn from her breast no sooner than they were born.

Brother Arros gently took hold of Elena's clenched fist, unfurled her fingers, and tugged the medallion from her grasp. She stared dully at her palm. An imprint of the Oto design was pressed into her flesh.

She raised her eyes to his.

All at once her hand began to throb.

18

Spring, 1505
Castle Oto, Aragón
Elena

ELENA STRAINED TO HEAR the usual sounds of castle life. The creak of the gates opening, the clang of the blacksmith in his forge, the high voices of the laundry women singing as they worked. Nothing assailed her ears but the whisper of a cool wind flowing down from the north, sliding over the white peaks into the valleys below.

Rounding the corner to the tall wooden gates, she pulled on the mule's reins and sat staring. No guards stood on the walls, no shouts of greeting floated out from the high parapets. All was silent.

She called out a greeting. After a few moments a familiar-looking guard peered out the door hole cut into one of the gates.

"You!" he said, surprised. "Back again, are you? After all this time?"

"Are you going to let me in, or aren't you?"

He unbarred the door and stood aside.

Riding up the narrow alley to the keep, she felt unsettled. The stench was unbearable. Why was the alley clothed with so much filth? There were half as many faces as usual peering out from their doorways and windows. Some of the cottages were shuttered and dark.

In the courtyard of the castle keep, Elena dismounted, staring around with a growing sense of apprehension. She heard a voice. Tilting her head back, she saw a small head emerge from a window.

"Who are you?" It was the high, clear voice of a child. "What do you want?"

"Don't you know me, Alejandro?"

"Elena!" The suspicion in the boy's voice was replaced by joy. His head disappeared.

Within a few moments the great oak doors creaked open. A young woman Elena recognized as Marguerite's maid stood hand in hand with Alejandro.

"What happened here?" Elena asked.

The woman shook her head, dropping her eyes. Alejandro stepped forward.

"Mother and father are dead," he said. "Beltrán ran away. Pelegrín is gone." His eyes were bright with tears. He hesitated, his lips trembling. "But he is coming back to me. He wrote a letter. My brother sails across the sea, back from war. In summer, he comes. Autumn, at the latest. That is what he promised."

Elena sank to her knees and gathered Alejandro in her arms.

The maidservant who had opened the doors led Elena to the catacombs later that evening. In a shadowy cavern, two torches burned on either end of a stone tomb.

"She's in there," the woman said, pointing through the gloom. "Lady Marguerite. Beltrán's men waited for him to return until autumn turned to winter. One morning they put on their armor and rode away. Most of the cooks disappeared too, because no one is left to hunt."

"And now you act as nursemaid to Alejandro?"

"There's no one else. Four knights came as soon as the roads were clear in early spring, saying that Ramón de Oto was dead. They brought a letter from Pelegrín ordering them to watch over this place until his return. But many of the servants and guards had already left. Besides, those knights know nothing of hunting and fishing. They're city folk, from Barcelona."

"How do you eat?"

"Some of us have family in these mountains. They see to it that we'll not starve."

"You've taken it upon yourself to care for the boy. Why?"

"Lady Marguerite was kind to me."

"The girl who came to paint Lady Marguerite's portrait—when she disappeared, what was the kitchen gossip?"

"That Lady Marguerite helped her escape her fate, and died because of it."

"What do you think?" Elena asked.

The woman stared back at her unblinking. "I think the artist looked like Lady Marguerite."

A necklace dangled from the servant's throat, a rough cream-colored shell strung on a leather cord.

"I recognize that." Elena flicked her eyes to the shell.

The woman tucked the shell back into her bodice. "It was a gift."

Elena nodded. "I know the giver."

In Marguerite's chamber, Elena stood on the red wool Moorish carpet, lost in memories. She remembered the hateful rattle of the balcony shutters the night Mira and Pelegrín were born, and her desperation to escape these walls instead of helping

Marguerite de Oto through the agonizing labor. She recalled the horrible day Marguerite gave birth to Alejandro, alone, locked inside this chamber, determined to end her own life and that of her baby should the child be a girl. The sight of Ramón smashing his way through the door with a great axe, bellowing with fury.

Elena knew there was a false bottom in one of the storage chests. Inside it she found a pot of a foul-smelling concoction which she herself had made many years ago. Alongside it was a linen bag that held a set of keys. She smiled, rocking back on her heels. Lady Marguerite and her keys.

She went to the Tower of Blood and used one of the keys to enter Ramón's chambers. Crossing to a window, she unlatched the shutter and flung it open to the spring air. A lone hawk circled outside. Snow still dusted the notched ridges that rose up across the valley. At the sight of the world beyond the castle walls, the uneasiness in her core diminished a bit.

Alejandro needed a protector, and it would have to be her. Not only because Elena was someone he knew and loved, but because he was her flesh and blood. She had no choice but to stay until Pelegrín returned. Xabi would worry, but there was nothing to be done about it. As soon as the new baron reclaimed his castle and set it to rights, she would leave this place and never come back.

She carefully latched the shutter again and cast a look around the room. On Ramón's desk, sealed letters and parchment rolls sat stacked in an unruly pile.

For the first time in her life, Elena wished she could read.

19

Spring, 1505
Toulouse, France
Mira

THEY STOOD IN THE sun-drenched courtyard watching the mule carts roll in through the broad doorway from the lane. Mira clenched her hands to stop them trembling. Arnaud slipped his arm around her, loosening the tension in her shoulders. This was the moment of reckoning, and Mira held herself responsible for whatever unfolded here this afternoon. Would Lord de Vernier be pleased with what lay inside those carts? Would the fabric bear up to his scrutiny? Had Sister Agathe ensured that the quality of the weaving and dyeing was uniformly high?

Arnaud broke away from her to greet the drivers of the carts. The three men were natives of Ronzal who now lived in the village just outside Belarac's gates.

"We're lucky to be here, with our load, all in one piece!" declared one of the men.

"Why lucky?" Arnaud asked.

"Suffered a broken wheel halfway down the road from Belarac to here," he said.

"It split clean in half, cleaved itself somehow," one of his companions cut in.

Arnaud examined the cart's wheels. "All looks as it should. You brought a replacement?"

The first man nodded. "Always carry one. Adds weight, but it's worth the hassle. Turned out the wheel was the least of our worries. The real problem was bandits. Three men—they sprung upon us from the forest."

"It was their bad luck they picked us to ambush!" cried one of his companions.

"Evenly matched, we were," said the third man.

While the men talked, Mira dashed to the nearest cart and pushed through its canvas curtains into the interior. Bolts of cloth wrapped in canvas were piled in neat stacks on the cart floor, secured with flax ropes. She tugged a wrapper off the nearest bolt, desperate to see the quality of the fabric. Underneath, the blue wool glowed bright as a jewel against the dull gray of the canvas. She stroked it with a fingertip.

"Well?" Arnaud asked, poking his head through the opening of the curtains.

"This small corner of fabric is perfect. I pray the rest of it is too."

Her employer's voice floated in from the courtyard. Arnaud and Mira hurried back and stood alongside the cart drivers, watching an entourage of servants follow the merchant into their midst. Two footmen carried a table, which was deposited at Lord de Vernier's side.

One by one, he had servants pull bolts of cloth at random from the carts and spread the fabric on the table for his inspection. He was silent throughout the proceedings.

Mira bit her lip, watching Lord de Vernier's face. His expression betrayed nothing. He occasionally murmured to his assistant, who then dipped his quill in a pot of ink and scratched notes in a parchment book that lay on the table.

Beyond the merchant Mira could see through the doorway that led to the lane. A figure stood there motionless, watching the proceedings from afar, his face shrouded by the hood of his long black cloak. It was only when the sound of an approaching mule cart rattled down the lane that the figure moved out of sight to make way.

"Excellent!"

Lord de Vernier's voice pulled Mira back to the scene at hand.

"This wool is as promised. The colors, the quality, the amount. All is as we agreed."

He turned to Arnaud and Mira. "You are indeed as good as your word, and I've got the proof twice over, it seems."

"My lord?" Mira asked.

"Prior Johan Arros of San Juan de la Peña got my letter, and sent me one of his own. He vouched for the both of you, even promised wool from his own flocks as collateral in case there was a mishap with this shipment. But clearly there is no need for such an arrangement."

"We are pleased that you approve," Arnaud said.

"I hope you are confident now that the abbey will never fail you," Mira said.

The merchant let out a short laugh. "I am confident that this wool is as promised. And I hope the abbey will never fail me, but the future is always a mystery, is it not?" He glanced at the cart drivers, who were supervising the stablehands as they unhitched the mules.

"Tell the men to go to the kitchens when they are finished with their duties. I am sure they are famished. As for the two of you—please be so good as to accompany me to my sitting room. My wife has requested you join us for wine and cake. A celebration of sorts, she says, for the success of our partnership and the happiness of our daughters with their new governess. And for another venture that I believe you will find to your liking."

In Lord de Vernier's private study waited Lady de Vernier and the notary who had witnessed their signatures on the agreement they had forged with Lord de Vernier last summer. His record book lay open on the polished oak table. Next to it, in an elaborately gilded wooden frame, sat the portrait Mira had painted of Lady de Vernier.

Lord de Vernier picked it up and held it at arm's length, his eyes passing from the image on the wooden panel to his wife standing before him.

"This is as fine a portrait as I've seen in this city," he said, his voice tinged with admiration. "I have been to Flanders. I saw no portrait there that strikes me as better-wrought than your work."

Mira ducked her head, closing her eyes a moment.

"Thank you," she finally managed to say.

The nobleman's serious, sharp-angled face softened a bit. "My notary awaits your mark on this page. Read the agreement, of course, but know that we simply desire you to complete two more paintings: one of me, and one of us with our children."

Mira glanced at Arnaud. She could tell he knew her thoughts.

He shook his head, smiling a little. "We've already delayed this long. What's another month or two? Bayonne will still be there. Go ahead, Mira."

She advanced toward the book, bending to read the lines. The notary dipped a quill in an ink pot and held it out to her. Before she could write her name, Lady de Vernier interrupted.

"I know you share the name of your husband. But as a woman of the house of Oto, you should make the mark of your own family."

Mira straightened. A glistening drop of ink formed at the point of the quill. "I beg your pardon?"

"I advise you to do so with your future in mind," Lady de Vernier continued. "When you are finished with our commissions, you will be inundated with offers from other merchants."

Before Mira could speak, she raised a hand. "Yes, you have obligations to keep in Bayonne. But this is about your future, and it applies to any city where you may seek commissions. As a woman, you will be paid a scant amount compared to a male artist. If you are known to be of noble birth, you will command a much higher price for your work."

"My wife speaks the truth," Lord de Vernier said. "You would be wise to listen."

Mira looked at Arnaud. Worry twisted in her gut.

"I don't see the harm in it," he said softly.

After all, they were leagues and leagues from Aragón, in a land ruled by a French king. No one knew them here.

The notary caught the blob of ink just as it began to fall, slipping his ink pot under Mira's outstretched hand. She dipped the quill again, tapped it against the edge of the pot, and began to write.

Miramonde de Oto, she thought, staring at the freshly inked words. Oto. The word made her long for her mother with an ache that rarely visited her. She remembered the languorous weeks spent at the castle of Oto, building up the layers of a portrait while her mother stood just a few steps away.

After a lifetime of separation, they finally had that precious summer together. Mira had imagined it was just the beginning of a reunion that would take years to unfold. But it ended as abruptly as it began. Her mother died protecting Mira, fighting for her daughter's life to the last.

Where is my mother's portrait? Did the thieves abandon it? Burn it? Throw it in a river? Or is it even now on the back of a mule, destined for some city I shall never see?

Her eyes flew from the book to Arnaud's beaming face and back again. She watched the notary apply his florid signature to the bottom of the page.

A selfish, shameful part of her wished their future lay not in Bayonne but here, in the glittering city of Toulouse. Mira kept her eyes trained on the book before her, watched the ink slowly dry on the page.

But perhaps Lord and Lady de Vernier would write her a letter of recommendation when the time came to leave for Bayonne. She raised her head, brightening at the thought. Yes. She would create two masterful portraits for them, and their good word would follow her west.

Whatever happened, Mira could at least make sure of that.

20

February, 2016
Zaragoza, Spain
Zari

THE TRAIN SWAYED SLIGHTLY as it hurtled east along the tracks. The train car was half-full and, from what Zari could tell, most of the passengers were Spanish. She had a double seat to herself. Unzipping her long down jacket, she spread it over herself like a blanket, taking in the view.

The rain-soaked green hills surrounding San Sebastián had given way to arid, rocky plains. Watching the golden-brown landscape flash by, Zari slipped on her sunglasses for the first time in days. The sun seemed brighter in Spain than it did in France. Its intensity reminded her of the harsh California sun.

To the north soared the Pyrenees, their snow-crusted peaks capped by a fleece of gray clouds. Zari would never look at these mountains again without thinking of Wil. She leaned her head against the window, lost in memories of their summertime trek along the Camino, of their return to Belarac at Christmas. A shiver of anticipation snaked up her spine. Wil was on his way from Barcelona to Zaragoza now. They would meet at a rented apartment there in just a few hours.

Zari had not been able to get permission for Wil to join her in the archives of the sheep ranchers' collective, but at least they would have evenings together, and three precious nights in the same bed. She felt a twinge of desire at the thought. The constant ache in her heart during their separations had become part of her now, a dull weight that pulled at her like some amplification of gravity.

Zari had no expectations for Zaragoza itself, so fixated was she on the treasures within the collective's archives. But when she and Wil walked to the archives the next morning along the wide River Ebro, Zari was captivated by the graceful stone bridges that arched over the water and the immense brick and stone structures that dominated the heart of the city. At the sight of the Basílica del Pilar with its copper-capped towers and tiled domes, she stopped. Her mind churned, imagining the scene five hundred years ago—the Ebro teeming with barges, gondolas, rafts...whatever got cargo to the sea in those days.

"Carlo Sacazar was a Renaissance-era entrepreneur," she said dreamily.

Wil laughed.

"I'm serious." She glanced up at him. "How many merchants in his shoes would set up a satellite empire to the north? That was gutsy."

"There must have been a good reason. Probably involving money. Or politics."

"Or both."

"Put that on your list of research questions for the day."

"Oh, I will," she assured him.

Wil kissed her just outside the doors of the collective. She watched him walk away in the bright winter sun, savoring the sight of his long, easy strides, his lanky form, his semi-tamped-down hair. In his puffy blue jacket, he looked bulkier than he truly was. She imagined him without his jacket, and then without his shirt, and...

Straightening her shoulders and taking a deep breath, she reached for the door buzzer. It was time to rustle up her best Spanish accent and clear her mind of lustful thoughts. After all, she had been allocated two full days of research within these walls, and she could not waste a minute. Only a few research slots were granted each month to foreign academics.

Inside, her eyes adjusted to the dim light of an entry hall that had white walls and red tile floors. Her wrangler for the day was a soft-spoken young man who identified himself as a doctoral candidate at the University of Barcelona. He was doing his dissertation on the sheep economy in Aragón during the reign of King Ferdinand and Queen Isabella, and he conducted research daily in these archives.

Zari felt a rush of jealousy. She only had two days—and he had an entire winter.

He handed her a lanyard with the logo of the organization emblazoned on a plastic card, underneath which the word "visitor" was printed in large block letters. She slipped it over her head.

Following him down a corridor hung with medieval-looking iron light fixtures, she noticed all the doors were shut.

"It's quiet here this morning," she ventured.

"I'm always the first one here," he said over his shoulder. "Me and the foreign researchers. Everyone else will arrive in an hour or so."

He led her to a room outfitted with several long metal tables. A laptop lay open on one of them.

"You can see the digital images for all the documents in our archives on this laptop," he said, quickly showing her how to navigate the search engine. "The images are high-quality so you should have no problem seeing details." He clicked to another tab on the browser. "If there are documents you want the librarian to pull for you, fill out this form."

Next to the laptop was a sheet of paper printed with a list of names and numbers.

"Every citation for the name Sacazar is on this," he said, picking it up. "So you can go directly to the pages you need."

He pointed at another table piled with shallow cardboard boxes. On top of the pile was a ziplocked bag containing a pair of white cotton gloves. "I'll be over there."

"Thank you," Zari said, jealous again. He got to handle actual documents, while she had to scroll through a digital library.

He nodded. "Good luck."

Over the course of the day, Zari learned that Carlo Sacazar was a fairly regular attendee at the collective's annual spring meetings for several decades. His name was on the roster starting in the late 1470s, along with the names of two other Sacazar men. One of those names only appeared in the first few meetings Carlo attended, and the other disappeared in the 1490s. Carlo himself only sporadically attended meetings after 1495, and his name vanished from the register altogether by 1505.

Zari could not make any sense of the meeting minutes but she took photos of them anyway.

After a brief, mandatory lunch break, during which Zari stood at the bar of a nearby café and wolfed down a cured ham sandwich followed by a shot of strong, thick espresso spiked with two packets of sugar, she returned to the archives and moved on to the trademark books.

She let out an audible gasp when she navigated to the Sacazars' page. Before her was a pen-and-ink drawing of a sheep, its torso emblazoned with an 'S'.

The young scholar at the table next to her looked up. "What is it?" he asked, startled.

"I found something interesting," she said apologetically.

He nodded and turned back to his work. Zari watched him carefully turn the page of an ancient-looking manuscript with his gloved fingers. Before envy could strike again, she began scrolling through the trademark book. Unfortunately for her, the Sacazar trademark looked nothing like the design on the merchant's ring in Laurence's painting. Since the day she visited the Sacazar home in Nay, she had cultivated hope that the ring and the trademark would bear the same design.

She sighed, clicking through meeting minutes again, more slowly this time. On several of the pages, one of the signatures stood out: it was much larger than the rest and bore an excess of flourishes. Zari cleared her throat.

"Excuse me, I wonder if you can tell me why this name is larger than the rest?"

The researcher came to her side and studied her computer's screen. "Ah. It is the royal agent's signature."

"Who was that?"

"The agent of King Ferdinand and Queen Isabella."

"Was the royal family involved in the council?"

"Very. Especially after the merino wool trade made a lot of people rich. They wanted to keep merino sheep out of the hands of foreigners so other countries could not develop merino industries of their own." He pulled up a chair and sat next to Zari. "Scroll to the meeting minutes from 1500."

She clicked to the relevant document.

"See?" he pointed. "This is a royal decree ordering the council members never to sell a merino sheep to a foreigner." He pointed at the row of signatures. "The royal agent's name appears at the bottom, after all the members had signed."

Zari nodded, scanning the list of names. There was Carlo

Sacazar, about halfway down the list. And below it...

She stiffened in her chair and clicked the zoom button several times.

Below Carlo Sacazar's name appeared the signature of Baroness Marguerite de Oto.

She drew in a sharp breath.

The young scholar gave her a bemused look.

"That name." Zari tapped her fingertip on the screen, shaking her head helplessly. "The barons of Oto are very important for my research, too. More important than Carlo Sacazar." She stumbled over the words, her mind racing through possibilities.

"I showed you how to make a request to the librarian," the young man said without enthusiasm, returning to his table. "Fill out the forms and you can see the materials tomorrow."

"Will they allow me to handle the actual documents?"

"With supervision, perhaps."

Zari clicked to the tab containing the materials request form, typed in the requisite information with trembling hands, and e-mailed it to the librarian.

Then she clicked back to the tab containing the trademark book and scrolled slowly through the entire document. This time, her hope was justified: the barons of Oto had their own page, too. It showed their coat of arms: two ships, two sheep, two castles. And the pen-and-ink drawing of a sheep displaying their mark showed the same design as the gold medallion that hung from the belt of the noblewoman in the Fontbroke College portrait.

Zari reached out a finger to trace the image, feeling light-headed.

So much of her research led nowhere—it was like a massive jigsaw puzzle whose pieces did not interlock, no matter how many times she repositioned them. But this moment was different. A wave of excitement washed over her.

Finally, the pieces of her puzzle were beginning to click together.

21

THAT EVENING AT A small restaurant near their apartment, tucking into a spread of *tapas* that included tiny medallions of beef, scallops with lemon-butter sauce, and mussels cooked in beer, Zari recounted the discoveries of the day to Wil.

"The pieces of my puzzle are starting to fit together. Tomorrow I should have more evidence about just how the barons of Oto and the Sacazar families were intertwined," she concluded. "And I may even get to touch some real documents. I'm bringing my magnifying visor—I can't wait to fire it up."

"But what will those connections do for Mira and the paintings?"

"I don't know yet, Mr. Devil's Advocate. Let me savor the moment." She sipped her wine. "This is divine. What is it?"

"It's from the Priorat region in Catalonia."

Zari swirled the red liquid in her glass, breathing in the aromas of earth, ripe plums, cinnamon, oak. "Someday, let's go wine tasting there. We'll drive around the hills, stumbling on unknown little gems, buy a few cases to keep in our basement..."

Wil smiled. "We need a basement first."

"Details, details."

His knee grazed hers under the table, and she suddenly yearned for the check.

Well after midnight, Zari was awakened by an ominous sound coming from the bathroom. A grunting, retching, heaving sound. She rolled out of bed and slowly made her way across the room.

"Wil?" She tapped at the bathroom door. "Are you sick?"

A bout of groaning was his only response.

"Can I help? Can I get you anything?"

Finally the answer came. "A new stomach?"

"Oh, my love," she said in sympathy. "I'm so sorry."

Within thirty minutes she was fighting him for space over the toilet.

The fantastic spread of tapas had contained something not so fantastic after all, it seemed. Something that their bodies were now violently rejecting at a rate of about three times per hour.

Her precious second day of research was spent curled on the white tile floor of their flat's bathroom, sweaty, delirious, and drained of every ounce of energy.

At one point she glanced at Wil, who lay staring glassily at the ceiling clad only in his underwear. "I guess this is the 'warts and all' part of our relationship," she croaked. "The glamour has officially worn off."

A ghost of a smile appeared on his face. "You can joke at a time like this?"

"Gallows humor," she explained. A wave of nausea knotted her stomach and she assumed the position over the toilet.

Wil crawled to the sink, wet a washcloth, and waited until she was done heaving. Then he tenderly wiped her face and eased her down on the cool tile, a bath towel folded under her head.

"That was gallant," she told him, closing her eyes.

Even with the lights off in the bathroom, the sun beating against the frosted window was much too bright. A diesel engine started up in the street outside their building and idled noisily.

"My opportunity is blown," she murmured. "Those documents. Today was my only chance."

Wil opened one eye. "What do you mean? You'll be fine by tomorrow. Extend your stay."

Zari groaned. "You don't understand. Researchers are slotted in ahead of time, and priority is given to Spanish scholars. I tried to play the food-poisoning card when I called the administrator this morning, and it didn't fly."

"Fly?"

"It didn't work. I had to get in the queue all over again. And nothing is available until after Bordeaux." She curled into a ball, her stomach spasming.

"If there's nothing you can do, move on to the next thing."

She peeled back her eyelids. "There is no next thing," she said darkly. "That's the problem."

Zari squeezed her eyes shut again. She took his hand between her own and lodged it at the base of her neck, bending her head so her chin was touching his knuckles. The warm pressure of his flesh against hers was reassuring.

"Zari," Wil said, "Remember how you felt when I found you in that storm at Belarac?"

"Yes. Angry."

He chuckled wryly. "Angry at me, yeah. But you got over that. You knew exactly what you were doing in those mountains. You had no fear. So what happened?"

She winced, overcome by the throbbing behind her forehead. Hot tears slid down her cheeks. Outside, the diesel engine sputtered to a stop.

"I don't know, Wil," she whispered into the silence. "Maybe the idea that Mira's story can be brought to life is just as impossible as Dotie Butterfield-Swinton claims. The more I dig, the more she fades away. There's this huge cast of supporting characters around her and I'm thrilled every time I unearth something about them. But is all of that just a waste of time and resources? I mean, I can prove now that Marguerite de Oto is the woman in the Fontbroke College portrait—but that does nothing to bolster my theory that Mira painted it. And I thought Carlo Sacazar might be the man in the portrait of the merchant family. I came here hoping that the design on his ring would match some family crest or sigil in the record books. I was wrong. Even if I was right, how does it help me prove Mira painted that portrait?"

"You said it last night: it's like putting together a puzzle. Get enough of the pieces linked together and the bigger picture will start to..." His voice trailed off.

"Emerge."

"Yes." He put his hand on her breastbone and spread his fingers wide, creating a warm container for her heart. "Have faith, Zari."

She covered his hand with both of hers, too tired to talk anymore, and drifted into sleep.

22

Spring, 1505
Toulouse, France
Mira

T HE PERFORMANCE WAS ABOUT to begin. Arnaud, Mira,
Deedit, and Rose had arrived too late to get a spot close
to the stage, but it was better this way, really. Standing at
the back of the crowd, it would be easy to make a quick escape if
Rose started fussing. All around them jostled city folk dressed
in their market day best.

The marionette show was a favorite of wealthy merchant families as well as the commoners who frequented the market each
week. Lord and Lady de Vernier's girls were sitting in a choice
spot near the stage on a small bench that a footman had carried
from their residence. Blanca turned, spied Mira, and squealed.
All three girls waved at her, beaming. Blanca babbled excitedly
until she was hushed by Heloise, who gave Mira a curt nod.

Rose clung wide-eyed to Arnaud's neck, her tiny fingers digging into his flesh.

Two boys nearby began to shove one another, arguing about who had the better vantage point. An older girl, probably the sister of one of them, got between the boys and scolded until they fell quiet, scowling. The circle of people swelled.

The sounds of a high-pitched accordion wafted from behind the stage, which was just a modified oxcart. A drumroll began, signaling that silence was required. The audience stared in rapt attention as a simpering voice spoke behind the curtain and a doll dressed as a fine lady came to life. Now a priest strode into view, and next a fat merchant, his arms and legs jerking on their strings. Each new character brought a round of applause from the onlookers. When the dashing prince appeared, a sigh of delight went up.

Mira fell under the spell of the story, her attention unbroken until she felt the tug of someone's gaze. She looked to her left and saw through the crowd a figure dressed in a black cloak, the hood pulled down low over his forehead. The person was clearly staring in their direction, not at the stage. Distracted by a squeal from Rose, she turned back to the show. When she looked again, the hooded figure had vanished.

Now the crisis of the play was unfolding. The prince, who had declared his intentions to the fine lady, received news that he was to go off and fight in a war. How the lady cried! The merchant had a whispered meeting with the priest, during which he handed over a large sack of jangling coins. The priest took them with reverence. Next the merchant came to comfort the sobbing lady. He kissed her hand, knelt, and held out a pink rose.

"Don't take it!" voices cried. "Wait for the prince!"

The lady considered the rose, then turned back to the prince. She covered her face with her kerchief, gathering herself, and declared she would confide in the priest before making her decision.

Boos and jeers rang out. A roar of laughter swelled as the priest beckoned to the lady and the merchant danced a hasty little jig behind them both.

Mira laughed until tears streamed down her cheeks. She glanced around, catching sight of Deedit's face. Deedit, wide-eyed with alarm, watched something just past Mira's shoulder. Mira turned her head, searching for the source of Deedit's anxiety. In the next instant, she was pushed savagely to the ground. Deedit rushed in front of her, collided with a cloaked figure, and fell.

Mira screamed.

The man backed away, his pale face half-hidden by the hood of his cloak. Then he melted into the crowd, which had pressed forward around them. People were whispering and pointing at Deedit, some women covering the faces of their children with their aprons.

Mira gasped when she saw the dark stain spreading across the bodice of Deedit's dress. She dropped to her knees and pressed her palm against the wound, trying to staunch the flow of blood. Arnaud stood over them, Rose wailing in his arms.

"How did he know?" Mira asked Deedit, leaning close.

"It wasn't because I'm a Cagot. He wasn't after me at all." Deedit reached for Mira's hand, her eyes full of anguish. "I tried to push you aside. He was—he was coming for you."

Arnaud thrust the baby at Mira and swept Deedit into his arms. As they hustled through the crowd, Mira could hear Blanca's voice calling her name. They hurried along the streets, finally turning down the lane toward their lodgings. A curious group of onlookers tagged along behind them at a distance.

When they arrived, the landlord was waiting outside.

"I'll not let that one in," he declared, pointing at Deedit. "She's a Cagot, and so's her whelp." He jerked his head at Rose. "I've only just discovered it. Deceitful scoundrels, the lot of you!"

"She is gravely injured!" Mira protested. "Let us in. We pay you well, and faithfully. Allow us upstairs."

"No." The landlord spread his legs wide, fixing them with a glare.

"Do you want Lord de Vernier's men on your doorstep?" Arnaud asked. He stepped up close to the landlord, Deedit clasped in his arms. "When he hears of this, he won't hesitate to dispatch them. I doubt you'd welcome being the target of such a man's anger."

The landlord wavered at this. "Blood everywhere," he said in distaste, staring down at the red stain on Deedit's bodice. "You'll ruin my bed and my floors."

"We can pay," Arnaud growled. He took another step forward. "The lord will hear of this within the hour if you don't let us in."

"Fine," the man relented, standing aside. "You'll pay all right. Mark my words, you'll pay."

Arnaud muscled past him through the door and Mira followed. Upstairs, they bound Deedit's wound with clean linen and made her comfortable in the bed. But the color was draining from her face and she did not respond to their entreaties. Her breath came shallower and shallower, her chest ceased to rise and fall. The pale afternoon light faded to darkness as the life bled out of her.

Mira rocked a sleeping Rose back and forth in her arms. She was not even aware she was weeping until she felt an odd tickling sensation on her cheek, wiped a hand across her face and felt dampness on it. Arnaud paced back and forth, grim and silent, stopping frequently at the shuttered window to listen.

"Why?" Mira said in a strangled whisper. "Why would someone do this?"

Arnaud said nothing.

"Who was that man?" she asked.

"I didn't get a clear look at him."

"Before this happened, I saw a person shrouded in black from head to toe in the crowd. I could swear he was staring at us. I could not see his face."

Arnaud stopped his pacing and looked at her.

"I saw a person shrouded as you say, the day the shipment came from Belarac," he said. "Staring in through the doors of the merchant's home."

"Yes," Mira said. "I saw him too."

Fear roiled in her chest. She kissed the top of Rose's head and breathed in her sweet scent. Panic would serve no purpose at this moment, she told herself.

"Deedit said he meant to kill me, Arnaud. Why?"

"Who knows what she saw? There's no telling what he truly meant to do."

He was gruff, but Mira could tell from his voice that Arnaud was worried.

"How did our landlord know Deedit was a Cagot?"

Arnaud shook his head. "She said as much to you just now, in the square. Others could have heard, could have run ahead of us and told him."

Mira tightened her arms around Rose, her eyes on Deedit's lifeless form sprawled across the bed.

"Someone has been watching us, Arnaud."

He did not disagree.

23

Spring, 1505
Toulouse, France
Mira

MIRA SLEPT LATER THAN usual the next morning. She found Arnaud in the sitting room, carving a block of oak with a sharp-nosed tool. Rose sat fussing on the bed, mystified by the absence of her mother.

Arnaud wiped the blade of his tool on his apron. "I took Deedit to the Cagot cemetery outside the city walls in the night."

"Did you see her buried?"

His expression tightened. "I could have been jailed for that. I found a Cagot man nearby. He promised to do it. I paid him well."

"And you trusted him?" Her voice grew shrill. "How could you..."

"Stop!" Rarely did Mira see Arnaud lose his temper, but he was very close to doing so at this moment. "We can't risk a tangle with the bailiff. I've been working illegally for months. They'll lock me up or worse if word gets out. We've already drawn too much attention to ourselves as it is." Before she could protest again, he shook his head wearily. "The other tenants complained to the landlord about Rose. They want us out, and he's willing to go along with it. Only the threat of the lord's wrath convinced him to let us upstairs. If that threat turns out to be empty, he'll turn us out."

"What harm can a baby do them?"

"She's a Cagot. They must live apart from other folk."

"Those rules are wrong!"

"You'll find little sympathy for that view. It could get us into trouble."

"I do not care!"

Rose began to scream. Mira scooped her up and jiggled her.

"She's hungry," said Arnaud. He resumed carving the wood. "Wouldn't take what I offered her."

"Boiled millet and goat's cheese is all we have. She will learn to like it."

"We should find her a wet-nurse."

Mira transferred Rose to the other hip. "Who would nurse a Cagot baby?"

"We'll find a Cagot family. They'll be glad to take our money. Let her go to one of them, and improve their fortunes at the same time."

"What?" Mira was incredulous. "She can't live with strangers. Deedit brought her here for a better life. At my urging. I want to keep Rose with us."

Arnaud put down his work again. "Is that truly what you want?"

"I just said so."

"It'll change the course of our lives forever. Raising a child is no small thing."

"You forget I helped raise many children at the abbey."

Rose let out a piercing shriek. Mira realized she had stopped bouncing. She began jiggling the girl again.

He watched them thoughtfully. "I fear you won't like the consequences."

"You want to give her up because she is a Cagot," Mira accused him. "Are you like all the rest of them?"

There was reproach in his brown eyes. "You know the answer to that."

She dropped her gaze. "Forgive me."

"I only want you to understand the hardships you're taking on."

"I swear to you I do," Mira said. "Please let us keep her."

He regarded them for another moment, then stood and made for the door.

"Where are you going?" she asked.

"To find another place for the three of us to live."

"Wait. We can go to Lord de Vernier, as you said. There's no one in Toulouse more powerful than he."

"And if he despises Cagots as much as every other citizen?"

She shook her head. "No. He is bound to us now. We have a contract. I know he will want to help us, and his wife will too."

Arnaud's expression darkened, but he stayed silent.

"You shall see. I'll go at once, and make things right." She handed Rose to him.

Her fingers trembled and her heart thudded as she threw on a cloak and slipped out the door of the lodging house. She dreaded another confrontation with the landlord or other tenants, but luck was with her. No one was about.

Quickly she strode through the streets, praying that her employers would show more mercy than the common citizens of Toulouse, would use the power of their position to help them keep their lodgings and protect baby Rose. The lord had finally warmed to them, and his wife was Mira's true ally.

The thought of turning Rose out to the crumbling alleyways of the Cagot slums was unbearable.

24

Spring, 1505
Toulouse, France
Mira

AT THE DOORWAY, HELOISE blocked Mira's path into the kitchens.

"If you think the leading lady of Toulouse will allow a woman who lives with Cagots to trespass on her generosity, let alone teach her daughters their lessons, you are the biggest fool in this city."

The hostile words hung in the air between them. There was a look of triumph in Heloise's eyes that made Mira want to slap her.

"That is for Lady de Vernier to decide," Mira said coolly.

Before Heloise could respond, a cook dropped a copper pot on the floor, spilling hot milk everywhere. In the resulting chaos, Mira slipped out of the kitchens and up the curving staircase to the nursery. In the corridor, Lady de Vernier emerged from a doorway and intercepted her.

"Follow me," she said in a low voice.

She led Mira into a small room furnished with Moorish tables and Venetian oil lamps made of jewel-toned glass.

Lady de Vernier shut the door and went to stand by the window, gesturing at Mira to draw close. The faint sound of voices floated up from the street below. Through the window, Mira saw dark clouds racing toward the city from the mountains in the south.

"There is nothing I can do for you unless you give up the child," Lady de Vernier said. "My husband will turn you out."

"So Madame Heloise has sounded the alarm." Mira folded her arms across her chest. She made no attempt to hide the bitterness in her voice.

"A Cagot will only bring heartache and troubles upon you."

"Perhaps if we simply find work and lodging across the city in a different quarter..."

"It will follow you, this scandal." Lady de Vernier looked out the window and sighed. "Gossip flows like wine through these streets."

"We will go someplace where Cagots are unknown, then," Mira said resolutely. "No one will know who or what Rose is."

Lady de Vernier studied her a moment. "I sympathize with your plight. You have a mother's instinct, and I commend you for it."

Mira was taken aback by the compliment. "I—thank you."

"You and your husband have obligations in the west. You may want to reconsider your plans, for I happen to know the Cagots are fewer in the east. If you go far enough in that direction, you'll find people who have never heard of a Cagot. Do you know of Perpignan?"

Mira shook her head.

"It is a great city by the sea, with a history far more illustrious than Toulouse can boast." Lady de Vernier toyed with the ruby that dangled at her throat. "I have a cousin there who longs for portraits of her family painted in the Flemish style. Apparently her great rival has a Flemish painter in her employ and talks of nothing else. I will write to my cousin and tell her you can do the work in the style she desires. You will still be employed as an artist, though unfortunately not by me. With my cousin's good word in hand, you should find steady employment amongst the merchant classes there."

Tears stung Mira's eyes. "I shall not forget this kindness, my lady. One day I will return and fulfill the contract we made."

"I would be pleased if that should ever come to pass. As for this agreement, it will stay a private matter between us. No one else here, not even my husband, will know I've made the arrangements for you. From one woman of Aragón to another, I am glad to do this. My daughters will sorely miss you. As shall I."

She smiled. In her eyes there was a sadness Mira recognized: a longing for home.

25

Spring, 1505
Nay, Béarn
Carlo

C ARLO SACAZAR HAD SENT his most trusted servant on
an errand. Upon his return, the two of them retreated
to the study and barred the door. When Carlo was satisfied with the man's answers, he passed him a handful of coins
and sent him on his rounds again. Then Carlo sat staring into
the fire until suppertime, his mind snarled with questions and
worries. It would not be possible to carry out any meaningful
task while he was caught up in this mess.

Amadina had told Carlo she was called away to Pau because
a notary there desired to introduce her to a merchant who
traded in lace. She was attempting to build relationships with
merchants from the north, especially Paris, where lace was all
the rage.

Carlo often dropped in unannounced at the convent when
his sister went abroad. It was for security's sake, and she was

grateful for it. After all, he was the only person in Nay—in all of Béarn, for that matter—whom she trusted.

So when he made his appearance at the convent's door, it was a matter of routine. What was not routine was his timing—he chose an hour of prayer. He navigated the kitchen courtyard with long strides, batting aside the linens that hung from flax ropes affixed to the walls, stepping over chickens and skirting the giant wicker baskets that lay ready for the laundry once it had dried. In the stable, he stood for a moment letting his eyes adjust to the dim light. He went into the mules' stalls one by one and ran his hands along the beasts' flanks, searching for their brands. One was different than all the others. His eyes widened in recognition. Then he turned and slipped out the stable door.

Inside the main building, he took the back stairs to his sister's chambers on the second floor. The corridors were empty, since everyone was in the chapel. He softly opened the door to Amadina's private rooms.

Methodically Carlo searched the bed chamber. Then he turned his attention to the sitting room. In the bottom of a great chest, his fingers searched for a secret latch. When it sprang open, he found a rectangular canvas-wrapped parcel in the space below. He slipped it from the wrappings and leaned it against the chest. Rocking back on his heels, he shook his head, regarding the find in astonishment. He passed a hand over his brow and it came away damp with sweat. Slowly he got to his feet, looking around the room again grimly. What else had his sister hidden away?

A collection of silver boxes atop a low table caught his eye. Some had been in Amadina's possession since she was a girl. In fact, one was a gift from the Moorish family who had for generations pole-barged Sacazar wool down the River Ebro to Tortosa, on the sea. He remembered working the fastenings of the box as a child, delighting in the clever way it was secured. Amadina had struggled to open it even after he patiently taught her how. Now he opened each box in turn, saving for last the gift from the Moors. As if no time had passed, he slid open the silver bars in just the right order and the box clicked open.

The fury that overcame him upon seeing what lay in that box rarely visited Carlo. He was a man of even temperament. But when something of this magnitude presented itself to him, he was capable of rage. His cheeks grew hot, his hands trembled. With great care he placed the contents of the silver box in a pouch he carried round his neck.

The morning after her return, Amadina sat next to her brother in the convent's parlor, sipping wine and snacking on almonds. Her eyes showed her impatience with this meeting. She drummed her fingertips on the curved arm of her chair, registering no reaction when he waved the servants from the room.

"I only just returned, brother," she complained. "I have not even unpacked my things. What is it you wish to discuss with me?"

He set down his cup. "Tell me about your trip to Pau."

Her fingers ceased their motion. "It was nothing out of the ordinary," she said after a moment, her eyes on the hearth.

"But you were away much longer than a trip to Pau would warrant. It must have been a most extraordinary visit, with much to tell."

"The lace merchant was delayed," she said airily. "I had to wait nearly a fortnight to see him."

"Ah." He sipped from his cup again. "While you were gone, an unfortunate mishap arose in your stables. The servants hastened to inform me, of course."

She looked at him, astonished. "I've heard nothing of it."

He put down his cup with a thump. "Are your servants lying to me? That is grave indeed."

"I know not. I shall investigate the matter."

"I have an idea. Let us investigate it together this instant." He stood. "Come."

"What is the meaning of this?"

"You are skilled in deception, Amadina. But even you make mistakes. Your confidence has bloomed. It outpaces your discretion."

She made no move to stand.

"Do you wish to have your allowance cut off?" he said in a hard, low voice. "We are within a hair's breadth of that occurrence. Consider wisely your next course of action."

Finally she rose, her lips pressed into a thin line, and followed him out of the room.

In the stables he walked up and down the central aisle between the stalls, examining the mules.

"I know from my own records that this convent owns ten mules. And here before me I see eleven. This is strange, indeed. For their numbers have not dwindled but increased by one."

He made a great show of entering each stall and examining the brand burned into the flank of each mule. When he got halfway down the row, he stopped.

"This is odd," he remarked. "The brand is unlike the others."

He glanced at his sister. Her face was stricken.

"Look into my eyes and tell me why you possess a mule of Ronzal," he said.

"I am as ignorant of this development as you, brother," she began, in a voice dripping with false innocence.

He took a great breath and exhaled, staring into the courtyard. Two chickens pecked aimlessly at the cobblestones.

"You and I both know that is a lie. Tell me where you went on this recent journey of yours. I will not suffer any more falsehoods about Pau." He took a step closer to her.

"If you must know, I was settling a business matter in Toulouse. I thought it prudent not to burden you with the affair. Now are you satisfied?"

"I think not, Amadina. Let us make haste for your chambers to continue our talk."

She was taken aback. "My chambers? No, no. The parlor, that is the place for conversation."

"Not today. Your chambers." He flung an arm in the direction of the door. "After you."

In her sitting room, he pointed at the collection of silver boxes. "Open them," he ordered.

She crossed her arms over her chest.

"Your allowance is dwindling by the minute," he growled.

Reluctantly she began to unclasp the fastenings of box after box. They were all empty. When she came to the last one, she hesitated.

"You see. They are empty. Can we stop this ridiculous exercise now?"

"It is not complete until every last one is opened."

She fumbled with the silver locking mechanism of the tiny box. "I do not remember how this opens. It is quite complicated."

"On the contrary," he said, plucking the box out of her grasp.

Her face froze. He deftly slid a series of silver bars this way and that, and the box clicked open.

"But how did you...?"

He overturned the box and shook it. Her face registered shock.

"You are surprised to see this one empty," he said softly.

"Where is it?" she spat.

Carlo retrieved a tiny silken pouch from a pocket and tipped something glittering and gold into his palm. "Is this what you refer to?"

"That ring—it fell into my possession. I wanted to keep it safe," she said carefully.

He twirled it between his thumb and forefinger.

"Remember, your last chance for the truth. How did this come into your possession?"

She looked away.

"This is the signet ring of Béatrice of Belarac," he said. "As you well know. Do not act the innocent with me any longer, Amadina. It wears on my patience." He stepped back, restraining his anger, batting it down with long, deep breaths.

Her lips tightened. "Sometimes matters get complicated. It is so with the business of wool. There were others who saw Béatrice of Belarac standing in their way. Why do you not interrogate them?"

"Because *they* do not possess *this*." He turned the ring over and touched a finger to the blue enamel surface inlaid with a golden sheaf of wheat. "The ring that has been missing since the day she died."

"I did not kill Béatrice of Belarac!"

"No, but you paid someone else to do it. I have done some investigating of the matter. It seems a stablehand who now works at the Abbey of Belarac lately bragged of undertaking such a job. He was easy to ply with drink and silver, my man said. The words poured out of his mouth like a great river, I hear, as soon as he saw those temptations."

Her jaw worked, but no sound came out.

"He said the first job went off without a hitch. He was paid handsomely for it. The second job was a bit messier than the first, and he missed his intended target."

Amadina's face registered pure terror for a fleeting moment.

"What was the second job, Amadina?"

She struggled to compose herself. A few moments passed in silence.

"The mule," he said calmly. "Let us return to that. How did that animal appear in your stables?"

Amadina stiffened.

"You cannot find the words? No matter. I am sure the residents of Ronzal will be happy to share the story of their missing beast. Mules are greatly valued by the mountain people. They mourn the loss of each as if it were a child." He circled her, noting the tension in her coiled hands, the trembling of her shoulders.

"But back to the more pressing matter. How did you do it, sister?" He approached so that their faces were nearly touching. "How did you arrange for Béatrice's murder? You cannot find the words? I will imagine myself inside your mind, then, and lay out your plan."

Two nearly perfect circles of color, scarlet as summer plums, stood out on her cheeks.

"You sent your spies up and down the market road, and they learned she had made a contract with the merchant of Toulouse whom you considered your best customer. They also learned she was heading home again, by way of Arudy. You sent your evil-doer there and bade him ply her with poison. Then he brought her ring to you as evidence that the deed was done."

The corners of her mouth quivered and the light went out of her eyes.

By her expression, he knew he had got it right.

BOOK III

Pulvis et umbra sumus.
We are dust and shadow.
—*Horace*

1

Summer, 1505
Perpignan, Aragón
Mira

T HEY LEFT TOULOUSE AT dawn in steady rain that poured
from a leaden sky, riding away from the wealth of the
merchants with their soaring brick towers, away from
the prosperous citizens clothed in layers of blue wool and silk,
away from the fields planted in woad that stretched across the
wide plains to the distant foothills of the Pyrenees. They headed
east to Perpignan, where the kings of Majorca had long ago built
a palace overlooking the Mediterranean Sea.

Mira hugged baby Rose to her chest. She would finally glimpse
the sea after a lifetime of dreaming about it. If only she could
muster a thrill at the thought. Instead she was numbed by the
events of the past few days, grieving the loss of Deedit, and
overwhelmed by Rose's needs.

Arnaud saw to it that they traveled in the footsteps of merchants who plied the roads between Toulouse and Perpignan.

Oxcarts with their billowing canvas covers forged ruts through the mud. The plains were clothed with a skim of new green shoots that stretched on monotonously to the horizon day after day.

Mira sat in silence on her mule, one arm wrapped around Rose, watching the mountains standing sentinel over them to the south. Her mind shuttled through memories of Elena, of Mother Béatrice, of the Ronzal villagers. She tried not to think of her mother, because that always brought on a rush of sorrow. Or the impending return of her father and brother to Oto. They would never find her now, she told herself—if indeed they were still alive.

Each evening she and Arnaud searched for convents and monasteries bearing the carved scallop shell that indicated a welcome awaited them inside. Many nights they lodged at inns whose overpriced, filthy rooms crawled with fleas and lice. On the most desolate stretches of land they knocked at farmhouse doors, welcomed by farmers only too willing to trade supper and a night's lodging for a few silver coins.

Rose was even-tempered for the most part. She slept well on the road, lulled asleep by the rhythmic movement of the mule. She accepted food eagerly, and she already had a few teeth pushing through her gums. One night in a convent's guest house she pulled herself up to standing, her little hands clinging to an oak chair. Her face broke into a proud grin. Arnaud and Mira both burst out laughing, then exchanged a look.

It was the first time either of them had laughed since Deedit's death.

One afternoon Perpignan rose up before them on the dusty plains, its walls of pink brick impossibly high. Above the city gates was a tower studded with arrow slits. Armored guards looked down at them from the parapets.

"What business have you in Perpignan?" asked the gate guard, his eyes on Arnaud.

"Work awaits me with the Moncada family," Mira replied.

The guard ignored her, staring fixedly at Arnaud.

Arnaud said, "My wife speaks the truth. For my part, I intend to join the cabinetmakers' guild." He shook the leather bag strapped over his shoulder to impress the guard with the sound of tools clanking.

"Let me see your faces and hands." The guard strode closer, examining them. Mira held out her hands, mystified. Rose shrank back against her chest and let out a wail.

He peered at Rose, inciting another shriek, then straightened his shoulders. "There's talk of the plague again. Any travelers with spots or boils are turned away."

"The plague?" Mira looked up at the tower again, at the impassive guards in their leather armor and metal helmets. A gust of wind tore her hood from her head. Suddenly she was overcome with an urge to turn and flee.

But at that moment the man waved them on. Arnaud clucked to the mules, nodded his thanks to the guard, and led them through the gates.

There was no turning back now.

Mira's new employer was a nervous woman with a habit of blinking rapidly as if to chase away some speck of dust in her eye. The home she lived in was elegant and large, and her image was carved into stone above the courtyard doorway alongside her husband's.

"How quickly can you finish the portrait?" she asked, waving Mira into a chair opposite her own.

"If you do not mind daily sittings, we can finish it within a few weeks."

Lady de Moncada clapped her hands in excitement.

"Do you know," she said in a tone that implied she was sharing a delicious secret, "my dear friend Lady de Berral employs an artist too. I have it on good authority that the woman is ill. She no sooner picks up a brush than she falls into her bed again. The first work she completed was exquisite, I'll admit, but it took her nigh on half a year to do it. Now she attempts another, but the poor thing barely has the strength to stand."

"Your friend's artist is also a woman?" Mira asked in surprise.

"Yes."

"She is ill, though?"

Lady de Moncada sniffed. "The only reason she still walks the earth is that her husband nurses her day and night."

"How devoted he must be."

"He works for the family as well. A musician." Lady de Moncada rolled her eyes. "There is nothing practical about employing musicians. Feeding them, sheltering them, is quite extravagant. And for what? A nightly strum on the lute? What a waste of good silver. But then what does that family know of economizing?" She blinked several times for emphasis.

Before Mira could take a breath to answer, the woman went on.

"They pour gold into that home of theirs in the valley of Maury. It lies in the shadow of a great castle that falls into ruin. Their home, come to think of it, was likely built from the very stones of the place. Every time this city sees a case of sweating sickness or plague, off they run to the countryside." She leaned forward, lowering her voice. "In my experience, if sickness wants to find you, it will."

"Indeed," Mira said.

"Here." The noblewoman retrieved a small sack and gave Mira a handful of coins. "Buy what you need to create the best portrait in all of Perpignan."

Mira looked at the small mound of tarnished silver in her palm.

"Thank you," she said. "But if you want me to use the finest pigments, I shall require more than this."

"Oh?"

"Lapis lazuli, gold dust, saffron. They are what the Flemish masters use to achieve the richest, most vibrant colors. Colors that glow and shimmer."

More blinking. Then the hand went into the sack again and withdrew more coins, gold this time.

"I expect the results to be exactly what you just described." The coins clanked into Mira's palm.

She bowed her head. "You shall not be disappointed, my lady."

On the next market day, Mira walked to the bookmakers' stalls. She was after a particular tool that she could not do without, the lead stylus that Sebastian de Scolna had taught her to use for underdrawings all those years ago. The one she had used in Toulouse remained in Lady de Vernier's sitting room, along with all of the other supplies she had purchased to complete the family's portraits.

One of the stalls was staffed by a short, jowly man with a laugh so infectious that a small crowd had gathered around him.

"Rumbach is my name, you'll not see a finer craftsman in this city!" he cried in a voice tinged with some guttural northern accent. "The finest Venetian silk covers my books. Straight off the ships it comes. Inside, you'll see illustrations lustrous with gold, with crimson, with the finest blue. Come, come, see for yourselves. You'll not be disappointed, I swear it."

Catching the eye of a merchant's wife, he opened a book to a page covered with a lacework of colorful painted patterns. A blank rectangle sat at the center of the page.

"This could be your image, madame," he said in a silky voice.

The woman took a few steps forward. He held the book out.

"Your lovely visage surrounded by this opulent design," he purred. "Just imagine it."

The woman simpered, took the book in her hands, stroked the cover. The bookmaker's face split into an enormous grin.

Mira made her rounds of the market and returned to the bookmaker's stall when the crowds had thinned. He was busily directing his apprentices to dust and oil the leather covers of a pile of parchment books. He glanced up as she approached.

"Yes, madame, may I be of service?" he asked.

"I wonder if you have a lead stylus."

"I might. What would you be needing such a tool for?" He rummaged in a wooden box.

"I am an artist."

"Oh?" He squinted at her.

"Yes. A painter."

"And what would a painter use a lead stylus for?" He pulled a small glinting thing from the box.

"Underdrawings for portraits, mostly. But I have also used it for the kinds of illuminations your books contain."

"I am the only bookmaker in Perpignan who offers such a service. Who employs you?"

"Lady de Moncada. But for portrait painting only, not illuminations."

"Ah. I know the family. Nearly sold them a prayer book just last week." He gazed at her suspiciously. "Where did you receive such training?"

"At an abbey in Béarn. I began illustrating books as a child, and then a master painter from Flanders taught me how to create a portrait."

She examined the tool he held out. "How much?"

He responded with a question of his own. "What say you to striking a bargain? You take this book..." He picked up the silk-covered prayer book he had tried to sell to the merchant's wife just a few moments before, opening it to the page with the bare rectangle. "Paint a miniature of yourself in this space. Bring it back to me here, next week on market day. If it is a fine likeness, expertly made, the stylus is yours. But even better, you will find yourself with a new business partner."

"Who?"

"Me. I have no end of apprentices who can draw a bit of filigree and fill it in with paint or gold leaf. But I am the only one who can create a likeness that meets with the approval of a wealthy man or woman. And truth be told, even my skills fall short for the most discerning customers. Prayer books are reflections of their owners, the best ones sell for ridiculous amounts. You'd get a cut of that."

"You would entrust me with a book this fine?"

His jovial expression darkened. "I know the streets of Perpignan as well as I know my wife's face, and I know its people better. If you do not fulfill your end of the deal, I will find you within a day."

2

Summer, 1505
Perpignan, Aragón
Mira

MIRA SOON LEARNED THAT Lady de Moncada was a
late riser, only interested in sitting for her portrait in
the afternoons. Mornings, therefore, were spent in the
bookmaker's workshop, painting tiny portraits of merchants in
prayer books. Each afternoon she marked the steps between her two
employers by the chiming of church bells as she passed from the
workshop through the quarter of the fabric merchants and finally
to her mistress's grand home. Her days passed in a blur of work.

They had found another convent with a shell carved above the
door. Its cramped guesthouse overlooked a busy lane. The enter-
prising abbess, who had a kind gleam in her gray eyes, assigned
a novice nun to care for Rose during the day in exchange for
Arnaud's labor on whatever needed fixing.

At night the three of them lay in one narrow bed, Mira and
Arnaud silent and still until the baby fell asleep. Then they whis-

pered back and forth over her head, sharing tidbits about the day until the cathedral in the square chimed midnight. Sometimes Mira complained to Arnaud of her exhaustion.

"At least you have work," he would remind her.

He had no master's recommendation for the cabinetmakers' guild and no chance of entering it as a journeyman, though he visited a tavern frequented by members of the guild nearly every day in hopes of chancing on an opportunity. He had finally, reluctantly, turned his sights on the docks. There was usually carpentry work to be had in a river harbor, as well as an over-abundance of disreputable characters. But, as he often told Mira, he could take care of himself.

Mira waited with Rose in the shadow of a half-timbered house across the square from the Consulate of the Sea. The sun glared down relentlessly. It hurt her eyes to look up at the cloudless blue sky, so she lowered her gaze to the crowded square before her. The citizens of Perpignan were not clad as richly as the people of Toulouse. The merchant classes were dominated by tanners and fabric makers. Artisans in leather aprons and dye-splattered smocks mingled with merchants' wives. Shipmasters congregated in small groups outside the Consulate of the Sea, their heads bent together in conversation.

Mesmerized by the parade of people across the dark cobble-stones, Rose was pliant in her arms. A servant woman carrying a basket of turnips slipped and lost her balance nearby; two turnips slid to the ground. She stooped to pick them up but a passing tradesman loaded down with squares of tanned leather stomped on the bigger of the turnips, squashing it into a white mass under the heel of his boot. Rose pointed at the mound of pulp, letting out a cry of amazement. The servant woman shook her head and tucked the remaining turnip back in her basket, then hurried on.

Mira gently blew on Rose's long eyelashes, eliciting a giggle. Rose amused herself for a few moments by closing her eyes and waiting for the quick burst of air from Mira's breath, then fluttering them open again. Soon enough, though, she began to squirm and fuss.

Arnaud had been inside that building for too long, Mira thought. His sole errand was to introduce himself to the harbor master and inquire about work repairing hulls, decking, and rigging—far less skilled work than he was capable of. But he had no other choice.

She thought longingly of their rented rooms above the quiet square in Toulouse. Here, they still lodged at the convent because they could not afford to rent rooms elsewhere. And for its access to women who would watch Rose for a morning or afternoon as needed. Now that they were responsible for a child everything revolved around her care.

Mira found herself wondering what their life would have been like had Deedit never found them. She tightened her arms around the baby and kissed the top of her head, ashamed at the thought. Rose was their child now, and she loved her.

The door burst open and Arnaud strode out into the bright sunshine. When he closed the distance between them, Mira saw relief on his face.

"The harbormaster said at first he had no use for my skills," Arnaud said, nearly shouting over the indignant braying of a heavily laden donkey in the alleyway next to them. "But a shipmaster overheard us and he offered me work sprucing up the captain's quarters on a craft anchored at Port-Vendres that just arrived from Venice. Then the harbormaster said if the shipmaster was pleased with my work, there'd be a job for me on the docks in the river harbor when I return."

"Port-Vendres?"

"On the sea. I'll have to journey there. It's not far, I'll just be gone a few days."

Rose squirmed in Mira's arms, watching the donkey retreat into the half-light of the alleyway. Arnaud reached out a hand to touch her cheek.

"What's that?" He examined a raised, red spot under her eye.

"This place swarms with insects. They feast on her by night."

"She doesn't seem bothered."

"Not much bothers this little one. And I dab her with rosemary oil to ease the itch."

Arnaud hoisted Rose out of Mira's arms and swung her up on his shoulders. Her little hands latched onto his ears.

"Let's be off," he said, taking a few elaborate bouncing steps forward and back.

Rose let out a cascade of joyful squeals, causing various passers-by to smile in their direction.

Mira laughed at the pair of them. Perpignan might not have the most pleasant climate, nor the most desirable surroundings, nor the opportunities for skilled work that Arnaud needed. But Rose seemed to like it.

That was something.

3

Summer, 1505
Perpignan, Aragón
Mira

MIRA STOOD IN FRONT of the oak door, hand poised over the polished iron knocker. She sighed, imagining her patron's face, the greasy pomade that made it glisten, the lips darkened with beet juice, the brows plucked and redrawn with charcoal. And the stream of prattle discharging from her mouth without cease, fueled by copious helpings of wine.

The portrait was nearly done, she reminded herself. And Lady de Moncada had offered to pay Mira handsomely to undertake a special job which she was to lay out in detail this afternoon. Reluctantly, Mira lifted the knocker and let it fall against the door with a resounding thump.

"May the saints above take note of this achievement," crooned Lady de Moncada, standing before the portrait with a cup of wine in hand. "You have done justice to my shining hair and my almond-shaped eyes. I chose my dress well too. The red velvet looks soft enough to touch, and the way you arranged the silver plate on the table and the mirror behind me complements my figure quite nicely. What's more, the light coming from the window truly makes my skin glow."

Mira bowed her head in thanks.

"I have been giving much thought to a scheme that I believe you will find amusing and even exciting. My friend Lady de Berral, you know of whom I speak..."

Mira nodded. All Lady de Moncada wished to do was gossip endlessly about this rival who spent much of her life a few days' journey to the west, in a valley studded with lavender fields near a crumbling palace built by long-dead kings.

"As you know, Lady de Berral has in her employ an artist whose skills she claims to be unsurpassed, who works in the style of the great Flemish masters, which is a rare thing indeed in these parts." She took a gulp of wine. "Apparently the woman can no longer work at all. She is simply waiting to die. What say you to traveling to my friend's home and finishing the portraits that her own artist cannot complete?"

Mira corked a jar of pigment and wiped a brush dry, not wanting to reveal the interest in her eyes. "I have never met another artist who is a woman," she admitted.

Lady de Moncada nodded enthusiastically. "I imagine you would have much to discuss with her. I could write at once and tell my friend you are coming. Just as a loan, of course, because I want you to return to me when the summer is done and stay for at least two seasons more...there are a number of other portraits you can paint for my family, and then perhaps I will parcel you out to other leading families of Perpignan."

Mira's employer has the unfortunate habit of speaking about her as if she were property. Lady de Vernier had never spoken thus. And neither had Carlo Sacazar. The only person she had ever worked for who truly made her feel inferior was Amadina Sacazar.

"I shall discuss the matter with my husband," she said.

"If you were to undertake the journey, I would provide you with my own fine wagon and a team of swift horses, and you would pass through the most beautiful lavender fields in the region. Imagine that—a lavender-scented journey in a comfortable wagon, during which all you would be required to do is stare in wonder at the snowy peaks of the mountains in the south. It would be more of a lark than anything else, I swear to you."

Mira rolled up her brushes in their canvas case.

"My friend Lady de Berral, for all of her faults, is a very generous woman," said Lady de Moncada, leaning close. "I know she would compensate you in a fashion you would find more than adequate. And if you agree, I shall gift you a dozen jars of those salted anchovies you so love."

Lady de Moncada frequently offered Mira tastes of the foods she snacked on during their painting sessions. The small, tangy fish, rinsed and soaked in olive oil, had proved particularly delicious.

"I thank you," Mira said, straightening up and looking Lady de Moncada in the eyes. "But I have my husband and daughter to think of, and we only lately arrived here in Perpignan. A journey is more difficult for a little one."

"Let me assure you, the wagon is covered—and there are soft cushions for her to rest upon. She would find the journey much more pleasant than what she will encounter here. I know you suffer from the heat and dampness, and believe me, this is only the beginning. In high summer it is absolutely stifling within these walls. Though the sea lies nearby, not a shred of breeze can be felt in these streets. That is why so many of our finer citizens leave the city of a summer and go to the countryside. And I would not dream of allowing you to make the journey without an escort of my finest footmen. The road is not dangerous in the least, but I know how a mother worries."

"Clearly you have thought of every possible impediment to the scheme and put them all to rest."

"Well? What say you?"

Mira hesitated. Rejecting this carefully constructed proposal with its attendant arguments would not sit well with the woman. In fact, saying no at this juncture, when Lady de Moncada was so invested in the plan, would possibly jeopardize Mira's employment.

But she hated feeling like a commodity to be passed from one noblewoman to another. It made her feel powerless, and that was something she could not abide.

"Forgive me," she said. "I cannot agree to the plan, not now. But I vow to you that I will broach the matter with my husband and give it the consideration it deserves."

She dropped into a curtsy.

Lady de Moncada's lips twitched. Disappointment was plain on her face. But instead of protesting, she abruptly changed the subject.

"I have decided on a new project which you can begin this very day," she said crisply. "I wish to have a prayer book made for me by that fellow who hawks such things at the market. His illustrations are very poor indeed. Vulgar, in my view. But I've heard that recently he has employed some new artisan whose skills are far superior."

Mira suppressed a smile.

"At any rate, I want *you* to make the illustrations. And I want my image to adorn every one of them."

"Even the Virgin Mary? She is to have your face as well?"

The tiniest hint of consternation showed in Lady de Moncada's eyes. But only for a fleeting instant.

"Of course. Though a younger version of my face. Imagine me when I was your age, fresh as a rose." Lady de Moncada reached into the sack that hung at her waist and withdrew a few coins. "Take these to the bookmaker to buy your supplies and tell him I want the finest calf's leather for the cover, not that gauzy fabric he sells to the merchants' wives. In this damp heat, a silk cover will not last more than a few years."

Mira pocketed the coins and bowed her head, praying that her employer would drop the matter of lending her out to Lady de Berral entirely. But it was not to be.

"Do not forget," Lady de Moncada reminded her. "Discuss the other matter with your husband. I am quite eager to know his thoughts. I will begin composing a letter to Lady de Berral tonight, proposing the idea."

"It is too soon for that, my lady," Mira protested.

"Nonsense. The best ideas benefit from good planning." Lady de Moncada blinked several times in quick succession and waved Mira toward the door. "Now, run along. The bookmaker awaits."

4

Summer, 1505
Perpignan, Aragón
Arnaud

ARNAUD WIPED SWEAT FROM his forehead with a sleeve. The sun blazed at him from a stark blue sky. The docks stretched out before him, strewn with trunks, parcels, and ropes. He spied another rotting board on the gangway he'd been tasked to repair and pried out several rusty nails with a hammer. Quickly he selected an oak plank from the cart at his side and laid it into place.

He had been relieved when the harbormaster hired him. But he hated sweating in the squalid air, breathing the fetid odors of rot and piss and vomit that lurked on the quays. Mostly he hated being on guard. Ravaged-looking, hollow-eyed men materialized at his side from time to time, entreating him for money or food. When he refused, they sometimes resorted to violence. He was never without his dagger, and he kept his tools strapped to a leather belt around his waist.

A group of wharf rats—young boys who hung around the docks—trotted by and congregated at the river's edge, pointing at something in the distance. He stood and shaded his eyes with his hand, staring at the wide, meandering river. Ah—there they were. More boats bound for these docks, carrying men and cargo from some great ship anchored at Port-Vendres on the nearby coast. Once the cargo was unloaded, the crew would disperse into the streets of Perpignan, swallowed up by its seedy quarters until it was time to board again. The ships were usually in dire need of repair, which was good for Arnaud. He sometimes traveled with a crew of carpenters downriver to the sea harbor, supplying wood and tools to the captains and making repairs as needed. It was backbreaking work, but he was grateful. It got him away from the river harbor.

Arnaud knelt and began hammering the board into place.

When he finished his task, the boats had docked at the far end of the harbor. His curiosity got the better of him. He followed another group of wharf rats to the easternmost dock and hung back in the shadows. The boats were in fair shape from what Arnaud could see. They flew the flag of Aragón and also another flag, made of blue and red fabric. He watched the passengers disembark. First came a ragtag group of soldiers, some of them limping, some supporting one another as they made their slow passage along the dock.

Then a group of knights emerged. They wore red leather armor. Longswords clanked at their sides. Their shields bore a herald that Arnaud had seen before. When he recognized it, he stepped into the shade of a tall stack of canvas sails.

The knights walked by, some of them staggering as their bodies adjusted to flat terrain after weeks of sailing. Two of them argued about the order in which the group should achieve its goals of wine, women, and food. The rest were silent. Arnaud scrutinized each face as they passed. Without thinking, he stepped out into the light and took a few steps in their direction.

"You!" a voice shouted. "Where d'you think you're going?" The harbormaster waved his arms at Arnaud from down the quay. "The work's not finished yet!"

Arnaud felt irritation rise in his chest. The knights disappeared up the gangway.

The harbormaster spread his legs wide, crossed his arms over his chest. "Well?"

There was nothing to do but turn and walk back to the docks.

5

Summer, 1505
Perpignan, Aragón
Mira

Mira trudged across the dusty cobblestones from the bookmaker's workshop through a humid cauldron of stagnant air, following the sound of the cathedral bells that echoed over the fabric merchants' quarter.

As she crossed a square that led in the direction of the river harbor, Mira spied an approaching group of knights. They wore red leather armor and longswords dangled at their sides. Two of them carried rectangular shields. One was taller than the rest and walked at the center of the group.

She slowed her pace, curious. A group of knights in armor was a sight she rarely saw.

A merchant couple and their entourage moved between Mira and the knights. She stood on tiptoe to get a better look, grateful for the barrier of flesh between herself and the men.

At that moment, she caught the eye of the tall knight at the center of the group. He had a short, pointed beard and a severe countenance. Seeing her, his face took on an expression of surprise. His pace flagged as he held her gaze.

Mira's heart thudded against her ribcage.

The tall man spoke to his comrades. They all turned in her direction, hunting for her. Mira's mouth grew dry. She backed away and slunk to the edge of the crowd. Slipping into a narrow passageway, she walked as quickly as she could to the next busy lane, her entire body trembling. Then she hastened to her employer's home, making sure to stay on streets well-populated with pedestrians.

All that afternoon she was distracted. She had found a way to delay Lady de Moncada's plan to lend her to Lady de Berral. It had been easy to do, in truth. After a few false starts with the prayer book illustrations, when Lady de Moncada found fault with various elements of her appearance in the small images that adorned each page, Mira had developed a habit of sketching a preliminary drawing on a piece of linen paper. After long-winded analysis of various aspects of the drawing (the drape of a sleeve, the curve of her waist, the size of her nose, the angle of her eyebrows) Lady de Moncada would give her approval and Mira would paint a copy of the edited drawing in the book. Today was no different. The drawing was based on one she had seen in several of Albrecht Rumbach's other prayer books: Judith slaying Holofernes. But when Lady de Moncada's eyes fell upon it, she drew in a sharp breath.

"A woman murdering a man! With a sword! Whatever possessed you to draw this?"

"It is all the rage, my lady. The bookmaker says in Barcelona, no woman commissioning such a book would think of omitting this image. Judith killed Holofernes to protect her people. She is no common murderess. Her loyalty and love, her courage are all on display here."

Lady de Moncada looked doubtful. "That may be. But my husband would not tolerate the sight of me with a sword in my hand, about to lop off a man's head." She scrunched up her face, considering the matter. "I like the idea of it, I must admit. The leading ladies of Barcelona know what is fashionable, and I am nothing if not fashionable." She gave Mira an appraising look. "Put *your* face on her. If you can stand being associated with a woman such as she. No matter her reasons, she is still, in my mind, a murderess."

"I would be happy to do so," Mira said smoothly.

If only her employer knew the truth: that she had killed not one, but two men.

As the afternoon wore on, Lady de Moncada chattered about the ladies of Barcelona, the fashions there, and her childhood in that city. Mira half-listened, caught on the memory of the tall knight's dark eyes searching the crowd for her.

"So, what are your thoughts on the matter?"

Mira's mind resurfaced.

"I...my thoughts?"

"Yes, on the matter of necklines. Square, or round? Which do you prefer?"

"To be truthful, my thoughts were with a strange and unsettling sight I saw on my way here today."

"Oh?" A look of rapt attention came over her mistress's face. "What was that?"

"A group of knights coming from the harbor. They were dressed in red leather armor. I have never seen such a sight, I confess."

"A ship home from the war for Naples, I would wager," Lady de Moncada said with confidence. "I had heard they might arrive one day. Covered in glory, having won back the kingdom of Naples for their queen. God rest her soul."

Mira blinked. "Queen Isabella is dead?"

Lady de Moncada nodded. "Word came in the spring. In any event, the king still lives, and no doubt he shall find a new queen in due time. Now, as for the knights you saw. They will be coveted by our city's merchant class as husbands for their daughters, so that their girls can be titled. Tell me, was one of the men finer dressed than the others? Did he walk at the center of the group?"

"Yes." The tall knight had clearly been the leader.

"He was their captain, then. Mark my words. He is of noble blood, and he shall soon be snapped up by a leading family of this city as bridegroom for a daughter."

Of course, Mira thought. The soldiers who fought in the battle for Naples would make their journeys across the sea, returning to Aragón. And her father and brother might one day be among them. Might have already come ashore.

A sick feeling took hold of her gut.

"Do you fear the walk home, with knights lately come from war roaming the streets?" Lady de Moncada asked, a look of concern on her face. "I see it in your eyes, my dear. I know I would. Let me dispatch two manservants to accompany you to your lodgings. It will put your mind at ease."

6

Summer, 1505
Perpignan, Aragón
Arnaud

ALL THE REST OF the afternoon Arnaud chafed with impatience. The moment the harbormaster released him from work, he strode in the direction the men had gone and asked passersby if they had seen the group. He entered shops and taverns, quizzing workers about the men. Slowly he nosed his way along the path the knights had taken from the docks to an inn that was reputed to serve the best food in Perpignan's merchant quarter, where the fabric-makers' workshops were located.

He hesitated outside a moment, wiping the sweat from his brow again, and pulled a cap over his head. Then he entered the noisy inn.

The knights were seated at the best table in a small alcove that had its own fireplace. The wreckage of a meal lay before them, the table studded with tankards of ale and cups of wine.

Arnaud slid into a seat at a table in a shadowy corner that had just been vacated by a pair of tanners. When the ale wench came, he ordered a tankard of ale.

"That's a fancy lot," he remarked when she brought it, jerking his head toward the knights.

She followed his gaze. "Indeed. A lord and his men. Returned from the battle for Naples. We got another lot of 'em a fortnight ago, full of talk about their dead queen and their empty coin purses."

"Dead queen?"

The girl nodded. "That's what they said. 'Course, the king still lives. But..." She glanced around, lowering her voice. "They complained that they've not been paid. If it weren't for the Great Captain sharing his war spoils with his favorites, they'd be poor as mice."

She turned away, distracted by a roar of laughter rising up from the group of knights.

Arnaud covertly raked his eyes over the men at the large table. Which one was the baron? He leaned forward, craning for a better view, and saw something gold flash on a man's finger. Were any of the others wearing jewels? Not that he could see. The man was large-framed, with lanky limbs. His hair was dark, his beard short and pointed, his face dominated by wide, jutting cheekbones. His eyes continually roamed the room, occasionally flitting back to settle on a companion's face as he spoke, then darting away again.

Arnaud caught snatches of the conversation. Talk of Naples, of battles, of pay owed them by the crown. Talk of homecomings.

There was a commotion at the door. An impeccably dressed merchant and three servants swept into the room and made for the knights' table. Chairs scraped the floor as the group stood and made their introductions. The merchant made a long speech. The knights all seemed to lose interest after the first few sentences, except for the tall man with the ring, whom the merchant seemed to be addressing. The merchant hovered, warming to his monologue, apparently intent on receiving some assurance from the man. When he eventually got it, he bowed and made a quick exit, followed by his servants.

As soon as they were gone, several of the knights burst out laughing.

"He wishes to be your father-in-law, my lord?" one said. "I pray his daughter talks only half as much as him, for your sake."

"Shows you know nothing of women," another said, shaking with laughter at his own wit. "She'll talk twice as *much* as him, I wager."

The tall man smiled. "At least I'll have fine lodging while we await the ship's repairs."

Arnaud leaned forward, listening intently. One of the knights asked a question he couldn't hear.

Then the man with the ring said something unintelligible, followed by: "Our parents are dead. Alejandro needs looking after."

Arnaud stiffened. He tightened his fingers around his tankard.

Another muffled question was asked.

"Oto," the man said, nodding. "Yes, home to Oto."

Arnaud kept his eyes trained on his hands, concentrating on steadying his breath. So Ramón de Oto was dead. And sitting not a stone's throw from him was Pelegrín, the new Baron of Oto. Mira's twin brother.

Somehow fate had conspired to bring them both to the same city, to breathe the same humid air, to tread the same worn cobblestone streets. He thanked the sun and stars that Mira had told no one here she was an Oto. As far as anyone knew, she was Madame de Luz.

For now, she was safe.

7

Summer, 1505
Perpignan, Aragón
Mira

THAT EVENING, MIRA SAID nothing to Arnaud of what she had seen. The knights, the tall bearded man at the center of their group whose dark eyes sought hers. Each time she recalled him a panicked feeling took hold of her chest.

Arnaud seemed even more drained than usual. The work on the docks was wearing on him. He had to be on his guard all the time, she knew, for the disreputable characters who frequented the harbor made a habit of preying on the carpenters who worked there. Anything of value was fair game to them: the odd iron nail, a plank of finely planed oak. And whatever was stolen, Arnaud was responsible for replacing. The harbormaster cared not for excuses. A missing nail was a missing nail, he said. Arnaud was armed, but what was a dagger against a thieving gang? She hated thinking of it.

In the gathering twilight, Rose fell asleep on Arnaud's shoulder. Mira looked at the two of them from her perch on the chair next to the bed. Rose's face was flushed, her mouth open. Her little chest rose and fell so rapidly, with the quick, fluttery breaths of a songbird.

"Stay away from the harbor gates," Arnaud whispered to Mira. "There is a sweating sickness in the quarter. The people are shut up in their homes, afraid to go abroad. No one's about but wharf rats and thieves."

Mira looked at him. She knew that was untrue, since the streets were as crowded as ever in the square that led to the harbor gates today. It was unlike Arnaud to fabricate a tale. In fact, she had never known him to do it.

"The quarter bustles in its usual fashion, Arnaud," she said in a low voice. "I was there today myself."

"What?"

"I saw something there." She hesitated. "A group of knights."

He extricated himself from Rose and stood up, running a hand through his hair. "What did they do?"

"Nothing. They just looked...fearsome, I suppose." She recalled the tall knight's gaze, the look of recognition in his eyes. "And one of them seemed to know me."

"He *saw* you?" There was a hard edge in Arnaud's voice.

"He seemed to recognize me, though I had never seen him before. I slipped away before they could approach."

"Thank the sun and stars."

"What do you mean? Why are you worried?"

He sighed, wiped the sweat off his brow with a sleeve. "That man was your brother. Pelegrín de Oto."

Mira felt cold, despite the sweltering air.

"I saw them disembark from their ship," he went on. "After work I followed them to a tavern and gleaned what I could. Your father is dead. Pelegrín is returned from Naples, on his way back to Oto. He stays here in the company of a merchant who seeks a groom for his daughter, awaiting repairs on his ship."

Mira's throat felt as if it were closing up, all the moisture stripped from it.

"Did you know ships from Naples would anchor at Port-Vendres?"

He nodded. "The shipmaster said a few have come. I decided not to tell you because I did not want to upset you."

"We never should have come here!" She sprang up and went to the window. "I felt it the day we arrived, when we walked through the city gates."

"Calm yourself. Nothing bad has happened to us. As for Pelegrín, he does not know you. He will be out of the city soon, back to Oto."

"True, he has never laid eyes upon me before, yet he did seem to know me. Why?"

Arnaud was silent, waiting for her to puzzle out the answer on her own.

"My mother. I look like her, enough so that the resemblance would not go unremarked. Our eyes, our hair. The shape of our faces. He saw me and was reminded of his mother, that was all."

One of her knees began to tremble. She sank back down on the bed, twisting her hands in her skirts.

"My patron proposed a silly scheme to me that now I think might prove a wise course of action after all." Mira looked up at Arnaud. "There are some portraits that were begun by another artist who has fallen ill and no longer has the strength to do the work. The place is a few days' journey from here. What say you to traveling there so I can complete the work? By the time we return, my brother and his men will be gone."

Arnaud folded his arms over his chest. "Nothing ties me to this place," he said. "The harbormaster pays me day by day; I've no contract. I'd leave tomorrow if I could. But things are different for you. What of your contract with Lady de Moncada?"

"I wish I had never signed it."

"Mira, have you ever considered what *I* wish for?" There was an unaccustomed coolness in his gaze.

She swallowed. "What do you wish for?"

"I wish to work as a cabinetmaker instead of fighting off wharf rats. I wish to go to Bayonne as we planned, to the life that awaits us there—to fulfill the obligation to my family in Ronzal. We told them we would send word as soon as we'd arranged barge transport for their oak. How much longer must they wait?"

"I have not forgotten," she snapped. "I worry over it too! But what about Rose?"

"Where's it written on her face that she's a Cagot? Even if we return to lands where they're plentiful, no one will know Rose is one of them."

Mira shook her head. "She will be tiny like her mother. The Cagots are known for that, even if they do not all look alike. You cannot hide your size. Rose will not become the object of abuse, not if I have anything to do with it."

"Are you telling me you wish to stay in Perpignan for the rest of your days?"

Mira glared at him. "Of course not. I shall tell Lady de Moncada that I agree to her scheme. We shall go west, I will complete the work at her rival's estate, we will return here so I can finish out the contract with her. By then my brother and his men will be gone and we can devise a plan for returning to Bayonne."

Arnaud slapped at a mosquito on his arm. "Yet one more delay. What will be the next one, Mira? I wonder." There was a bitterness in his voice she had never heard before.

Mira stayed quiet, kept her eyes on Rose's sleeping form. In silence, they took their places on either side of the baby. After a long while, Arnaud's breathing became deep and regular, and she knew he was asleep. For her part, she stared into the darkness, ruminating, until the dawn sky brightened.

8

Summer, 1505
Valley of Maury, France
Mira

THE CLOP OF THE horses' hooves on the hard-packed, dusty road rang out in a crisp rhythm. A breeze blew softly from the south, where the undulating waters of the Mediterranean glittered in the sunlight. Rose was nestled on a pile of cushions on the floor of the wagon, and Mira and Arnaud sat on a bench behind her. Lady de Moncada had been true to her word: they rode in style, with two footmen accompanying them.

The childish dream that had guided Mira's desire to visit the crashing waves of the sea and witness the rivers pouring off the ends of the earth—it no longer propelled her forward. It had been diverted, she realized, twisted up with the threads of other peoples' stories, with mishaps and illnesses and death. Her eyes fell upon Rose's tiny hands clutching Arnaud's arm. *And with love*, she thought. *Mostly with love.*

"What are your thoughts?" Arnaud asked, glancing at her.

"The sea. Remember how I yearned to see it? Now I have, and it is not at all what I imagined."

She shaded her eyes and peered between the flapping canvas curtains of the wagon at the shimmering blue horizon.

"This isn't the same," Arnaud said. "The sea near Bayonne is what Brother Arros described to you. It crashes and rages and flings creatures up on the sand."

"And the sea monsters he spoke of?"

He nodded seriously. "The prows of ships are plastered over with monster bits from all the collisions."

She doubled over laughing, relieved that his bitterness was gone, replaced by a lightness she had not seen in him for months. At the sound of laughter, Rose began to giggle. Even Arnaud allowed a smile at his own joke.

The house of Lord and Lady de Berral stood near a village, looking out over a valley planted with crops. A great field of lavender spread out before it, and in the distance, on the crown of a low hill, was a ruined castle.

Inside, a servant girl ushered the three travelers to their new quarters, a modest suite not far from the kitchens. The main room held a bed much bigger than any they had ever slept in before, a carved oak chest, a table, and two chairs. The adjoining room was much smaller, but had a bank of windows overlooking a courtyard planted in roses and lavender, the shutters flung open to allow fresh air and sunlight inside. A tiny bed had been made up there for Rose, and a wooden cart and horse sat upon it.

Rose's eyes lit up when she spied the toys. She toddled to the little bed and took the cart and horse in her hands. Turning back to Mira and Arnaud, she hugged the toys to her chest, a look of wonderment on her face.

The servant girl smiled. "She can play in the courtyard. And if she gets hungry, go to the kitchens as it pleases you. The cooks'll give her biscuits and plums. Or porridge if you'd rather. A tub and bathwater are coming. You'll hear a bell ring later when it's time to eat."

She curtsied and left the room.

Arnaud let out a low whistle. "What are the likes of us doing here?"

"I'll remind you of my noble origins." Mira tossed her head and scooped up the hem of her skirt, miming the walk of a fine lady.

"Ha!"

"I beg your pardon, sir?"

"Any woman who can hunt for her own supper, swim in a mountain stream, and wield a blade the way you do has no right to call herself a lady."

"Any man who can read Latin, work figures like a Moorish scholar, and craft furniture much finer than anything in this place is nothing less than a gentleman."

Arnaud offered her his arm.

"Shall we take a turn around our chambers, then?"

"Why yes, m'lord, I would be honored."

Mira laid her fingertips delicately upon his dust-streaked sleeve. They sashayed here and there, Rose following behind dragging the cart and horse, until they both collapsed laughing on the chairs.

Rose regarded them in amazement for a moment. Then, waving the wooden horse in the air, she let out a scream of laughter herself.

"Mama!" she cried, her sparkling eyes fixed on Mira.

Mira swooped down and picked up the girl, swinging her around in a circle.

"She called me Mama!"

"I heard," Arnaud said wryly.

Mira's chest felt delightfully loose. The dread she carried in her abdomen like a clenched fist had vanished. In its place was something she had not felt for a long, long time. She scooped up Rose in one arm; with the other she reached out for Arnaud. The three of them stood swaying, breathing the lavender-scented air.

Rose repeated her new word in a soft, insistent voice. "Mama. Mama. Mama."

Arnaud grinned. "You're the favorite."

Mira kissed Rose's soft cheek. Her eyes stung with tears.

"Arnaud," she whispered. "I almost forgot what joy feels like. I have not felt this way since..."

"...Since Deedit died?"

She nodded.

"Seize your joy," he murmured into her hair. "Don't let it go."

Mira took his hand and pulled it to her heart.

9

ZARI HAD FINISHED A freelance job that evening, building a website for an organic cosmetics company based in San Francisco. Now she sat in the dark, clicking link after link on her laptop, combing through the archives of auction houses in search of unsigned Renaissance-era portraits painted in the Flemish style. It had become a habit. And it was needle-in-a-haystack ridiculousness, she knew. But she was fueled by a buzz of anticipation, a searing curiosity, and—most of all—desperation.

It could be worse, she told herself. *I could be up all night watching cat videos.*

The refrigerator hummed in the tiny kitchen. She got up and flicked on the kitchen light, rummaging in the cupboards for a teacup and a packet of crackers. Waiting for the kettle to boil, she stared at the photo taped to the refrigerator. It was a selfie she and Wil had taken in front of the cabin at Christmas. Their cheeks and noses were pink from cold. Her head was tucked under his chin, and they both looked radiantly happy.

If Zaragoza hadn't ended so badly, she probably would have another adorable selfie to tape alongside this one. Instead, Zari could barely remember saying goodbye to Wil when she boarded her train back to San Sebastián. Both of them had been dazed, nauseous, sallow-faced wrecks at the time.

She poured boiling water over a chamomile tea bag, watching the steam rise from the cup. Now Wil was in Indonesia on a sourcing trip, searching for reclaimed teak wood to use in his furniture design business. Soon after returning from that trip, he would head to Croatia with Filip. The connection Zari had made between Filip and her brother's disabled friend had blossomed quickly into a friendship. For the first time since his accident, Filip was preparing for an adventure again, and Wil would be at his side.

All of this travel meant that the conference in Bordeaux—two months away—was the next time she would see Wil. Zari traced a fingertip over their smiling faces in the photo. She felt completely at ease with him, absolutely herself. She had never longed for someone so hungrily before, which exhilarated her. But the aching loneliness she experienced when they were apart was terrifying. It made her feel trapped, locked into something she had no control over.

Tears blurred her vision and she blinked them angrily away. She had never been much of a crier. She became an expert at tamping down her emotions during the long years of fighting between her parents, and then even more so when her brother Gus struggled with addiction. Yet somehow since Mira and Wil came into her life, tears had become a regular—and irritating—occurrence.

She smiled, tossing her tea bag in the trash. How weird was that? Mira was as real to her as Wil. She had formed a deep attachment to someone who'd been dead for centuries.

Back in her seat, Zari could hear the sounds of her own eyelids lifting and lowering every time she blinked. The familiar shuffling steps of her nocturnal upstairs neighbor made muffled creaking noises overhead. She sighed, rubbed her eyes, and leaned back in her chair. Just a few more clicks, she promised herself.

Maybe ten more.

There was a tremendous crash from above, a heavy, ominous thud that sent the light fixture on the ceiling reverberating, and then—silence.

Zari sprang up. She walked swiftly to the front door, slipped out and climbed the stairs to the floor above. The crash had come from his apartment.

She stood at the door, hesitating, looking up and down the corridor. No one else had come out. She felt foolish for a moment. Then she knocked.

There was complete silence.

She knocked louder. Then called out, "*Monsieur! Bonsoir!*" She felt somewhat ridiculous saying 'good evening' at three in the morning, but nothing else came to mind. "*Monsieur!*" she called again.

A neighbor poked his head out his door, eyeing her in bleary annoyance. He was tall and pale and wore light-blue pajamas that looked like something Gregory Peck might have sported in a circa-1940 movie.

"What's wrong?" he asked.

"I heard a loud noise," she said.

He did not look impressed.

"Very loud. From this apartment."

The man frowned. He moved out from the doorway, adjusting his pajama top, and came to stand next to her.

"Monsieur Mendieta," he called, rapping on the door with his knuckles.

There was no response.

Mendieta? He has my mother's last name. Zari turned the thought over in her mind, staring dumbly at the door, willing it to open.

The man wheeled and headed to his own door again.

"Where are you going?" Zari asked, feeling abandoned.

"To call for help," he replied over his shoulder.

"We're getting help, Monsieur Mendieta," she said through the door. "You'll be fine. We're getting help."

When the paramedics left, after wrestling Monsieur Mendieta onto a stretcher and navigating him down the stairs, they thanked Zari for checking on him. He had collapsed due to dehydration, they said. He was not critically ill or badly hurt by his fall, but they would take him to the hospital anyway and keep him under observation for the night.

"Does he have any relatives?" she asked the neighbor who had first come to her aid. His partner, a sinewy man with russet-brown skin clad in a tank top and running shorts, had emerged from their apartment during the commotion and stood beside him, rubbing his eyes.

"I don't know." He turned to his partner. "Have you ever seen any?"

The man shrugged. "No one ever goes in there but him."

Before they returned to their respective apartments, they introduced themselves and promised to check up on Monsieur Mendieta once he returned home.

The next day was Sunday. Zari slept until noon. When she awoke she set the kettle boiling, fixed a pot of Irish Breakfast, washed her face, and settled back in front of the computer, which still sat open on her desk. She hadn't shut it down properly last night after Monsieur Mendieta's crisis. Taking a sip of tea, she scrolled through her e-mails and saw one from an unfamiliar sender with the subject heading "ADL."

The brief note, accompanied by several attachments, was from a man named Andreas Gutknecht who said he had been in the audience at John Drake's presentation in Amsterdam last fall. When he saw a painting at auction in London that had the 'ADL' stamp on the back of the panel, his interest was piqued. He searched online using the hashtag 'ADL' and found Zari's posts about Mira de Oto on various social media platforms. He concluded the note by wishing Zari luck with her research.

Zari sat up straighter in her chair. She leaned closer to the screen and clicked on the attachments. The first was a small image of a portrait listed in an auction catalog. The subject was a wealthy woman dressed in luminous blue, her hair concealed by a jewel-studded veil. Behind her was a window that was open to a courtyard dominated by a pink brick tower. Zari zoomed in on the accompanying text. The work was oil-on-panel, a circa-1500 portrait of a merchant's wife. Artist unknown.

The last sentence made her catch her breath: "The reverse side of the panel bears the mark 'ADL.'"

Zari slid to the very edge of her seat, zooming in on the image until it was a pixelated blur. She adjusted it again and again, trying to get a clear view of the details, of the woman's eyes.

"Don't get your knickers in a twist," she said firmly. "Verify first, celebrate later."

She drank the entire pot of tea while writing to the auction house, explaining her interest and requesting access to high-quality digital images of the painting.

Then she began typing an e-mail to John Drake, hesitated, and hit 'cancel.' In just a few days she would see him in St. Jean de Luz. They would have ample time to discuss this new find—unless she had a major surfing wipeout and was sucked under the waves to a watery grave. It had been years since she'd climbed on a surfboard.

It's like riding a bike, she told herself, attempting to dislodge the pit of worry in her stomach. *Your body will remember what to do. Trust it.*

10

March, 2016
St. Jean de Luz, France
Zari

S EAMS OF WHITE FOAM stretched to the glinting horizon. Zari stared at the swells, mesmerized by their rhythmic rise and fall, the salty sharp air filling her lungs. John strode toward the water, his surfboard tucked under one arm. She started after him. Sand squeaked under her neoprene booties.

She could get used to this.

Zari followed John into the water and lay flat on the surfboard, paddling with her arms and pushing the nose of her board low to dive under the surface of each oncoming wave. She paddled furiously to get out to deeper waters. Her shoulders and arms burned with the effort. She probably should have been doing more planks and push-ups in preparation for this little adventure.

Oh, well. She was in it now.

The first few waves she tried to catch rippled away from her and crashed on the shore, and her efforts to stand up on her board resulted in one wipeout after another.

For a while she sat on her surfboard, bobbing in the waves, watching John. Obviously at home in the water, he picked his waves wisely and rode them with sure-footed grace. He had a surfer's body. His muscles were defined even under the wetsuit. After a while, she became uncomfortably aware that she was no longer admiring his technique, but ogling him.

Finally she found the proper balance on her board. Relaxing her knees, she rode a wave until it began to foam and weaken, then dropped off and paddled out to deeper waters again, a huge grin on her face.

Nearby, John whooped at her accomplishment, his voice echoing over the water.

"Not as rusty as you thought, eh?" he shouted.

She paddled closer. "It's like riding a bicycle," she said airily. "Your body never forgets."

The next five waves she attempted eluded her, and when she caught up with John again, he gave her a pointed look.

"Bragging never gets me anywhere," she admitted. "But defeat only makes me more determined. We might be out here all day."

"Suits me," he said, glancing over his shoulder at the horizon. "Here comes a great set. Get ready, Zari!"

She paddled with all her might and caught another wave. Her confidence soaring, she followed that one with at least a dozen more. The energy sapped from her limbs little by little, but she ignored the voice in her head that told her to take a break.

A little while later she lost her balance and wiped out hard. Pushed underwater by a crumbling, messy wave, her lungs burning, she felt panic begin to overtake her. When she surfaced, disoriented, she waved at John.

"I'm going in!" she shouted over the roar of the surf.

Her legs were shaky as she made her way to the beach and sat down on a bleached log that lay near the water's edge. Even though the air was cold and the water even colder, she was hot inside her thick wetsuit. She peeled off her booties and pulled back her hood.

Too exhausted to do anything but sit, she watched John catch wave after wave.

Then he wiped out and disappeared under the roiling waters. She stood, shading her eyes, and strode into the shallow waves that licked at the sand, her heart beginning to race. Where was he?

His board popped up, followed by his neoprene-encased head. He turned to look for her and waved, gave her the thumbs-up sign. Relieved, she turned and waded toward shore again.

A terrible stinging pain seized the sole of her right foot. She looked down in the water to see a streamlined dark shape darting away. She must have stepped on it, though why stepping on a fish would cause such intense pain was a mystery.

Zari limped back to John's car and changed out of her wetsuit. The pain in her foot was worsening. There was a dark red spot on her sole where the skin had been broken. The surrounding flesh was beginning to swell. She rummaged in her handbag for ibuprofen tablets and retrieved her mobile from the car, then sat on the beach waiting for John to finish his set. Two plump seagulls settled nearby on a dark ribbon of sand littered with shells and pecked at a washed-up crab, occasionally pausing to give Zari accusing stares.

A white-plumed seabird with elegant black-tipped wings appeared over the waves, flying south. She took a few pictures of it cruising low over the whitecaps, then scrolled through the photo library on her mobile. There were images from Zaragoza (pre-food poisoning), Wil grinning at her in his blue down jacket with the River Ebro in the background. Dozens of shots from their snowy idyll at the mountain cabin. She idly swiped through the photo stream, glancing up now and then to watch John ride a wave.

When she got to the series she had taken at the Sacazar home in Nay, her heart began to thud a little faster. The shot of the orange cat stepping daintily across the stones on the courtyard floor gave her pause. There was something about the proud arch of its back, the curve of its tail, its command of a space that had just been swarming with energetic children.

But for the first time, it wasn't the cat that caught her eye.

11

JOHN JOGGED ACROSS THE beach to Zari, looking as energetic as he had going into the water hours earlier.

"Ouch." He put aside his surfboard, kneeled down, and took her foot in his hands. "You stepped on a *vive*."

"A what?"

"In English it's called a weever. A flat fish with a stinger. Hangs out in the shallows around here."

"Stinger is the right word. I took some ibuprofen to ease the pain."

"It also helps to immerse it in hot water." He retrieved his surfboard from the sand. "Come on. I'll take you back to your hotel. Run a hot bath and you'll be right as rain in time for dinner tonight."

Zari limped back to the car. Once in her seat, she eased her socks on. But when she tried to insert her right foot into her shoe, the pain made her gasp.

John flinched. "I feel responsible. I stepped on one of those things years ago. I should have warned you not to take off your booties."

"It was just an accident, John. Life has thrown worse at me. It'll make a good story one day."

He smiled. "That's one way to look at it."

In the low-ceilinged restaurant that evening, a wash of pale light from a reproduction oil lamp illuminated their battered table. The server plonked down silverware and paper napkins, then promised to return with a carafe of white wine. Zari studied John across the table. He wore a brown wool sweater and dark jeans, and his hair was still wet from the shower. There was a faint red ring around his throat where the wetsuit neckline had rubbed against his skin.

A few tables down, two young boys sat with their parents, tucking into a spread of tiny whole fried fish and salad.

"Wow," Zari marveled. "French kids are adventurous eaters. My niece and nephew wouldn't touch that meal with a ten-foot pole."

"I'm not acquainted with the world of children, nor their interests, I'm afraid. I'm an affirmed non-parent."

"Have you always felt that way?"

"Yes." John's expression tightened. "It's been a bit of a problem for me."

"I can imagine."

"I lost two partners over it. I'm upfront about the kid thing. But sometimes people think they can change you."

"That must have been rough."

The server deposited their wine and a plate of piping hot fried sardines between them.

"It's not that I don't like kids." John poured them each a glass of wine, then picked up his fork. "I do. The idea of them, anyway. It's—fear, more than anything, I suppose."

"Fear of what?"

He put his fork down.

"My brother was diagnosed with leukemia when he was eleven. I was fifteen when he died. It was agonizing for all of us. My mother never recovered, really. She and my father divorced when I went to university. The grief took over her life. My dad managed to move on—he remarried and found contentment. But my mother's health deteriorated and she died five years ago."

"I'm so sorry, John," Zari said haltingly, surprised that he had confided something so personal to her. Shifting in her seat, she accidentally knocked her injured foot against the table leg. She drank deeply from her wine glass, hoping the alcohol would numb the pain.

He speared a sardine on the tines of his fork. "There's more to life than having kids, I'm happy to report."

"Absolutely. Like surfing."

"I'm a bit obsessed. I do at least one big surf trip a year if I can get away with it. I've been to Bali and Hawaii, I'm going to Costa Rica next year. This is a good budget adventure, St. Jean de Luz. There's something special about it."

Zari nodded. "These streets are filled with stories, I know they are."

He looked at her intently. "You're a story chaser."

Something in his gaze made her heart beat a little faster.

"Especially Mira's story," she said.

The words hovered between them like a protective barrier, an antidote to the charged atmosphere.

He shifted in his seat, leaning back. "She existed. You proved it. And I'm guessing you've found at least a shred or two more of evidence to share with me."

"I've found some interesting clues in a notary register from Toulouse and a prayer book from Perpignan," she said. "And I found evidence of Marguerite de Oto in the archives of a sheep-breeders' collective in Zaragoza."

Zari took out her mobile and showed him the photo of the Oto trademark page. "Do you recognize this?"

"It's the medallion on the woman's belt in the Fontbroke College portrait."

"And there's something else you might recognize from Laurence's portrait of the merchant family," she added, scrolling to the photo of the cat.

"There's no cat in the painting, if I recall correctly."

She shook her head. "See the design in the stones on the courtyard floor?"

John studied the photo a moment. "Ah! The merchant's ring has the same design."

She nodded, watching him refill her wine glass. "Which proves the merchant is Carlo Sacazar—one of the people who signed Mother Béatrice of Belarac's mortuary roll. The courtyard is at his home in Nay." Zari sighed. "I went all the way to Zaragoza to find evidence of that connection and failed. Then today when I was waiting for you on the beach I pieced it together. I took this picture months ago and I never made the connection because the scale of the design in the courtyard is so big."

"Excellent sleuthing." John chewed a forkful of fish. "You've still found nothing that ties Mira herself to any of these paintings, though."

"True." A defensive tone crept into Zari's voice. "But I'm hopeful about a painting that recently sold at auction in London, a portrait of a woman in blue. The 'ADL' mark is burned into the back of the panel."

He set down his fork and looked at her in surprise.

"I know." Zari smiled. "It could be huge for my research. The buyer was anonymous so I've hit a dead end there, but the auction house was kind enough to send me a high-resolution image. Would you please look at it? I need your expert eye."

He glanced away, swirling the last of his wine. The muscles in his jaw tensed. "Zari, I hate to disappoint you, but—"

"Please, John. You see things I'm completely blind to. And remember that pep talk you promised me in Amsterdam? I could really use it right now. I'm trying to stay positive." Zari tried for a light tone, but her voice betrayed her.

"You're asking the wrong person for a pep talk, I'm afraid." John's dark eyes settled on her again. "While I'm impressed with your research, I don't want to give you false hope. At the moment, I regret to say Mira is still not much more than a lovely idea." His tone was different now, too—flat and businesslike, just as it had been the first time they met. "Convincing the art world that she was a master painter will take far more evidence than you've got."

Zari crumpled her napkin in a ball and tossed it on the table. She stared at it in silence, listening to the animated buzz of conversations all around them, a prickle of anxiety tracing a path along her spine. If she had kept her findings to herself, maybe her confidence would still be intact. She bit her lip, wishing she had been more guarded.

"I'll check out that woman in blue," John said after a moment, more gently. "I just want you to be ready for what's coming in Bordeaux. You've done excellent work, but your status as a newcomer will make you a target."

"Then there's the fact that I'm American," Zari said dully. "And female."

"I wish it weren't the case, but to a certain breed, yes—you'll be seen as an outsider, subject to suspicion."

"And by a certain breed, you refer to Dotie Butterfield-Swinton and his friends?"

John nodded. "The very same."

John drove Zari back to her hotel through a maze of quiet streets. Tourists had not yet descended upon St. Jean de Luz, and the town felt deserted at this hour. He regaled Zari with surf lore as they drove, describing his encounters with dolphins, seals, sharks, and eccentric locals. He was funny and loquacious, spinning one story after the next. Zari forgot her bruised ego, dissolving in laughter at his tales.

He pulled up near the entrance to the hotel. Exiting the car, Zari stepped up on the curb, putting all her weight on her sore foot. The tender spot on her sole where the *vive*'s stinger had penetrated her flesh flared with pain. She lurched to one side and nearly fell. John dashed around the car and put a steadying hand on her back.

The warm pressure of his touch sent a jolt of electricity through her.

Zari squeezed her eyes shut and opened them again, woozy from wine and painkillers. The idea that John was attractive had not even occurred to her until she saw him surfing this morning. Was that because she was a completely shallow person, easily taken in by the sight of a fit man in a wetsuit astride a surfboard? Or was her loneliness the culprit?

She longed for the solitude of her room, eager to escape the tangle of confused thoughts plaguing her brain. But instead of stepping away when they reached the awning of the hotel, John pulled her closer.

For a moment she melted into his embrace, her heart thudding wildly. Then Wil's face floated into her mind. What was she doing? She wanted Wil's arms around her, not John's. Didn't she?

Zari pulled away, flooded with consternation. "That was... unexpected."

John took a step toward her, his desire radiating like a magnetic aura, drawing her in. To her chagrin, she felt her body responding.

"I can't," she said in a voice so quiet it was almost a whisper, more to herself than to him. "I can't."

She stared at the ground, unwilling to look him in the eyes again for fear she would give in to her loneliness, to the electric charge that was fizzing between them.

He took another step.

"No," she said more sharply. "I'm sorry, John."

Without another word, he turned away to the car.

"Wait," she called out.

He stopped in the street, looked back at her.

"I'm in a relationship. That's why. If circumstances were different..."

"No worries, Zari," he interrupted levelly. "I understand. Good night."

12

Summer, 1505
Nay, 'Béarn
Carlo

IT WAS WELL PAST midnight. Carlo had been in his study for hours going over his accounts by candlelight, ensconced in his favorite leather-backed oak chair. When the numbers began to swim on the page before him, he got up and paced around the room, pausing occasionally to peer out the window. The courtyard was veiled in darkness. Overhead, a sickle moon hung suspended in the sky, glowing faintly behind a shroud of mist.

For months he had wrestled with the dilemma of what to do about his sister. The truth about Béatrice of Belarac's murder hung over him day and night, casting a shadow on his happiness.

He had long wondered if some malady plagued his sister's brain. And this was the proof. She was not fit to move through the world independently, let alone preside over a convent.

He did a few more laps around the room, hands clasped behind his back, breathing deeply of the comforting aromas of parchment and beeswax.

And yet—and yet. The Sacazars were respected, even feared in Nay. In the entire principality of Béarn, only a handful of families possessed wealth rivaling his own. More important still was his family's reputation in Aragón. The brotherhood of sheep ranchers in Zaragoza had been shaped by Sacazar men since the time of the Moors. Carlo himself worked tirelessly to curry favor with the royal family as the merino wool business grew more lucrative. He even received a letter a few years back from Queen Isabella thanking him for his efforts to bolster the wool trade into the north.

Yes, his power was at its pinnacle. He would not allow his sister's transgressions to spoil that. Too many generations of Sacazars had toiled to build the family's wealth and reputation. He was bound to protect their legacy for his own children and grandchildren.

He would have to find a way to punish Amadina without bringing shame upon them all. An idea—a solution—had been idling in his mind for a while. He would find a convent for her in Aragón, someplace remote and desolate. He would not buy her a title this time, though. He would tell her she was going to rule the place as she had done here. But in reality he would put her into the care of others. Amadina would become a common nun, cloistered behind bars, no longer in possession of power. Perhaps then she would learn to be penitent and remorseful. Though he was no longer confident she had the capacity for remorse.

Carlo stopped at the window. The sky was silvering now, the moon fading as dawn approached. He stared out at the multi-hued river rocks on the courtyard floor that artisans had installed under his supervision over the course of a sweltering summer.

He held up a hand, turning it this way and that, admiring the ring that adorned his middle finger. It was gold, inlaid with a swirling design of black enamel that matched the pattern on the courtyard floor exactly. He had purchased the ring from a jeweler in Florence during one of his early trips abroad, when his wool business relied on Florentine merchants. The ring had belonged to a duke, the jeweler swore, and the design was a whimsical play on the letter 'S'.

Stepping away from the window again, he brightened, thinking of a way to assuage his burden of guilt. He would send Mira's portrait of Marguerite de Oto to Sebastian de Scolna in Flanders. There was no better man to undertake the task of repairing it.

He slipped the portrait from its canvas wrappings and propped it against the wall on an oak sideboard, overcome once again with the sick feeling that had twisted his gut the moment he had found it hidden in Amadina's oak chest.

Once again he was taken by the marked similarity between Mira and her mother. Their eyes, the color of their hair, their angular jaws and high cheekbones, their arching dark eyebrows. And most remarkable of all, they had the same calm expression of confidence, a challenge in the eyes, a knowingness. It made one feel seen in a way that was almost unbearable.

Carlo ran a finger over the damaged area on the portrait. Luckily the face had escaped the worst of it. The bodice of the dress was destroyed, but Sebastian and his apprentices would have an easy time repairing that. They would have to plug the hole with something, smooth out the raw splinters of oak.

He bent closer, squinting. What had caused the damage, anyway? A knife? An axe? Something wickedly sharp, whatever it was.

Suddenly he wondered if Amadina had inflicted this scar on the painting. It was not unimaginable that she would do such a thing. He sighed, wrapping up the portrait again. He would have it sent to Flanders within the week.

And the matter of his sister? He would begin the process of finding the appropriate environment for her on his next trip to Aragón.

13

Summer, 1505
Valley of Maury, France
Mira

L ORD AND LADY DE Berral sat in gilt-covered armchairs, staring in Mira's direction. They were dressed in silk, he in a short yellow doublet and matching hose, she in a dress of brilliant blue, its white sleeves adorned with black ribbons. Her hands were laden with rings; her throat ornamented with pearls as big as chickpeas.

The windows were open to let in the morning breeze, which was scant and warm. A servant hovered nearby, blotting the couples' faces wherever beads of sweat formed.

Mira wiped her hands on a rag and assessed the wooden panel before her. The artist who had begun this work was highly skilled. The brushstrokes were reminiscent of Sebastian de Scolna's.

She struggled to match the blue of the lady's dress. She suspected lapis lazuli was needed, but none was in the supplies she had been given. There was no simple solution. She would either have to paint the entire dress again with the inferior blue she had managed to mix, or hunt down a different type of pigment.

"My lord, my lady...?" Mira ventured.

The lord's eyes settled on her. He raised an eyebrow inquisitively.

"One of the colors your artist achieved is not possible with the pigments at my disposal. Perhaps she has materials tucked away that I might use."

He let out a barely perceptible sigh.

"Madame Van der Zee is very ill. But we shall send a servant to inquire."

"I would not dare to hope if I were you," his wife said through thin, cherry-colored lips. "The poor woman is rumored to be near death."

"And yet she lives on," her husband said in mock surprise. "She eats, she breathes. If death comes for her, it has been delayed."

The lady looked at Mira. "Do not fret on your child's account. Our own physician assures us the woman's illness cannot pass to others. She simply wastes away from the inside. She has always been frail, her husband told me. Those cold Northern winters, I suppose. Flanders."

"You trained in Flanders, did you not?" her husband asked Mira.

"No, my lord. My teacher was from Flanders, but I trained in an abbey in Béarn."

"Interesting," he mused. "How did you procure your first commissions?"

"I traveled to a nearby market town called Nay."

"You've a patron there, then?"

"Yes."

"What is his name?"

"Carlo Sacazar."

"Ah. And do you intend to return to Béarn one day?"

"I do, my lord. It is our hope to settle in the west, closer to family."

"How unfortunate," said Lady de Berral, frowning at the open windows. "We have lost our breeze." She narrowed her eyes at Mira. "Can you not continue? It is simply too tedious, sitting here of a morning."

"Of course." Mira picked up her brush again.

The servant led Mira across the great central courtyard of the manor house, through a back wing, and out again to a field of lavender. On the edge of the field was a modest house of sand-colored stone, its shutters painted blue. They approached it through a small garden planted with vegetables and edged with rose bushes.

"Ever since she got sick, they've lived here," the servant said. "The husband, he plays in the evenings with the other musicians. That's why they've allowed them to stay, I suppose." She rapped on the door. "Poor thing—"

"Thank you," Mira said sharply to the woman, whose hopeful expression turned sour. "You can go back now."

The servant turned away reluctantly.

Gossips, Mira thought. *Always eager for a story.*

The door creaked open. A man of middle age stood in the doorway, wisps of pale thinning hair crowning his bony skull, his face twisted in an expression of either worry or annoyance.

"You're the new artist?" He gestured at her to come inside.

"Yes, Mira...Mira de Luz," she said, stumbling over her name. Why did the word Oto suddenly press against her tongue, threatening to slip out once again?

"Today is better than most for my wife. You're fortunate."

He led her into a bright room that faced the lavender field. A gaunt woman lay on a bed near the window, which was flung open to allow the sunshine inside.

"Cornelia, your visitor is here."

He busied himself for a moment tucking cushions behind his wife's back to prop her up. She turned her head slightly and eyed Mira.

"Ah. Sit, please."

Cornelia's husband left the room as Mira sank into the chair next to the bed.

"Thank you for receiving me," Mira said. "You are the first woman painter I have had the honor to meet."

"There are a few of us about." Cornelia's lips twitched in a faint approximation of a smile. "Mostly lurking in the shadows, I'm afraid."

Mira realized the artist's voice had the same inflections as Sebastian's, which made sense because they were both Flemish.

"The shadows?"

"We learn at the knee of an artist father, or by the grace of a brother or husband. We train in their shadows."

"Ah. I learned from Sebastian de Scolna."

"That is what I was told. A fine master. A good man, too."

Mira nodded. "I miss him."

"You nursed him back to health, I heard."

"I was trained as a nurse in a convent along the pilgrim's way, and he came to us nearly dead. He was attacked by a bear—that is what we believed, anyway. I did what I could, but God saved him in the end."

Cornelia shifted her position and a low moan escaped her.

"Do you have anything for the pain?" Mira asked.

"Yes, the odd tincture. Mysterious syrups and pastes. Nothing helps much."

"Where does it hurt?"

"Everywhere."

Cornelia's eyes were sunken into her skull, the skin around them dark and puffy. Her forehead was creased with lines and her lips were nearly as pale as her skin. A faint aroma of disease emanated from her. Mira recognized the scent from her days in the abbey's infirmary.

"The pain began in my stomach," Cornelia said weakly. "And there it remains. But it journeys up and down each of my limbs and settles in my head most nights."

"How long have you felt it?"

"It began soon after we moved here from Flanders."

Without thinking, Mira reached forward and laid a hand on Cornelia's brow. The skin was cool to touch.

"No fever, anyway. That is good."

"Once a nurse, always a nurse, is that it?"

"I suppose." Mira was embarrassed to have been so forward.

"Before I lose strength to speak, tell me what you wished to ask."

"The blue of Lady de Berral's dress. I cannot replicate it with the pigments in your palette. What am I missing?"

"Ah yes. Ground lapis. I have more in that drawer." Cornelia pointed at a small walnut desk that had two deep drawers on either end.

Mira stood. "May I?"

"Please."

Mira opened the drawer and found a black velvet bag cinched with a silken cord. She loosened the cord and drew out a Venetian glass jar filled with brilliant blue powder.

Cornelia nodded. "There should be more than enough for the dress."

"I am grateful." Mira put the jar back in the bag. "You are a fine artist. I hope I can do justice to your work."

"If you were trained by Sebastian de Scolna, I imagine you are a finer artist than I."

"Do you sign your work? I could do it for you, if you show me your mark."

"I signed the back of the panels at my lord's command. That is always the way. I am no celebrated painter, and no man. You should sign them on the back as well, next to my name."

"Me? No, I am only finishing what you began."

Cornelia smiled. "What is a half-finished painting worth? Nothing. You must sign it. I insist. Two women conscripted to paint the same portrait. A rarer occurrence is hard to imagine. Or try the trick I do sometimes. Paint yourself into the portrait."

"How do you manage that?"

"In a reflection. A vase, a silver plate, a window. It is not so difficult. The key is to make it well hidden, impossible to see unless you know exactly where to look."

Mira smiled. "I have done the same in prayer books I illuminated."

"Ah?"

She nodded. "I conceal my name in a thicket of pen strokes, or I use my face in an illustration. Only I know that my mark and my image is there. But there is always the chance that one day, someone else will find them."

"Then you know exactly how I feel."

"Does anyone ever discover what you have done?"

"Of course. And my patrons are always amused by it. They find it clever, charming. An artist should leave her mark upon her work, whether she signs it or not."

Mira smiled. Then, because she couldn't help herself, she eyed the bottles lined up on a low table by the bed.

"Do you have bark of the willow there? Lavender oil? Poppy milk?"

"Yes, all of those things and more. Truly, the lord is a generous patron. He has spared no expense to care for me. He installed us in this home away from the household so I can rest in tranquillity. I only wish I had been able to complete my work."

"Perhaps you will recover your strength," Mira said encouragingly.

Cornelia raised her eyes to Mira's. "Only God knows. But I am weary of this pain. Each day brings new torment, and the nights are interminable. If I could hasten my own death, I would."

Mira held her gaze, remembering the day so long ago when Elena showed her how to harvest death caps in the forest. Sometimes it was merciful to take a life, Elena had said. Mira could still remember the rage that consumed her at Elena's words.

For the first time, she understood the compassion behind them.

14

Summer, 1505
Perpignan, Aragón
Pelegrín

PELEGRÍN SAVORED HIS FIRST experience at Perpignan's market. He had walked with his men past the livestock pens, the leather goods, the iron works, the bronzer, the cabinetmaker, the flax and rope purveyor, the merchants of oil, salt, wine, salted fish, silk, lace.

In a bookmaker's stall, he watched, amused, as the man cajoled potential customers, hawking his prayer books, holding them open and displaying the jewel-toned colors of the illustrations within.

The man approached Pelegrín. "Can I interest you in your own prayer book, my lord? Modified for your pleasure, with illustrations painted to your specifications?" He flipped through the pages of a book, holding it up for Pelegrín to see. His words were inflected with some guttural accent. He must be a northerner, Pelegrín guessed. Not from Flanders, but from someplace else like it, where people spoke as if they were scraping the words up from their lungs and coughing them out.

"Fine work," Pelegrín complimented him.

"Your likeness could go inside, painted specially by an artist trained in the Flemish style. See?" The bookmaker pointed at a small rectangle of black ink, within which was a woman depicted from the shoulders up, a figure with golden skin, wide, slanted gray-green eyes and hair the color of aged copper.

Pelegrín reached out and took the book, holding the page up to get a closer view of the image. It was so like his mother's face.

"Who is she?"

"The artist I speak of. She painted her own image there."

The woman he had seen in the streets. He realized a few days later why she had struck him so—because she had his mother's face. The eyes, the curve of the cheeks and the jaw—and he had seen a glimmer of coppery hair under her cap.

"What is her name?"

"Madame de Luz."

"Where can I find her?"

The man's demeanor changed. A guarded look came into his eyes. "I know not. She lately left the city."

"When will she return?"

"It is anyone's guess, my lord. Why might you be seeking her?"

"It is a family matter. Do you know where she went?"

There was no response. The bookmaker smoothed the cover of the prayer book and flicked an invisible speck of dust off the spine.

Pelegrín retrieved a sack of coins from his vest and gave it a little shake. "Are you sure there is nothing you can tell me of her?"

The bookmaker stared at the sack, his mouth quivering a bit. "They went to the countryside. To the home of some gentlewoman, that's all I know. There was a painting job that needed doing."

"They?"

"She and her husband and their little girl."

"Have you seen them? Her husband and daughter?"

"Never. But she said something once about the mountain folk, speaking of her husband's family. She talks high-born, herself."

Pelegrín thrust out some coins. "I will take that book, if it's for sale."

The man pocketed the coins. "Done."

Pelegrín spent the night awake. A thick beeswax candle burned on the table by his bed. The prayer book lay next to it. He opened it to the image of the woman and stared at it in the flickering light. Restless, he got up and crossed to the window, the book in his hand. His chambers overlooked the interior courtyard. Its stone floor was laid in an ornamental pattern that alternated black and white stones. In the moonlight the white stones glowed as if illuminated from within.

As soon as his ship was repaired and reloaded with the goods he had purchased here, he and his men would sail to Tortosa. Then they would ride through the arid plains north of the Ebro River all the way to Oto.

A constant thrum of worries about Alejandro plagued his mind. He had sent a squire and several knights to look after him, but with their parents both dead, he felt the burden of responsibility for his young brother all too keenly.

He opened the book again, tracing the outline of the woman's face with his finger. She did look like his mother. But that was not enough reason to change his plans, go searching through the countryside on a hunch. There was no more to this than hope, he realized. He would probably see his mother's face everywhere he went from now on. He might as well resign himself to it.

Pelegrín returned the book to the table, blew out the candle, and got into bed. He was ready to leave this place, bored of the interminable evenings with the merchant and the oddly contrived interactions with the man's daughter. She could not have been more than fourteen, he thought. Her face had a perpetually startled look. When he spoke, she flinched. He knew his stature, his deep voice, and the severe angles of his face made him intimidating, a quality he had inherited from his father. But he sometimes grew tired of the effect it had on others.

Her father was typical of the merchants who saw titles for their daughters as the crowning glory in their economic achievements. He wanted nothing more than the word 'baroness' in front of her name. And he was willing to pay handsomely for the privilege.

Pelegrín folded his hands under his head. He would string the merchant along, leave him with a reason to hope. But he would not commit to a bride until the rest of his family was accounted for.

15

April, 2016
Toulouse, France
Zari

ZARI SCRAPED HER CHAIR away from the desk and covered her eyes with her hands. The conference was just weeks away. And what did she have? A prayer book from Perpignan, a page in a Toulouse notary's record book, a design set in stone on a courtyard floor in Nay, and the Oto medallion she had found in the archives at Zaragoza.

Four precious bits of evidence. But none of them tied Mira directly to a painting. So what were they really worth?

She groaned aloud.

The portrait of the woman in blue was constantly in her head. Zari had e-mailed the high-resolution image of it to John Drake as promised, but she had heard nothing back from him. Whether he was simply busy or was embarrassed about their awkward encounter, she had no idea. For now, at any rate, it seemed she could no longer rely on his help.

The past few days she had turned her focus back to Toulouse, to the second record book of Jean Aubrey, the notary who had witnessed the contract Mira and Arnaud had signed with Lord de Vernier.

She scoured the internet for details about the chief archivist, who had repeatedly cancelled their appointments. Apparently he was a budding photographer who took evening courses at an art institute in Toulouse. She studied the course catalogue of the institute and made a few calls. It seemed an exhibition of student work would be on display next week, and the chief archivist was among those whose photography would be displayed.

Zari chewed her lip. She had never stalked anyone before. But she had never felt this desperate before, either.

On the appointed day, Zari boarded a bus and headed to Toulouse with a portfolio of Mira-related documents.

Outside the doorway of the art school, she smoothed her hair, checked the buttons of her crisp white blouse and eyed her clothing to make sure no smears of chocolate or crumbs from the *pain au chocolat* she had consumed earlier were visible on her olive-green jacket or black jeans. She had purposely jettisoned her usual vibrant colors in favor of a conservative ensemble. She could look vaguely European with a little bit of effort.

Just before entering the gallery where the student art show was hung, Zari put a hand to the hollow at the base of her throat and touched the tiny scallop shell that hung from a silver chain around her neck.

Here goes, she thought.

Silently chanting self-affirming mantras, she pushed the door open, portfolio in hand. The walls inside the gallery were hung with photographs of people, animals, urban landscapes, and the broad plains that dominated this part of France. A bar was set up in a corner. Clusters of people were scattered around the room, conversing in low tones.

Zari blazed into their midst with all the confidence she could muster. She took a glass of red wine from the bar counter and set off through the crowd.

She knew which photographs were his. They were stark urban landscapes that reminded her of the work of an American photographer, dead now, who rose to prominence in the 1970s. Scanning the faces in the room, she finally spotted the chief archivist, whose image she had studied in her online snooping sessions. He was a tall, thin man with skin the color of milk, his graying hair clipped close to his skull. He wore a blue and white checkered button-down shirt, dark pressed jeans, and polished black leather shoes.

Zari moved closer. She had learned that a big smile was often greeted with suspicion in France, so she maintained an expression that she hoped conveyed sober interest. Approaching one of his works, she peered at it critically.

"It has the air of an Arlo Winfield," she remarked to no one in particular.

The chief archivist turned to her in surprise. "Thank you," he said. "That is a great compliment. He is one of the artists who inspires my work."

"I can tell. Those who have gone before us can be quite inspiring."

He nodded, eyeing her. "What accent is that? Swedish?"

She smiled. "Now it is my turn to thank you. I am American, but I am happy to be taken for a Swedish woman."

There was an unmistakable gleam of interest in his eyes. "What brings you to the exhibition? I'm sure you did not simply stumble upon it. This gallery is well off the tourist routes."

"Actually, it was you."

He looked startled. "Me?"

She nodded. "I have been wanting to meet you for some time."

A look of guarded pleasure came over his face. "And why would that be?"

"I am, I think, a lot like you. A lover of art and history."

His eyes widened slightly at that, but her next words chased the light out of them.

"I'm on the trail of a great artist, a woman who once spent time in Toulouse. And I think you can help me find her."

"Why do you think I can help?"

"Because you are the chief archivist of the city's history."

Now he looked annoyed. "You're that American?"

She nodded. "Every appointment I made with you was cancelled. This was the only way I could think of to get your attention."

"I see," he said tightly.

A sudden panic clutched her chest. Had she just torpedoed any chance she'd ever had of getting back in the archives again?

"I apologize for the way I approached you," she said quickly. "I truly don't want to interfere with your event. I know you are being honored for your work today and it was quite bold of me to appear here."

Was it her imagination, or did he look a little less irritated?

Zari decided to be brave. "Can I come to your office tomorrow? I will only take a few moments of your time." She hefted the portfolio in the air. "I think you will appreciate what I have to show you."

A group of students approached, calling out the archivist's name.

"Fine," he said quickly, his eyes lingering on the portfolio a moment. "Meet me there tomorrow at two o'clock."

Feeling as if someone had just removed the cartilage from her knees, Zari wobbled through the crowd to the door.

16

April, 2016
Toulouse, France
Zari

Z
ARI FOUND A HOTEL in downtown Toulouse that was
clean and sparse. Then she went to a Monoprix store
and bought a prepared meal of couscous and chicken,
two bottles of mineral water, a toothbrush and toothpaste, a
stick of deodorant, a tiny bottle of laundry detergent, and an
Indian-print scarf. Hopefully the archivist wouldn't notice that
she was wearing the same clothes tomorrow. She would bungle
the scarf-tying, of course, but she wasn't trying to pass herself
off as French or even European now.

After eating her food at the small desk near the window, she
lay on the bed, half-watching an American television drama
dubbed into French. Her mobile buzzed with an incoming video
call. It was her mother.

"Mom! How are you?"

"Great, honey." Portia beamed at her. "Obsidian and I have two more scuba diving classes in the practice pool and then we head down to Monterey for our first dive in a couple of weeks."

"Do you feel ready to tackle the ocean?"

"We won't be diving very deep, not much deeper than the pool, and we've practiced everything a million times, so I'm not worried."

Zari's chest constricted at the thought of her mother entering the cold, murky waters of Monterey Bay, loaded down by weights, an oxygen tank, and other assorted gear.

"How are things there?" Portia asked. "How's your neighbor doing?"

"Monsieur Mendieta? He's fine. He even lets me help carry his groceries upstairs for him. I told him Mendieta is a family name for us, too, and he said his people originally came from a town in Spain just over the border from St. Jean de Luz. I told him I'd find out where our Basque ancestors came from."

"Your dad was the one who collected genealogical information. He had a file going for a few years and I know he talked to some of my cousins about the Mendieta history at family reunions. You should start with him."

"I bet he threw that file away the day you divorced," Zari said darkly. "I doubt he would even remember it."

"He'd appreciate a call regardless of the reason, honey."

"I used to call him a lot." Zari got up from the bed and walked to the window. "I just gave up after a while."

"Try again."

"Mom, you're so forgiving. He was such a jerk to you. To us."

"That was a long time ago. If I had hung onto my anger all these years I would have keeled over by now. I've never been one to focus on the past, Zari. I live in the now. The past is history. Tomorrow's a mystery. Today is a gift..."

"...That's why we call it the present. I know, I know."

"You laugh at all my sayings, but you secretly love them."

"Lately they've been getting me through a lot of rough patches," Zari agreed. "But for the time being, just to keep my own sense of balance intact, I'm going to avoid calling Dad. So who else could tell me about the Mendietas?"

"I have a second cousin who used to hand-draw family trees and bring them to gatherings. Your father got a lot of the Mendieta information from her. She lives in Oregon now, though. Way out in the middle of nowhere near a place called Wallowa Lake. I'll see if I can track down contact information for you."

The next afternoon when Zari was ushered by the grim-faced receptionist into the chief archivist's office, he did not stand to greet her. Instead, he stayed seated behind his desk and waved her into a chair.

"Now that you've got my attention, you had better show me what's so important," he said, his eyes stony. "And quickly. I don't have much time for you, I'm afraid."

She swallowed, pulling a handful of papers from her portfolio. Images of the Fontbroke College painting, Laurence's portrait of the merchant family, and the painting of the woman in the blue dress. Mira's miniature self-portraits, one with the words 'Mira, painter and servant of God' written in tiny Latin script around it. Photos of Arnaud's mark on the backs of the panels. The prayer book image with Mira's inscription, 'Mira illustrated this book.' The mortuary roll with the signatures of Mira, Marguerite de Oto, the Sacazars. Mira and Arnaud's marks on the walls of the cave in Aragón. The Oto family trademark and the corresponding medallion in the Fontbroke College portrait. The design on Carlo Sacazar's ring in the merchant family portrait—and in the stone courtyard of his home.

The archivist inspected the documents one by one in silence, then raised his eyes to Zari's.

"Mira de Oto was an artist who lived and worked in this area five hundred years ago," she said with conviction. "It was here, in the notary Jean Aubrey's record book, that I found evidence that Mira was married to Arnaud de Luz. He made the panels for the paintings I've shown you. I need more evidence of Mira's life and work, and that's why I have to see Jean Aubrey's other book. Forgive me for the way I arranged this meeting, but I am almost out of time. I have to present evidence at a conference in Bordeaux soon. I had no choice."

He pushed back his chair and stood up, expressionless.

Zari felt her composure begin to crumble. Her cheeks were hot.

Without another word, he walked to the door.

Apparently her presentation had failed to impress him. The thought of looking him in the eye again was unbearable. She began gathering her papers together, wishing she could melt into the floor.

"Well?" he said. "Are you coming with me, or not?"

She choked back a cry of delight, snatched up her portfolio, and followed him out the door.

At a long metal table in the room where Zari and Laurence had seen Jean Aubrey's elaborate signature for the first time, an assistant laid the notary's record book in one of the miniature bean bag supports. The chief archivist pulled on a pair of latex gloves. Zari stood at his side.

"*Allons-y,*" he said. "Let's go." With great care he lifted the worn leather cover of the book.

The parchment pages were stained, some of them clearly beyond readability.

"Water damage?" Zari asked.

He nodded. "And more. This book has been through hell."

Delicately he slid a narrow metal tool with a pointed edge between two pages and separated them.

"We can't open the book all the way," he explained. "It would stress the spine too much. That's why we haven't digitized the contents."

Zari bent down and tilted her head, examining the pages.

"Each notary had his own mark, you see," he explained. "Some of them were quite ornate. In Toulouse at that time, there were a dozen or so very powerful families who ruled the city. This Lord de Vernier that you saw in the notary's other book was one of them."

"The notaries went from house to house, or sometimes set up a stall at the local market. The entries reflect that. A debt to be repaid, a sale of wool, an agreement to take a loan, a wedding dowry...they all appear randomly." He pointed to various entries. "See here, a contract for manufacture of shoes between a grain merchant and a shoemaker. Here, a contract for carpentry work between a merchant and a group of Cagot men."

"Cagots? The people who had to wear red badges?"

The archivist nodded. "It's an ugly history. Cagots who worked within the city walls weren't allowed to live inside Toulouse itself, so each night after work they had to leave. They had their own graveyards outside the city walls, too."

"But they could worship in the same churches as everyone else, with restrictions," Zari remembered. "What happened to them?"

"After the revolution, a group of Cagots managed to destroy most of the records about themselves in the city's municipal buildings. Eventually they vanished into the fabric of society. Their culture disappeared." He paused. "But we are here to talk about a notary, not Cagots. Sometimes, for a very rich merchant, a notary would be exclusive to him and even travel with him. Lord de Vernier seemed to prefer this notary, Jean Aubrey."

He turned the page. Zari's eyes were instantly drawn to the signatures at the bottom. There, next to the notary's mark, were four names: Lord and Lady de Vernier, Miramonde de Oto, and Arnaud de Luz.

Zari heard the thudding of her own heart and nothing else, staring at the words in disbelief. She had found Mira again. And this time, Mira had identified herself as an Oto, with a notary as witness.

The archivist glanced at her, the shadow of a smile on his face. "You are happy? There is something else, too. Some illustrations you will find interesting..."

His words bled together, buzzing in her ears. She just breathed in and out, tears blurring her vision. Once again she felt a tug of connection to the woman she had spent so many hours pursuing through layers of time and history.

Miramonde de Oto. The words seemed to float off the page and hover just before her eyes. All along she had harbored the belief that Mira wanted to be found. In this moment, it seemed her belief was grounded in truth.

The crumbling book before her bore the evidence.

17

Summer, 1505
Valley of Maury, France
Mira

IN THE STILL HOURS before dawn, Mira was tugged awake
by a sound, a piteous moan that threaded its way into her
consciousness. Drowsily, she sat up, listening in the dark.
There it was again, that tiny, insistent moan.

Rose.

She padded across the cool stone floor to Rose's room and
knelt by her bedside. The silver light of a three-quarter moon
illuminated Rose's tiny shape sprawled in the center of the
bed. Her nightdress was twisted around her hips, the coverlet
bunched around her ankles. Rose's face glowed with an eerie
luminescence in the moonlight. Mira frowned, put her palm to
the girl's forehead; it came away damp with sweat. She rested
a hand on Rose's chest, felt the furious pumping of her heart.

"Arnaud!" A jolt of terror overtook Mira. "Rose has a fever."

In a moment he was beside her.

"We need bark of the willow," he said. "I'll go to the kitchens and wake someone."

He was back in a few moments. "No one's about. I'll go to the servants' quarters and find a cook."

"No," Mira said. "Go to the artist's house in the field. She has what we need. I know she would share it."

While he was gone Mira did her best to comfort Rose. She poured water from a ceramic pitcher on a length of linen and folded it into a rectangle, then placed it on Rose's forehead. She took another cloth, wet it, and wiped Rose's limbs one by one. The girl lay still, silent except for those occasional tiny moans.

Where was Arnaud? Fear began to leach into Mira's mind. Fevers in a child this small came on like a quickly burning wildfire; one moment a small glowing ember and the next a towering flame.

Finally he returned with a small bottle and a ceramic jar.

"Bark of the willow and herb salve for her chest." He thrust the items at Mira.

She cradled Rose in one arm and administered the willow bark syrup.

"Go back to the kitchens and find some watered wine," she ordered.

He disappeared again. Mira smeared the salve on Rose's chest, then perched on the edge of the bed, not wanting her own body heat to increase the fever. For the first time since they arrived in this place, tears welled in her eyes. She sat staring at Rose as dawn approached, aching to hold the girl in her arms, to rock her and soothe her, to cure her of this agony.

When Arnaud returned and she tried to pour a little watered wine down the girl's throat, it was no use—Rose thrashed and moaned and spluttered, her breath coming faster and shallower with each passing moment.

Birdsong sounded in the courtyard. Mira realized dawn had bloomed in the sky. Rose's hair was dark with sweat, her cheeks a brilliant scarlet. Arnaud crossed his arms over his chest, taking in the sight of Rose's feverish little body with worried eyes.

"She's so small." His voice was ragged, barely a whisper.

He sank down on his knees next to the bed.

18

Summer, 1505
Perpignan, Aragón
Pelegrín

A FORTNIGHT PASSED. THEN another. Summer was at its end. Pelegrín's restlessness grew. Finally the ship was loaded, its decks washed, the damage it had sustained during the crossing from Naples mended with pine pitch, oil, and glue. He had done his best at diplomatically indicating interest in the merchant's daughter while remaining vague about his ultimate intentions.

The last morning, he checked the trunk that contained his few belongings. On top lay the prayer book. He pulled it out one more time to riffle through the pages. The small portrait of the pale-eyed woman stared out at him. So like his mother's image, so familiar. He traced the frame around the image, a cross-hatched pattern of Moorish designs. His finger came to rest on a series of lines and squares. He peered more closely at the drawing.

There were words within the maze of pen strokes, he realized. Letters had been cleverly inserted one after another inside the design.

"*Mira pinxit hunc librum,*" he read aloud.

Mira illustrated this book.

He flipped to the last page of the volume and studied the bookmaker's mark. Then he sprang up, clattered down the stairs, and burst out the door, leaving a trail of bewildered servants in his wake.

At the bookmaker's workshop, he banged on the door until a terrified servant answered. Without waiting, with no words of introduction, he pushed past the man and shouted for the bookmaker. It was early yet, not much past dawn, and the man appeared blearily tying a wrapper around his nightshirt.

"How can I be of service, my lord?" he said.

"The artist. Where did she go?" Pelegrín opened the book to Mira's image and pointed.

"To a great house in the countryside. I told you, my lord."

"Yes, but which great house?"

Pelegrín took a step forward, impatience plain on his face. The man shrunk back.

"It was a few days' journey away to the west, near a castle falling into ruin. In a valley planted with lavender. I remember that because she said she loved lavender, like her mother before her. I swear it to you, my lord."

Pelegrín shook some coins into the bookmaker's hand and left without another word.

19

Summer, 1505
Valley of Maury, France
Mira

LITTLE ROSE'S STIFFENING BODY lay before them, her skin taking on a milky pallor, the sheen of sweat fading from her brow. Mira's eyes burned with a searing pain that would not go away. Her training as a nurse had meant nothing in the end. She had been powerless to stop the fever raging inside Rose all night. It had swelled and festered like some furious beast, impervious to her ministrations. And it had dealt its death blow swiftly, so swiftly.

She smoothed Rose's nightdress back into place and tenderly lay the sheet over her again. Carefully she fitted herself next to Rose's small form, curling her arms around the girl, and began to weep. Arnaud knelt beside her, smoothing her hair.

They startled at the sound of footsteps in the hallway. A knock at the door.

Mira and Arnaud exchanged a bleak glance.

Their employers sent word via servants, along with a small sack of silver coins, that they were to leave immediately. The baron did do them the kindness of offering a spade with which to bury Rose and a mule to carry their burdens. They packed the mule and led him to a field that lay fallow, just past the lavender beds on the far side of the Van der Zees' home.

As Arnaud dug a hole under the baleful eye of the sun, Mira clutched Rose to her chest and stared unseeing at the little house, numb with grief. A movement within it startled her. She could just make out the form of Cornelia van der Zee's husband, framed in a window. He reached out and quickly pulled the shutters closed. Within a few moments he had shuttered each window that looked out over the field. Perhaps he feared that whatever killed Rose was capable of drifting across the fields and slithering into his home. Or perhaps, with his wife so close to death, he could not bear the sight of her own unfolding fate in the small, linen-wrapped corpse that Mira held in her arms.

She dropped her eyes, filled with despair at the thought of relinquishing her little girl. Their patrons had not even allowed her to bathe Rose with lavender water, so panicked were they that the illness would spread and fester within their walls. So now her tiny body would be laid unclean in a shallow grave and covered with soil, with no protective layer of pine or oak between her and the wriggling creatures of the earth. She gripped Rose's small form tightly, thinking of Deedit. First the father, then the mother, now the child. An entire family extinguished in the space of a few seasons. Why would God let such a tragedy occur? Why not at least spare Rose, innocent Rose? Tears welled in her eyes. She choked back a sob, bit the inside of her cheek, tasted blood.

The door of the small house opened and Cornelia's husband slipped out carrying a wooden chest. He lugged it across the field and laid it next to the hole that Arnaud was digging.

"My wife bade me bring you this," he said. "For the girl."

Mira searched the shuttered windows of the house, desperate to communicate her thanks. As if he knew her thoughts, the husband shook his head.

"Cornelia is poorly today. Even the light of day pains her."

"Thank her for us—please," Mira entreated him.

He bent and opened the chest. Inside was a layer of blue wool, upon it a hand-stitched silken doll with pearl eyes and hair made of yarn.

"She always wanted a child but we were never blessed. These are for your girl, to ease her passage into the heavens."

Tears blurred Mira's vision as she laid Rose gently in the chest and placed the doll beside her. The two men settled the chest into the ground and Arnaud spaded soil into the hole. Cornelia's husband helped cover it with stones.

The three of them stood silently for a few moments. A breeze carried the scent of roses from the garden. The sweet odor repulsed Mira. She took a breath to clear her head, then bent down and was violently sick.

"Mira!" Arnaud stepped forward and steadied her.

She was trembling.

"You should stay on," Cornelia's husband said to Arnaud. "Your wife is ill."

"We can't," Arnaud replied, jerking his head back toward the manor house. "They've ordered us out."

"But what if..." the man broke off, his eyes on the mounded stones. "Where will you go?"

"West. All the way to the sea, if the fates allow."

"The pilgrim's route would be safest for you, then. There's an abbey called Camon about a week's journey from here, near a market town named Mirepoix. That's where the road connects with the pilgrim's way. Your wife will find sanctuary with the nuns there until she's well enough to make the journey to the sea."

"You're very kind." Arnaud's voice faltered. He swallowed, ducked his head at the man in thanks, and reached for Mira. "It's time to go."

Mira stared vacantly at the dark clods of fresh earth Arnaud had dug from the ground, at the neat stack of stones on the tiny grave. Arnaud squeezed her hand.

"May God watch over you both," Cornelia's husband said.

He trudged back through the field to his house.

That afternoon they rested in a copse of juniper trees near a stream just off the roadside. Arnaud settled Mira in the shade and rolled up his cloak for a pillow.

A passing farmer driving an oxcart full of hay paused at the sight of them.

"Will this road take us to the pilgrim's route west?" Arnaud asked him.

"Aye, it's several days' journey from here."

"And there's a convent along the way?"

"Aye." He peered at Mira's prone form. "If you're in need of shelter, the farmers hereabouts will put up a couple like you, if you've a few coins to offer for their troubles."

He drove off.

"See?" Arnaud said, his voice soothing in her ear as the sway-backed oxen pulled their load away. "Soon we'll find shelter. Once you're recovered, we'll follow the pilgrim's route west to the river Pau and find a barge to float us to Bayonne."

He held her hand until she fell asleep.

Mira woke a little later feeling flushed and agitated.

"Stay back." She rolled away from Arnaud.

He shook his head. "Never. I'm not afraid of a fever."

"You should be." Her tongue felt thick and mossy. "It struck Rose down in one night."

"A child that small is a fragile thing. She couldn't fight it off."

Mira felt tears coming again. "What will become of us, Arnaud?"

"We're going to Bayonne, just as we planned," he said firmly. "We've lost our Rose. Now we've nothing to stop us."

A bluejay screeched in a branch overhead. Mira caught sight of its shiny dark eyes. It cocked its head at her and rasped, the scratchy timbre of its call burrowing into her brain.

She covered her ears with her hands and wept.

20

Summer, 1505
Valley of Maury, France
Pelegrín

PELEGRÍN AND HIS MEN cantered along the road, making
good time. The oppressive summer heat had waned. It
was a perfect day to travel.

When they got to the first farm in the valley, Pelegrín sent
one of the men to the farmhouse to make inquiries. It seemed
the house they sought was half a league farther along the road.
They resumed their journey, the horses sending fine yellow dust
into the air as they pounded through low, rolling hills that were
all planted in lavender.

Finally they saw it: a sand-colored stone house near a village,
set back from the road along a narrow lane. And beyond it, on
a stubby hill, the ruins of a castle.

Inside, Pelegrín asked the housekeeper to fetch Mira. At her
blank look, he pulled the prayer book from his vest and opened
it to the miniature image of his sister. The woman shrank away

and refused to speak, telling another servant to run upstairs and fetch their master. Soon the lord of the manor descended the stairs. He made an elaborate show of introductions and said he was loathe to stand and discuss anything. He invited Pelegrín to the sitting room and ordered refreshments.

Pelegrín fought off his impatience. He sat and waited while his host settled himself in the chair opposite.

"Now, what is the urgent matter you have come to inquire about?"

"This woman." Pelegrín held up the prayer book, opened to the page with Mira's likeness. "Mira. I heard she was in your employ."

"Ah, yes, indeed." Lord de Berral sucked in his breath and tut-tutted. "What a sad story. She was sent to us by another family as a portrait artist. Our own artist is infirm and cannot go on painting." He pointed to the image on the page. "This young woman proved to be an equal in talent. Or perhaps superior. But do not mention that to my wife if she appears."

He gestured at a portrait of himself and his wife that hung on the wall.

"Young Madame de Luz completed the work you see there. I would have had her paint another portrait or two for us, but it was not to be. Their daughter fell ill with a sweating sickness. She died, poor thing. Of course, we had no choice but to turn the couple out of our home." He leaned forward and his voice took on a conspiratorial tone. "My wife is quite nervous about the sweating sickness."

"And where did they go?" Pelegrín's voice was dangerously low.

"West. I know not where. Though once she said she painted for a patron called Sacazar in a market town in Béarn...what was its name?" Lord de Berral drummed his fingers on the arm of his chair. "Ah, yes—Nay. Perhaps that is where they went off to. I was surprised at the direction they chose, in truth, for I thought they would return to Perpignan."

A tingle of anger crawled up Pelegrín's neck. "When did this happen?"

"Not a fortnight ago. The father dug the girl's grave himself." Lord de Berral crossed one silk-clad leg over the other. "Sad business all around, I must say."

"De Luz is their family name. But what does Mira's husband call himself?"

The man snapped his fingers at a servant. "What was the name of the young artist's husband?"

"I know not, my lord."

"And the little girl?" Pelegrín asked, struggling to keep his voice even. "Do you know her name?"

The servant nodded. "Everyone knew Rose."

Before they left, Pelegrín walked to the site of the grave. The soil was dark where it had been overturned and patted down again, and it was mounded with a layer of stones. There was a rose bush twining along the low wall that surrounded the small house near the field. He plucked a handful of blooms from it and laid them on the grave.

Closing his eyes, he said a prayer for the girl's soul. Rose. His niece. Buried with no ceremony, nothing to memorialize her passing. A slow burn crept up his neck into his cheeks. For a moment he was overcome with rage. He longed to turn and enter the manor home again and run its master through with his longsword.

A faint breeze bathed his face with cool air. He gathered himself, breathing deeply, his lips moving as he resumed his prayers.

Mira and her husband had only one mule between them—they could not have gotten far. He and his men would track them down quickly. And then he would do what his father could not: welcome Mira into the family. If he could persuade her and her husband to return to Castle Oto with him, so much the better.

As he turned to go he saw a shadow move in a window of the little house. He shaded his eyes with a hand, trying to make out what it was.

But nothing revealed itself.

21

Summer, 1505
River Arazas, Aragón
Elena

WITH A BASKET OF mushrooms hooked over her elbow, Elena took Alejandro's hand and followed the men along the stream that twisted through the narrow valley. The dry crack of a branch rang out. Elena shook her head, frowning. The knights took no care where they stepped. But then they had never learned the ways of the mountain folk—they were city men, born and bred. What did they know of wilderness? The clanking weapons, high black boots, red leather armor—it all looked absurdly out of place here.

Further on, a wide meadow populated with ancient oaks spread out before them. Crumbling stone cottages rose up from the grass near the silty waters of the stream. Elena headed toward a tree whose branches drooped nearly to the ground, digging stick in hand. After a lifetime of foraging, she read the signs that nature provided as well as any scholar read Latin.

Sunlight broke through the wispy clouds overhead. Two great shadows moved across the grass. Elena squinted, peering up.

Griffon vultures. Guardians of kings. They ruled this canyon, their flat black eyes raking the forest and grass for movement, for any sign of illness or death. They circled endlessly, waiting to swoop down and strip a carcass to the bone, leave it bleaching in the sun. Elena had witnessed what they could do to a body. For that reason she always vowed that if she were injured in the mountains, she would drag herself under cover of the deepest woods, into the hollow of snarled tree roots or the lee of a boulder. She would rather take her chances with a bear or a wolf than these silently gliding agents of death making their bleak rounds in the sky.

She watched Alejandro and the knights explore the ruins in the sunlight. Arazas was a village of ghosts now. Elena had no memories of it, had left this place when she was a girl old enough to walk but not old enough to talk. Here in the shadow of a mountain, the village was returning to the earth stone by stone.

"Why does no one live here anymore?" Alejandro shouted, standing in the doorway of a half-ruined structure.

"The plague, my boy. It destroyed all but one in the town."

"Who was the one?"

"Me."

Alejandro fell silent, intrigued. He came to her side, watched her poke the stick into the soft soil. She rooted around briefly, felt resistance, and pried out a dense black truffle.

"How did you stop the plague from taking you?"

She shrugged. "The gods were smiling on me that day, I suppose. Keeping me on this earth for another purpose."

"What was that?"

"To take care of you." She smiled.

The boy looked doubtful. "What about all the other things you did before you came back here? Maybe you were kept on earth to do them."

"That's true. I've done quite a lot in my life. Traveled these mountains too many times to count."

A snow finch trilled a warning at them from the top of the oak.

"You've told me of all your adventures." Alejandro spread his legs wide, dug his heels into the earth. "I missed your stories when you went away. I used to tell mother I wished you lived with us always."

The corners of his mouth trembled and she knew he was holding back tears at the thought of his mother. He kicked a stone and watched it roll.

"What was your favorite adventure?" He looked up at her again. "The best of all?"

"The best of all? Now, that takes some thought." She pretended to mull it over. "I believe it was my summers with your sister Mira, at Belarac."

He looked confused. "I have no sister."

She squatted down so their eyes were level. "You do. She lived at the Abbey of Belarac as a child. Grew up without your mother at her side. But I did my best to love her as a mother would. Each summer, I tried."

"Will I ever see her?"

"You have seen her."

"When?"

"Remember the artist who came to paint your mother's portrait?"

"Yes."

"That's her."

He stared at her, astonished.

"What is her name?"

Elena picked up a glossy brown oak leaf and twirled it in her fingertips. "Miramonde. One who sees the world."

He was quiet a moment, his forehead puckered in a frown.

"Where is the portrait?"

"Mira has it." Elena had no idea if that was true. She hoped Mira and Arnaud were safely ensconced in some city dwelling, the portrait of Marguerite repaired and hanging on a wall in their home.

"If she is my sister, why did she never live with us?"

"The true answer to your question would take too long, and the knights come this way. When your brother Pelegrín returns, we will ask him to explain."

"Is he coming back soon?"

"It's my great hope. I know he would never forsake you."

A smile broke out on Alejandro's face. He stepped forward, his arms outstretched as if to embrace her, but at the sound of the knights' footsteps behind him, he let his arms fall back at his sides.

Elena felt a strange rush of tenderness and despair collide in her chest and squeeze her heart until it ached. The thin chain of the Oto necklace pressed into the flesh beneath her undergarments, each link of gold leaving an imprint on her skin. She was bound to this family, carried the same blood in her veins. There was no other choice but to wait by Alejandro's side for Pelegrín to reappear and assume the role of baron. She could only hope that he would show more kindness to those under his thumb than his father ever had.

The full moon of high summer had come and gone. She had missed her own wedding. Sadness tugged at her with every thought of Xabi, but it was eclipsed by the profound relief she felt at being extricated from his clamorous, gossiping family. The thought of being forced to live within their walls for the rest of her days—it made her shudder. Brother Arros had often remarked to her that she had more in common with the wild creatures of the mountains than with her own kind. It was true. There was a wildness in her that would never be tamed.

The thin wavering cry of a wolf pierced the air. It floated into the valley on a northerly breeze.

"Wolves," Alejandro said, his eyes wide.

"Don't fret, my boy. There's nothing for them here."

Overhead a griffon vulture circled lower, its wings dark against the blue sky. Elena could feel its sharp gaze upon them. The dry oak leaves around them rustled in the wind, sounding like a thousand whispering voices. Uneasy, she slipped an arm around Alejandro's shoulders and drew him close.

The guards were nearly upon them now.

22

May, 2016
Bordeaux, France
Zari

ZARI SIGHED, FLIPPED OVER on her stomach, shut her eyes. Sleep was elusive tonight. She had never dreaded a presentation with such intensity, and now here she was, twelve hours before showtime, wide awake when she should have been recharging her brain and body with healing sleep. The rock-hard couch probably had something to do with her uneasiness, too. The door to the bedroom was shut; Laurence at least was getting some rest.

When Zari had reserved this place a few months ago, a one-bedroom was exactly what she wanted. Wil was her intended companion for the space. But several days ago, he had called her from Croatia. Filip had developed an infection from a cut on his leg that had gone unnoticed for too long. He had been sent to a Croatian hospital to get intravenous antibiotics. Wil would stay at Filip's side and see him safely home to Amsterdam when he was ready to travel again. Zari could not fault him for that. It was the right thing to do.

Still, there was a hollow feeling in her chest. Wil's presence at the conference was something she had banked on. The idea of his slate-blue eyes gazing steadily at her from the audience made the whole thing seem a little more palatable. But now she would have to steel herself and forge ahead without him. Besides, she had Laurence. She was lucky to have a supporter in Bordeaux, no matter who it was.

Zari got up and padded into the kitchen. She had heard nothing from Wil in two days, but his last text reported that Filip was getting the antibiotics he needed to kick the infection. Though it was late, Wil was probably killing time in a hospital waiting room, bored out of his skull. She impulsively decided to call him. His mobile rang twice, then a woman answered in Dutch.

"Hello?" Zari said hesitantly, confused. "I'm calling for Wil."

The woman switched to unaccented English. "This is Hana. Filip's sister."

There was a short silence while Hana's words sunk in.

"Hello, Hana. How are you?" Zari stumbled over the words, feeling idiotic.

"Not good," Hana snapped. "My brother's life is in danger."

"What?" Zari's breath caught in her throat. "Oh, no. I'm so sorry."

"He told me it was you who gave him the idea to do this trip." Hana's voice was like ice.

Zari sank onto a bar stool, stunned. She heard the muted voice of a man speaking Dutch in the background and Hana's sharp retort.

"Zari?" Wil's familiar voice filled her ear.

"Wil!"

"Why are you calling so late?" His tone was tight and distant.

"I...I thought you might be bored and needing a chat."

"Bored? Filip is in crisis. It's crazy here."

Zari felt as if the breath had been knocked out of her lungs. "Wil, I had no idea how bad things are. Your text said..."

"Things have changed," he interrupted. "Filip isn't responding to the antibiotics."

She heard him talking in Dutch again, an undercurrent of anger in his voice. A woman—it must have been Hana—replied, her voice rising, the words coming faster and faster.

"Look, Zari, I'll call you later." His voice was curt, formal, the voice of a stranger. "Hana's mobile died and she's using mine to text with her family. Filip's parents will arrive tonight but until then Hana and I are watching over him."

"Of course, Wil. I'm so sorry and I'll be thinking of Filip every minute. Please..."

Before she could finish, Wil ended the call.

Did Wil think Filip's infection was her fault, too? Tears began to gather in Zari's eyes.

Oh, God. She dropped the mobile on the kitchen counter, staring at it in horror. *What have I done?*

23

Summer, 1505
Abbey of Camon, France
Mira

THE DAYS BLURRED TOGETHER into one long, nauseating ordeal. Arnaud walked alongside the mule from dawn to dusk while Mira slumped in the saddle, staring blankly ahead. The clop of the mule's hooves blended with the sound of crickets chorusing on the roadside. She felt hot, then cold, then hot again. A searing pain throbbed in her head. The thought of food made her gag. And the tears came without warning, roiling up in her chest and spilling out.

Mostly she closed her eyes, shutting out the bright sunlight, wishing for a mantle of fog to descend, to hide her from the world, to cocoon her in layers of soft gray oblivion.

Arnaud said it was a sickness brought on by sorrow, and only time would mend it.

They plodded past the jutting branches of pine trees and the tall spires of junipers, past rolling fields of lavender, flax, barley, and millet. Past winding rivers, market towns on hillsides, the occasional manor house or farm. They saw grain merchants driving oxcarts; they fell in with mule trains bound for points west and north; they lodged in farmhouses and inns along the roadside.

Mira caught herself straining for the sound of Rose's laughter, the sudden infectious joy of it rippling in her ears. Her sweet round face, her little mouth curved in an 'o' of surprise or pulled wide in a radiant grin. The life, the promise, the energy contained in that sturdy body, had all vanished.

She was simply gone.

One night Arnaud paid a farmer's wife to let them sleep in a cottage on the edge of a field that was marked with deep furrows from the plow but had never been planted. Arnaud fell asleep immediately on the thin woolen pallet lent to them by the farmer's wife. Mira could not get comfortable.

She went to the small window overlooking the field and pushed open the shutter, breathing in cool evening air that smelled of earth and straw. The moon sent a wash of silvery light over the field, illuminating a lone oak that stood at its center. Under the oak was a tall stone reminiscent of the granite markers the mountain people erected in summer grazing meadows.

Mira stared at the furrows of soil radiating from the tree, wondering why the field had never been planted. Perhaps the seed stock had been plundered by rodents. Perhaps a disease had taken root in the soil. She glanced at the stone again. Perhaps the farmer met with some disaster after he carved those long gashes in the soil—and that was his tombstone.

She shuddered, imagining Deedit in her unmarked grave outside the walls of Toulouse. Cagots did not merit coffins or tombstones. No, Deedit was just one of a jumble of bodies in an earthen hole, a reeking scar that was dug up and filled in without end. At least Rose, poor sweet Rose, rested in a box of solid wood.

Mira backed away from the window, sank to her knees, curled up on the pallet next to Arnaud. He reached out sleepily and held her in silence. Tears slid down her cheeks. Desperately she tried to regulate her breathing, to regain control. She wondered if she would ever recover from her grief. Was she now doomed to twist the sight of every good thing in this world into something grim?

The woman she used to be was apparently gone, lost in the lavender fields, still watching over Rose. This shell of a person was some other Mira. She felt sorry for Arnaud. He was mourning the loss of Rose, too, and now he was saddled with a weeping, useless wife who could no longer sleep or eat, whose sound mind had deserted her somewhere between the curving shores of the Mediterranean Sea and the lavender fields of the Valley of Maury.

One morning after a few hours on the road, they came upon a little rise. A long, narrow valley opened up before them. A high-walled structure of dun-colored rock built atop a small hill was visible at the far end of the valley.

"This is the place. Camon. We'll stay until you're recovered," Arnaud promised. "And when you're ready, we'll follow the pilgrim's way west."

She said nothing, just watched the shimmering green fields waver in the sunlight and listened to the call of songbirds in shrubs alongside the lane. At the base of the hill where the abbey stood, the road forked. The more northerly route was marked with a stone bearing the scallop shell symbol of the pilgrim's way.

"See, Mira?" Arnaud pointed at the marker. "That's how we'll go to Bayonne. We'll follow the shells and stars all the way to the sea."

Mira looked absently for a moment in the direction he indicated, then bowed her head.

When they reached the abbey's tall iron gates, she slumped in the saddle while Arnaud talked in low tones with the gatekeeper, her eyes fixed on a tiny yellow and black bird that busied itself building a nest in the stone wall.

In the convent's infirmary, several elderly women lay on straw-filled pallets. Only one, whose breath was labored and who periodically unleashed an ominous gurgling cough, seemed gravely ill.

Mira lay with her eyes closed while a young woman in a novice's habit and veil washed her body tenderly with lavender water, then dressed her in a rough, clean flax shift and tucked a wool blanket over her.

"When was the last time you bled?" the woman asked quietly.

Mira thought. It had been in Perpignan, soon after they arrived.

The woman laid a hand on Mira's belly and smiled.

"I think it is no illness you suffer from," she said.

The realization came over Mira like a thunderclap. Why her ill feeling never left, why she had no appetite, why she felt such bone-crushing fatigue—all the symptoms pointed to one obvious explanation. Another life grew within her.

The image of Rose's face came to her then. She took a long breath. Her exhalation came out with a raw, ragged sob. The woman's eyes grew round and she withdrew her hand.

Mira turned her head to the wall. This was what she had yearned for since she wed Arnaud. But all she could think of was little Rose. No baby could replace her. The grief she carried was like a stone slung around her neck. It would dangle there, pressing against her heart, for the rest of her days.

The woman scraped back her stool.

"Please." Mira gathered herself, wiped the tears from her eyes. "Do not inform my husband. I wish to tell him myself. We only lately lost a child, you see. It is a shock. It is all of it a shock."

A look of understanding passed between them.

"As you wish. Sleep now, and in the morning I will have you taken to a room of your own in the convent dormitory. There is no point having you stay on amongst the ill if your condition is a happy one, but a rest from the attentions of your husband will also do you good. He will be comfortable in the guesthouse. We shall tell him you are recovering well and simply in need of quiet."

When she had gone, Mira regarded a faded fresco that adorned the opposite wall. The paint had peeled away in spots and soot had darkened much of it, but the overall composition was still intact. She went through a mental list of the materials one would need to restore it. Vermillion, charcoal dust, yellow ochre, iris flower, moss, white lead, lapis lazuli.

Her eyelids fluttered. *Linseed oil*, she thought. *Gold dust. Brushes made of marten hair.* A sudden memory of Elena and their days spent gathering herbs and plants rushed back to her. She caught hold of it, forcing her grief aside, recalling tiny details like the twitch of Elena's long black braid as she strode through meadow grasses in search of asters and lilies, the scent of woodsmoke from the fires she built under Elena's watchful eyes, the digging stick Elena carried to prod roots and tubers from the soil.

The dull leaden feeling that had pinned her to the earth for days eased. A curious sensation of lightness overcame her. Hands cupping her belly, her mind transfixed by the memory of pouring and mixing and scraping and brushing, by the mingling scents of oil and oak and minerals and plants, Mira drifted out of consciousness.

24

May, 2016
Bordeaux, France
Zari

ZARI AND LAURENCE STOOD together in the dim light just offstage, waiting for Zari's turn at the podium. The academic who was speaking, an Italian whose expertise on early Renaissance Florentine painters was unparalleled, gave his closing remarks. Zari took a deep breath, fighting off the butterflies that batted against her rib cage, desperate for air. She had not slept at all after speaking to Hana and Wil. A sick feeling had taken root in her belly. The thought of facing an audience normally inspired her, but right now it filled her with dread.

"You need some color." Laurence pulled a burnt-orange silk scarf from her handbag and, stepping forward, knotted it expertly around Zari's throat. She smiled. "Good. You are wearing my necklace."

Since Toulouse, Zari had not removed the scallop shell necklace that Laurence had gifted her last summer. This morning, after some hesitation, she also slipped on the matching shell earrings Wil gave her at Christmas.

Zari forced a smile. "I'm afraid to take it off now. I need all the luck I can get."

Laurence reached out and took her hands. "You will get through this," she said in a fierce low voice. "There is nothing you can do about Filip or Wil at this moment. You are here for Mira."

Zari squeezed Laurence's hands, smiling her gratitude. Then her mobile began buzzing in her pocket. She fished for it, hoping it was Wil. But it was Gus. She pressed 'decline.' Gus's latest report on the antics of her niece and nephew could wait.

The Italian professor finished his presentation. A few questions were posed and answered. Polite applause filled the auditorium.

It was time.

Zari gathered her things and headed to the stage. Though she normally enjoyed giving presentations, today she was stricken with exhaustion, heartache, and worry. She wondered how she would ever stumble through this.

Behind the podium, Zari ran her eyes over the assembled crowd, quailing for a moment. A tremor began to flicker in her left knee. Then she took a long breath, drew herself up, felt energy coiling in the muscles along her spine. She could almost hear her mother's voice: *Channel your courage, Zari.*

She introduced herself, injecting each word with as much power as she could muster. The atmosphere in the room grew charged with anticipation. Reassured by the confidence she was projecting, Zari began to relax.

One by one she pulled up the slides showing all the evidence of Mira's existence: the portraits, the mortuary roll, the prayer books, the underdrawings, the carvings from the cave in Aragón. The Oto trademark that was identical to the medallion around the waist of the woman in the Fontbroke College portrait; the ornate design that appeared on Carlo Sacazar's ring and also on the floor of his stone courtyard. And finally, the pages from the Toulouse notary's books. When the slide showing the translation of the second agreement appeared on the screen, Zari read it aloud, her voice clear and strong.

"'I, Miramonde de Oto, at the wish and consent of the two of us together, bestow myself in labor and in my works to you, Lord Esteven de Vernier, merchant and lord of Toulouse, to produce portraits of you and your family painted in oil, with fine colors and with blue. Said portraits will be painted on panels of dry, good quality Pyreneen oak constructed by my husband, Arnaud de Luz....'"

The room was hushed as she finished reading the words.

The next slide showed the signatures of Miramonde de Oto, Arnaud de Luz, Lord and Lady de Vernier, and the notary Jean Aubrey.

Excited whispering rose up around the auditorium.

Zari smiled and pressed her clicker again. She had saved the best for last.

A sixteenth-century illustration appeared on the screen. It showed a noble couple, both dark-haired and dressed in various shades of blue.

"These are Lord and Lady de Vernier, who contracted with Mira de Oto to paint their portraits. The archives of Toulouse contains an illustrated book showing the images of leading merchant families of the time."

Next, she clicked to the portrait of the woman in the blue dress.

"This painting was recently sold at auction in London. I believe the subject is also Lady de Vernier. On the back of this painting appears the mark of Arnaud de Luz. His mark is on the back of Fontbroke College's portrait of an unknown woman—and on the portrait of the merchant family owned by my colleague Laurence Ceravet."

Zari clicked to the last slide, which showed all three of the portraits side by side.

"As you just learned, Arnaud de Luz was married to Mira de Oto. He made the panels for all of these portraits. The stylistic similarities between the works are obvious."

She turned to the audience, took a deep breath, and let it out. "The findings I have shared with you today all point to one conclusion: Mira de Oto was a masterful portrait painter of the early Renaissance who worked in what is now Southern France and northern Spain."

Zari fell silent.

There was a pause, and then hands shot into the air all over the room.

The questions flew at her in quick succession, and she answered them with the assurance of one who knows her subject intimately. The stress she had felt before the presentation melted away. She felt completely at ease. Until a familiar voice rang out.

"Miss Durrell, you neglected to mention the one factor that not only complicates your conclusion but likely renders it impossible."

The crowd quieted again.

Dotie Butterfield-Swinton. The feeling of joyful relief that had overcome Zari as soon as her presentation ended was replaced by dread. Her exhaustion flooded back. She put a hand on the podium for support.

"The much more likely possibility," he went on, "is that the paintings you refer to were made by Bartolomé Bermejo. At my side is the foremost European expert on Bermejo himself, and while his English is not up to the level of this discussion, let me say that he vehemently disagrees with Ms. Durrell's theory."

The rotund, dark-haired man at Dotie's left glowered at Zari.

She felt her confidence waver. Then she caught sight of Laurence standing at the back of the room. Gratitude pricked her heart. Laurence had been right: this moment was for Mira, and Zari would be damned if anyone stole the spotlight from her.

"Are you truly not going to address the issue of Bermejo?" Dotie needled her. "His hallmarks are all over the paintings you discuss."

A buzz of chatter broke out around the room.

"Professor Butterfield-Swinton, you are welcome to explain the details of your own theory on your own time," Zari shot back, "but I would never dream of doing it for you. The topic at hand is Mira de Oto, a Renaissance-era artist who has not yet claimed her rightful place in history."

She stared back at him, the words reverberating in the air between them.

"My colleague's presentation on Spanish Renaissance artists is tomorrow, and I urge everyone in the room to attend," he said finally, in a clipped tone that indicated his tolerance had been sorely tested. "We have the results from tests done on the painting of the merchant family that will prove most interesting to you all, especially in light of Ms. Durrell's claims about the origins of the work. In addition, you might be intrigued to learn that I am the owner of that new find Ms. Durrell mentioned. The portrait of a woman in a blue dress."

Zari stared at him, flabbergasted. The overhead lights suddenly felt hot on her face. One of her knees buckled. She reached for the glass of water on the podium in front of her and drained it.

"Furthermore," Dotie went on, "the painting is in the process of analysis as we speak. Like the other portraits Ms. Durrell discussed, this one bears several hallmarks of the master Bermejo's work. Particularly the detailed backgrounds. So if you are seeking the truth about what Ms. Durrell claims, you might do well to attend my talk tomorrow. A translator will be on hand, I assure you, so that you get the full benefit of my Spanish colleague's expertise."

The Spanish scholar gave one sharp nod at that, his dark eyes fixed on Zari in a disapproving glare. Dotie sat down and crossed his arms over his chest.

The audience turned to look at Zari. She felt her lips begin to quiver.

"Are there any other questions about what I presented today?"

Her voice sounded thin and high, like a little girl's.

There were none.

25

May, 2016
Bordeaux, France
Zari

ARI WALKED UNSTEADILY OFFSTAGE, completely shattered. She leaned against a wall, closed her eyes, and tried to gather the shreds of her courage. *It could have been worse,* she told herself. After all, she hadn't thrown up or passed out in front of all those people.

But now she would have to face them for the duration of the conference, enduring their stares and silent judgement while she watched Dotie and his Bermejo guru trot out their theory to anyone who would listen.

Her mobile buzzed again. Gus.

Zari's temper flared suddenly. Gus knew nothing of the stress she dealt with in her professional life. He was a stay-at-home dad whose biggest challenges were coordinating carpools and making lunches. He could call her whenever he wanted, but she wasn't always available, especially if she was busy being publicly humiliated by a man whose smoothly modulated voice sounded like that of a crumpet-eating member of the British royal family.

She snatched up her mobile and took the call.

"Yes, Gus, what is it?"

"Mom's had an accident."

Her irritation evaporated. "What?"

"She and Obsidian were driving back from their diving lesson in Monterey and got in a car accident on the coast highway."

Zari's bones turned to rubber. She slid down the wall and collapsed on the floor, staring dumbly at her splayed legs, a hundred questions crowding her mind.

"She's going to be okay, Zari," Gus went on before she could speak. "But she's got broken ribs and whiplash."

"What about Obsidian?" Zari's voice was a dull rasp.

"He's in much better shape. Nothing broken, at any rate. He'll have some monster bruises, though."

"Listen, I'm coming back. I'll book the next flight I can get on."

"What about that conference? Isn't it happening now?"

"Yes, but I can leave."

"What? No, Zari, stay there. Mom's in stable condition, on a lot of pain meds. She's going to move in with us for a few weeks. It'll be fine."

"How can you say it'll be fine?" Tears slid down her cheeks. "Can I talk to her?"

"She is so drugged up right now she wouldn't recognize your voice."

"I have to come home." Zari's voice broke. "She needs me."

"Look, if she were dying, I would say get your ass back here. But she's going to be fine. It's not even like you could help that much if you were here, because our guest room is going to be booked, the couch is really uncomfortable, and we both know my wife can only take so much of the Durrell family."

"Gus, I feel so useless. What am I even doing here?" Zari whispered. "This isn't my world. I should be in California, where I belong."

"*So* not true. You belong right where you are. Besides, you know exactly what you're doing," he said briskly. "You're getting Mira de Oto out of the shadows. Don't stop now."

Zari succumbed to sobbing for a moment.

"Pull yourself together," her brother ordered. "You know what happens when you really start crying. It's a train wreck."

Zari fought to stabilize her breath. "Don't tell your sister what to do," she said, smiling a little.

"That's the spirit. Now get back out there and kick some asses."

Zari skulked to the women's room and spent fifteen minutes rinsing her face with cold water, taking deep yoga breaths, and doing damage control with tinted moisturizer and lipstick. She regarded herself in the mirror one last time before heading to the reception. Her eyes were still red-rimmed but the puffiness had gone down. The dark raspberry lipstick she'd applied might serve to distract attention from the top half of her face. She made a tentative attempt at a happy expression. The hollow wisp of a smile that emerged made her look like a demented escapee from a Halloween frightfest.

Turning away from the mirror, she steeled herself.

At the reception, she scanned the room feverishly for Laurence. The crowd parted before her as if she glowed with radiation or had the plague. People seemed to eye her with curiosity, amusement, disdain. She told herself it was too easy to misinterpret the stares of strangers as judgement, especially when one was a paranoid wreck whose entire life was in the process of blowing up.

Before she could find Laurence, her path was blocked by a slender man about her height whose skin had the reddish-brown gleam of mahogany. He held a glass of red wine in each hand.

"Zari Durrell?" He offered her a glass.

"Yes." She accepted the wine gratefully.

"I enjoyed your presentation very much." His English was tinged with a slight accent that she tentatively identified as German. "I'm even more intrigued with Mira now than I was when I first heard her name."

"When was that?"

"Amsterdam. My boss and I sat next to you during John Drake's talk."

Zari peered at his name tag.

"Andreas," he said, sticking out a hand. "Andreas Gutknecht."

She took the proffered hand and shook it.

"I remember now." Zari felt as if she'd aged ten years since that September day. "And you e-mailed me about the portrait of the lady in blue."

He nodded.

"It was a great lead—at least I thought so, until today." She took a sip of wine. "So what got you interested in Mira?"

"I'm an art broker. My boss is an art dealer; he specializes in Renaissance-era portraiture." He handed her his card. "We hire art historians and conservators as consultants when we're considering purchasing a painting with dubious origins, or to verify that a painting was indeed made by a master."

"That sounds expensive."

"Once, my boss sold a painting that had been attributed to Raphael by an expert. Then analysis proved it was a copy made two hundred years later. He was sued by the collector who had purchased the painting. *That* was expensive. It makes far more sense to analyze the paintings before he sells them to collectors."

"Which explains why you're here, in a perfect storm of academics and conservationists."

"Exactly," he said. "Great networking."

Over his shoulder, she saw Dotie and his Bermejo expert friend holding court, surrounded by a rapt group of junior academics. She dragged her eyes away and focused them firmly on Andreas.

"So that Bermejo theory...?" He raised an eyebrow.

She took a sip of wine. "I think he pretty much summed it up out there. Not much more to report from my end."

"It would be quite a career boost for him, I imagine, if these portraits turn out to be the work of Bermejo."

"He's well-connected; these are his people. Bermejo is lucky to have him for an advocate. Mira, on the other hand—well, I'm all she's got. And I'm a fish out of water in this world."

"I understand better than you might think."

"Why's that?"

His eyes crinkled in amusement. "Did you not notice that I'm quite brown-skinned for a Swiss man?"

"I've never been to Switzerland so I'm clueless about the physical characteristics of the Swiss," Zari confessed.

He laughed. "They're a bit short in the melanin department. I was adopted. When I was very young, my father was an administrator at international schools all over the world, but he died when I was twelve and my mother and I returned to the town in Switzerland where she had grown up. In my school there, I was the only brown face in the room."

"That must have been tough."

"You know what I learned, though?" Andreas' expression grew sober. "Sometimes being an outsider has its advantages."

"I'll try to keep that in mind."

"Mira may not have a following yet. But there is a market developing for art by women of this era. Of course, much of what exists is unsigned, or buried in museum vaults and dusty attics."

"That's my line," Zari said, unable to repress a wan smile. "But as you heard, my theory has its opponents and they're quite influential. As much as I want to keep digging into those vaults and attics, I doubt I'll get any more grant money to keep going with my research—especially after today."

Andreas studied her a moment, swirling his wine. "Grant money isn't my area. But you might be the kind of researcher my employer will support. Have you ever considered a private contract?"

"It's not exactly in line with my career trajectory. I have to start applying for professorships." Her mind turned to Wil. Then to her mother. Then back to Wil. "I don't know. I would have to learn more about the opportunity and the compensation."

"I think you would find the compensation more than adequate after a post-doc salary. Get in touch with me and we'll talk about the possibilities." He raised his glass, which was empty. "Time for another. You?"

She shook her head. "I've had enough, thanks."

Across the room, Dotie's eyes caught hers.

The look of triumph on his face was unmistakable.

26

Summer, 1505
Abbey of Camon, France
Mira

MIRA WAS MOVED INTO a small room that overlooked the convent's rectangular courtyard, directly opposite the guesthouse, the stables, and the gates that led to the road. A tiny window covered with a wooden shutter let in a bit of light and air. Occasionally she heard the sounds of muted voices and footsteps in the courtyard, the soft clang of the gates, the strike of hooves on stone.

For several days she mostly slept. She ate plain meals of porridge, bread, and barley soup that were delivered by a young novice nun with rosy cheeks and a ready smile. Slowly her strength returned, though memories of Rose still sent her into a fog of grief. She resigned herself to accommodating the dark thoughts. The sadness had worn a groove in her heart, a tender spot where Rose's absence throbbed day and night. It was part of her now.

Though it felt strange to be apart from Arnaud, Mira was relieved that he had a respite from her grief. She had seen something in his eyes these last few days that frightened her—not the exasperation that he displayed when he was displeased with her, but something else. A flatness, a distance in his gaze.

She had asked too much of him. Now that Rose was gone and a new baby was coming, they could make a new life together, she resolved. They could put the sorrows of the past behind them.

On the third or fourth morning—she had lost track of the days—Mira awoke feeling rested and refreshed, her mind still caught on a dream. In it, she had been walking through the lavender fields near the place where Rose was buried. The sun warmed her face and the sky was the deep blue of lapis lazuli. She breathed deeply, luxuriating in the scent of the lavender and the heat of the sun. And though she was close to the spot where Rose's body lay, she felt only peace.

A gusting wind set the shutter rattling. Propping herself up on an elbow, Mira looked drowsily around the dim room. When the wind died down, the faint sound of voices floated up from the courtyard, or perhaps the road. A horse whinnied. Then the sharp clang of metal rang out.

She sprang out of bed, went to the window, and peered through the slats of the shutter. Laundry hanging on flax ropes in the courtyard flapped in the wind, partially obscuring her view of the gates. There were several horses and riders on the road. Were there three men? No, four. They had the look of knights, dressed in red leather armor and carrying swords. One of the men dismounted. He was tall and broad-shouldered, long-legged, and when he pulled off his silver helmet a cascade of dark hair plummeted around his shoulders.

Mira's heart lurched with a sickening thud.

Pelegrín.

He approached the guesthouse adjacent to the gates and disappeared around the corner of the building. The wind settled for a moment and she heard a dull thwacking sound. He must have been pounding at the door. The other men led the horses away from the gates, out of her sight.

Arnaud was in the guesthouse.

For a moment Mira stood frozen, overcome with terror, her mind churning with horrifying possibilities.

She pulled her clothes on, laced up her bodice with shaking fingers, quickly stuffed her hair under a flax cap. Struggling to open the shutter for a better view, she realized it had been nailed shut.

After a few moments the men were in the road again, massing before the gates. Were they about to burst through? Mira took a shaky breath, pressed a hand against her chest to steady the wild pounding of her heart. Then she forgot about breathing, forgot about her racing heart.

There was a fifth man in their midst.

It was Arnaud.

Without thinking, she screamed his name. But the sound of her voice was lost in a gust of wind that swooped into the courtyard, whipping the laundry into a froth.

She whirled, snatched open the door, and ran to the end of the corridor. The door there was locked. She turned and sprinted in the opposite direction. The door on that end was locked, too.

"Let me through!" She pounded on the door with both fists. "Let me out!"

No one came.

She ran frantically up and down the corridor again, entering first one room, then the next. None of them were occupied. *It must be the hour of prayer*, she thought. The nuns were in the chapel.

Back in her own room, she pressed her face against the shutter, but the view revealed nothing. No horses, no men, no movement at all near the gates or in the road. The wind had died as well. All she heard was a pair of doves cooing somewhere in the eaves above her window.

Mira sank to the floor, arms wrapped around her knees.

What had Pelegrín and his men done to Arnaud? Had they hurt him? Would they force their way into the abbey through the guesthouse? Would they come for her next?

She instinctively put a hand to her waist, seeking the reassuring touch of her dagger. But Arnaud had kept it in the guesthouse. A dagger was not a welcome accessory in a convent.

She looked around the room for anything she could use as a weapon. Her eyes fell on a brown ceramic pitcher in a bowl that stood upon a small oak table to the left of the door. She hefted it in her hand. It could be used as a bludgeon.

There was no latch on the door. Slowly Mira pushed the table across the floor to block it, the muscles in her back and arms straining with the effort. It was not much, but it would delay anyone trying to gain entry to the room.

A door creaked open in the corridor, then shut with a muffled thump.

Mira tightened her grip on the pitcher.

27

May, 2016
Lacanau Beach, France
Zari

Z ARI AND LAURENCE WATCHED the waves foam and break
on the sand. Their deconstruction of the conference proceedings had gotten underway during lunch in a nearby
village, but it was not quite over.

Dotie's colleague, the Bermejo expert, had not revealed anything groundbreaking in his presentation. There was still no
definitive proof that Bermejo had painted any of the portraits
that Zari believed were the work of Mira de Oto. But the man
had claimed that attribution to Bermejo was likely, and would
probably be made official after an exhaustive analysis of the
portrait of the woman in blue.

"There was nothing you could do to stop this, Zari," Laurence
said.

A fishing boat motored slowly past, several hundred yards
from shore.

"What I don't understand is how Dotie got that painting of the woman in blue," Laurence mused. "And why."

"I shared the news with him last year about the 'ADL' stamp being on both the Fontbroke College portrait and on your portrait of the merchant family," Zari said. "When I told him about the word 'Bermejo' under the layers of your painting, he had his aha moment."

"What do you mean?"

"When that word 'Bermejo' came to light, he went to Pau to see your painting, right?"

Laurence nodded.

"Dotie wanted to dig up more connections between the 'ADL' stamp and Bermejo. He probably put the word out about the stamp to a billionaire art collector friend who has contacts at every major auction house in Europe, some guy he's been trading favors with since they were in diapers. When the woman in blue came to auction, I'm guessing it was already earmarked for Dotie."

"Listen to you," Laurence said approvingly. "You are starting to sound French."

"I was so naive, Laurence! I thought I was doing the right thing, sharing what I learned with him out of courtesy." Zari slipped her arm through Laurence's. "I'm pretty clear-eyed about this. I don't have the credibility or the experience to inspire confidence on the level of the world's foremost expert on Bermejo. And let's face it, Mira doesn't have a place in the historical record—Bermejo does. Everything about those paintings that correlates to Bermejo is explainable. Nothing about them that correlates to Mira is. It's that simple."

"What will you do?"

Zari contemplated telling Laurence about Andreas Gutknecht, but decided against it. She had analyzed their conversation too many times to count during her mostly sleepless nights these past few days. Finally she had rejected the idea of working with him. Going off on a private contract was not going to help her land a professorship. In fact, it would hurt her chances. She would lose her place in the queue, so to speak. Her commitment to the academic world would be called into question.

It would be a stupid thing to do.

Wil hadn't returned her texts or calls since their tense conversation the night before her presentation. She felt a deep sense of shame every time she recalled the moment when she had flippantly suggested to Filip that he resume the adventuring that had nearly taken his life. Of course his family would be furious with her. She was an outsider who knew nothing of their private struggles.

Her eyes stung each time she thought of Wil. Maybe the cultural differences and the distance were all too much. They had both dreamed of experiencing daily life together—the banal details of shopping and working and cooking that so many couples took for granted seemed exotic and compelling. But perhaps their love wouldn't have survived all of that. The deep loneliness of their separations might have been the critical fuel for the passion and joy of their brief times together.

Now, Zari feared, she would never have the opportunity to find out.

"I talked to Vanessa this morning. She said several people who were at the conference reached out to her in support of my research. And she said my habit of posting about Mira on social media sites is paying off. Mira's starting to attract a following in the art history world."

Zari turned to face Laurence, blinking back tears. "I know we've made some good progress, but I also feel like I've wasted your time. Mira is still a ghost, a silenced story."

A fat seagull landed nearby, its unblinking yellow eyes fixed on them.

"Mira is not a silenced story," Laurence said. "She is coming to life, little by little. And it is because of you. Listen, research is a *long* game. You cannot solve a mystery from five hundred years ago all at once. I am sorry to say it, but this is..."

"A very American way of thinking," Zari finished, wiping her cheeks with a sleeve.

"Yes. You must be patient."

They began strolling again. The gull scuttled away as they approached, then unfolded its wings and flapped out over the sea.

"I wish I could keep going, keep digging for Mira," Zari said. "But what I have to do now is go home and start applying for jobs. And my family needs me."

"Your brother is taking care of your mother, I thought?"

"He is, but..." Zari broke off, listening to the rubbery squeak of their shoes scuffing the dry sand. "It's a long story. He can't do this on his own."

Laurence was quiet a moment, kicking a small object ahead of her, watching it roll across the sand, then kicking it again. She stooped and picked it up. It was a small scallop shell, worn nearly translucent by the action of wind, sand, and water.

"I see. What about Wil?"

Zari watched a quivering lump of sea foam explode into tiny white puffs that skittered along the sand like miniature tumbleweeds.

"I sometimes wish I'd never met him, because it hurts so much to be apart. It's hard to plan a future with him, especially now. He's not very happy with me at the moment."

"But you told me he is the love of your life."

"He is. Was. I don't know." Zari sighed, staring out over the sea.

"I had love." Laurence's voice was rough with emotion. "When my husband died, a part of me died. There is nothing more precious than life with a companion you love. You have found one—find a way to keep him in your life."

"Don't hold back on the advice, now," Zari said drily.

Laurence laughed. "If there is one thing age gives us, it's the ability to look back in time and see the choices we made, good and bad."

A band of gulls skimmed along the waves, their bodies hovering just above the cresting whitecaps.

"How do they do that?" Zari marveled. "A rogue wave could come along and knock them into the water. But it never does."

"Always curious. That is what makes you good at your job." Laurence's eyes were trained on the south, where the green hills of Basque country rose up on the flanks of the Pyrenees. "Your people came from those hills, Zari. Your mother's people. The Mendietas. One day you will search for them, I know it." She placed the scallop shell in Zari's palm. "Whatever you decide to do, I will keep looking for Mira. She's not lost to us. Not yet."

Zari folded her fingers around the shell and slipped it into her pocket.

28

THE THICK OAK DOOR rattled against the table once, twice.
"Leave me alone!" Mira tried to shout the words, but
they came out in a croak.

"It is I, the abbess. Let me in at once."

She set down the pitcher with trembling hands and inched the
table away from the door just enough for the abbess to slip through.

"Why did you block the door?"

The abbess's angular face was grave, her dark eyes cool. Something in her assessing gaze reminded Mira of Mother Béatrice.

"I heard the voices of men." Mira folded her arms across her
chest to quiet the tremor in her hands. "I was afraid."

"Your husband left with those men on the road east to
Fanjeaux."

Mira stared at her, dumbfounded. "Did they take him by
force?"

"I know not. The gatekeeper saw them approach. She was afraid. Your husband told her to stay inside, that he would talk to them. They were knights, that was plain to her. She said your husband spoke some foreign tongue with the men. He bade her have a stable boy fetch his mule, then they all left in haste. Their shields bore a coat of arms, she saw. Two ships, two sheep, two castles."

The question that had haunted Mira for weeks pounded in her skull: *Does my twin wish me well, or does he wish me dead?* She would be a fool to assume anything but the worst. She balled her hands into fists and dug her nails into her palms, forcing the panic away.

"You know those men?"

"Perhaps one of them."

The abbess's gaze hardened. "Does he seek you?"

Mira dropped her eyes, unable to lie to this woman who had offered her care and shelter. "Yes."

Crossing to the window, the abbess peered through the shutter's slats. "We have no defense save those gates. The women here are under my care." She faced Mira again. "What if they come back? We cannot take the risk. You must leave here at once. You may give me a message for your husband. If he returns without the other men, I will see he gets it."

"But..." Mira's voice faltered. "I am with child."

"I know." The abbess's face was difficult to see, standing as she was with her back to the window. "I will escort you to the guesthouse. Your husband left your things in his room."

There was not a trace of sympathy in her voice.

In the guesthouse, Mira questioned the stout, nearly toothless gatekeeper, who declared that Arnaud had indeed left in haste with the men on the road to the market town Fanjeaux. He had told her nothing of what the men had said to him, the woman declared. He just turned to her and raised an arm in farewell, said he'd be back.

Mira went into his room. It was slightly larger than her room in the convent dormitory, with the same narrow bed pushed against one wall, but instead of an oak table it contained a desk and chair. All of his things were gone. Her leather satchels were piled neatly on the bed. She pawed through them. At the bottom of the smaller satchel she spied the bag of coins Lord de Berral had given them. Next to it was her dagger in its sheath.

She opened the bag of coins, gave it a shake. Had Arnaud kept any for himself? This was more than enough to purchase a mule from the abbess and pay for lodging elsewhere. Pulling the sheath out, she laid it gently in her lap. At least she could arm herself.

She sank down on the chair, remembering the stench of the humid air the day she saw the tall nobleman in Perpignan, the determined stride of his long legs, how his dark eyes had searched for her in the crowd.

Somehow her twin had pieced together the truth. If it was Mira he wanted, why had he taken her husband away? Elena had once told her Pelegrín had a good heart. But what had war done to him? Did their father's cruelty lurk in his blood?

She ran her fingers over the dagger's polished bone hilt, half-pulled it from the sheath, eyed the gleaming blade. Her father had stolen it from the dead body of a Moor after a battle and gifted it to her mother long ago. For years, Marguerite hid the dagger in a chest. When Mira was eleven, Marguerite gave it to Elena and told her to instruct the girl in its use.

The thought of her father usually made Mira's heart thud faster. But not today. In fact, for the first time since Rose's death, she felt strong. It was as if an unseen well inside her had been sucked dry and then replenished again. After succumbing to the grief of losing Rose, after nearly drowning in it, she knew she could survive anything.

Since she learned Ramón de Oto was her father, she had wondered if his blood gave her courage or simply the capacity to perform monstrous deeds. She had murdered twice, after all. But the truth was, Mira's courage came from another source entirely—from the three women who had mothered her each in their own way. They were responsible for Mira's strength, her knowledge, her capacity for love, her very survival. She was alive because of the discipline Béatrice had instilled within her, the skills Elena taught her, the hope her mother had nurtured that, one day, Mira would live a life of her own choosing.

And now, there was another reason to be brave: the life within her, pulsing with promise. She pressed a hand on her belly, reassured by its flatness under her skirts. Then she slipped the dagger entirely free of the sheath and laid it on the bed beside her.

Her mother's ivory shell necklace on its thin chain of gold lay coiled at the bottom of the sheath. The sight of it always gave her comfort. She tipped the necklace into her palm. Another object tumbled out, too: a tightly rolled strip of linen paper.

Mira unfurled the paper, eyed the familiar lettering scribbled in charcoal. She whispered the words aloud.

"'I go east so you do not have to meet the past again. Keep to the pilgrim's road west, and I'll follow. If you require aid, remember the one who promised it.'"

She sat frozen, holding the paper by its edges, Arnaud's words repeating themselves on an endless loop in her head. Her heart flailed in her chest. For a long moment, she was nearly consumed by panic. She struggled to breathe, to push aside the fear that threatened to engulf her.

Staring fixedly at her mother's necklace, she willed herself calm again. She would find a mule train to join and continue west, on the pilgrim's route through the plains and woad fields—just as she and Arnaud had planned.

An anxious voice in her mind pointed out that Pelegrín might turn his sword against her husband. For a brief, terrifying instant, she imagined a world without Arnaud.

Mira squeezed her eyes shut and shook her head, vanquishing the fear.

If Arnaud did not follow as promised, she would continue to Nay and seek refuge with the Sacazar family until her baby was born—for 'the one who promised aid' had to be Carlo. She dreaded crossing paths with Amadina again, but there was nothing to be done about that. Her baby's well-being was all that mattered now, and Carlo Sacazar would offer protection.

In the desk she found the other half of the slip of linen paper, torn along one edge, along with a broken stick of vine charcoal. She stared unseeing at the paper for a long time, composing the words in her head. Then she willed her hands to stop trembling and wrote several lines of script all at once.

If the abbess was true to her word, Arnaud would read her message when he returned. They would be reunited well before she reached Nay—and they could sidestep the town entirely on their way to Bayonne.

The Sacazars would never be the wiser.

She emerged from the guesthouse into bright sunlight. The abbess stood near the stable doors, dispensing orders to a pair of servants. Hens pecked at bits of straw that lay scattered over the cobblestones. Mira crossed the courtyard, ducking around linen sheets that billowed and writhed in the breeze, her mind caught on a refrain that kept rhythm with her steps—words that had been her guide since the day of her birth, though she did not know it then.

"I am Miramonde," she said aloud, in a voice so forceful that two red hens flapped squawking away from her, their wings frantically beating the air.

The wind gusted then, catching the rest of her words and sending them swirling into the blue sky just as she reached the abbess. But in her head they rang out fiercely, like the strike of iron on stone.

One who sees the world.

29

May, 2016
Pau, France
Zari

THE WINDOWS IN ZARI'S bedroom were flung open to the warm spring air. The chug of a diesel truck floated up from the square below, then the high-pitched bark of a dog. Sunshine spilled into the room, illuminating the piles of belongings she'd stacked on her bed.

One by one she rolled up the shirts and tucked them into sleek rows in the bottom of her suitcase. Wil had taught her that trick—rolling instead of folding. She remembered how ingeniously he organized his backpack during their days on the Camino. His waterproof topographical maps. The Belgian chocolates he carried all the way up the mountain for her. She became acutely aware of the thudding of her heart. Each beat marked another second of silence between them.

She glanced again at the mobile sitting on her pillow, buzzing with an incoming call. Wil.

"Zari." His voice was hoarse, low.

"How is Filip?"

"He's stable. We arrived last night in Amsterdam and he's in a hospital here."

"Are you with him now?"

"Yes."

"Wil, I'm so sorry I ever mentioned adaptive sports to him." The words tumbled out in a rush. "I wish I could take back everything I said that night at dinner. I feel horrible."

"What?" He sounded astonished.

"If I hadn't told him about Gus's friend, offered to make the contact, he wouldn't have gone on the trip."

"That's crazy, Zari. Why would you think that?"

"Hana said it, when she answered my call. She said it was my fault."

There was a long silence.

"Zari, he would have gone back to adventuring whether you encouraged him or not. He was so happy on that sailboat...I can't even describe it. He was alive again. And Hana will not admit it, but the infection probably started before the trip began."

Zari's entire body felt like it had turned to gelatinous mush. She began to sob.

"I've been worrying that Filip is going to die because of me for more than a week now."

"The hospital in Croatia was horrible, Zari," he said wearily. "Hana got no sleep. The stress made her say things she should not have said. Not just to you."

Zari wiped her eyes, steadied her breath. "Do you miss her?" The question sounded like an accusation.

There was a tiny hesitation before he responded. "No. I mean, I miss our happy times, but we were really young when we got together. We've both changed."

She stayed silent.

"Zari, I love *you*. But Hana is part of my life and will always be, because Filip is my closest friend, and our families are close too. You have to accept that."

Zari got up and went to the window, watching a group of students pedal across the square on battered bicycles, book bags slung over their shoulders.

"I'm going back to California," she said. "After I give my report to the Mendenhall Trust in Oxford, I'm flying home."

"Wait. What happened to Amsterdam? You were going to come here."

"Filip's not the only one having a crisis. My mother was in a car accident last week. I need to go home. And frankly, after that conversation with Hana and your silence, I figured I was no longer welcome in Amsterdam."

"Your imagination gets you in trouble, Zari."

"If you had communicated more, maybe I wouldn't have imagined the worst," she pointed out, her voice rising. "I wish we could live together and give real life a try. But I think real life, for me, is six thousand miles away."

Muffled voices sounded in the background. Wil said something in Dutch and then asked if he could put her on mute. Zari shoved her mobile in her pocket, feeling ready to explode.

To distract herself she went to the kitchen and grabbed a nectarine from the fruit bowl on the table. Next to the bowl was a final to-do list and a printed itinerary for her flights back to England and then California. Chewing her nectarine, she ran her finger down the list. All the items had been checked off.

Except one.

She tossed out the pit, washed her hands, and walked barefoot into the living area, contemplating the map that Wil had hung for her on the wall. The routes of the Camino he highlighted last fall were marked by bright green and purple slashes, by circles and question marks and scrawled notes that made long, blurry trails. Zari slowly removed the pushpins and folded the map into a tiny rectangle. Then she returned to the bedroom and slipped it into her messenger bag.

Pulling her mobile from her pocket, she saw that the call had dropped, or Wil had ended it.

She sank down on the bed with a sigh and picked up a small framed color copy of the prayer book page she and Laurence had discovered last summer in the university archives. It had been a parting gift from Laurence. Zari gently traced the features of Mira's self-portrait with a finger, then picked out the words hidden in a bramble of black ink squiggles and curves: '*Mira pinxit hunc librum.*'

She closed her eyes, listening to a pigeon coo on a nearby windowsill. She had held tight to those threads of connection binding her to Mira—had dragged herself hand over hand along each one, clinging to hope that when she reached the end Mira would be waiting for her, gray-green eyes aglow.

"We got so close, Mira," she whispered, blinking back tears. "We were nearly there."

Carefully Zari folded a long-sleeved black shirt around the frame. Something in one of the pockets poked at her palm. She fished it out. Andreas Gutknecht's card. She folded it in half and tossed it in the Monoprix bag she was using as a garbage bin. In the next moment, she pulled it out again and entered his contact information into her mobile. After she typed in the data, she accidentally touched his number on the screen. The call went through.

Zari cancelled the call immediately, scowling in irritation. One of the few things she didn't like about the modern age was the fact that accidental calls, or 'butt dialing' as her nephew described it, could not be kept anonymous.

The next morning, she stood at the window of her apartment one last time. The rising sun bathed the city in golden light, illuminating the green ridges of the Pyrenees in the south. Two massive white clouds scudded diagonally down from the mountaintops. Zari squinted up, gauging the distance between them, the speed of their movements. A collision was imminent, she realized. And it would be directly over her building.

Looking down, she saw the cobblestones in the square below gleaming, still wet from a rain shower in the night. Several pigeons gathered around a stormwater drain near the sidewalk. While Zari watched, another bird flapped into their midst, setting off a flurry of strutting and cooing from its comrades. Laurence's charcoal gray Renault motored into the square then, pulling up in front of Zari's building. The diesel engine spluttered for a moment and went silent.

Zari dashed upstairs and left a bag containing a bottle of Priorat and a goodbye note for Monsieur Mendieta by his door. Carefully she made her way down the curving staircase to the lobby, lugging her roll-aboard and her messenger bag, sweating in her winter coat.

When she pushed open the door, the bright morning sunlight reflecting off the slick cobblestones made her eyes ache.

"Ready?" Laurence said, popping open the trunk of her car.

Zari fought back tears as Laurence helped load her things into the back of the Renault. She stripped off her coat and slid into the passenger seat.

Her mobile buzzed. She pulled it eagerly from her handbag, hoping it was Wil.

Laurence buckled her seatbelt and glanced down at the mobile's screen.

"Country code 41. Switzerland." She inserted the key in the ignition and the car roared to life. "Who do you know there?"

Zari sat frozen, staring in consternation at the device in her hand, her thumb hovering over the 'decline' button.

The mobile buzzed a fifth time, then a sixth.

"Are you going to answer it?" Laurence pulled away from the curb. The pigeons vaulted into the air and scattered in all directions.

Zari took a deep breath and slowly let it out, wondering what her mother would say at this moment. The answer came to her immediately.

Sometimes accidents are miracles in disguise.

Overhead the clouds collided, muting the light.

With one swift motion, Zari pressed 'accept.'

THE END

AUTHOR'S NOTE

THE HISTORICAL RECORD IS full of holes. We know history is written by the victors, by people whose wealth and education gave them the opportunity to describe what they saw and experienced through their own narrow lens. That narrative is rife with misrepresentations, with silenced voices, with stories that were suppressed or ignored.

The Miramonde Series is an attempt to fill in the blanks about women artists during a particular time and place: the early Renaissance era in what is now France and Spain. With these stories, I weave what I have learned from the historical record with my own imaginings.

The Cagots were a mysterious people who lived in and around the western Pyrenees, first entering the historical record during the late Middle Ages. The scant documentation about them offers conflicting accounts of their origins, customs, and characteristics. What is generally agreed upon is the fact that they were ruthlessly segregated, demeaned, and abused. Today the Cagots have vanished, mostly by quietly assimilating into French society, their stories buried under layers of time and history.

The Abbey of Camon was inhabited by a Benedictine order of monks beginning in the middle ages and offered shelter to travelers and pilgrims passing through the region. I took the liberty of transforming it into a nunnery for the purposes of this book.

Casa de Ganaderos is a cooperative of sheep breeders in Zaragoza, Spain, that dates back to 1218. The organization has kept kept meticulous records since its inception, some of which are archived online.

The city of Toulouse has archived many historic documents online, including the record books of notaries dating from the early 1500s.

The city of Perpignan passed from Aragónese to French rule and back again more than once over the course of history. During Mira's time, Perpignan was controlled by Aragón.

Bartolomé Bermejo (c. 1440-c. 1495) was a Spanish artist who, unlike most of his contemporaries on the Iberian Peninsula, painted in the Flemish style. He is known for his exceptionally detailed backgrounds.

The character of Cornelia van der Zee is based on Flemish portrait artist Caterina van Hemessen (c. 1528-c. 1587).

The character of Albrecht Rumbach is based on German book printer/publisher Jean Rosembach, who established a business in Perpignan in 1500.

For information about other aspects of the research behind this book (or if you just love to geek out on history) please e-mail the author at info@amymaroney.com.

CONTEMPORARY CAST OF CHARACTERS

Zari Durrell..*Art historian*

Portia Durrell...*Zari's mother*

Gus Durrell...*Zari's brother*

Vanessa Conlon..............*Professor at Fontbroke College, Oxford*

Dotie Butterfield-Swinton..........*Professor at Fontbroke College,*
Oxford

John Drake...*art conservator*

Wil Bandstra............................*Adventurer and furniture builder*

Filip Holst...*Wil's best friend*

Hana Holst..*Filip's sister*

Laurence Ceravet..........*Professor at University of Pau, France*

Monsieur Mendieta........................*Zari's elderly neighbor in Pau*

Andreas Gutknecht.....................*art broker based in Switzerland*

HISTORICAL CAST OF CHARACTERS

ABOUT THE AUTHOR

AMY MARONEY LIVES IN the Pacific Northwest with her family. She studied English literature at Boston University and worked for many years as a writer and editor of nonfiction. *Mira's Way* is her second novel. The third book in the series is underway.

If you enjoyed this book, please take a moment to leave a review online or spread the word to family and friends.

Join Amy's readers group and get occasional spam-free e-mails with news about her next books (plus giveaways and deals on other great reads) at www.amymaroney.com.

ACKNOWLEDGEMENTS

MY GRATITUDE ONCE AGAIN to everyone I thanked last time around for *The Girl from Oto*. In addition, I wish to thank the following people. They helped make *Mira's Way* what it is and assisted me with the marketing and promotion pieces of this journey.

Deepest thanks to art conservator Nina Olsson, for her generous gifts of time, resources, and a delicious cup of tea. To Sara Starbuck, for insightful and comprehensive editing, and for her support of my writing and my story. To Amy Compton, for being a superfan and for helping me tackle the murky waters of marketing and promotion. To my parents-in-law JoAnn and Paul Maroney, for tirelessly promoting *The Girl from Oto* and getting it into the hands of influencers. To Margie Goodman, for her faith in me and her advocacy of my work. And to everyone who read and enjoyed *The Girl from Oto* and took the time to leave a review or spread the word to friends—thank you from the bottom of my heart.

Printed in Great Britain
by Amazon

19602201R00226